Justin Hill has won the Geoffrey Faber Memorial Prize, the Betty Trask and Somerset Maugham Awards, and has been shortlisted and nominated for a host of other awards, as well as enjoying the rare achievement of being banned in the People's Republic of China. *Shieldwall* is the first of a series exploring England's epic tale: 1066, and the Norman Conquest. The *Sunday Times* heralded it as a Best Novel of 2011.

He studied Old English and Medieval Literature at Durham University and his books have been translated into fifteen languages.

www.justinhillauthor.com

Praise for *Shieldwall*

'As close to an eyewitness account of this major Dark Age conflict as you could hope for without getting caught in the line of fire. Bracing and real'
Dan Abnett

'Hill's sense of place, landscape and home is really good . . . I shall be waiting for the next novel in the trilogy'
Observer

'*Shieldwall* is the first foray into historical fiction by the acclaimed novelist Justin Hill. I was delighted to discover that this was no mild-mannered ingress into the genre, but a grand, full-blooded entrance. Lovers of history and historical fiction, sit up and take notice! *Shieldwall* is a magnificent story, full of complex historical and fictional characters. Hill is a master at describing the politics, lifestyles and conflicts of eleventh-century England; ordinary, domestic scenes and the madness and gore of set-piece battles are described with equal aplomb. I loved every page and will eagerly look forward to the sequel. Do not miss it'
Ben Kane

'Intensely likeable and moving . . . Hill hints that the people of past times had inner lives as complex and ambivalent as ours'
Roz Kaveney, *Independent*

'Much the best was Justin Hill's *Shieldwall*, which superbly evoked the wordplay of the period's poetry as it unfolds a compelling story of Earl Godwin's battles against the Norse'
Sunday Times Pick of 2011 Historical Novels

Shieldwall

Shieldwall

JUSTIN HILL

ABACUS

First published in Great Britain in 2011 by Little, Brown
This paperback edition published in 2012 by Abacus
Reprinted 2012

A CIP catalogue record for this book
is available from the British Library.

ISBN 978-0-349-12337-0

Typeset in Garamond by M Rules
Printed and bound in Great Britain by
Clays Ltd, St Ives plc

Papers used by Abacus are from well-managed forests
and other responsible sources.

 MIX
Paper from
responsible sources
FSC   FSC® C104740
www.fsc.org

Abacus
An imprint of
Little, Brown Book Group
100 Victoria Embankment
London EC4Y 0DY

An Hachette UK Company
www.hachette.co.uk

www.littlebrown.co.uk

Shieldwall

JUSTIN HILL

ABACUS

First published in Great Britain in 2011 by Little, Brown
This paperback edition published in 2012 by Abacus
Reprinted 2012

A CIP catalogue record for this book
is available from the British Library.

ISBN 978-0-349-12337-0

Typeset in Garamond by M Rules
Printed and bound in Great Britain by
Clays Ltd, St Ives plc

Papers used by Abacus are from well-managed forests
and other responsible sources.

Abacus
An imprint of
Little, Brown Book Group
100 Victoria Embankment
London EC4Y 0DY

An Hachette UK Company
www.hachette.co.uk

www.littlebrown.co.uk

For Percy, Madison,
Isabella and Edmund

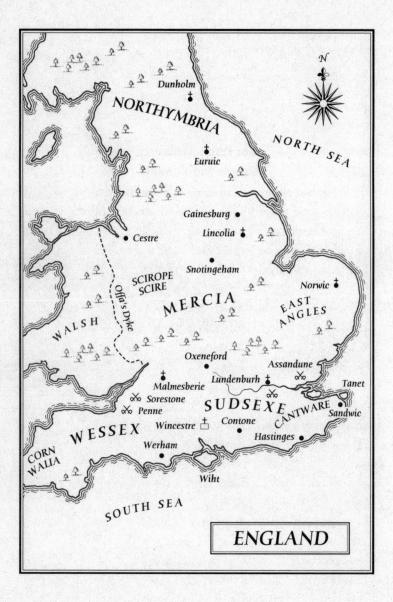

PLACE NAMES

Old English spelling was an uncertain and fluctuating art, with variations used according to time and accent, and the vagaries of the particular scribe. I have used spellings from the *Oxford Dictionary of English Place Names* for the nearest year to the events recorded in the story.

Adelingi	Athelney
Adewic	Adwick-le-Street
Ældgate	Aldgate
Athelingedean	Dean
Assandune	Ashington
Bade	Bath
Bebbanburge	Bamburgh
Beiminstre	Beaminster
Boseham	Bosham
Breguntford	Brentford
Bricge	Bruges
Burgenda land	Burgundy
Burne	Westbourne
Cantebrigiescir	Cambridgeshire
Canturburie	Canterbury
Cantware	Kent

Ierusalem	Jerusalem
Iseldone	Islington
Knightridestrete	Knightrider Street, London
Langelete	Longleat
Leomynstre	Leominster
Liguera ceastre	Leicester
Lincolia(scir)	Lincoln(shire)
Lindesi	Lindsey
Lundenburh	London
Malmesberie	Malmesbury
Meredone	Marden
Mide	Munster
Midelsexe	Middlesex
Nordfolc	Norfolk
Normandig	Normandy
Northantone	Northampton
Northweg	Norway
Northymbrelond	Northumbria, much larger than the current county of the same name: then it included Northumbria, Durham, Yorkshire and much of Lancashire.
Norwic	Norwich
Orcanege	Orkney
Oxeneford(scire)	Oxford(shire)
Penne	Penselwood
Peteorde	Petworth
Sandwice	Sandwich
Sciropescire	Shropshire
Selesie	Selsey
Snotingham	Nottingham
Soluente	Solent
Sorestone	Sherston

Sudfulc	Suffolk
Sudrie	Surrey
Sudsexe	Sussex
Sudwerca	Southwark
Sumersæton	Somerset
Tanet	Thanet
Tanshelf	Now a suburb of Pontefract (which derives from the Latin, Ponte Fracto – Broken Bridge)
Tatecastre	Tadcaster
Temese	River Thames
Thornei Island	Thorney Island
Ulfastir	Ulster
Wæcelinga Stræt	Wæcelinga Street
Walingeford	Wallingford
Werham	Wareham
Wiltunscir	Wiltshire
Wincestre	Winchester
Wiht	Isle of Wight

BOOK I

CHAPTER ONE

The Unforgotten

Dyflin, midwinter 1013

Christ did not come again that year. The Lord kept to His churches and the pages of His Book, and Wulfnoth sat in the half-timbered hall, watching rain drip down through roof-thatch, puddling on the floor, while the peat fire smoked. His remaining men sat round him, the wooden benches drawn close, cloaks and hoods pulled tight to their chests. Their round-bossed shields hung in the hall shadows; their spears were sheathed; their swords kept to hand like favourite hounds.

The midwinter days were short and dark; thin shadows stretched long on the ground. No one spoke. It was bad business, these days in Dyflin. The slave markets were still busy, but day by day rumour grew of the size of Brian Boru's warhost.

War was coming, like a mounted horseman. A blood-red horse, the Lord's Book said, Hell and Judgement following after. The seagulls sensed it, that distant scent of battle. They fought and cawed in chaotic multitudes; swooped low over the small fishing boats; plucked cold flapping fish from the slate-grey waters.

The dull winter day was cold and grey and bleak. Wulfnoth stood at the quayside and looked out towards the estuary. He watched the masts of approaching warships appear amongst the riverside trees; the rain unceasing as it stripped the boughs; wet leaves plastered along the smooth river water.

Wulfnoth shivered, despite his blue cloak and hood; the shaggy lining beginning to wear thin. The silver brooch held the wool cloth close to his chest, the disc patterned with three swirling hounds. The midwinter days were short and the afternoon light was already beginning to fail; the hounds' blue glass eyes were dull, one eye setting blind and empty.

Wulfnoth stood still as an ancient oak, gnarled and hollowed by too many winters, staring eastwards, over the waves. His thoughts were far away from this muddy dockside in the shadow of the high Dyflin earthworks, topped with a wall of split timbers. They crossed the grey and restless waves, made their way back to the fields of his youth, to his hall's hearthside where warm and gentle hands welcomed his return; when there was good food on the table and warm-hearted words; when music and laughter rose like abbey plainchant; when he slept without cares under home rafters and a heavy thatch.

'Brian'll not dare come back,' an Orcanege man, from his accent, shouted out at the sight of the new boat crews, and Wulfnoth snorted.

'You're a fool, or a wishful thinker,' he called out over the men's heads. A few bystanders laughed. 'Brian's emptied Mide and Connacht and Ulfastir of fighting men. He does not fear you Spear-Danes!'

Some men voiced agreement; few doubted the tales that Brian Boru, Emperor of the Gaels, High King of the Irish, was gathering his men for battle. But the Orcanege man heard the English accent in Wulfnoth's voice and laughed. 'What is it to

4

you greybeard? Go back home, if you still have one! When Brian is dead we will come and use you as a woman every third night!'

Wulfnoth paused and strangers about him grinned, hoping for a scrap. He had killed for less, but now he was wiser and more assured. His look stopped the laughter. He held it long. Spat into the black mud. Walked slowly away, his hand tight on his sword hilt as the taunts grew more distant.

Wulfnoth had carried his guilt for five winters, and that morning as he walked home it weighed more heavily down on him, weighted each step, like a bag of silver.

'Silent and empty, former hall of laughter,' he heard his slave girl singing in her clear voice as she carried water up from the river.

> The once-lord wanders
> Sorrow and longing as companions
> The solitary man awaiting God's mercy

She was waiting in the hall when he stepped through the door. She took off his cloak and laid it near the fire to warm. The woollen cloth steamed gently. The embers crackled as the crude hall hunched over them, bracken-thatch eaves dripping rain. His slave girl teased a snagged thorn-twig from the hem of his cloak, threw another log of split holly on to the fire. A few red sparks flew up, but the log was still damp; it hissed and foamed as it warmed in the flames.

'Any news?'

'None,' Wulfnoth said, and sat in silence, staring deep into the twisting flames. He had questioned the longbeards at the quayside, but they shook their heads; they did not know; there was nothing they could tell him; there was no salve for the unhappy man.

He signalled for the slave girl to throw more wood on to the fire, ignored the small brown rat that scurried along the wall edge, took in a deep breath of the smoky air to buoy his flagging spirits. He hated the cramped houses, the stink of sewers, the constant noise of men and animals passing along the city street. He liked to step out of his door and feel the wind on his face and see a wide green horizon before him, his own little kingdom of fields, woods and pasture, liked to see who approached his door from a mile down the road.

It had been like that at his manor in Sudsexe, high on the shoulder of the South Downs, with a view over an ordered landscape of fields, rich meadows and clear and gushing streams.

Contone was the manor's name, a small and unimportant stead in the scheme of things, but it had been given to Wulfnoth's family by Alfred himself, and it was home – an uncomplicated word, unnoticed until it went missing, like hope, and cheer, and family. Contone was as familiar as the lines of his palm or the moods of his men. He knew its seasons by heart, the busy calendar of sowing and coppicing, shearing, mowing, fattening and slaughter. He knew the exact number of villars and bordars and slaves, knew the number of ploughs and closes, how much tax the manor was worth and how much it paid.

Wulfnoth stared deep into the fire and the flames filled his whole vision. He kicked through drifts of fondly remembered days and friends and incidents: the great autumn feasts, ere winter came on; the blazing and hospitable firesides; bright candlelight gleaming on close-gathered faces; laughter and songs keeping the long dark at bay. The quiet mornings after feasting when the hall smelt of stale beer and ashes; the cool summer evenings when the doors were thrown wide open to the midges and the blackbird's evening song; the long lingering late-summer twilight when no fire was lit, when bat shadows flittered low overhead and white stars glimmered in the northern sky.

Wulfnoth drank steadily, brooding on the fate that had brought him to this end.

'You should eat more,' the slave girl said and Wulfnoth looked up from the worn lines of his palms and the untouched bowl of barley bread and salt pork.

Kendra was a pretty Cumbraland girl: black hair, blue eyes and a gentle manner. When she undressed, her skin was pale and cold like frost. Three years earlier, when they had bought her from the Dyflin slave market – dirty and flea-bitten, bites on her forearms and shins scratched into scabs – she had not a word of English. No one could pronounce her real name, so Wulfnoth and his men called her Kendra: 'All-Knowing'. It was a joke that had amused them at first, as she learnt their language and the ways of their lord, but they had long ago stopped laughing at her. She had been a good handmaid to Wulfnoth, and he would remember it.

'You haven't eaten,' Kendra said. 'Here, this is hot.'

Wulfnoth stretched his hands out to the flames but they did not warm him. Nothing did. Not even the silver coin he had amassed selling captured slaves to Moorish salesmen, for expense and profit held only a passing interest; it was honour and loyalty that consumed him. And duty, Wulfnoth reminded himself. A simple word, a blood bond that bound and fettered freeborn men.

Twilight grew; the day sank; their faces up-lit by the warm hearth, a heap of red and brittle embers. It was good to sit with kinsfolk and kettle-friends, to drink and eat without the need to talk. Twenty-six men Wulfnoth had, where once he had led more than a hundred. But stout men they were, with good hearts, loyalty long tested by the hunger and cold of the exile's path. In battle they were a shield of bodies; on dull nights like these they raised their lord's spirits with tales of strange sights, distant harbours, men they had killed, feuds and manslayings, half-remembered tales of the long-past.

Tonight they drank thin barley ale as the steersman, Caerl, told the tale of Troy, the valiant fighters doomed to failure. His hands plucked the harp strings as he spoke of the ships and the battles, and the steadfastness of the heroes, doomed warriors massed like winter thickets. But Wulfnoth was not in the mood for stories. He had been brooding afternoon and evening, drinking away this dull, grey Dyflin day, and he felt this story was somehow pointed at him. Just before Caerl told of Priam's grandson, skull-smashed on the heathen altar, Wulfnoth slammed down his horn of ale and the harp-notes faded away. His cheeks were red; he had the manner of a knackeryard bull: angry and caged and impotent.

'I did not break my vows!' Wulfnoth slurred his words. His eyes were small and pink. 'None of them stood up for me. None of them!'

Wulfnoth's hand shook and the slave girl wanted to go to him, but it would not be seemly. His men looked down into the night's fire, as if there were answers to be found in the lick and flicker of elf-lights dancing above the embers.

Wulfnoth held out his hands, more like a carpenter's than a lord of men. 'I would have held hot irons if I could have brought my son away with me. I would have walked on coals!' he said. 'They held me back, kept telling me that the king would have me killed. All of them. They told me to flee. Your son will have to fend for himself, they told me, and I left my own sweet child. Why did you let me do such a thing!'

The change of pronoun escaped no one. The men froze. In Wulfnoth's mind he gripped the hilt of a sword. The knuckles of his fist whitened before it fell back to the rough wood grain.

There was a long pause. The fire crackled. A spark flew, landed on the flagstone next to his foot, cooled to black and grey.

No sane man would have trusted Ethelred with any of his children. Look how he had treated the sons of Alderman Elfhelm – their eyes torn out by pressing thumbs, their father's corpse dumped in a forest ditch. But Wulfnoth was not sane that day five winters unforgotten. Terror had seized him, as it seizes men in battle and unmans them. Wulfnoth clenched his teeth and remembered the oaths he had sworn, the oaths Ethelred had sworn in reply: to be a good lord; to uphold the laws; to protect the people. They were the three vows of a king and Ethelred had broken each one. It was surely God's judgement that the Spear-Danes had come.

'I gave him my own son,' Wulfnoth whispered. The words hung in the air for a moment. 'I gave the king my own son as hostage! What has he done with my son?' Wulfnoth demanded of the borrowed hall shadows, but his voice was dulled by the damp dripping thatch; the drenching sound of rainfall was the only answer.

The luckless man bottles his feelings, Kendra hummed silently to herself,

> Seeks one who would love him
> And entice him back with joys.

At last Wulfnoth stood unsteadily for bed. His slave girl hurried from the stool in the corner, opened the door for him and followed him inside. That night her skin was as pale and cold as ever, her hair dark as the night shadows. He held her close to his side, and her fingers played with the hair on his chest, almost as a child would.

They lay for a long time under the furs and the blankets. After a while he was aware of the unease in the stiffness of her limbs and the position of her body, half turned away from his. From the harbour came the distant singing of Norse voices, a drunken battle song riding on the night's calm:

> One sword among swords
> has made me rich.
> My sword is worth three swords
> in sword battle-play.

Wulfnoth's girl tried not to listen to the northern word play. She knew the language of the Norse, all right. It brought bad memories of a cold time. She lay for a long while without speaking.

'Why go back?' she said at last.

'Why not?' he asked her.

She sat up then, spoke loudly enough for the men in the hall to hear. 'They will kill you, that is why,' she said.

Wulfnoth did not answer. An image came to him: a meadow in flower, a clear and stony stream, a fisherman staking his reed fish-trap into the salmon-brimming water, and his mother's voice calling him home at the end of the day.

All men die, he thought, and he had lived in exile long enough.

That night as Wulfnoth lay in bed, he tossed and turned and tried to sleep, but the room began to spin a little and he could feel cold sweat upon his forehead. His hands were dry but the rest of his body sweated. He sat up and felt his stomach churn, up and down, like making butter. He raised himself over the body of the girl, his blind hands fumbling for his cloak which he threw around his shoulders, felt for the door latch stepped out into the smoky dark of the hall.

He could hear his men breathing; from the dull red ember's light could make out their sleeping forms, lined like corpses along the floor. He wiped the sweat from his lip again, cursed the beer and the stink of Dyflin; the war and Ethelred, and the fate that had brought him to this moment: leaning on this rented doorpost, the cold night air on his face, ragged night-clouds being chased past a gibbous moon – and he puked out of the doorway of the rented barn.

Wulfnoth bent double to vomit again, gagged and spat a long string of saliva from his mouth. He drooled like a dog, knew that more was coming, but rather than wait he opened his mouth gannet wide and put his hand in, two fingers searching for the back of his throat. He knew the spot, behind his tonsils, could taste his own skin and the dirt under his nails, the black hairs on the back of his hands rough against the roof of his mouth. He gagged again. Spat more. He slid his fingers back inside and his stomach heaved in response and he pulled out his hand, pulled the hem of his cloak up as his stomach clenched like a fist, emptied itself of beer and lumps of half-chewed bread and pork and parsnips in an impossibly long stream.

Wulfnoth thought this would ease the sweat on his skin, but he heaved again. The third time he gagged, nothing came from his gut, but his stomach squeezed a fourth time and he could taste foul black bile.

When he had finished, Wulfnoth poured water on his pale and hairy shins, swilled the backsplash from his skin.

His feet were still wet when he fumbled his way back into bed.

He wanted to wake the girl, but he could smell the vomit on himself and knew he was drunk and tried to wipe himself down with the lining of his cloak. She moved a little to make room for him, but he liked to sleep on the usual side and clambered over her again, careful not to rouse her.

But he could not sleep. The room did not spin, but his body still sweated. Wulfnoth opened his eyes to the night black. It was still raining. A puddle had formed somewhere on the mud floor of the chamber. The sound was very intense in the silence. He could hear the drip, drip, drip marking the long and sleepless watches of the night.

The next morning Wulfnoth woke and found that the slave girl was up already, sitting on a milking stool by his bedside, washing the dirt from his cloak.

'You were sick,' she said, and Wulfnoth remembered.

He closed his eyes and put his hands to his head as if he could massage away the pain inside.

'You talked of your son,' the slave girl said. He winced and pushed himself up from the bed, saw the puddle on the floor and the long-dripping roof.

He stood up, felt a little light-headed, pulled on his trousers and tunic, strapped his belt on tight. The men would not want to see an old drunk come stumbling forward into the day. They had sworn him oaths and shared his food, but there was no tighter bond than respect and love, and after a night like last night Wulfnoth felt he must give them an entrance to admire.

He could feel his slave girl watching him as he put his hand to the door-latch.

'Wait,' she said, and stood up from the three-legged stool. The hem of her dress was wet. Her hands were white and wrinkled from the washing water; they reached up to his throat and the skin on his back shivered for a moment, as if they were the wet hands of a drowned corpse.

'Here,' she said, and he closed his eyes and let his breath out. She straightened his clothes. She said something in her own language, pulled dried lumps from his beard.

'You look like a Dane,' she said, her voice soft and rebuking.

'I should shave it off,' he said.

She looked at him. She took one of the grey hairs between her fingers and pulled quickly.

He winced as the lichen-grey hair wrenched free from his skin.

She pulled another one out. And another. They were like slaps to the face, waking him up.

'There,' she said, and nodded towards the door, as if to tell him he was free to go.

Wulfnoth had once held court with the finest of the land and had, when that dread time came, buckled on mail shirt and sword, taken up his spear and shield, and led his men in battle. Shield of his people, he'd earned a great name in fighting the Danes: Wulfnoth Cild, the king had named him – the 'Young Hero' – and, as he strode out and greeted each man in turn, he was Wulfnoth Cild again.

'Someone should teach the Irish to brew decent ale,' Wulfnoth said, clapping Beorn on the back. The big man smiled; his crooked teeth gave him a fearsome look. 'So you think you have more scars than me? Not yet, young Beorn!' he boomed. 'A good night indeed! Caerl, how is the wind?'

'She has shifted a little to the south,' Caerl told him.

'Good,' Wulfnoth laughed. 'Good! The gale cannot last all winter. Soon it will relent and blow us home.'

Wulfnoth grew sicker. He hid his pain and spoke in a fine and expansive mood as he gave orders to his men to sell this and buy that, to bring in loans that had been given to men in the city, to prepare the boat for the crossing to Sudsexe.

That night Wulfnoth did not sleep well. His mind raced and his stomach rumbled; he tossed and turned and feared his son might now be drowning on an Irish beach. He dreamt of a high green wave washing over a floundering ship. He woke with a start.

When news came that a ship had foundered in the gales two days before. Wulfnoth was sure his son Godwin had drowned. Words would not sway him; he insisted on riding out to see the place. The gale had calmed and the sky was clear and blue and wind-scrubbed as Wulfnoth and his men took their horses, spears and shields, and rode to the bay. The tide was ebbing and the waves were gentle, almost apologetic, as they nudged the wreckage ashore. Sand and surf swirled; the broad beach was littered with scraps of timber and sacking and the shattered sea-chests of the crew.

Caerl stuck his tongue into his cheek and looked at the capsized ship. She lay on her side about three furlongs from where he stood, her barnacled timbers turned up to the sky. A barrel of arrows had burst and the sodden bushels now made the high-water mark, while in the shallows a few seaweed-tangled corpses, stripped by locals, lapped the shore with each nudging wave.

'This is an English ship,' Wulfnoth said. 'That is English oak. And look, this cross is an English cross.'

'Come,' Beorn shouted, 'let us take our countrymen from the shore and give them a decent burial.'

The soil was light and sandy, and it did not take long to dig a hole deep enough for the bodies. One of the corpses was a tall and handsome fellow with long blond hair. Beorn felt the man's skull and the head swung up at a gruesome angle; the man's throat had been cut almost to the bone.

Beorn looked about him. Poor soul, he thought. He could

picture the man staggering ashore only to be met by the local shipwreckers. But now there was nothing but the wind and the grasses, and the stranded arrows.

'No sign of your son,' Caerl said to Wulfnoth.

Wulfnoth stared over the grey sea. The 'whale road', men called it, and there the great beasts were, rising like hillocks from under the waves, wandering through the cold grey water, breaking the surface in turn, strange voyagers hurrying to the ends of the earth.

That afternoon the pot was just starting to steam when one of the men handed Wulfnoth a bowl of dark beef broth. Wulfnoth took it in both hands, felt the warmth come slowly through the hand-polished wood. His stomach cramped as he watched Beorn airing the sheepskins that would keep off the damp; Wulfnoth gritted his teeth while the pain eased.

'Lord,' a soft voice said. His slave girl was standing next to him. The hall was almost empty. It was dark and cold and quiet. His men had all gone out on their errands. It was still raining softly; the light was thin and dull, he could not tell how long he had slept, just saw the raindrops dripping onto the ground outside, counting.

Wulfnoth shivered and shut his eyes.

'Would you like me to sing?'

Wulfnoth shook his head. There was a pain low down in his gut. He did not want music today. 'I will sleep. Wake me if the wind changes,' he said and pulled his cloak tighter to him. He rested his chin on his chest, thought of Contone and his wife and son, and that long-lost feeling of contentment and joy.

Wulfnoth slept for three more hours, drifted on the dreams of a man who yearns for kinfolk but cannot steer his ship homeward. As he slept he could hear voices outside.

He called for Kendra.

'Who is that?' he asked when she came hurrying.

'Men from Sudsexe. The winds have turned to the east.'

'Any news?'

She shook her head and Wulfnoth put his head back to his rolled-cloak pillow.

As he slept again, the temperature dropped and a thick winter mist rose from the river. It steadily filled the streets till the roofs were like islands in a sea of white. Trees loomed up like the weird figures of giants. Men groped their way home, the dark shapes of buildings and wicker walls looming closer and darker and more sombre. The fog kept rising till it began to feel its way down through the smoke hole, making the fire cough and splutter.

Wulfnoth had a dream that he was underwater and woke with a start. He pushed back a blanket that had been spread over his legs and threw the door open to the clawing fog. A wall of white faced him. He felt his way along the narrow walkway along the side of the hall to the privy.

When it was over Wulfnoth used a handful of moss to rub himself clean. But he was back half and hour later, with the same urgent need, but with nothing coming.

Wulfnoth sat in the outhouse for more than ten minutes, and when he came back to bed, he asked his slave girl to bring in a bucket.

'You're sick?' she said.

'Cheap beer,' he told her, but he knew it wasn't just the beer that made him feel light-headed and faint and he was up many times in the night.

When morning came, he was so hot and feverish that the slave girl threw the covers off, opened the high shutters to let the smell out and the thin winter light in.

She bent to pick up the bucket and carried it out through the hall. It was only when she was out of the hall door and picking her way through the puddles that she saw what was inside. She tried not to breathe – held her breath till after she had tipped the contents out – and then threw the bucket after it.

No one would use it now. Not after what she had seen.

She hurried back, splashing through the puddles this time, and opened her mouth and heaved in a great gasp of air. She washed her hands and lingered at the chamber door, as if the whole room had become infected.

Wulfnoth lay on his side, his arm curled under his head, one white foot sticking out from the bedclothes. His breathing was slow and regular. She touched her hand to his forehead, felt the fire that burnt inside.

She had seen this sickness before. His bowel movements had not produced anything brown or liquid or familiar, but clots of blood floating in a translucent gruel of mucus. She knelt next to the bed and clasped her hands and prayed: Forgive me, Lord, and forgive Wulfnoth for the sins we have committed. She prayed for mercy and hope and for Him to cast a forgiving eye on her master.

After a long while, when the men were already up and talking in loud morning voices, Wulfnoth opened an eye and saw her kneeling next to his bed.

'What's wrong, child?'

She looked at him and did not know what to say.

He shut his eyes and smiled.

'Praying for me already?' he said.

She blushed.

'How is the wind?'

'Fair.'

'And *Swanneck*? Is she ready to sail?'

She nodded.

'Good. When this has passed, we shall go down and push her off the shore,' he said, but the next day his cheeks were sunken and he spoke fitfully.

'I saw my son,' Wulfnoth said, and she saw a feverish light in his blue eyes. 'I saw my lad and he opened his arms to me, welcomed me back home.' Wulfnoth closed his eyes for a moment, then said in the quiet, 'No, not yet. Don't get the monks yet.'

Kendra knelt for a little while and wondered if he would keep sleeping.

'I saw my son. I saw Godwin,' Wulfnoth whispered after a while, but his eyes stayed shut and she sat and watched the slow rise and fall of his chest, took his hand, was reassured when he squeezed her fingers in reply.

Beorn filled a jug with ale, set two cups before him and waited by the hearth for his lord to come out. But Wulfnoth did not come. Beorn grimaced, filled his own cup and emptied it, refilled it and kept drinking. He grew quiet and then gloomy and took out his sword, Doomgiver, and polished her till she gleamed red in the firelight.

'Does he not value our jokes any more?' he said.

'He is sick,' Caerl told him.

There was nothing they could do. It tested them both.

'Another cup?'

Caerl shook his head. 'No,' he said, then rested a hand on Beorn's shoulder. 'But drink one for him.'

Caerl went down to the muddy Dyflin quayside, where the tethered boats sat low in the water, their reflections close round them like uneasy sheep. He climbed aboard, stood at the prow and watched the other crews casting off. He threw back his cloak and rubbed his eyes clear. The boats were loaded and ready; all they needed was Wulfnoth's word.

But Wulfnoth was almost past giving orders.

Caerl listened to the lapping water along the ships' flanks, the departing sound of the morning's sailings, the crews working quietly, with only the occasional voice drifting through the morning calm. As each ship readied, they pushed off and rowed out, the long oars dripping. They rounded the end of the harbour, then unfurled the sails and caught the wind and the river current and the ebbing tide.

Caerl hated being left behind, even by strangers' boats. He always had this feeling when watching other boats leave, the tug of the wanderer. He tried to keep himself busy, to keep his mind off thoughts of the many journeys they had been on together. He stayed at the boat all morning, going through the hundred little tasks that keep crews busy: checking and coiling ropes, inspecting sails, oiling oarlocks, trying to foresee anything that might break or fail at sea.

'Look!' Caerl shouted, and aimed a blow at the boy, who was stitching the blue-striped wool sail with a sturdy whalebone needle. 'You need to pull this tighter.' He slipped his fingers into the hole and ripped the boy's stitching wide open.

The boy said nothing, and Caerl thought about explaining but said nothing. Idiot, he thought, remembered hard gales that had torn sails from top to bottom, the shreds clearing the deck in a berserker's fury.

He left the boy for a few minutes, checked that the provisions of salt pork and hard-baked barley bread were not getting damp under their oilskin tarpaulin, then came back and watched over his shoulder. The lad was biting his lip. His cheeks were pink. He held up his stitching and Caerl tugged it. It gave a little, but not enough to make a fuss about.

'Better,' he said, and walked over to the other side of the ship and leant on a stretch of sealskin rigging, felt it give a little under his weight. The boy was a fool, he thought, then shook his head. No, it wasn't the boy, he told himself. It was the death of his lord, waiting like twilight in the evening woods.

When Caerl returned, he met an Irish blood-letter carrying a covered vessel out of the hall. His monk's robes were soiled around the hem, his head shaved in the Irish fashion, with a long tuft running over the top. There was a razor and a leather strap crossed over the bowl, and blood on the man's hands. He smiled, but Caerl gave him a wide berth.

The slave girl was mopping his brow and Wulfnoth's eyes were closed. A cloth had been wrapped round the forearm wound. His face gleamed with a light covering of sweat.

'How is he?' Caerl asked.

'Weak,' she said. She looked tired and busy and smiled in a way that told him all he needed to know. 'But he is comfortable.'

Caerl nodded and stood and watched for a long time. Lif is læna – life was only lent to us, to do as well as we could manage, before returning our body to the soil, and our soul to Heaven.

Beorn stumbled in. His smile was unsure. 'Where is he? Still abed? Wait till he hears what I have to tell.' His face was flushed and his eyes bloodshot, but the sight of Wulfnoth drained the colour from his cheeks. 'What is wrong with him? Why is he no better?'

Kendra sat down and let out a long sigh. His lord was not sick, he was dying.

'It is the flux,' she said.

Beorn nodded. Kendra looked at Caerl and an understanding passed between them. 'How long?' he said.

She let out another tired sigh. 'Not long,' she said, walking back and forth, performing little jobs to keep her busy.

Beorn belched. Caerl said nothing. The Three Wyrd Sisters, who wove men's fates, were readying the shears.

A church bell began to ring for evensong. Wulfnoth lay in his bed and heard the same ringing, summoning the faithful. He heard the words of the Magnificat in his head; his lips moved for the final blessing: Gloria Patri et Filio et Spiritui Sancto – felt another bowel movement, was too weak to climb out of bed. He wanted to sit up, but the girl was there. She pressed him back down into the bed and he struggled to push her away. He understood then how weak he had become. This hand, which once held a sword, was now too weak to fight off a serving girl.

It made him laugh.

His laugh was like a faint croak. The noise worried her. She finished wiping him clean, rinsed her hands in the bucket and dried them on her skirts. Caerl slipped out, tears in his eyes, glad that Wulfnoth had not seen him. A warrior humbled, a lord passing, the last glimpses of a dying friend. It was a good reason to go and pray, Caerl told himself, and made his way, after too long absent, back to the home of the Nailed God.

There was a tiny mud-and-wattle chapel on the other side of the cattle market, ill lit with smoky rush lights, with a packed earth floor and white quartz stones embedded around the altar. A carved stone cross was set there, with a painted Christ staring out with wide blue eyes. Caerl bowed his head and knelt, shut his eyes and prayed. The words did not come easily at first, but his wish was simple, and he said it out loud for Christ to hear as he had done once before. It hadn't worked then, and as he opened his eyes the rush lights flickered as before, the statue did not bleed or weep or move. The Lord gave him no sign.

Caerl pushed himself up, but he paused at the door, unbent

the silver arm-ring that Wulfnoth had given him years before and tossed it on to the altar table.

God would understand that, he thought.

When Caerl had gone, Wulfnoth lay silent for a long time, and his slave girl sat next to his bed and repeated the words of the paternoster.

'Thy kingdom come, thy will be done . . .' she said and Wulfnoth felt those words as never before. *Et dimitte nobis debita nostra*, 'Forgive us our trespasses, as we forgive . . .' Wulfnoth's lips moved in time with hers.

Beorn prayed with her. It took a while before he realised that Wulfnoth was awake. Beorn met his gaze and then looked away.

Wulfnoth understood. He shut his eyes, remembered the first man who'd died in his arms. It wasn't on the battlefield, but in the low meadow in Contone. A young lad – a freeman's son – who'd been trampled by a plough team of four oxen. That boy had clung on to life like a man who feels he is drowning, had not gone gently.

Old memories came so easily now, clustered round him like a crowd of friends at some last and final reunion. Wulfnoth had stood and watched the soul go out of that boy. Ælla, they had called him. Cenhelm's son. It was very clear to him now. In the year of Our Lord's incarnation 997. A frosty morning after Yuletide. Pale and still. The fields fixed with frost, blades of green grass sheathed with white hoarfrost, splattered with red blood. Ælla's last rattling breath on Wulfnoth's cheek as a dawn rook flapped low across the unploughed field.

Wulfnoth slept for a while and woke and saw his men crowding in the doorway, their watching faces pale. Beorn still sat by the bedside. His face was strained. A rosary was twisted about and through his fingers. The other hand held Wulfnoth's.

Wulfnoth opened his eyes at the touch. 'Who ever saw Beorn pray!' he said.

Wulfnoth caught Beorn's eye and he would have laughed, Beorn thought, if he had the strength, but Wulfnoth seemed barely to have the will to signal Caerl forward. The other men made space for Wulfnoth's shipmaster and kinsman. Caerl stood close now, so close he could smell his lord's sickness. Wulfnoth's flesh and skin were parchment-thin; the links between bone and tendon and gristle were obvious.

'My lord,' he said, no other words coming to him.

Wulfnoth shook his head, as if warding off argument, and pointed with his chin to the end of the bed, where his sword leant against the bedpost. There was a bundle of cloth as well, tied close with knotted leather thongs. Both men knew why it was there. 'It is my sword. Take it to him.' The slave girl propped him up on his rolled-up cloak. 'And the bundle,' Wulfnoth's voice was as thin and soft as the night rustle of leaves.

'Save him!' Wulfnoth croaked.

Caerl nodded.

'Promise me,' he whispered.

'I promise,' Caerl said.

'Help him,' Wulfnoth said to Beorn and Caerl, and both men nodded.

Wulfnoth held their gaze a long while and then sighed and shut his eyes. There was a heavy silence and some of them thought that he had already gone. Beorn wiped his cheeks with his rough warrior hands. Caerl stayed kneeling by the bedside, his head bowed. Wulfnoth's breathing became ragged. He opened his eyes for the last time. His voice was so faint that only Caerl could hear him. They watched as Caerl nodded again, then hung his head and started to weep.

They did not hear what Wulfnoth said, but they heard Caerl's response: 'I shall.'

Wulfnoth nodded and gave Caerl's fingers a final squeeze. There was a smile on his lips, as if, on the border of death, the grey rain curtain of the world had lifted. and the sun shone and he heard beautiful singing, smelt sweet incense and looked out from his hall down across a broad, green and ordered country. They sat waiting for long, dragging moments before Wulfnoth's breathing paused and then stopped. It was as if he had forgotten to draw in another breath. They waited for the next but it did not come. The stillness stretched on impossibly long and they bowed their heads and some made the sign of the cross; all were silent.

Beorn spoke. 'Here passes Wulfnoth Cild, son of Athelmar, Marshal of the Southern Shore, Beloved Lord! No longer shall we share a cup. No longer shall we ease your cares or stand shoulder to shoulder in the battle play. Alone and leaderless, we lament your passing.'

As they stood, the slave girl slipped out of the chamber, head bowed, one hand to her mouth. She hurried through the hall, which her memory still filled with Wulfnoth's shape and voice and touch and laughter, thrust the doors open and stepped outside.

The evening air had deepened to darkness; the mist had cleared; the night air was cold, the air damp. High, ragged clouds were tearing apart; the cold stars were glimmering overhead. Wulfnoth would have loved this night, she thought, would have breathed deep the presence of the old and unforgotten gods, entertained her with a tale of ancient times before his people had sailed out of the Nameless North when great heroes won eternal fame. His stories were sad but never gloomy. Most of them were encouraging and uplifting and Wulfnoth's favourites were when the hero knew he was to die and all that was left was to die well. It wasn't the end that was important, but the choices men made.

Kendra took a deep breath and turned her face to the pale and starry Heavens. Sad tales gave comfort where happy ones did not. The wise took strength from sorrow, for sadness brought beauty and wisdom and, when all else failed, steeled men with the courage to continue against the tallest odds.

CHAPTER TWO

The Easter King

Godwin was born in the shire of Sudsexe in the summer of the year 998. 'He looks sickly,' one of the village women whispered as the babe was washed and swaddled. 'Should we fetch the monk?'

'Hush,' his mother, Gytha, said. She reached out and held the babe close to her chest. 'Don't speak so. He's fine. Aren't you, my son? There is no need for monks tonight.' The infant jerked his head towards the finger that touched his cheek. 'Look – he thirsts for life. Here, drink deep.'

The women gathered round the childbed, as the animals had done for Jesus, and cooed over his little toes and fingers and face. Gytha helped him take the breast. She felt her milk begin to flow and Godwin opened his eyes for the first time – indistinctly blue and unfocused – and she was so proud that she began to cry.

Of course, Godwin did not remember any of this, but he heard the tale many times from his mother, and it formed in his head as if it were a memory.

The next tale Godwin remembered was his cold dip in the marble font at Cicestre Abbey.

'Godwin had a cold. I began to fear for him, but he coughed

and spluttered his way through the baptismal mass,' Gytha told visitors as their children played at their feet with soapstone marbles. Godwin was four. He heard himself discussed and sat up.

'Hold his right hand from the font so he may wield a sword without fear of sin,' Gytha had whispered to Wulfnoth, and Wulfnoth did as she bade him, but the monk noted the gesture. He was an ill-looking man, who had not seen a bath for a month too long.

'It is not just by swords that men sin,' the monk said.

Wulfnoth laughed. 'Shall I hold that away too?'

Wulfnoth liked to retell his joke. It always got a laugh. But on that day the monk did not smile. He was not a humorous man. He lifted his head to the roof-timbers and called out in a loud voice: '*Agnus Dei, qui tollis paccata mundi, miserere nobis. Agnus Dei, qui tollis peccata mundi, dona nobis pacem.*'

Young Godwin felt that the story had strayed a little far from himself and tugged at his mother's skirts. 'Mama! Mama! Mama!' he called till she paid him attention. 'Did I cry?'

'Yes,' his elder brother Leofwine said quickly, though he didn't remember either. 'You always cry!'

Contone – 'coombe-ton', the village in the valley – was Godwin's patch of Middangeard – Middle Earth. The agricultural year started in March, when winter was over and spring beckoned and day grew as long as the night, and then longer. Dark diminished and oxen were driven out to be yoked for ploughing and sowing. For as long as they could remember Godwin and Leofwine helped goad the oxen, and when the fields were done and the beasts were returned to their warm hay and stabling, they dashed up to the high stone shielings, where their father was bringing down the sheep, fat with this year's crop of lambs, to the low pastures for lambing.

The long fast of Lent made a virtue out of necessity, as their mother liked to tell them, for even though the world bloomed and budded and began to ring with birdsong – the crops were still too young to eat, and the store of last year's wheat was thin. But they never starved. There were berries and turnips, and, in the autumn, crab apples and cabbages, and beer of course – a thin and fizzy small beer that they drank at breakfast, lunch and dinner. In fact Wulfnoth prospered selling wool and worked iron that he bought from high in the Weald, and he did not forget to pay his due to God.

When Godwin was five his father built a stone bell-cot on the wooden village chapel and bought a copper bell that became a thing of wonder.

'It is glorious!' Godwin's mother said. 'Like Christ's angels calling us to prayer.'

At Easter men came from three valleys away and waited for the priest to ride up from the valley bottom on his brown rouncey, with his wife and children sitting on a stubborn mule.

The priest was a cheerful man; he greeted Wulfnoth and Gytha, pinched the cheeks of Leofwine and Godwin. He walked about and shook hands liberally as he slaked his thirst on a mug of small beer. He always took his sword off to say mass, and left it at the church door where it remained untouched and the boys stared at it in wonder.

'*Bene!*' the priest began in Latin, pronounced with a thick Sudsexe accent, before switching into English as the boys bowed their heads. 'Let us pray . . .'

But when the priest left, they solemnly carried the corn dolls, that had spent all winter in the shelter of the home, out into the field to be ploughed into the first cut furrow. Easter was a goddess from heathen times, when the doll was a real man, killed as a blessing to the Earth. That man was a slave, but when great calamity came the king knew his calling and went willingly to sacrifice, like a prize stallion. 'For sacrifice is always the price of leadership,' Wulfnoth taught his sons. 'As Our Lord Christ sacrificed himself on the cross on behalf of sinners. Now when the enemy comes, the king still stands at the forefront of the battle and marches against our enemies and dies there, if necessary.'

It seemed a hard job to be king.

'Who was the last king to die in battle?' Godwin asked.

Wulfnoth frowned. Kings were murdered and overturned, but no Wessex king had fallen on the battlefield. 'None,' he said.

'Why?'

Wulfnoth was tired of the list of questions. 'God is on our side.'

Autumn was Godwin and Leofwine's favourite season. It was hunting time, and they would ride behind with the other boys. Hunting was good training for a young thegn, for he should always be ready to take his best men and ride at his king's bidding. But the best were the great harvest feasts. The hall doors were thrown open and the whole valley filled the benches in noisy and excited crowds. In the morning there were games, in the afternoon eating, and in the evening, when they were all merry with ale, there were songs and tales and laughter.

Leofwine and Godwin shared a narrow closet along the side of the hall, shared a blanket as well as each other's warmth, and they lay listening to the harp music fading into the night.

'Your feet are cold,' Godwin told his brother.

Leofwine moved them. He lay in silence, and Godwin could see his eyes were open. They gleamed darkly, and he wondered if he had upset his brother, tried to think of something to say.

'Leofwine, when we are men and we fight in battle, I will stand by your shoulder,' he said.

'You're too young,' Leofwine said.

'So are you.'

'I'm three years older than you. Father has said he will take me to court next time the king rides through Sudsexe.'

'He will take me too.'

'No, Godwin, you're still a baby.'

'No I'm not!'

'Yes you are. You stay with the women all day. That means you're a baby.'

'I won't be a baby any more. Who else will guard your back in battle?'

Godwin and his brother loved tales from the elder days. There was a fine store that went back to the days of yore: of Goths and Ostrogoths, who killed Caesar and sacked Rome. Great heroes, oaths and honour compelled them to go out and face a formidable foe. One foe was followed by another, until eventually the hero, overmatched, went down fighting gallantly. The message was clear: although Fate conquered all men, word-fame never died.

Godwin's people were Saxons and they came across the water in the time of the Roman emperor Justin I, who was born a peasant. They brought their stories and their heroes, oath-bonds and law codes. Godwin's folk were brave warriors, and Wulfnoth's great-great-grandfather had carried King Alfred's banner, the White Dragon of Wessex, at the Battle of Ethandun. At the height of the battle, when both sides thought they had reached the limit of their endurance, he beat back the Danes who tried to seize the king's banner, and lost a hand in the struggle.

Alfred's reign was the dawn of England, from which the bright day began to shine out. Godwin's family prospered; Alfred's sons and grandsons drove the Norse and Danes and Welsh and men of Cumbraland back from the ruined kingdoms of Mercia and Northymbria and united all the English-speaking peoples in the Isle of Britannia. A hundred or so years since King Alfred's death, the Wessex kings were kings of the whole of England. And England prospered.

Godwin and Leofwine loved the saga of King Alfred: how he was driven into the fens of Adelingi and burnt the cakes as he wondered how to beat the Danes. They sat at their father's feet, knees drawn up to their chests, eyes wide as they heard how Alfred secretly gathered a great fyrd, the name for an expedition, and defeated the Danes, then ordered the land with laws, organised men into boroughs and shires that would last more than a thousand years.

Just a part of Wulfnoth's tale could fill a night, and just one night of great tale telling lived for weeks after inside their heads.

The fact that Alfred had once owned this manor added magic to the history.

'Perhaps Alfred sat on this very rock,' Godwin said to Leofwine as they sat by the willow-choked stream.

Leofwine jumped up. 'I'll be Alfred,' he said, 'and you be Guthrum!'

'No!' Godwin said.

'All right. I'll be Alfred and you be Athelstan, and the nettles are the Danes!'

Godwin and Leofwine drew their sticks, stood back to back and slashed at the ring of nettles that hemmed them in. They slashed and hacked till the air was full of shredded nettle, which stung their cheeks and necks and knuckles.

'Good fighting!' Leofwine told his brother, when there was no nettle left standing.

'It was close,' Godwin said. He watched how his brother held himself and tried to stand the same way. But there was a hollow in the slashed nettles and Godwin twisted his ankle and it swelled up to twice its size and Leofwine's face was grave. 'You're wounded,' he said. 'I'll carry you home.'

Leofwine put Godwin over his shoulder as if he were dead. Englishmen did not leave their own on the battlefield.

That was the year that Godwin first heard men speak of the Army. The Army was the name they gave the Danes who came each summer in increasing numbers, and soon began to over-winter. The Army claimed to be led by kings, but they were little more than a band of brigands who burned and ravaged. They avoided battle, preyed on the weak and relied on terror and vio-lence to subdue the people about them. They only left once a tax had been raised to buy them off and soon men grumbled more about the tax than the Army.

'It's evil. Even Archbishop Wulfstan says so. It turns folk to hunger and hatred. The only way to deal with these heathens is to meet them in battle and bloody their noses,' the local priest argued with a neighbour.

'Alderman Byrthnoth tried that.'

'And he died, I know that. But at least he gave the Army a kicking it'll not forget.'

They turned to Wulfnoth to adjudicate, but he was not con-vinced by either. 'Of course we should meet them in battle. If we paid them to leave then we could use that respite to organise our-selves to repel them next time. But we don't! We give them silver. Each spearman in the Army returns home rich. Look how easily the English are cowed, their neighbours think, and when the next sowing season comes, the Army has twice as many hea-thens!'

Wulfnoth rode from hall to hall soldering alliances with the good men of the district. He took Leofwine with him but left

Godwin behind. When they returned, Leofwine was smug with news.

'The king has found a new wife. A Norman princess named Emma.'

'Who are the Normans?'

'People who live in Normandig.'

'Why should the king marry a Norman?'

Leofwine bit his lip as he tightened his sword belt another notch. 'To stop the Army using Norman harbours. It is the king's new plan. Though Father says the Norman duke's oaths are not worth a bronze brooch.'

Godwin was six when the Army returned with a hundred and twenty ship crews, three kings and their battle-hardened retainers. The Norman ports remained open to the Danes, and now the king was saddled with a treacherous brother-in-law and a meddlesome wife. The Army plundered Exonia and all Wiltunscir while the king and his chief men bickered. They crossed from Wiltunscir to Hamtunscir and Leofwine and Godwin climbed to the high points and saw the land was burning.

Wulfnoth summoned the biggest men from the farms about. They arrived in twos and threes, dressed for battle. The bearded men slapped each other's backs while the lads too young to sport a moustache stood a little awkwardly with spear and shield or struck poses for the local girls. Godwin admired the shield-devices painted on the raw hide: crosses and axes and entwined wolves, on fields halved or quartered with bright blues and reds and yellow and white. He took a warped shield from the hay barn and pretended to be a warrior, and stood guard as Wulfnoth rode off, he and his men singing proud war songs.

But the king dithered, and the man he put in charge of the

English fyrd fell sick. That man – a foolish king's thegn – was named Elfric. The closer the Army came, the sicker Elfric grew, till he refused to get up from his bed and asked another man to take the lead. The English lost heart then and began to disband. News came that Norwic had been plundered.

'Nordfolc burns, but Sudsexe is saved,' Wulfnoth said bitterly as he hung his unmarked shield on the hall wall.

Wulfnoth was among many who clamoured for the king to act, but the king sent messengers to make terms with the Army, who said they would keep burning and killing until another great tax was raised to buy them off. They demanded twenty-four thousand pounds of silver. The amount was staggering. Men had never heard of such a quantity. It hurt them to think that their labours were being stolen by violent thieves. Wulfnoth cursed so hard he made the boys' mother blush, but there was cold fury in his eyes when he came back from the barns.

'Tighten your belts,' he told his sons as they loaded up the carts. 'This will be a lean year.'

Godwin looked at the money his father had collected. It was a sorry collection of ha'pennies and farthings; the proud and distinguishing features of the former kings were worn away. He dipped his hand into the leather sack. The crowned heads were smooth and blank and fearful, they slipped from his hand like cowards before battle.

Alderman Elfhelm was the lord of Northymbria. He had once fought alongside Wulfnoth and had given him the gold-worked sword hilt set with blood-red garnets that hung upon the hall wall. He was Wulfnoth's benefactor, and in the spring of 1006 he declared that he would pass through Contone on his way to the king's Great Easter Court at Wincestre.

Alderman Elfhelm travelled with a great company of retainers and squires and farriers, but thankfully the Downs roads were too steep for them all, so he sent the packhorses and covered wagons on to Wincestre by gentler roads.

'He is one of the great men of the kingdom,' Leofwine told Godwin, as if he should know this already. 'Now quick! Mother is calling you.'

Gytha was filled with horror when she thought of so many grand and hungry mouths. She wiped her hands on her apron and did not know where to begin. 'How long will they stay? They will eat us out of house and home! He will want game three times a day, and his men will not be content with oats and salt pork. They'll want venison and snipe and goose and swan. There's not enough food in the parish to last more than a week of hard feasting! And the alderman is a northerner, and we know how much they drink. Tell the ale-wife to malt more grains.'

Godwin and Leofwine watched in wonder as the hall was scrubbed and swept and the wainscoting hung with new tapestries that came from Boseham on ox-drawn carts, the wide-horned beasts bellowing as they dragged the carts up the narrow stony path and left it a mess of ruts for weeks after. Their mother hurried to and fro, keys jangling at her girdle, sleeves rolled up to her elbows. An air of tense and nervous expectation filled the household as the day approached. Harbingers arrived two days before the alderman and set their mother in a final frenzy of activity.

'When is the alderman due in court?' She bobbed. 'Does he intend to stay long? He is welcome, of course to stay as long as he likes. We are honoured indeed.'

That night Godwin's mother combed his hair and picked out lice eggs and flicked them into the fire. She dressed him in a fine kirtle of blue lambswool that was a hand-me-down from his brother, and over his shoulders she pinned a cloak of fine English cloth, hemmed with silver thread.

Godwin and Leofwine stood together.

'Godwin, how you are growing!' Gytha said.

Godwin looked sideways and saw that his head came up to Leofwine's shoulder. He'd be taller than him soon, he thought.

'Now, off to bed!' she told him, and kissed his head. 'God bless you. It'll be a long day tomorrow.'

Godwin and Leofwine were up with the larks. They climbed the high ash tree and spied out the end of the road that led through the thick woods of the Weald. When they saw the company ride from the forest they let out gasps of pleasure.

'Look! Elfhelm rides a white palfrey with a silver bit,' Leofwine said.

Godwin said, 'And at his right hand rides Father!'

They scuffed their new kirtles as they slid down the tree and ran to the hall.

'Mother! Father is here riding at the head of the finest company ever seen. Every man wears a gold armband, and their belts sparkle with cunning cut gems!'

Alderman Elfhelm dismounted at the door. He was tall and balding, with greying hair and a war wound that left him with a stiff hip and a slight limp.

'Thank you,' he said and took the bowl of welcome from Gytha's hands. He took a loud and appreciative sip, looked about at the land, not the people, and seemed pleased. 'Wulfnoth, this is a fine spot. It reminds me of the great moors of Northymbria. But this manor bespeaks of comfort and gentleness in the windy heights, like a great shoulder of the land.

'Aha! So that is the South Sea. See how it glitters silver in the sunlight!'

Elfhelm strode a few steps futher, put his hands on his hips and let out a great breath. He stared down as the valley sloped down to the sea, hands on his hips in a defiant gesture. 'You're right, Wulfnoth. We've paid too much too many times. Look at that!' Elfhelm pointed to the gentle and ordered landscape of little strip fields and woods and rivers and villages. 'That is a land worth fighting for!'

Elfhelm was the grandest man Godwin had ever seen and he watched him closely. His manner was magnanimous and to Godwin he seemed like a leader out of legend: high-born, educated, fierce, brave and generous. Godwin and Leofwine had never seen so many swords and shields stacked against the walls, so many bold and bearded men crammed along the benches.

'So, you are Godwin,' Elfhelm said as he ruffled Godwin's freshly combed hair.

Wulfnoth was eager his sons would make a good impression and he watched as Godwin puffed his chest out. Any boy who listened to poems knew how to announce himself in men's company. 'I am Godwin, son of Wulfnoth, son of Athelmar of the folk of Aelle, who came across the sea. My mother is Gytha, of the Hastingas, and they are the bravest of warriors!'

Elfhelm laughed. 'Are they?'

'Of course,' Godwin said and ignored the look Leofwine gave him. 'Except my father. He is even more brave! And you are the alderman of Northymbria. Your great-great-grandfather was one of the Danes that King Alfred beat. My ancestor fought there too. He lost his hand and in return for his hand he was given this manor. King Alfred hunted here!'

'Did he?'

'Yes,' Godwin said. 'But you are welcome here, to come in peace. Hunt or no.'

Alderman Elfhelm let Godwin talk, but the longer he went on, the more a smile began to tickle about his mouth.

'You're a fine talker, Godwin Wulfnothson!'

Godwin almost forgot what he wanted to ask, but he had thought long about his question and it tumbled out. 'My father says you are keenest to fight the Army. But if your ancestors were Danes, and they come from Danemark, why do you want to fight them? I have heard men say that when the Army comes again, you will support them against us.'

'And who told you that?'

'It is what the men in Cicestre say.'

Elfhelm laughed, not because this wasn't true, but because it was a rumour not worth the retelling. 'Men – from Cicestre or not – say many things, Godwin, son of Wulfnoth. If you wish to sleep well at night, it is best to ignore the tattle you hear by the well-side. Where I am from, we say, "Whither the needle leads, the thread will follow."'

Riddling wordplays were popular and Godwin had a sharp mind and a quick tongue. '"An upright man does not throw a crooked shadow,"' he said, and his mother tugged at his elbow.

'Come away, lad,' she said, but Elfhelm put his hand up.

'No, but men might see a straight shadow and the evil in their own eye makes them see it crooked. Decide your path, and stick to it come rain or shine.'

Godwin thought the alderman was talking to him, but then Elfhelm lifted his voice so that the whole assembly could hear him. 'Hear me, all of you. This lad speaks well. It is true that there are some in England who say that because our blood and speech are Danish we support the Army. But we are good and honest Christian people. We have lived in the Isle of Britain for a hundred and fifty years. Our loyalty is to the White Dragon.

We follow the English king into battle. And it has been thus for generations of man.

'Who are the Army? In Danemark kings are ten a penny. In Frankia they choose the eldest son of the eldest son, as if age were the best qualification for kingship. But in England we have one king, and when one king dies the Wise – clergy, warriors and wise greybeards – assemble all the princes of the royal house and choose from the athelings the one most suited to kingship. And so our land is governed by law and custom, not by might or terror or the whims of a king, nor yet by the rule of the spear and the sword.'

'So what makes a man wise?' Godwin asked him later, when the dishes were cleared away and the tale-teller tuned his lyre in the corner.

'A man is considered wise when he is respected by men of his shire and by the men of other shires.'

'And are you one of the Wise?'

Elfhelm laughed. 'So other men say,' he said.

'And are you here to choose an heir to Ethelred?'

Elfhelm laughed again. 'No. That only happens when one king dies. But as well as choosing a new king, it is also our part to witness the actions of the king and counsel him if he should, by anger or greed or poor judgement, be led astray.'

Elfhelm spoke well, and Godwin liked him, and the alderman took a shine to Wulfnoth's lad because he reminded Elfhelm of himself when he was young: bright and freckled and inquisitive.

At the farewell feast Alderman Elfhelm set Godwin on his knee. It was a great honour. The spring days were lengthening and they were allowed to stay up later, and Elfhelm laughed at his many questions.

'So why is it that the Danes sail to England and we do not sail to Danemark and burn their halls?' Godwin asked.

'That is a good question, Wulfnothson. Some say that we have become too sinful. Others that we are badly led. Others yet say that we are too gentle and that we have been blessed with too many comforts. But the truth is that in England we prosper and trade and, with Christ's blessing, grow rich. And as long as men exist the hungry will envy another his bowl of gruel. Law does not rule in Danemark; it is the sword and the axe that rule their land, and they grow fierce and violent from a young age. Even father and son come to blows. Look at their new king, Swein Forkbeard. He has raised the sword against his father, and now his father, that hoary-headed and unblessed man, has been driven into exile and drifts from hall to hall, begging for a cup of ale. There is no end to their violence. Neighbours are smoked out of their halls by their freemen. Freemen are cut down in cold blood and the killer pays no weregeld.'

Godwin shook his head. Lawlessness brought manslaughter and murder.

Godwin was sorry to see Elfhelm and all his great company depart, his father among them. 'It is my duty to go and witness the king's business,' Elfhelm said as he held Godwin's chin and winked at him. 'Both for his benefit and for ours. For in England we keep the king to our laws, as well as us to his. Elfhelm held out his arm and Godwin grasped his wrist and they shook hands in farewell.

'Farewell, Godwin Quick-Tongue!' he said and ruffled his hair. Godwin ran alongside the horsemen till he was more than a mile from home and his father gave him a look that told him that enough was enough.

A month later, as May filled the hedges with white, Wulfnoth returned with his closest retainers. They were stiff and formal, and Wulfnoth's shoes were dusty as he swung down from the saddle.

'Back into the hall!' he told them. 'Ring the bell. Summon all the men. There is dire news to tell.'

It took twenty minutes for all the retainers to assemble. Wulfnoth's eyes bored into them. His brows were tight-knit; his mood smouldered. The hubbub stilled. Godwin felt his heart hammering away as his father drew in a deep breath.

'There is murder afoot – against both the king's and our common law. Our recent guest the beloved Alderman Elfhelm has been most foully murdered.'

'No!' someone shouted. 'Surely not!'

More voices were raised. Godwin realised one of them was his. No, surely not, but Wulfnoth told the tale that he'd been told. 'Elfhelm went to the hall of a Sciropescir thegn named Eadric Streona. This Eadric is a man with an evil name and had long feuded with Elfhelm's people. A battle-shirker and braggart, loud on the benches, timid in battle. He welcomed Elfhelm as with a warm embrace. Took gifts and gave his own, and full friendship was restored on both sides. But on the fourth day as they rode to hunt, a bought man leapt out in ambush and drove a spear into Elfhelm's back till the steel-thorn stood a hand's breath from his belly.'

The hall listened in appalled silence and Godwin did not know what this meant.

'So passes Elfhelm,' Wulfnoth said. 'But there is worse to tell. As soon as the appalling deed was done, the king had Elfhelm's sons seized and their eyes put out and forbade their family from taking either weregeld or vengeance.'

News of Elfhelm's murder spread faster than the cattle-blight. It was told in the hall that evening, as if one of the ancient tales had come alive: Elfhelm the hero; Eadric the villain, who had feuded with Elfhelm's family as God had feuded with the brood of giants ages long.

That night the storyteller played Elfhelm. He did not have the old man's kindness, but he copied the limp well enough. Godwin wanted the story to hurry along to the moment of his death, for in dying a hero's character shone through.

The storyteller recounted Elfhelm's dying words as if he had witnessed the event. The murderer's hidden spear was thrust through him and the man's hands clenched in agony. He let a rivulet of ale dribble from his lips, dark in the firelight, like blood. He staggered a few steps forward, staring at the imaginary spear, red with his own hot gore, then stopped as he saw Eadric's face and understood he had been lured here to be murdered.

> *You welcomed me with open arms,*
> *But hotter than fire between false friends*
> *Does friendship burn. My heart's fire cools*
> *Mauled by the spear, men shall hear of this foul murder.*
> *For ages to come Eadric's folk*
> *Shall wander without land rights.*

The storyteller turned and in an instant he was no longer Elfhelm but Eadric. The transformation was horrifying. Absorbing Eadric was like swallowing hot coals. The man's face twisted, his back bent, and his lips peeled back in a grim rictus. He looked like a hunched hound as he crept forward filled with malice: moor-walker, master of the fen-fortress, kindred of Cain.

Eadric's hiss filled the hall; he drew his knife, grasped the old man's hair and pulled back his head, so his throat was exposed beneath the white beard. Godwin wanted to look away, but could not. Silence plunged in. It was as if they had witnessed Elfhelm's murder in that Scirospescir wood.

No one spoke. The shock was palpable.

In the days that followed Godwin saw assassins everywhere. He stood close to his father, was ready to fend off the darting shadow, the hidden spear. When his father was out in the black-smith's yard, sleeves rolled up to his elbows, helping the farrier nail a new set of shoes on to his pony, Godwin kept watch.

'Eadric won't bother about me,' his father said as the new shoe sizzled as it touched the cold hoof, but Godwin was not con-vinced.

'Why would Elfhelm go to such a man's hall?' Godwin asked later that day as they castrated lambs.

Wulfnoth stretched up to his full height. Godwin was almost of age, and it was time for him to understand men's business. 'Well, he went at the king's bidding,' he said.

Godwin caught the look in his father's eyes. 'But why should the king act against him?' Godwin said. 'What did Elfhelm do?'

'The king has evil advisers,' Wulfnoth said, 'and evil men see the world crooked.'

News came that Eadric was betrothed to the king's daughter. Godwin saw the light in his father's eyes. So the king was com-plicit in Elfhelm's murder.

'Why would King Ethelred do such a thing?' Godwin asked.

Wulfnoth did not know, but his mood was grim, and he set a guard on his land. For if the highest cannot claim recompense, then what hope have small men when the storm blows?

Godwin and Leofwine knew enough of their letters to read a charter or a list of laws, and they knew murder went against all the laws of the land, both written and unwritten. It was as if the nation's mast had broken and England wallowed dangerously in the swells, and instead of drawing together the great families struggled against each other, like a shieldwall that fragments as each man turns his back and runs – and is cut down from behind.

There was a gloomy air as Wulfnoth and his men sat around and discussed the news. It was almost all bad. Distant slave markets thronged with English voices; whole swathes of Oxenefordscire and Hamtunscir were waste; while along the coast corn rotted in the autumn fields, wind whistled through the charred roof slats, and abandoned doors banged angrily in the sea breeze.

At harvest time Godwin and Leofwine spent the day winnowing the wheat so the chaff was carried away on the wind. There were husks in their hair and clothes. Their faces were freckled with sun. They stole a jug of ale and hurried out into the half-light of the summer evening. It was approaching Lammas Eve 1006, and the evening sky was a pale green ribbed with darkening clouds. They drank and stretched their toes out and sighed.

Far off, by the coast, a light caught their eye.

'Look!' Godwin said.

Leofwine looked.

The beacons had been lit. The wind was blowing the smoke inland and the columns curved as they rose. The two boys stared and there was no mistaking: the darker the evening grew, the brighter the flames.

Wulfnoth nodded. Yes, it was the beacons. He cuffed the boys ahead of him and then turned and saw the twinkling fires growing brighter. 'The more silver we give, the quicker they return. As if our troubles are not enough,' he cursed, 'the Army chooses this moment to return.'

The hall soon filled with excited warriors. They talked of where the Army might land, who their leaders might be and where the king would muster the English forces to meet them. The fires were piled up, and ale brought out, and a supper of oats and bacon was served in bowls while the harp was passed from hand to hand, rose late the next morning and sat in the hall rubbing their heads and looking to their weapons.

Wulfnoth did not wait for the shire summons to call out his retainers. He had the horses brought in from the fields and their manes braided, and he summoned all the men who owed him service. He was grim and determined and warlike as he dressed in steel-knit shirt and helmet, took ash spear, grasped shield of linden and spoke brave words: he would pay a tribute of spears, stand toe to toe with the Army, and see who fell first.

CHAPTER THREE

The Hall Stands Empty

It was six weeks before Wulfnoth returned. Half the horses were riderless; Wulfnoth's face was sour. The campaign had been a shambles. Kites and crows now picked at the stubbled fields of English dead.

When one man tried to chant a poem to honour the dead Wulfnoth grew angry. 'Hush! We sing too much of defeat. Let no song be sung till we drive the Army back into the surf and send the hated longships back hollow to their homelands.'

'How did you lose?' Godwin asked when he found Beorn sitting in the smithy. 'They only had a hundred and twenty ships. Didn't we outnumber the Army?'

'We did,' Beorn said, 'but it takes more than numbers to win a battle. The Danes are united and determined. When their king speaks, all the men listen to him and obey because he brings them to victory.'

Godwin swung his legs and screwed up his face.

'So what now?'

'If your father was king he would summon all fighting men into a great fyrd and give the Army battle. They dislike battle. It is a dangerous place for any man, Dane or no. But King Ethelred sends other men, and they ask themselves why should they die for him. And they refuse, or feign illness, and then their men think, Why should we fight when our lords do not? And they go home to their farms and pray the Army does not come.'

'There must be something we can do,' Godwin said, and Beorn laughed bitterly.

'Yes, Wulfnothson. Pray.'

When they saw that the will to resist had been crushed, the Army broke up into raiding parties that rode about the valleys and exhorted food and coin and women. A few brave men tried to defy the Danes and their homes were burnt, their wives seized, and they were left cut down.

Wulfnoth had buried his silver and sent his womenfolk under his wife's command deep into the Weald. The boys refused to go.

Wulfnoth glared at them. 'Go with your mother,' he repeated.

'No, Father, we want to stay and fight,' Godwin squeaked.

Wulfnoth was furious. His look silenced him.

'Father,' Leofwine said, 'I am older. Let me stay.'

'And what would you do?'

'Stand by you,' Leofwine said, 'when the Army comes.'

Wulfnoth was angry and trapped between duty and his oaths to the king, and the combination was too much and he roared with sudden anger, 'Why have I been given fools as sons? Listen, both of you! We are not going to fight,' Wulfnoth said. 'No! There will be no killing. That is the last thing we need. The Danes will come and pray God they will leave when they have what they want.'

'And what do they want?'

'Silver, food and ale,' Wulfnoth said.

'So why are the women being sent away?'

'Out!' Wulfnoth shouted.

Wulfnoth was in a furious mood. He feared his wrath when the looting Danes came, feared that he would be unable to contain his pride, and would strike out in anger, and be cut down in turn, and leave his sons, like wolf cubs, to raise themselves. The Devil preyed on each man's weakness. Wulfnoth would endure the Danes. He would protect his people.

Gytha saw the look in his eye. 'Come with us,' she said.

'I shall not.'

'You are in a dangerous mood.'

Wulfnoth said nothing.

She took his hand. 'I am worried. Husband, I am fearful.'

'You have spear and knife. I will send what men I can spare. Take the dogs as well. They will keep animals away.'

'No,' she said, and took his other hand so that he had to look her in the eye. 'We do not need noble corpses. A blind man is better than a corpse. You are the shepherd of the folk. We need you, Wulfnoth.'

Wulfnoth had no words for her, but he held her gaze and nodded solemnly.

Godwin took his father's hand and squeezed it.

Wulfnoth could not look at them. His voice trembled. 'When it is safe to return I will send word.'

They had never been so deep into the woods before. It was full of pits and mounds, all overgrown with nettles and weeds, and the trees were thick and unmanaged, although a few ancient pollards showed that men had once lived up here.

The deeper they went, the darker and more tangled the forest and the narrower the deer-paths. In the heart of the Weald there were more and more lime trees. They trailed long beards of moss and lichen, and it was in the centre of this woodland fortress that they camped, in a wide and marshy clearing ringed with alders. They penned the livestock with wattle fences, and the dogs spent a long time warily sniffing the air. The boys helped gather firewood. There was plenty of it about, and they could hear the redbreast and the song thrush in the trees above their heads.

They kept to the dry land and built a great fire to keep wild beasts away, but at night they could hear wolves howling, and the dogs barked. Gytha set a watch each night on the horses and milch goats. The fringes of the Weald were home to charcoal-burners and men who still worked the ore pits and smelted pig iron. But the deeper tracts had a reputation as a haunt for monsters and outlaws, so they avoided all strangers until it became clear that the strangers were other refugees. Then they visited each other's camps and traded tales of horror and rape and violence, as if they were at the market and were chatting about the weather and the coming fair.

Godwin and Leofwine found a spot a bowshot from the camp, where they liked to sit and talk. They were changing from children into young men, and the world about them was changing too.

'We shall stand with Father when he next meets the Army,' Leofwine said as he chewed on a stalk of wild grass.

'You will hold his standard, and I will hold your shield,' Godwin said.

When the time to return came, the boys were almost sad to leave. In Contone the people seemed altered, the fields empty.

But it was better not to talk about it. The paddocks were empty, the milch cows had gone, and all that was left of Wulfnoth's prize bull was the skin that hung in the hall and the

49

four hooves that waited to be boiled up for glue or paint for a shield.

The only time the Danes were mentioned was almost a year later, when one of the freemen's daughters lower down the valley had a child. She had married in the spring, and there was nothing uncommon about betrothals after the fact. But Godwin was in the dairy as the women were talking of the birth.

'It's dead,' one of them said.

'Not surprised,' another girl said.

'In the stream, poor mite,' said another.

'What's a "poor mite"?' Godwin asked, but they all fell silent.

'A baby died,' his mother told him as she shooed him back outside. 'Now off with you.' And as Godwin went outside, he heard her say, 'Poor Danish bastard.'

One day a tall, blond thick-set man was standing by the hall door. His feet were bound with rags, and his cloak was muddied and weather-stained. He fell to his knees when Wulfnoth came out, and begged for food and shelter.

Wulfnoth took him in; he looked like a good man. 'Can you wield a sword?'

'Yes.'

'And are you content to do farm work?'

'Yes.'

'Where is your old lord?'

'Dead.'

'You survived him?'

'Alas I did. And I have been punished by the North Wind and Jack Frost, and I wish that I had died with him. But he fell to a feud while I was at market and we hunted down his killers and killed them as they staggered from a feast.'

'What was your lord's name, and who did he feud with?'

'His name was Little Helm, on account of his size – he was a big man. But his foe was one of Eadric's retainers. An ugly man with ginger hair and orange freckles. A giant of a man, with a sneering manner.'

'What is your name?'

'Hemming.'

Wulfnoth did not ask any more questions, but put out his hand and pulled the man up. 'Well, Hemming, fetch yourself a bowl of soup. See if we have a better cloak for you. You sleep in the hall with the other retainers.'

Hemming ate like a horse, and when Gytha saw the lice eggs – small, dark grey pebbles in the hems of his clothing – she had the man stripped and those of his clothes that could be mended were boiled in the cauldron that hung from the roof-beam. His hair and beard were combed, and even though he was dressed in borrowed clothes he looked like a retainer, not any common fellow.

'Why don't the kings of the Army kill Ethelred?' Godwin asked that night as the fire dwindled to a red and baleful glow.

Wulfnoth laughed. 'He is the ring through the bull's nose.'

'What do you mean?'

'They need him. He is their milch cow. Have you seen Ethelred's eldest son, Athelstan?' Wulfnoth laughed and Godwin understood, he thought, something more about his father. He had seen Athelstan Aetheling fleetingly. He was older than Leofwine, and proud and warlike, like a king of legend.

'Athelstan is come of age this year and he is champing at the bit. King Ethelred cannot die soon enough. Do you think his son will sit at home while the Army kills his people? He is eager for glory. So the Army are content to leave Ethelred alone, and we are led a merry dance, like a ringed bull is led to the slaughterer's axe.'

Throughout the autumn of 1006 the Army rode about unhindered. Wulfnoth's hall stood silent and empty, and their stomachs ached as they licked their bowls clean of nettle and field-grass gruel and the cook chased the boys out when they came to filch.

They sat on a rock and groaned with hunger.

That evening Godwin devoured his meal, and there was nothing left but an empty bowl. He licked it out. Twice. In the end Godwin started crying. Leofwine looked at him and sighed. Then he reached out and took Godwin's bowl and gave him his own.

In the summer of 1007, the king announced yet another tax, of thirty thousand pounds of silver. Wulfnoth went pale, because he had given so much already, and he could not look his people in the face.

But he, and the rest of the country, paid, and the Army went home, but before the wheat could be brought in heavy rain and blight ruined much of the crop. November came with heavy snows that killed many sheep and left the people shivering in their beds.

'We have seen the backs of the Danes, but it is not the end of our troubles,' Wulfnoth said as he poked at the fire with a charred stick. 'Fetch your spears. It is time to hunt.'

That winter was the coldest that men could remember and, after the long year of hunger, made the people weak. The old went first, then the sick and the weak, and men prayed. When the young and the healthy and the beautiful went too, men tugged their beards and wept.

Leofwine began to cough, but he refused to stay home. The people needed him. They needed deer and meat and fat and the thin brown broth that the marrow bones brought, and Wulfnoth needed his elder son's help.

The hounds were as lean and listless as the rest of them, but when they got the scent they were as vicious as starving men. One day Leofwine and Godwin caught their first wolf. It was old and grey and lame in one leg, but they cornered it in one of the high fields and killed it with stabs to the heart.

Wulfnoth was proud of them. 'Come, let's skin it before it freezes.'

Leofwine and Godwin refused to stay in the hall, and Godwin, determined to show he was as big a boy as his brother, insisted on riding and hunting and hawking. Each evening his energy was spent and he fell asleep at the benches and had to be carried to bed.

Leofwine's cough failed to get better once the frosts had passed. Days turned to weeks and one day Leofwine coughed and then looked at his hand and said, 'Look – blood!'

He was bemused more than shocked, but when Gytha saw the blood at dinner that night her face went pale.

'Come,' she said, 'sit by the fire. No more running wild for you. Rest, child.'

'I cannot,' Leofwine said.

'Your father will have to do without you for the moment.'

Leofwine argued, but she refused to listen.

'Godwin will have to help,' she said. 'And I shall fetch the priest to come and bless you.'

Gytha gathered all manner of herbs, brewed up coltsfoot with honey and held the bowl for Leofwine to sip.

Godwin was jealous of all the attention his brother got and wished he could cough up blood too.

'Don't be silly,' his mother told him. 'Now out you go and make yourself useful!'

'Useful' meant keeping out of her way, and Godwin went about the manor looking for trouble, or something that might snag his attention. When he came back to the hall, Leofwine made faces at him as the women rubbed goose fat into his chest.

'I would gladly swap places,' Leofwine said as he buttoned his kirtle, 'but Mother says I must stay here till the weather warms. Tell me, has anyone caught the white hart yet?'

'I don't know.'

'Go and see for me. We can't let our neighbour snag him. He'll mount the antlers over his chair and we'll have to sit there while he gloats that he caught him and not us!'

Leofwine started coughing and the cough wouldn't stop and Godwin was shooed out of the door.

'What's the matter with him?' he asked as the door was shut behind him.

'Your brother is sick,' one of the women said. 'Now off with you and don't let in any more draughts.'

Godwin found himself standing on the doorstep looking out into the world. The sun was just starting to break through the clouds. It stabbed down and lit up strip fields and hedgerows, pasture and hall, church and glebe, and the far-off acres of blue water. Godwin pursed his lips. It was a day he and Leofwine would have disappeared together over the distant hedge, and come back at dinnertime, dirty and ravenous. He set off alone, with stick and knife, into the fringes of the forest. He saw nothing, not a white hart or a brown hind, nor elf or goblin, friend or foe.

He picked up stones and tossed them out into the sunlight.

The day faded and he shivered.

When summer came he would bring Leofwine up here and

share this spot with him, he thought. They would sit here and laugh at the time when Leofwine was sick. Maybe they would return as old men, when they had sons of their own and great victories to remember.

These thoughts made Godwin cheerful again, and as the day began to fail, he pushed himself up and started back down the narrow sheep track of trodden grass, half whistling odd notes.

'I'm going down to Cicestre,' his mother announced that evening, 'to fetch holy water.'

'Can I come?' Godwin said.

'No,' she said.

The holy water came in a red clay pot stamped with a cross and a little image of a pair of angels looking up into the clouds. It cost his mother ten shillings.

'It was drawn from the Saints' Well and blessed by nuns and monks of the highest purity,' Gytha said.

'Can I try some?'

'Godwin,' she said. 'Please!'

Godwin waited till Leofwine had been given the water to drink before he dipped his finger to see what this holy water tasted like.

It wasn't like the water in Contone, and he guessed it was the holiness he could taste and dipped his finger in again.

'Godwin!' his mother said, and he jumped at the sound. 'Will you please stop!'

Leofwine took to his bed, and Godwin had to sleep in a corner of the hall floor where the sacks of seed corn were kept. After a week and a half their father was summoned home, but it took a long time for the messenger to find him, and he could not find a physic to bring back with him, so it was their mother and her ladies who tended to the boy, with charms and prayers and poultices of stinking herbs mixed with goose fat.

'You smell like a goose!' Godwin told his brother, and Leofwine smiled.

'I feel like a goose,' he said.

Godwin went in to see his brother each morning, and even though the leecher came and opened up vein after vein, his brother did not get better.

One morning Leofwine said, 'Men say the Danes will come in the spring, and then we will ride out with Father,' and he seemed so much brighter that Godwin hugged him.

'You are looking much better!' he said.

'Am I?'

Godwin nodded. 'Much. When the Danes come, Father said we can ride with the fyrd.'

That was something to look forward to, and Leofwine started to come out of his bed and sit by the fire.

But it was like the light of the setting sun that shines full in the face, warming the skin, blinding the viewer.

'Of course we will,' Leofwine said, as if these things were certain, though life could be as brief as a sparrow's flight.

A week later Leofwine was confined to bed and weaker than a girl.

'Are you going to die?' Godwin asked when the days were at their shortest and it was easiest to slip from the world.

'No,' Leofwine said, for his coughing had improved, and it seemed that the spotting of blood had lessened. 'You will grow up and we will ride and hunt together. I'll take you to catch a falcon for yourself. I can see it. You will grow a pitchfork moustache!'

The two boys laughed.

'Down to your chest,' Leofwine assured him, and his laughter turned into a thick, rattling noise in his chest. and even as Leofwine struggled for breath his humour was still good. 'It'll be so long you can sieve your ale.'

Godwin smiled and his brother laughed again, but the laughter made Godwin wince, and he wished that his brother would not tell any more jokes.

Gytha took Godwin aside for their daily prayers one day.

'Your brother does not have long for this world,' she said.

'What do you mean?'

'He is almost ready to slip across into the Lord's care.'

'Will the Lord look after him?'

Gytha nodded.

'But why should He take Leofwine?' Godwin asked. 'He has done nothing wrong.'

'None of us has done anything wrong,' she told him. 'It is just the way of the world.'

'The world is wrong,' he said as if it were his mother's fault.

There was nothing Gytha could say. 'You're right, it is.'

Godwin was angry. 'I thought you brought a priest!'

'Godwin,' she said. Her tone was low. It was almost like a warning.

He turned away and kicked the door.

'Can't you do something!' he shouted. He punched the door as well.

Punched it again.

Leofwine lasted all the next day. He seemed to rally during the afternoon, but he had grown too weak to talk, and for the brief moments they were alone Godwin spoke. The words did not come easily, for he did not know what to say, so he told Leofwine all the things they would grow up and do together.

Hunt, hawk, marry, have sons. He kept talking even as the wan winter light began to fade about them, and Leofwine closed his eyes and his chest moved very slowly, and then Godwin didn't talk any more. and someone put their hand on his shoulder and patted it, and Godwin looked up and saw Beorn's face.

'How's he doing?'

'Well,' Godwin said.

Beorn nodded. Godwin could not tell what he was thinking, but then he forced a smile, and patted Godwin's shoulder again. 'Good,' he said. 'Good.'

Day seemed barely to have begun before night came creeping back among them all. The candles burnt steadily down and on Christmas Eve Leofwine opened his eyes, saw his family near and smiled. But he was past hearing and almost past caring, and the angels came for him in the darkness when Godwin's head had fallen forward in sleep.

When Godwin woke he looked up and could sense his brother's soul had departed. He could see it in the maid's face as she swept the hearth ash into a bucket, feel it in the silence of the heavy roof-thatch, the taut look about his father's mouth, the dull clang of the chapel bell where the monks' prayers had failed them.

Wulfnoth did not cry, but stood silent and nodded to his son as if he understood. He should have fought the Danes. He should not have given them his food. He should have died in battle rather than watch his eldest son starve and sicken. Wulfnoth sat by the embers and his eyes gleamed red, a slow and angry flame, stoked to fury. His nostrils flared and his hands open and closed; his eyebrows came together and he refused ale or milk or whey. His loss weighed on him, and it was all he could do to sit upright and not curl like a child in grief.

You are a coward, Wulfnoth Cild, he told himself. God has punished you for your cowardice. And as he sat his hands opened, as if about a Danish throat, and he looked down and imagined slowly squeezing his fury out.

Better to revenge, Wulfnoth decided, than wade through mourning.

Early the next day, Godwin came in and knelt with his father and mother, and the monk led a prayer in Latin. Leofwine was propped up on down pillows, his arms had been tucked in under the blanket, a cloth had been tied about his jaw, and the king's silver coins weighted down his eyelids. The monk talked and the words flowed over Godwin and he was jealous and angry, and did not know how his brother could leave him like this.

As the day drew on, Godwin half expected his brother to sit up or stop playing dead, but day turned to night, silence to tears, tears to a sudden wail in the middle of the night that chilled men's hearts.

Godwin thought it was his mother, at first, but slow dawning he understood it was his father's voice, ripped from the gut, and it spoke of pain Godwin knew he did not understand.

> *Open doth stand the gap of a son*
> *Woeful the breach where grief floods in*

Godwin didn't know what to do or say any more and for a few weeks he decided he wanted to become a monk.

'Father, can we bring Father Cuthbert back so I can study?' he asked one night, and Wulfnoth's face paled.

'No,' he said. 'And do not speak to me of this again.'

When dawn came, Wulfnoth shook Godwin awake. 'Godwin! Awake, there is much work to be done.'

Godwin did not pause for his day meal, but threw on cloak and boots and hurried after his father. He worked like a churl with wedge and mallet splitting timbers for the new barn his father was building. He chopped firewood from crooked timbers; wove hazel rods into wattle; warmed sick sheep with his own body; carried water; laid hedges; trapped foxes; helped foal a colt by the light of a candle; and bore the weight of two sons upon his growing shoulders. There was no time for grief, but Godwin saw the absence of Leofwine everywhere: in the stables, the bed closet, the benches, the hillsides, even at the pregnant grave mound, which slowly fell back into itself. He steeled himself, vowed to survive and vowed to live for Leofwine as well as himself, and to do the things that they had promised each other in the depths of the Weald.

Wulfnoth saw the look in Godwin's eye. 'Come, I can smell our night meal,' he said, and he and Godwin trudged through the darkening day. At the hall door Wulfnoth and Godwin scraped the caked mud from their shoes and Wulfnoth held the door open for Godwin, as if he were an equal, and that gesture meant more than a saga.

On Godwin's tenth birthday Wulfnoth presented him with his first sword. It was a simple blade of patterned steel: the swirling clouds of light and dark where nine rods of iron and steel had been welded into a perfect blade. The hilt was unadorned, except for a wolf's head in silver on the cross guards.

'I had this made for Leofwine,' Wulfnoth said as he held it out in two hands. 'But it is yours now. Practise with it. You might need it soon enough. And here!' Wulfnoth gave him a new-made shield. It was unpainted yet, but had already been covered with rawhide. The pattern of the fur looked familiar.

'It is the prize bull's skin,' Beorn whispered as they boiled up the hooves for paint. 'So that you will stand in battle and remember!'

Godwin took sword and shield with pride and did not go anywhere without his sword strapped to his waist. It was heavy and slapped against his thigh, but he felt like a king already. He puffed out his chest, put his hand on the hilt and swaggered about as Elfhelm's men had done. But when his mother saw him, her face hardened.

Has it come to this, her look seemed to say, that we arm boys to fight when the king himself will not.

Wulfnoth met her gaze without flinching. Yes, it said, the world has come to this.

Wulfnoth brooded all winter on the death of his son. Leofwine's death seemed entwined with the decline of England, and after the months of long, dark nights and even darker tales he was eager for the chance to slake his fury in Danish blood. As soon as the spring sea lanes reopened Wulfnoth rode off with his steel-shirted retainers. In March he caught three Danish ships in the Soluente and killed their crews to a man. Godwin was not there, but Beorn was and told him how Wulfnoth leapt like a berserker into the Danish captain's ship and set about him with his sword as if he were reaping hay. Wulfnoth's fury did not abate till he had burnt their ships and watched the thick columns of black smoke bring the news of the slaughter to God and His angels.

His father revelled in the bloodshed. He strode up to their leader and killed him in single combat, then had the dead man's skin nailed to the church door, while the survivors were sold off into slavery.

Godwin begged to be taken to the coast next time, and a month later another slaver tried to run the gauntlet, but

Wulfnoth knew the Soluente better than the pirates and on a gloomy Thursday morning, in a fine drizzle, he caught them as they stumbled drunkenly back to the coast, loaded down with slaves and booty. Godwin watched in astonished fascination at the fury of Wulfnoth and his men as they butchered the drunken rabble.

Their leader had a fine coat of Frankish mail, and Wulfnoth gave it to Beorn as a reward. The steel shirt was worth more than the manor of Contone made in a year. It was a fine prize and all looked on in admiration as Beorn threw it over his shoulders. Godwin looked up at him in wonder.

'Norman pirates,' Wulfnoth said as he wiped the blood from his sword. 'So much for their oaths!'

The more Wulfnoth hunted pirates, the unhappier Godwin's mother became. She sat by the afternoon fire and held up the square cloth she was embroidering with the face of Jesus.

'Back from the hunt?' she asked.

'Yes,' Godwin said.

'Did you catch anything?'

'A hind.'

'Make sure Agnes hangs it,' Gytha said.

'Yes, Mother,' Godwin said, and pushed himself up and started back towards the door.

Gytha flung a question after him. 'Have you heard?'

'What?'

'Your father is planning to go back to sea.'

'I know.'

Gytha looked back to her needlework and pursed her lips as she stabbed the thread through Christ's eye. She worked quickly, the black thread forming Christ's pupil. 'He is intent on making himself a noble corpse. There is nothing useful in a corpse. A blind man can sing, but a buried man is good for nothing but tears.'

'Better to die than to suffer shame,' Godwin said, and his mother was up in a moment. Her slap startled him.

'You were brought up to talk more sense than that!'

Godwin's cheek stung. At that moment Wulfnoth strode in, wiping his hands on his kirtle front. He looked from Godwin to his wife and back again.

'What's this?' he said. Godwin's eyes gleamed with anger but he held his tongue.

'We were talking about how you are making a name for yourself,' Gytha said at last.

Wulfnoth sighed. He threw his cloak back and warmed his hands near the fire. 'Want to come to sea?' he said to Godwin.

Godwin nodded.

'Good,' he said, and winked. 'We'll catch some Danes and feed them to the fish.'

CHAPTER FOUR

The Wolf Hunts

Wulfnoth's favourite ship was named *Seawolf.* She was a sixty-oared craft, deeper and stouter than the Army's longships, a sturdy sea-mount for the roving warrior.

That summer they sailed up and down the south coast. Wulfnoth knew many of the sea captains, buff and tanned men with thick salty beards and bulging forearms. At night they moored the boats behind headlands and in sheltered inlets; each day they rowed out to catch the wind. They rekindled friendships, traded news and raced each other round the Needles. There were a lot of drinking games, which Godwin joined in, and learnt to hold his own and not let the ale talk for him. But he was only ten years old and each night he fell into his blankets and snored like a pig.

When they sailed as far as Cornwalia, Godwin stared towards the shore to catch a glimpse of either hut or hall, but all he could see was sheer black cliffs and pounding black water wild with white spray.

Cornwalia was a foreign land. The name made that clear for 'wal' meant 'stranger' or 'foreigner'. In the far west lived the Walsh; nuts came from the hazel tree, but from the south came the walnut, and the strange stone circle high on the Downs, where witches played at night, was named Wal-Ditch.

'The West Walsh are a strange and secretive people,' Wulfnoth said. 'Each man has two names – one Saxon and one Walsh – and outside the towns no man speaks a word of English.'

'Two names and two faces,' Beorn said. 'And two sets of laws.'

Which meant no law at all, Godwin knew.

As they stared up to the top of the black cliffs they saw a cloaked figure step to the lip and lean on his spear, silhouetted against the sky.

'To them we are pirates,' Wulfnoth said.

As he spoke, three more armed warriors came to the edge of the cliff. One of them lifted his spear and pointed. It was a foreign gesture, something between a salute and a threat, and it thrilled Godwin, and stayed with him long after.

At Lizard Rock, the last headland of the Isle of Britain, five grey seals were basking on the rocks, and Godwin felt the boom of the sea and rocks deep within his bones as they turned for home with a great flapping of sail and creaking of timbers and sealskin ropes.

That night on the whale road they saw the great beasts rising like hillocks from under the waves. One came so close that its spray was blown into the faces of men along the boat's edge. It half rolled in the water, one great eye open to the moonlight. Whales were mysterious and malevolent beasts and one rubbed along the side of the boat. There were shouts of alarm as the well-caulked planks began to spring leaks.

'They're trying to turn us over!'

'He'll break our keel!'

Beorn's crooked teeth were clenched. He grasped a spear and thrust down at the terrifying beast. The point caught it just behind its baleful eye, and it let out a great blast of water as it sank. The sudden and bloody upwelling rocked the vessel violently and Godwin was almost thrown over the side, but he clung on and Wulfnoth grabbed the tiller and righted the boat.

'Are these my brave warriors!' he laughed. 'Who face Danes in battle but take fright at a sea monster!'

So the year 1008 passed waiting for Danes who did not come.

In Normandig Duke Richard II's court imposed the ducal family's rule through Church and State. In Rome there was plague and famine, while in the Middle Sea heathen Saracens used their base on the rocky island of Sardinia to ravage the coasts of Italy.

In England life seemed so hopeless that men talked of the End Times, when Christ would return in all his glory. It had been over a thousand years since Christ's birth. His return was imminent. To think, men said, that it should come in our time!

Autumn arrived and the fields were full of golden strips of wheat and barley. Wulfnoth decided to end his summer's sailing. They brought *Seawolf* back to the royal port of Boseham, a rich town at the end of a muddy inlet that fed into the Soluente. It was a royal port. There the king kept his well-painted boats and there the best shipwrights worked on the stretches of beach that doubled as marketplace and open factory.

'So it's true,' Wulfnoth said, as they admired a row of half-built warships. 'The king is building a fleet.'

'Will walls of wood help us?'

'No,' Wulfnoth said. 'Unless we fill them with wills of iron.'

Wulfnoth ordered *Seawolf* to be dragged up the beach. She was caked in weed and barnacles and all manner of sea-slime. Her timbers had been eaten through by worms, and she bore scars from the whale's back that ran almost the whole length of the craft. They propped her upright on thick ash staves, scrubbed her free of weed and barnacles, cut out her caulking, mixed coal tar and horsehair, set to work making her watertight again and sent word to the womenfolk in Contone to stitch two new sails of red-and-white striped wool.

By the time they had finished *Seawolf* looked like a newly built craft. There was not a blemish on her, and Godwin and Wulfnoth spent the last afternoon – a cool September day with a faint breath of air and low-dripping clouds anchored over the shingle beach – stripped to the waist rubbing her down till the wet planks gleamed.

'Done?' Wulfnoth asked when Godwin came back exhausted, polishing cloth slung over his shoulder.

'Done!' said Godwin, and let out a long sigh as he slumped down beside him and shared a horn of ale.

At the harvest festival the talk was all of the new king's fleet. 'Every man possessed of three hundred and ten hides was to provide a galley; every man possessed of eight hides only to find a helmet and breastplate.' The document was read from market crosses and the law mooted.

'I shall provide six ships,' Wulfnoth boasted. 'If I can find enough men to crew them!'

'That is a proud boast,' Gytha said.

Wulfnoth laughed. 'Only the hollow man boasts. I say what shall be! Let God Almighty, Creator of Heaven and Earth, be my witness.'

The idea of the fleet excited men. This would work; they would never fear for folk and food, never endure Dane's Rule again.

Wulfnoth was optimistic, and the year ended well, for it was said that the king had heard of the exploits of the Sudsexe thegn Wulfnoth Cild. Hemming had become a trusted member of the household, and now he had a silver ring on his arm and a sword at his belt, and there was no man more loyal or meek, for he always sat at the far end of the benches and slept furthest from the hearth.

The winter passed, but with spring came rumours that another Army was gathering in the islands and inlets and earth-castles of Sealand and Danemark.

'How many ships?'

'Two hundred,' the seafarers said. Wulfnoth laughed at the number.

Throughout Lent they fasted on bread and herbs and water, processed barefoot to the church. Godwin alone rang the church bell now. The same priest arrived and left his sword at the chapel door and then the service began with the Kyrie eleison, a list of Christ and his Saints, and then they sang Psalm 3. Godwin learnt it off by heart, and with the thought of a vast ship Army arriving, the words were very real to him:

> Lord, how are they increased that trouble me!
> Many are they that rise up against me . . .
> Arise, O Lord; save me, O my God:
> For Thou hast smitten all mine enemies upon the
> cheekbone;
> Thou hast broken the teeth of the ungodly.

Wulfnoth put his faith in steel and courage. He rode up and down the neighbouring valleys picking out the biggest lads, bright enough to make good warriors. The first thing they had to learn was how to hold a spear and shield. Second was their foot play, and most important they had to learn the shieldwall, where each man stood shoulder to shoulder, shields overlapping, a wall to the enemy: a spear hedge, a shieldburg, a rocky and defiant shore for the Army to dash themselves upon.

'Hold that shield up!' Beorn ordered. 'Think about you and the man that stands next to you. A mail shirt is only as strong as the weakest link.'

'What's the point of learning to fight?' one of the lads muttered to the man next to him. 'If Ethelred leads us, perhaps we should learn how to turn and run faster than the men about us!'

Wulfnoth heard that last man speak and knocked him flat, sent him home in shame.

His nostrils flared with anger as he turned and glared at the rest of the men. 'Who else wants to go home?'

No one moved. Wulfnoth slapped one lad who was slouching. 'Stand tall! Stand proud!'

The new recruits braced themselves together as a shieldwall as Wulfnoth and Beorn and Caerl and Hemming took wood axes. The first charge bounced off but they charged again and hammered their shields, turned and kicked and thrust and kneed. The shieldwall held – just – and Wulfnoth seemed content.

'Better,' he said. 'Now, see those grain sacks? One under each arm and run round the lone hazel!'

The lone hazel grew halfway up the far side of the valley. Hardly any of them could manage to carry the sacks without dropping them, but Wulfnoth did, and jogged past them, sweat dripping from his nose and chin.

'Again!' he said when the last stumbled home. 'Come on! Do you think the Army is sitting at home and picking their noses? No! They're rowing to England and they're dreaming of splitting your dumb skulls!'

It was nearing Lent when Wulfnoth took Godwin down to the coast. The shipyards stretched as far as they could see. Nailworkers beat out flat-headed nails, and painters were mixing great copper cauldrons of stinking colours, and there she was, a sixty-four-oared craft, six rods long from end to end, a raised platform at the front where spearmen and archers could stand.

Wulfnoth swung down from the saddle.

'Look at this!' he said. 'My new ship. She's a fine craft, is she not?' He ran a hand lovingly down her clinker planks. 'Her name is *Swanneck*. Sixty-four oars, the longest keel we could find, and just look how lean she is!'

There was a delight in his father's gaze as he stood back. It was as if he saw the ship filled with warriors, and himself at the prow, ready to leap into the enemy's midst.

Swanneck was a warship through and through. Her lean, low, arrow-thin design was built for speed, not cargo; she was the finest ship on the Boseham strand: lean like a hunter.

That evening the wind sharpened, brought angry waves up from the deep. Wulfnoth stood, dark against the westering sunlight. He spent a long time staring out to the horizon. The sun began to set; the sky was a pale lavender; the sea shifted in colour, dark and gloomy and uneasy.

'What is he looking for?' Godwin asked.

Caerl said, 'Pirate sails.'

'And how will he know one square sail from another?'

Caerl laughed. 'That I do not know, but I have learnt to trust your father when he smells a pirate.'

A week later when the winds turned to the east and Wulfnoth spotted three sails skimming the horizon. He shinned up a tree to get a better look. They were Norse ships with square sails, stiff with the brisk tailing wind, loping over the waves like a pack of hounds. They were too sleek to be merchants, he thought, too close to be heading for Burgenda land.

He sent Godwin up into the tree to keep watch as they crossed the horizon. For a long time they drifted along the coast, but when the sun began westering they tacked sharply towards shore.

Wulfnoth caught a branch and swung himself up.

They were warships and he saw the glint of steel flashing in the sunlight.

'That's it!' Wulfnoth said, and jumped up. 'To sea!'

Swanneck was still only half painted, but she slid into the waves and her eager timbers were buoyed up.

It was a rough day and Godwin held fast to the mast as the ship nosed out of the estuary. He was eleven and this was to be his first battle. He would brag about it later, as men bragged about the first girl they bedded. Godwin checked his sword was loose in its sheath, went through everything he could remember about war and battle. The men about him had the air of huntsmen on a morning jaunt. Each thrust of the oars lurched the prow forward, swan-flapping low over the water, the banks of oars rising and falling like wings. Godwin looked behind and saw the foaming wake widen behind them as the land grew more distant.

They cleared the headland and Godwin felt the breeze on his face. It smelt of salt and seaweed, and a young lad's first battle. The wind on his cheeks settled his roiling gut. Godwin let out a tentative belch, but no puke came, so he let out another, and took in a deep breath.

'They are making for Wiht!' the lookout called, but just looking up at the lad, swinging back and forth from the mast top, made Godwin's stomach lurch. The wind was driving the waves onto shore, and as it grew in strength the boat began to roll and pitch and the seasickness came all of a sudden with a cold sweat and a mouth full of spit.

'I see them!' the lookout called out, and Godwin clutched the mast and let out another belch, which failed to take away the awful feeling in his stomach. 'Three furlongs off. Square sails!'

'Come!' Wulfnoth said to Godwin as he strode past. Godwin made the mistake of leaving the mast, and before he had got to the end of the boat the cold sweat spread from his back to his hands, and he knew he was going to be sick. He wished, like the dying man wishes for death, that it would just come and be done.

'Look!' Wulfnoth said and Godwin tried to listen as his father pointed out the dim shadows breaking through the mists, but he puked over the side and the spit flew back up at him and then sailed along the side of the boat and caught Beorn in the face.

Beorn smiled his crooked smile, wiped it off and gently patted Godwin's back.

'We shouldn't have brought him,' Hemming said. 'He is too young for sea battle.'

Beorn said nothing, but Hemming came over and put his hand on Godwin's back.

Godwin vomited three more times. They were loud retches, with nothing left to bring up. Wulfnoth didn't pause, and Godwin stood up and wiped his mouth, and thought that he had shamed his father, but he could see that the men about him were smiling.

'That's it – get it all out,' one man said. 'It's better than shitting yourself!'

Godwin tried to make it back to the mast, but the sickness overcame him and the men about him groaned and shoved him towards the side of the boat.

'Keep to the edge!' one of the men told him, and Godwin leant over the side and stared down into the water, and wished he had been left ashore. There was a fathom of clear green water before the light-shafts faded. He broke the surface with his fingers and the tomb-cold touch made his stomach feel better, but with each roll the wave-crest skimmed along the side of the boat. Godwin felt sure that the next wave would swamp them and wanted to warn someone, but could not open his mouth.

Fear had cold and numbing talons, and each grip left him more and more miserable. Bit by bit the Norse ships plunged closer.

'They think they can outpace us,' Hemming called.

'Faster!' Wulfnoth ordered, but *Swanneck* was not sailing; swan-skimming, she barely touched the water while the other four ships butted each wave and fell behind, and poor *Seawolf* looked like a lumbering old hound as she tried to keep up with the sleek sprinter.

The first Norse boat was a light craft of forty oars, with a red-and-black striped sail that bellied out with the gathering breeze. The next was a lean wave-cutter, with white sail silhouetting the shaven-headed warrior at the prow. The third was the largest and slowest – butting the waves rather than slicing through them. Silver fish leapt to safety from their cutting prows, rising and falling in flashing shoals like the flight of many arrows.

'Larboard a little!' Wulfnoth shouted. 'Larboard!' he shouted again and waved frantically, but the day was waning and the tide had gone too far out, the water was too shallow for them to cross the sandbanks. *Swanneck* slowed as her keel grated on the bottom, and then stopped.

'Damn!' Wulfnoth cursed. 'Back!'

They pushed and heaved. Godwin scooped up a mouthful of seawater and spat out the taste of vomit as his father stamped up and down the boat, shouting orders as he swung himself under the rigging.

'Are we going to go back to land?' Godwin asked hopefully.

Beorn sniffed and wrinkled his nose. 'No. It will not be long until the bore sweeps round the other side of the isle and lifts us again.'

'Will there be a battle?'

'Let us hope so!'

Godwin did not share his enthusiasm. The sagas never spoke of seasickness, and he did not want to go to his grave feeling like this. Come on, Godwin, he told himself. Only a fool feels no fear, and even fish fear the sea.

Wulfnoth looked over the side of the boat and back to land to check his bearings. He spotted his son and saw him for what he was – a boy among men – and felt a moment's indecision. The Norsemen jeered; he turned to face them and grinned. Wulfnoth smelt the air, for the wind was shifting.

The Soluente was a treacherous water, but it wasn't Wulfnoth who had been betrayed; it was the hope of the Norsemen. There were two tides here; as they lapped about the Wiht he could see the bore making its way towards them.

'Ready your oars!' he shouted, and with one hand on the rigging he swung himself over the side of the boat to check one more time, then called the first oar strike. 'But gently. Save some strength for killing!'

'Not long now,' Hemming said a short while later as he worked his oar and *Swanneck* broke over the sand banks. The Norse captains shouted to each other in alarm.

Wulfnoth put his lips to his horn and blew a great blast. It rang out from the watching hills and headlands and weed-strewn rocks as if there was a host of warriors, and despite his misery, it stirred something within Godwin – hard and brave and warlike – and with a low grunt all as one the men about him bent to their oars. Wulfnoth's four remaining ships had turned round the sandbank, where the channel ran deeper, but foam-throated Swanneck cut the green seawater, the banks of oars flapping her forwards, swooping on her prey as the gyrfalcon strikes.

Hemming peered over his shoulder. 'Keep to the mast,' he told Godwin.

Godwin nodded, but the warlike spirit that had entered him. He drew his sword, stood by the oarsmen, gripped his shield. Now they were sailing into the waves, the roll and pitch had gone and the boat skimmed forward.

'They will not make it!' Wulfnoth called out.

The first two ships were too far ahead. They were turning to try and help the third, but Wulfnoth laughed. He had waited hours – no, years – for this moment. 'We have them!' He laughed, and Godwin smiled with him and the boat lurched forwards. As the battle-joy coursed through him, Godwin saw the crew upon the last Norse boat. The captain was a fine-looking man with black hair, tight-meshed mail and gold rings. He marched up and down, shouting as Wulfnoth had done, and they furled their sails and looked to their weapons.

Wulfnoth waved his spear to the other boats. 'Faster,' he roared to the oarsmen, 'lest we have to share the glory!'

They can see that they will die, Godwin thought as the distance between them shortened to half a furlong, but still they ready themselves for battle. They have chosen a good ending.

Wulfnoth turned and saw Godwin behind him. 'Back to the mast,' he shouted, 'and stay there!'

But he did not stop to see if his son did as he was told, and Godwin stood in the prow and stared out at the doomed pirates. Their ship was wallowing in the water, and a few of the crew had taken their oars out to ward off *Swanneck*, while the captain – handsome in his war-rings – brandished his war spear.

'Bring us alongside!' Wulfnoth called, and *Swanneck* lurched as Caerl pushed on the steer board.

The men dropped their oars and leapt up, seizing shields and weapons. The bravest rushed to the gunwales, while others stayed in the middle to balance the boat, but still *Swanneck* rocked violently and Godwin put his hand out to steady himself and feared for a moment that they would be swamped with cold, green water.

The Norses had a few archers and arrows flew between the boats. One of the men from Contone fell back with a grunt, a Norse barb buried in his gut. The air between the boats was thick with missiles. A hammer blow struck Godwin and he tripped backwards over a sea chest and banged his head. He felt hands under his armpits dragging him to safety as the grappling ropes began to clatter and thud, and the narrowing gap of green sea became frantic with leaping fish and confused waves.

Wulfnoth was the first to leap across and he landed on his feet, felt his shield buckle under the weight of spear-thrusts that would have killed an unarmed man. He struck left and right, slammed his ruined shield into an ugly Norse's face, splattering the man's nose across his cheek with the steel boss, then tossed the ruined shield aside and rammed his spear blade into the mouth of a barefoot pirate. He saw it come out of the back of his head before the man jerked backwards and fell down, his heels drumming the deck as Wulfnoth roared over him. It was death to lose your footing in a sea battle, and Wulfnoth danced as the ships rocked and pitched with each swell.

The first warrior behind Wulfnoth was the son of Contone's blacksmith, Unferth. As he leapt across the gap a throwing axe caught him on the side of the head, his head spun round, his back teeth flew out in an arc and he crashed to the floor like a stunned ox. He almost knocked Beorn over as he took his death-leap into the enemy boat and felt a spear point graze up his left arm, his right hand jar as his sword blade clanged tunelessly on an iron helmet.

The battle was a blur. Only Caerl saw things clearly as he stood at the stern, grasping the steer board till the two ships were grappled together like knife fighters in a death grip. Both crews leapt into the other's boat. Caerl used a spear to fend off one hairy Dane. He had black hair and smouldering blue eyes, huge forearms from a life at sea and a thick sword that he used to hack at the ash spear shaft. The wood split in two and the Dane laughed as he raised his sword to murder Caerl.

The brute tripped on a grappling rope and Caerl took his chance and leapt up into him. It was knife work then. The Dane went for Caerl's eyes and Caerl groaned and whipped his head back and forth while he struggled to get his eating knife free. It came out at last, and Caerl had one of the man's hands locked in his teeth as he lifted the Dane's mail shirt, found the soft spot under the belt and drove the blade in. Caerl kept pushing deeper till the fiend stopped twitching, and only then did he spit the hairy hand out of his mouth and stagger to his feet.

It was short and bloody and brutal, and it was almost over before the second craft arrived, crashing into the paired boats, shattering her own steer board in her helmsman's eagerness. Only the Norse captain, unwounded in his coat of fine mail, remained. Wulfnoth strode towards him meaning to offer him a clean death, but the man denied him that, leapt over the dead and the dying and, with a great bound, hurled himself over the side. Arms wide like a crane suddenly launching itself from a high branch, he hung there for a moment, mouth open, laughing at death.

'Odin!' he shouted, and hit the water like a stone. Wulfnoth tried to grab him but he sank in an instant with a horrible sucking sound, as if the sea had swallowed him. Wulfnoth stared down; all that remained were a brief ripple of black water and a few bubbles that troubled the surface, and were gone.

Wulfnoth lost seven men in the fight, and another who slipped on the gunwales and sank into the waves before anyone could grab him. He was a cheerful lad named Osgod who was good at the harp and left a mother and wife with a pair of twins to care for.

'Are you all right?' Wulfnoth asked Godwin, who already had a large bruise starting to bloom on his ribs.

Godwin nodded.

'Good,' his father said. 'Now, let's get this craft back to shore before night comes in!'

That evening, Godwin was too wearied to join in the revelries, but Wulfnoth and his men spent the night feasting and bragging. Morning brought hangovers and headaches, and a scattering of dead Norsemen along the strand, wet like the regurgitated mice the owl brings to the nest.

Wulfnoth set his men to search for the captain's body, 'For he wore enough gold to buy a man a manor!' But the sea did not choose to return that treasure. Instead, on the next tide, in an apologetic act it carried Osgod back to land. Caerl found him two miles along the beach, lying on his side, with weed in his hair and a few tentative crabs crawling into his open mouth. Caerl flicked the crabs away, bundled the dead weight over his saddle and led the horse back to the nearest hall, which had a table where he could be laid out and dressed for burial.

Caerl looked at Osgod's wet body and, in an odd moment, brushed the sand from the left side of his face.

'My lord will pay whatever you need,' he said to the women

hurrying to fetch water. Then he went out without looking back.

Wulfnoth gave the captured ship to the king's reeve, to add to his fleet, and his victory gave Wulfnoth even greater wealth and fame – and it was the fame he valued most of all, for it brought men to his side who would obey his commands and fill his ships and, when that dread day came, meet the Army in battle. Songs about Wulfnoth Cild were sung as far west as Bade and as far north as Bebbanburge and the king heard them and it was rumoured that he intended to appoint Wulfnoth as commander of the king's fleet.

Wulfnoth's mood was optimistic as the year 1009 drew to a close, for he had been hailed by all as Wulfnoth Cild, Wulfnoth the Hero.

'Maybe the king will summon you to court,' Gytha said, as she and the women stitched the sail with needles of horn.

'Maybe he will,' Wulfnoth said, as he stretched his toes to the fire.

'Do not sound so pleased. Nothing good comes of the king. Remember Elfhelm,' Gytha warned, but Wulfnoth was a proud man, swelled with victory, and determined to lead where so many had failed.

'Godwin,' Wulfnoth said when the summons came, 'fetch your cloak and your sword. We are going to see the king.'

'You really intend to go?' Gytha asked that night as they lay in bed and stared up at the ceiling.

'Of course.'

'I do not like it,' she said. 'You should not have given him that boat. You should not outdo a king in generosity. He will have to repay you and nothing good will come of that.'

'Do not fret, wife.'

'I do fret!' she said, sitting up and leaning on her elbow. 'There are many jealous men whose bile will rise when they see you march into the hall with all those gold arm-rings, for you won yours in battle, when they took theirs from their fathers.'

Wulfnoth pulled her back down but she shrugged him off.

'Eadric Streona will be there,' she said.

'So? What care I of this Eadric!'

'He rules the king's mind with guile. Or worse.'

'Witchcraft?' Wulfnoth said.

'So some say,' she said, and turned towards him.

'Then say a prayer for me at the Virgin's Chapel.'

'Don't mock,' she said.

Wulfnoth put his hand up and kissed her cheek.

'I do not mock.'

CHAPTER FIVE

The English Fleet

That summer all England was abuzz with the news that in the Holy Land the Fatimid caliph had ordered the destruction of the Church of the Holy Sepulchre in Ierusalem. Preachers called for a holy war against the heathens, but Christendom was too riven with barbarianism and conflict, and England was fixated on the fleet and the Army that it was meant to defend against.

'This is our chance,' Wulfnoth said. 'If we cannot stop them this time they shall return even bigger and then how can we defend against them?'

'Bones in a field or slaves in the Moors' markets,' Hemming said.

'It is what was prophesied in the Gospel: "When ye see the abomination of desolation standing in the holy place",' one of the neighbours quoted to Wulfnoth. '"Woe unto them that are with child. Pray ye that your flight be not in the winter: for then shall be great tribulation."'

Wulfnoth listened, but did not seem dismayed. 'If this is the End Times, then I at least shall hold my head up high when the Archangel Gabriel blows on his war horn, and the Angelic Host meets the forces of the Devil in battle.'

But later, when he and Godwin were alone, Wulfnoth laughed at the doomsayers: 'Much nonsense a man talks who talks without tiring. The court is at Lundenburh. There you will hear more and bigger tales. Listen well and hold your tongue, for they talk much nonsense there. Now go and get your things ready. Bring your sword. We leave on the morrow.'

That evening Godwin washed and combed his hair, and his mother came and picked out the best clothing she could find. Most of them were Leofwine's old clothes, but she held them up to Godwin and nodded.

'This will fit you well enough.'

When Godwin was dressed in his best kirtle of sky-blue wool, and trousers of red, and a silk-lined cloak, he felt half a prince already.

'Here!' Wulfnoth said as the firelight gleamed on their faces, and he took a gold arm-band from his own arm and put it on to his son's. 'In honour of your first battle.'

It was a thin band of two plaited wires, with wolf heads at the ends. It barely made a circle about Wulfnoth's arm, but on Godwin it made almost two. He marvelled at the weight of it.

'The first of many, son,' Wulfnoth said and winked.

Next morning there was an air of optimisim and celebration as Wulfnoth's war band mounted up. They had all dressed in their finest, and Godwin sat high on his horse and looked back to wave to his mother and his childhood. He would have stopped and taken a better look if he had known how long it would be before he would see his home again.

It was three days' ride to Lundenburh and while Wulfnoth's ships sailed to Sandwice, he and his companions took the high roads along the Weald. The chalky soil made good going, the air was bright, the leaves were beginning to unfurl, and they filled the forest with a bright green light. On the second day the trees began to fail, and as they came out into a strange landscape, Godwin felt strangely exposed. They came to a town and were turned away.

'Why are men burning fires?' Godwin asked.

'There is plague in the city,' Caerl said.

Godwin nodded, though he didn't quite understand. He would rather have ridden with Beorn than the taciturn ship-master, but Beorn was riding at the front with his father, and Caerl had been put in charge of him this day.

That night as they lay down to sleep without tale or song, Godwin wished he had stayed at home.

Bear up, he told himself. Only half of all journeys take you home.

England held a million souls, and it seemed to Godwin that half of them were crammed into the narrow and dirty streets of Lundenburh. It was not the capital of England – that was Wincestre – but when King Alfred, Shield of the English, Shepherd of the Folk, united Mercia and Wessex he refounded the city within the old square of the Roman town and repaired the stone walls with ramparts of earth and timber, and since that time Lundenburh had thrived like lice on the fat man.

Lundenburh was Ethelred's favourite city, not least for the devotion its people showed to him and his family. When Wulfnoth's men went to the muddy shore market – little more than trading ships beached along the flat banks of the Temese – there were boats and voices and clothes from all the four corners of the world: the four corners of the cathedral maps, painted on square boards with Ierusalem in the centre, the continents arranged round it. Godwin saw such a map in St Paul's Cathedral and looked up at the world in wonder at how small was his corner of it, and how tiny the vast seas seemed when painted on a board.

'So where is Cornwalia?' he asked and, his father pointed.

'And that was four days' sailing.'

Godwin looked and wondered.

'So where have you sailed to?'

Wulfnoth pointed. 'With *Seasnake* I went to Flandran. With *Seawolf* we sailed all the way down the coast to Burgenda land, and saw the Moors there.'

'Are they evil?'

'They are heathen,' Wulfnoth said. 'As to evil . . . you will see some here in Lundenburh, then you may judge for yourself.'

Wulfnoth's men stayed at the hall of a rich and well-respected Snotingehamscire thegn named Morcar. He was broad and thick, like a barrel with arms and legs, and a round face with balding pate. He was a cousin of Alderman Elfhelm and greeted Godwin as if they had met before. But Godwin did not remember him, and he did not look like Elfhelm, though there was an air about him – honest and straightforward and slightly embarrassed, as if he felt his Mercian manners did not quite match up to those of Wessex men.

They did not drink, but spent a quiet night sipping butter-milk and chewing on their barley bread and cheese as they swapped news.

'Eadric continues to insult us and our people,' Morcar said. The words were hard for him, and Godwin felt his pain. It was hard to suffer without recourse. 'He has four brothers and they are bastards all. The worst is Brihtric, a one-eyed villain. He is an evil man. He covets land and power even more than his brother. He rides about the land and no one dares stand against him whatever mischief he commits. We cannot go openly against him, for he has the full backing of the king. But there are many among my people who call out for vengeance for Elfhelm and his sons. They grow more angry as each year passes. We pray that Ethelred will die soon and a better king will take his place.'

'He has passed his fortieth year.'

'That he has. And the lives of the kings of the House of Cerdic burn bright and fast.'

Wulfnoth said, 'Has Ethelred started burning at all?'

There were low chuckles. 'Well. It cannot be long till Athelstan is king.'

'The Wise will choose Athelstan?' Wulfnoth asked.

Morcar nodded, but there was hesitation. 'Yes, the Wise will choose Prince Athelstan,' he said. 'Unless Queen Emma gets her way. She wants her son Edward to be anointed.'

'He is barely ten years old.'

'Eight. But if Ethelred lives another six years, he might be old enough.'

Wulfnoth laughed at the idea. 'No. The boy is a weakling.'

'But he has a strong mother.'

'The Wise are not choosing mothers.'

'That is true. And let us speak no more of this. If Christ was to bless us, it would be to take Ethelred to his eternal rest sooner rather than later. Men in the north talk of finding a new king, perhaps one not born of the House of Cerdic.'

'Who?'

'In York they always took their kings from Northweg.'

'But they are heathen. They would break the country apart. That is madness.'

Morcar stopped. 'Indeed.'

'Well, pray that the king soon sees sense or the afterlife,' Wulfnoth said, and the discussion ended with the men crossing themselves.

As they brought out mattresses to sleep on, Wulfnoth took Godwin aside and spoke gravely to him: 'What you have heard tonight is not to be talked of to others.'

'No, Father,' Godwin said.

Next morning the summons came and they dressed in their finest clothes. The king's palace lay on Thornei Island, the Eyot of Thorns, which had long since been cleared of brambles. Now it was home to the Abbey of St Peter, the West Minster, which gave the place its name. Godwin and Wulfnoth rode at the head of the men as they passed reedy Tyburn banks on their left and saw the stone tower of West Minster Abbey rise above the green spring willows. As they approached, a church bell began to clang, and then another, till the air was discordant with their noise.

'The king's manor has no wall,' Godwin said. 'Doesn't Ethelred fear for himself?'

Wulfnoth laughed. 'The Army does not want him dead. If Ethelred was dead, then his sons would fight. They would have to. No. With Ethelred alive he keeps the country together and makes it easier for the Army to milk us dry.'

'Stay, strangers unknown! Who approaches Ethelred's hall?' an armed warrior called out as they rode along the causeway.

Wulfnoth spoke in a loud, proud voice. 'I am Wulfnoth, son of Athelmar, Marshal of the Southern Shore. Men call me Wulfnoth Cild.'

The man bowed. 'Greetings, Marshal,' the door ward called out. 'The king is waiting for you. It is good to see that in Sudsexe men remember how to defend our lands.'

The gates swung open and the man who had spoken walked out to greet them.

'Greetings, Gamal,' Wulfnoth said, and both men spoke in a friendly tone. 'How is the king?'

'He will be happy to see you and hear your news. There have been too many pirates and too little resistance. In the Walsh marches, where I was raised, men say that killing without resistance is not slaughter. We have heard you have killed five ship crews of Danes.'

'They were Normans.'

'Normans or Danes – there is little difference, is there not?'

Wulfnoth shrugged. 'It is a brief tale.'

'Then make it long! In court there are too many men who speak much and act little.'

The king's manor was a pleasant and peaceful place. There were ordered gardens, both physic and ornamental, and a trellis through which a stone path led down to a wooden quay lined with magnificently painted boats.

When they reached the entrance to the hall, Wulfnoth's men handed their reins to the king's servants, who took the horses to the long stables.

The king's hall was built of stone, with high gables and a great ornate doorway. 'Leave your swords here,' the door ward told them.

Godwin did not know the man, but, like Gamal, he seemed to know his father, for the two men embraced briefly and then the man looked at Godwin with surprise.

Wulfnoth put a hand on Godwin's shoulder. 'This is my younger son, Godwin.'

'Welcome,' the other man said, but he gave Wulfnoth an odd look.

'Died,' Wulfnoth explained. 'Two winters past. So, how goes the king?'

'He is still at prayer.'

'What is the news?'

'The king's fleet is gathering. There will be two hundred ships. Not even the Army can summon that many.'

'But the Army have a strong leader,' Wulfnoth said. There was a long pause. Even the finest swords were useless if handled by a fool. 'We do not.'

'Wulfnoth Cild!' a voice announced, and through the king's own doors Wulfnoth strode in. The black-and-white tiled floor rang with each heel-fall.

The hall had a cool church air, but instead of God, the House of Wessex was worshipped here, and the present king Ethelred, 'Wise-Council'. There were two lines of carved wooden pillars and in the shadows, from the corner of his eye, Godwin saw banners, with shields and crossed spears, and old coats of grey mail, and bright tapestries showing stories from the Old Testament, legend and the deeds of Ethelred's illustrious ancestors. At the end of the room, sunlight streamed in from high windows, and before the king a charcoal fire was smoking lazily.

And there! Godwin thought. That must be the king.

Once English kings were presented with a sword and helmet to show their role as protector of the folk, but now they were crowned and presented with an orb and a sceptre, such as was given to Roman consuls.

Ethelred was tall and fair, with shots of grey in his moustache. But there was nothing infirm about his eyes or manner. His look was hard and vital. He had a quick mind, listened to the monk next to him and then cut him off with simple and direct speech.

The king kept talking to the man seated to his left. Arrayed to either side of the king was an assembly of monks, bishops and warriors, and longbearded old men. Godwin realised that these were the Wise. They sat on long benches, a motley array of ages and faces, bishops and warriors, Mercians and Northymbrians, Walsh and Cymbrian, men from Cornwalia and even Lombards. They regarded Wulfnoth and his men with a mixture of resentment and curiosity.

'Wulfnoth Cild!' Ethelred said suddenly. He stood and threw back his cloak and greeted Wulfnoth all in one movement. 'Do not kneel,' he said, and lifted Wulfnoth. 'Come! Sit! Tell us your news.'

It was hard to dislike Ethelred. Godwin was struck by how handsome the king was. The history of England flowed through his veins; his face carried echoes of the kings before him. His father was Edgar, son of Edmund, son of Edward, son of Alfred, son of Ethelwulf, son of Egbert, back to Cerdic, who was a pagan and came over the seas, son of Elesa, son of Esla, son of Giwis, son of Freawine, son of Frithgar, son of Brond, son of Bældæg, son of Woden, whom heathens worshipped as a deity.

But Ethelred was more than a man. He was the anointed. The cyning – of the people – their king. The only man who could unite feuding families.

The meeting was long and Godwin could not stop his attention from wandering. He yawned. A bell was rung to announce that the day meal would soon be served, and the assembly rose and chattered amongst themselves as water and linen were brought for washing hands before the feasting.

At that moment a voice called out from the open doorway, 'Eadric, Alderman of Mercia! You are just in time,' said Ethelred. 'We would have waited but the thegns were hungry!'

'Not at all, my lord. There is plague in Oxeneford and the road was flooded and we had to ford the river upstream.'

Eadric was not the twisted monster of Godwin's imaginings. He was slender, short and well mannered. His eyes moved quickly along the faces before him, and paused for a moment on Wulfnoth.

'We have not met,' Eadric said.

'That is Wulfnoth, Athelmar's son,' Ethelred put in. 'The man we have spoken of.'

'The man who presented a pirate ship to the king. That was a fine gift. Have you men to crew it?'

'Of course,' Wulfnoth said, and stiffened. 'Though you are mistaken: we have met, Alderman Eadric. I came to court with Alderman Elfhelm.' The room went silent at the sound of that name, but Wulfnoth seemed to relish the moment to confront Elfhelm's murderer. 'Three years ago. Just before he died.'

'Oh?' Eadric said. 'I don't remember you. But let us not dwell on past matters. Mill water only grinds once; then it flows to the sea. Yes, I have heard of your exploits, Athelmar's son. How good that you have come here to share your wisdom with us. You will be part of the king's fleet?'

'I will,' Wulfnoth said.

'Good. We need men like you. In fact, the king is looking for a man to lead the fleet. Look, lords and bishops, who better than a sea captain with a record of catching the Danes?'

And with that Eadric turned his back and put his arm on the king's and they led the way to dinner.

At the feast Eadric sat near the king. Morcar stood at the far end of the hall. After the feast he waited outside for Wulfnoth and shook his hand warmly. 'Those were brave words,' he said.

'I spoke truthfully.'

'And Eadric will not forget it.'

'Who was he?' Godwin asked.

'Morcar. Elfhelm's kinsman.'

'If he is of Elfhelm's kin, and enemy of Eadric, then why does the king still bring him to council?' Godwin whispered to his father.

Wulfnoth's face was serious. 'The king must balance many men and opinons,' he said. 'Morcar is now the chief man among Elfhelm's people. He is held a great lord in his own country. The king cannot ignore any man of such power. And if he excluded him, then war – not feud – would soon flourish between Eadric and Morcar.'

The next day the king took them all hawking among the reedy islets of the Temese.

Eadric came with all his brothers – an ugly brood, Godwin thought.

At the head of the company rode the king and Eadric, with their falcons hooded on their gloves.

'Wulfnoth Cild,' Eadric called. 'Come forward! Take my hawk. Let us see who will catch the first heron for the king's table.'

Wulfnoth heeled his horse forward, and Godwin tagged along, but his father was busy and there was no time for boys. The business was an adult affair: all hand-shaking and private conversations, and downing cranes or swans or ducks for the feasting. Godwin grew a little bored as his father debated the rights and wrongs of Danegeld with the king's chaplain, a plump little monk with a high-pitched, earnest voice.

Godwin returned his horse to the stables. He was saddle sore and walked stiffly towards the king's hall.

'What is that?' Godwin interrupted as a strange beast emerged from the bushes. Godwin had heard the king kept a strange bestiary of animals, and the thing he saw was long and tailed, with a head like a snake: a wyrm or a cockatrice, or a hoard-guarding spawn of a dragon. The beast came towards him and as it walked out into the sun – Godwin saw a brilliant blue snake's head, long like a goose. It put its head back, its throat curling underneath, and let out a dreadful and haunting screech. Godwin's mouth hung open.

The king's door ward stood behind him and laughed.

'That,' he said, 'is the king's peacock. Watch!'

The bird – for bird it was – paced out into the sunlight, and then it spread its trailing tail and there was a gasp – and Godwin saw a crowd had gathered to watch the thing. Godwin's mouth fell open. The bird paraded its tail as it stalked forwards, turning the tail a little to the side and the feathers shimmered like silk, changing hue and colour. Godwin felt tears in his eyes and did not know why. The sudden and unexpected beauty left his speechless.

At that moment the tail folded in upon itself. 'You are lucky, Wulfnothson,' he said. 'Some never see that!'

At that moment Godwin heard shouting. There was a carefree note to it that awoke something in him that had long slept. Godwin walked towards the noise. It was boys shouting. Something flew past his nose and he ducked back as a herd of boys rushed after it. It was a bag of stitched leather. The boys almost crushed him as they dashed past. At the front was a blond lad. He grabbed the bag and kept running, looking over his shoulder for support. The young men – twenty or so in total – followed with all the determination of a hue and cry.

For a moment it seemed the blond lad would get away, before one of the larger boys tripped him up and he was promptly buried in a scrum of fists and bodies and screaming faces.

Godwin did not play games. He had no idea what was happening. Was it a lynching?

'What are they doing?' he said.

'They're playing football,' Gamal told him.

Godwin had heard of it, a dangerous game, banned by many parishes, after the deaths and feuds it caused. The scrum collapsed. The boys punched and pummelled each other. After an interminable delay the ball appeared and one of the boys booted it up the field. The mob of lads pushed themselves up and followed, left the blond boy lying on his back. For a moment Godwin thought he was dead. His eyes were closed and there was blood smeared down from his nose. Godwin knelt down and put his hand to the lad's chest. Godwin could see that he was a few years older than himself, perhaps fifteen or sixteen. He was breathing, but he did not move or open his eyes.

Godwin looked around for someone to call to, but Gamal had gone to greet some visitors. He was about to call for help when the lad sat up. 'Jesu!' he said, shaking his head. He spoke with a strong Northymbrian accent, touched his nose and saw that it was bleeding. 'Jes-fething-u!'

The boy pushed himself to his feet, dusted himself off and caught Godwin's eye. He was broad, with clothes made of the finest blue cloth, and a belt of cunningly plaited leather.

'Did you see that?' he said. 'It took three of them. Bastards! Should pick on someone their own size. They're Eadric's sons. Father gave him my sister to marry, so we have to let them play with us. They're all in my brother's team. He's Athelstan. He'll be king next, so everyone wants to be on his side. Anyway, what's your name? My name's Edmund. You're on my team. Come! Take your cloak off. There's no swords or daggers, so better leave your eating knife as well. We have to get the ball to that tree over there.' Edmund pointed along the length of the hall wall where there was a great crowd of boys all shouting and fighting. Somewhere in the middle of the ruck was the ball. A tall blond boy broke free and someone tripped him up.

'That's my brother Eadwig. He's a shit,' Edmund said. 'I had another brother, but he died.'

Godwin was speechless for a moment. 'My brother died too,' he said.

Edmund wiped the blood from his nose on the back of his hand. 'How?'

'He was wasted by sickness,' Godwin said.

'Mine had the king's evil. Ironic, huh? Hands of a king are the hands of a healer. Isn't that what they say? Bollocks, clearly. My father's Ethelred.'

'I guessed.'

Edmund made an oddly apologetic and embarrassed gesture.

Godwin didn't know what to say. 'When did your brother die?' he said after a pause.

'A month ago. Yours?'

'A year and a half ago.'

The boy let out a sigh and gave him a sympathetic look. 'Shit, isn't it?'

Godwin nodded.

'What's your name?' Edmund said.

'Godwin.'

'And who is your father?'

'Wulfnoth Cild.'

'Ah!' Edmund said. 'Good. You're on my team. Come on! Let's get stuck into these bastards!'

Godwin followed Edmund as he limped after the others.

As the royal hunt ended, the king led the nobles back towards the hall. Eadric's horse fell in alongside Wulfnoth's.

'Greetings, Wulfnoth. How are you enjoying your stay at court?'

'Very well, Alderman.'

Eadric smiled. 'Please. No need for formalities here, Wulfnoth Thegn. High and low, we are all the king's councillors. And his servants.'

'We are,' Wulfnoth said.

Eadric looked ahead and let out a great breath. 'The king's fleet,' he said, 'is a great venture. What think you?'

'I am proud to serve.'

'And how will you serve?'

'In whatever way the king needs me.'

'We need a commander to lead the fleet.'

Wulfnoth drew in a slow breath. 'We do. A strong commander who will meet the Army and prevent their landing.'

'You know all about sea battles?'

Wulfnoth shrugged. 'They are much like land battles. First you must find the enemy, and then you meet them in battle. The rest is up to courage, luck and God.'

Eadric listened wide-eyed as Wulfnoth recounted tales of sea fights, where ships were lashed together, so there was a large and stable platform for men to slaughter each other. 'Such bravery!' he said. 'Such resolution! You are just the kind of man England needs. When do you go to the fleet at Sandwice?'

'In two days' time. We go by boat.'

'You do not travel with the king?'

'I was not asked.'

'I ask you,' Eadric said.

'You are not the king.'

Eadric leant in and put his hand to Wulfnoth's arm, but Wulfnoth flinched.

'You're right, I am not. Ah, look! That is your son, is it not? He has made friends with the athelings. A fine future awaits you both, it seems. Farewell, Wulfnoth. You should come to my hall some time. I have a fine collection of Frankish swords.'

'Perhaps you should use them,' Wulfnoth said.

Eadric laughed, and as farewell he said, 'I like you, Wulfnoth Cild. You will go far. I can see it.'

When the time came, Godwin was sad to leave Edmund. The two lads stood side by side, not talking, as Wulfnoth paid his respects to the king. He was tense and irritable, and when he came out of the hall, he called to Godwin to come.

'I'm going,' Godwin said.

'All right then,' Edmund said, and rolled his eyes. 'And I have to go to Canturburie!'

'Say a prayer for me,' Godwin said.

Edmund laughed.

'Come on, Godwin,' Wulfnoth called again.

Wulfnoth was glad to take his leave from the king's court. The scheming appalled him, and he was tired of both Eadric and Morcar, for they were each obsessed with the other and Wulfnoth did not like being soiled by either.

They took boats down the Temese and reached Sandwice on the third day. They found *Swanneck* and all of the Sudsexe ships, pulled high on to the dunes well away from the crashing slow waves. The masts of Wulfnoth's ships were stepped, their hulls scrubbed clean, timbers caulked and painted, oar-locks oiled. They looked formidable, like a pack of hounds or a line of dragons, angry and fierce and ready to be unleashed at last against the country's enemies.

All through July the fleet gathered, till there were more than a hundred and seventy ships, and all their crews. They came from the coastal shires: Northymbria, Lincoliascir, Nordfolc, Sudfulc, Exsessa, Cantware, Sudsexe, Hamtunscir, Dornsætum, Defanascir and a few ships from far Cornwalia.

As the crews came together, they found that their stories were common to all of them, that whole tracts of England had suffered the same or worse.

Their grievances against the king's councillors – Eadric chief among them – were commonplace, and the longer they waited for the king, the louder their anger became.

Wulfnoth tried to calm them and went from camp to camp talking to the leaders.

'I met the king in Lundenburh,' he said. 'He will be here soon and then he will announce the leader. Have faith. The king is a good man.'

When Morcar arrived, Wulfnoth rode straight to see him. He was shown in to Morcar's tent, and the two men greeted each other warmly.

'Men are not happy,' Wulfnoth said. 'Many are talking of going home.'

'I do not blame them,' Morcar said.

'We need the fleet,' Wulfnoth said. 'England needs the fleet.'

Morcar looked at him. 'So you have not heard?'

'What?'

'At Canturburie, the king announced the captain of the fleet.'

Wulfnoth felt a thrill and a dread run through him.

'Guess,' Morcar said.

'I cannot.'

'Go on.'

'Tell me.'

'Eadric,' Morcar said.

Eadric, Wulfnoth thought later that night when he was finally alone. He had hoped that he would be given command, and he laughed at himself for that now. Foolish man. Of course it would be Eadric. Who else could it be? How could you imagine that you would be made captain?

Wulfnoth brooded. To either side, stretched along the long strand, the English fleet of two hundred ships lay prone on the pale shingle. The sea breeze turned from the west to the east and men began to look for the Danish fleet. The horizons were clear, but it focused men's minds. They reacted to the news of Eadric's appointment with fury.

'Who is this fool?' men raged. 'He does not live within a hundred miles of the coast!'

Before them was a watery grave or a Danish spear.

'I shall not risk my life for Eadric,' one man said.

The crews spoke hot words to their captains. The captains came together and spoke to their lords, and the lords sat unhappily, for the only man they had to complain to was the king.

'We need a leader who will speak to the king,' they agreed. 'If we all go together, he will have to listen.'

CHAPTER SIX

The Sea Captain

Wulfnoth was troubled. The country had poured all their faith into the fleet, but as it teetered towards mutiny it seemed their hopes were as fragile as the green glass beaker on the king's best table. Morcar refused to invervene.

'So you will sit here and let the Army burn your boats? Or will you sail home and cower and wait for the Army to come? Either way, your hall will burn, and your folk will curse your name and your memory!'

Morcar did not disagree. 'My men will not sail.'

'They will sail if you lead them!' Wulfnoth said.

'Do not shout at me, Wulfnoth. I am not one of your retainers. I am a lord of men, and my men have suffered more than most. The king allowed our lord Elfhelm to be murdered, and then he appointed his murderer to be our chief. Each day our shame is rubbed like salt into our weeping wounds, and yet we still came; but we cannot follow that murderer into battle.'

Wulfnoth was raging with grief. 'Then who will you follow?'

'I would follow a mule if it was set upon a boat, rather than that murderous bastard,' Morcar said.

'Yes, we will follow any man except Eadric,' the ship captains agreed. 'Let us follow the king.'

'The king will not lead,' Wulfnoth said.

'Then give us his son. Let Athelstan lead us!'

'The queen will not allow her own son to be upstaged.'

'Then who can lead us?' the men asked.

'We should give the king one of our names to be our leader,' they said amongst themselves. 'Which of us can lead us?'

There was a pause. 'Let Wulfnoth lead us!' Morcar said, 'For he is a Sudsexe man and he has already won a name for himself. Let Wulfnoth lead!'

Wulfnoth tried to still this talk, but he no more had the power over men's tongues than did any other man, and he secretly felt he was destined to lead the fleet. There was no one else who had done so much against the pirates, who knew so much about the tides and the coasts, and who had the courage to take the fight to the enemy's ships.

The ship crews lined the Sandwice beach as they waited for the king's painted barges next morning. When they arrived, their sails filled with a stiff westerly gale, many of the Wise lay seasick in the gunwales. Clinging nervously to the masts, the ship crews stared stonily out at them.

'Where is our captain?' one man asked. His words carried far.

'Look – there he is, clinging to the mast!' the contemptuous answer came.

Eadric was no sea-hand and his skin was green as he made his way forward to the prow of the king's barge, to show himself to the fleet. It was all he could do to stand tall, but as the ship turned along the shore, it began to wallow violently in the swell. The boat pitched and yawned and Eadric regretted leaving the mast. He had never felt so miserable, could hold his lunch down no longer, and bent over the side and puked, and all along the shore the English ship crews laughed and mocked.

Even King Ethelred laughed. 'Bear up!' he said. 'The men are looking at you.'

The crew of the king's barge caught the mood of their fellows lining the shore and they moved slowly, drawing the landing out. In the end Eadric could not wait. He saw the land so close and jumped over the side, thinking he would wade ashore, but the beach was steep and Eadric went under the waves. No one moved. Let's see if he can swim, they thought.

Eadric came spluttering to the surface.

Men wished that a sea monster might come and drag him under, and in the end it was Wulfnoth who strode in and pulled him out, vomit still clinging to his kirtle, looking like a drowned rat. He set Eadric upon dry land.

Morcar strode forward. 'Look what Wulfnoth has rescued, the finest sea captain the king could find!'

Wulfnoth went to see Eadric as soon as he had a chance to establish himself in a thatched tithe barn. He sat at a table with his four brothers, and Wulfnoth could not think of a more unpleasant row of faces. They were like evil and malice and treachery and guile all made manifest.

Eadric looked up. 'What is it, Wulfnoth?' he asked. His tone was brusque.

'There is discontent among the fleet,' Wulfnoth said. 'They will not sail.'

'Then they are fools.'

Eadric took a gold ring from his finger and held it out. 'We need brave men like you.' The hand remained outstretched. 'Take it,' Eadric said. The gold ring gleamed. Eadric's eyes were full upon him. His palm remained open.

Wulfnoth did not like this choice. He clenched his jaw and smiled. 'Thank you, but I take no gifts except from the king.'

'Take it.'

'I cannot.'

'Wulfnoth, I will not ask again.'

'The men want leadership,' Wulfnoth said.

'Do they? And what do you mean by that?'

Wulfnoth chose his words carefully: 'They want a captain they can believe in.' Eadric watched him closely.

'I hear a man who wants to be the king's sea captain himself.'

Wulfnoth smarted. 'I am doing this for England.'

Eadric left the ring on the table and spoke almost sadly. 'No, Wulfnoth. You are doing this for you.'

The king requisitioned a walled manor a few miles inland, where there was a suitable chapel – an ancient square stone building that had been built by the Romans – and the place was soon teeming with retainers and servants, erecting a small town of wattle houses for themselves.

At the council, a bell rang and each man took his appointed place. Ethelred came in state and stood at the head of the room. Wulfnoth looked to see if the king's sons were there, but neither the princes nor the queen were present. Eadric stood on the king's right. Three of the ship captains from Glowcestrescir, young and foolish men, stood with Eadric's retainers. They stood about him, self-consciously holding their hands where the dull gold gleamed.

'Eadric carries a chest of rings wherever he goes,' Morcar whispered to Wulfnoth.

'He tried to give me one.'

Morcar chuckled. 'Oh did he? You didn't take it?'

Wulfnoth gave him a look. 'No,' he said, 'I did not.'

*

Godwin looked for Gamal, and although the door ward stood behind the king with the other men of Ethelred's household, he did not see Godwin, or did not turn his way. There was an excited murmur as the king straightened his robes, but his brows were brought together and he glowered at the men in his council.

'Silence!' Ethelred ordered and fear fell.

Godwin could feel his heart beat in his fingertips.

Ethelred glowered about the room. 'I was just a boy,' he spoke in a voice choked with emotion, 'when I was brought to the throne. And I was misled by some men, who took land from the Church. But we have made amends and brought protection back to the Holy Church. Now the Lord has forgiven us, for by His grace and the efforts of all our people we have assembled this mighty fleet.

'For many years I have sat and worried too many times how we can best prevent the Army from murdering our people. It has been a long and wearisome trial, but God has appointed me for this task. I have always done my best, raising honest men to power, ensuring that good and religious men are appointed to the bishoprics, and petitioning Our Lord Christ on behalf of the whole country. This fair land is already groaning under the taxes that we have been forced to raise. I am not unaware of the privations each tax brings upon the great and the small, but I agree that it is better to spend the money with hope of deliverance than to sit like an old and toothless dragon upon its treasure-hoard, forever fretting against the day when the robber comes and steals a jewelled cup.

'But, when I arrived here, I have found that some men have spoken against me and my advisers. And it is men who I have feasted at my own hall who have spoken against me!'

Ethelred's tone was genuinely aggrieved, but nothing more was said on the subject, and the court business was taken up with an embassy from Normandig and another from Bricge, where the dukes had promised not to give haven to the Army's ships.

The council was dismissed. Men began to stroll towards the door when Ethelred called Wulfnoth to him. The king scowled.

'Fury grows in a far seat,' Ethelred said, 'but I have brought you to my hall and given you gifts.'

'Yes, my lord,' Wulfnoth said. 'And you have no more faithful servant.'

'Do I, Wulfnoth?'

'Of course.'

Ethelred seemed to ponder this.

'Have men spoken against me to you?' Wulfnoth said. 'For I swear that I have not said anything against your person. There is no man who has proven his devotion to you more than myself. Is there any other who has taken so many ships or killed so many pirates! If any doubt me, let them step forward and challenge me face to face.'

There were no challengers of course. Nothing but fireside whispers; private doubts watered and nourished; female murmuring.

'I have faith in you, Wulfnoth Cild,' Ethelred said, but his words had almost the opposite meaning.

'Eadric has betrayed you to the king,' Wulfnoth's men warned him that night. 'It is not right that that man, whose lands are far from the sea, has grown rich while the rest of us have suffered the Army's depredations. He is a coward. He cannot bear to see any other man in greater favour than himself. Eadric fears you!'

'Enough!' Wulfnoth said. 'I am tired. You are all as nervous as a girl on her wedding night. I do not fear this Eadric.'

*

Eadric remained with the king and soon the sea captains were so despairing that they said they were going to go home.

'You must go with us to see the king,' they said.

'I agree with you, but do not ask me to go to the king on your behalf,' Wulfnoth said. 'I do not have the influence that you believe. I cannot bring more of the king's ire.'

'Wulfnoth, we have no other who can speak to the king.'

The sea captains begged him and at last Wulfnoth relented. 'I will go with you, but I shall not speak for you all. I will go and ask the king to listen to you, but that is all.'

The next day the ship captains came together and made their way to the king's hall. Summer was at its peak and the fields were parched. There were thick cracks in the soil, and the barley corns, always the first to ripen, were gold as they bowed their heads. Reapers sat in the shade of the trees and sharpened their scythes.

Gamal, the door ward, stood waiting. He walked out to greet Wulfnoth, but his face was grave. 'Wulfnoth,' he said.

'Gamal.'

'Do not do this, Wulfnoth.'

'How can I not? We have a fleet to repel the Devil himself and the king puts that fool in charge. On land or wave, the man has never fought a battle. What use will he be when the Army come with two hundred ship crews? Will he lash his ships together and sail them towards Swein Forkbeard's craft? Will he be the first to jump into the enemy's boat? No, Gamal, he will not, and every man in England knows it except the king himself.'

Wulfnoth worked himself into a fever of anger, and when they strode into the king's presence, it was Wulfnoth who stood at their head. Ethelred's eyes were baleful.

'So, this is how you want to earn a name for yourself?' he said.

'No, lord. My care is only for yourself and the country.'

'And you think I am a fool?'

Wulfnoth's mouth opened, but the words he was about to use did not seem fitting. 'I think you have been misled, lord. A fleet is only as good as the man leading it.'

It was at this moment that Eadric stepped into the hall.

'Wulfnoth does not think you are up to leading our fleet,' Ethelred said.

'Does he not?'

Eadric strode between Wulfnoth and the king. He did not seem either cowed or perturbed by the news; indeed he seemed to relish the intrigue. He wet his lips as if savouring the moment, like a wolf that tastes the prey's fear.

'No doubt he thinks that he would make a better sea captain.'

'I would,' Wulfnoth said. 'But that is not the reason I came with these men.' He gestured behind him. 'They begged me to come and speak with you, lord, and I agreed I would come to lend weight to their argument, though I said I would not speak on their behalf. But it seems that it would be cowardly of me to come all this way and not speak my mind.

'When we were twelve, we all went to the Hundred Stone and swore oaths to you, King Ethelred. Not one of us stepped forward and spoke those words without feeling the weight of responsibility upon our young shoulders. I would be betraying my oath if I did not stand here and speak plainly to you.

'This country has suffered under poor leadership. Suffered more than men can say. I have been a lucky one, and yet I have lost my eldest son, as well as many of my people to starvation and disease and sickness. It is on the backs of the farm folk that my wealth and the wealth of the whole country rides. And it is from their sweat and labour that this great fleet has been brought together. Our people are hungry because of this fleet. They lie in bed at night and their stomachs groan for food. Nevertheless they are content to go without because we have promised them that we shall keep the Army from these shores.

'Never has the country put forth so great an effort for their protection. Not even Alfred brought together a fleet of this size and strength. I for one cannot go back and look my folk full in the face if we fail them now.'

There was a long pause; then Eadric began slow applause.

'I see through you as clearly as if you were a pane of church glass,' he said. 'You have only hunger for power and position. It demeans you and cheapens every word you have said. There is nothing but desire and avarice within you, Wulfnoth Cild. How dare you speak to the king in this manner and berate him as if he were an ale-wife who had forgotten how to malt her grains!'

Wulfnoth smarted. 'There is no desire within me, Eadric Streona, except for a peaceful and prosperous England.'

'I am glad to hear that, Wulfnoth.' It was Ethelred who spoke. 'And I have heard your concerns. But do not forget that I am anointed king of this land, not any Wulfnoth Cild, and it is my right to summon a fleet into being and appoint the man I think most able to lead that fleet in battle.'

Wulfnoth laughed as he looked at Eadric. 'And this is him?'

'It is. Now go back to your ships and await his command. And, Wulfnoth . . .'

Wulfnoth turned back and the king spoke almost kindly to him. 'We do not doubt your courage or resolution. Save your anger for the Army!'

Wulfnoth rode back in silence. It was a still and subdued day, with high and mottled clouds, and bright white sunlight. The heat had brought all the midden flies out, large and black and gleaming. Wulfnoth threw his cloak over his head to keep them off. The sea was flat as he approached; rain clouds rolled in later that day and flecked the slate-grey water, which swirled with mocking gulls.

From then on he kept to his hollow ships, did not allow other men to speak treacherous words to him. If anyone started to speak, he would stand up and walk away. But he could not dispel dissent by refusing to listen to it, and the mood of the fleet remained cantankerous.

He was summoned back three days later, and this time Gamal did not walk out to greet him, but took sword and dagger from Wulfnoth and his men, and showed them into the hall, where they sat on the bench.

The king had finished his evening meal, and only Eadric and the king's chaplain were present, along with their retainers. Eadric finished telling the king a story, and the king laughed and then wiped his mouth on a linen cloth he kept on his lap.

Arrayed along the table were Eadric's brothers. At the centre was Brihtric, the sour-faced murderer and robber, who had just returned from a pilgrimage.

'Is this the man?' Eadric asked.

Brihtric's solitary eye looked at Wulfnoth. 'It is,' he said.

There was a finality to the exchange, and Eadric turned to the king.

Wulfnoth did not know what was being decided. 'I am what man?'

'You are the man who was in Flandran in the spring, meeting chief members of the Army. To help them plan their attack.'

'I am not!'

'You are. Men have already testified that you took five ships out in the spring, and were gone for nearly five weeks.'

Wulfnoth burst out laughing. 'Eadric. Is this the best you can do? Drag out paid men who will swear oaths on your behalf.'

'Do you deny it?'

'Deny what?'

'That you sailed out of Boseham, on a mission unknown, and did not return for forty days!'

'No. Of course not. It is well known why I sailed out. All my men can testify. We sailed along the south coast looking for pirates. There is no mystery. All men know what deeds I have done. I do not hear men call you "Hero", Eadric Streona.'

'I am not on trial here, Wulfnoth.'

'Is this a trial?'

Wulfnoth looked to the king and his closest councillors. The king let out an exasperated sigh. 'Have we misjudged you, Wulfnoth Cild?' he said.

'No. You have not.'

'Brihtric is a good man, fresh from Rome, where he went with gifts for the Saxon School. And Eadric is his brother, my most trusted councillor, the husband of my own daughter. Why should either of them lie?'

Wulfnoth laughed. 'There are many reasons a coward will fling mud. Shame is one, when he feels that another man has outpaced him. Jealousy another.'

Wulfnoth felt increasingly isolated as he spoke for himself, for one by one the men who had sat about him shuffled away until Godwin alone sat beside him on the bench.

'Brihtric,' Ethelred said at last, 'these are heavy charges. Do you have men who will swear on this?'

Brihtric produced twelve men of rank who would swear what he said was true. They looked Wulfnoth full in the face and repeated the charge that he had betrayed them to the Danes. Wulfnoth glared at them. Bastards all.

'Can you summon men of equal rank who will swear upon your innocence?' the king asked.

Wulfnoth looked about him to see which of the council might volunteer.

Morcar stood. 'I will swear!'

Eadric seemed to gloat, waiting to see who else would betray themselves. Wulfnoth's temper flared, but he kept his mouth shut. If he had gone down on his knees to beg the Wise, their consciences would have been pricked to action, but Wulfnoth was too proud and they were too fearful, and Wulfnoth was disgusted by them all and sought to invoke heavenly judgement.

'I will take trial by ordeal,' Wulfnoth said. 'I will do whatever you desire, lord, to prove my worth. I put my faith in the Lord Almighty.'

'Wulfnoth,' Ethelred said, 'why trouble the Almighty Maker? If you have twelve men who will come here and swear oaths on your behalf, then it will be that Brihtric is mistaken. This is not a lynching. Leave your son here and go and find twelve men who will swear oaths on your behalf.'

Godwin could see his father pause, like the man who understands that he has stumbled – or been led into a trap – and sees no way out except to win a good name.

'I will not give my son, for he is innocent of any crime.'

'We do not doubt his innocence,' Ethelred said. 'It is yours that is on trial.'

'Lord! I swear what this man says is not true.' Wulfnoth went to put his hand on his hilt, but his sword had been taken. The move was enough for two of the king's guards to start towards him.

'I suggest you do as the king bids,' Eadric said. 'Leave your son in his care, go and bring your witnesses and let the king decide.'

Of all the room Wulfnoth looked to Godwin. There was no other face that he could trust for a response, and Godwin believed in him, heart and soul.

Godwin was fearless then. 'Go, Father!' he said. 'We all know that you are innocent. If my staying allows you to go and clear your name, then go.'

Godwin was nearly eleven, but he was old enough to make a choice, old enough to understand what he was giving his father. And despite all that happened after, Godwin's choice was good. He drew the attention of every man there, and it seemed strange that the Wise of England were witnesses there, not to the wisdom or good deeds of their king, but to the courage of a ten-year-old boy who believed in his father, as boys did. Generosity glowed within him, and he seemed to shine with an inner light, like an angel, filled with the glow of truth and right.

Wulfnoth – who would not kneel to save his own life – knelt before his son and held Godwin's head between both his hands and kissed his brow. He spoke in a whisper. 'Godwin, my son, these are lies.'

Godwin took his hands from his head and held them in his own. 'I know,' he told him. 'We all know this. Go! Bring twelve men, and when you return, the fleet shall keep the Danes away.'

Wulfnoth kissed his brow again. 'I will come back for you, I swear.'

Godwin pushed his father's hands away. Yes, he smiled, I know. Wulfnoth stood and Godwin remained. He was not afraid. He stood calmly as his father faced the assembly and swore an oath to return within twelve nights.

Godwin remained as his father strode to the hall door. Wulfnoth paused for a moment and turned to take in the hall. His cheeks were red, his nostrils flared; he hated them. But his eyes found Godwin and Wulfnoth's last act was to nod to his son, half confirmation, half farewell, it seemed, in hindsight. Godwin smiled at his father. Wulfnoth Cild found it hard to respond. He gathered his cloak about him and stepped out of the hall, stooped slightly against the rain.

Godwin did not know what to do then. He had played a role of willing hostage, but now it seemed he must submit to the king's authority.

At that moment Morcar stepped forward. 'I shall care for Godwin until Wulfnoth returns.'

Godwin turned his gaze on the king, and although the light had gone from his complexion, Ethelred had seen the same beauty that the rest of the hall had seen and was not unmoved. Even Eadric did nothing to protest, and so Godwin was led away from the hall with the remains of the party of Elfhelm tight about him.

'That was a brave thing to do,' Morcar's cousin, Sigeferth, said.

Godwin thought for a moment that he was talking to him, but when he looked up, he saw that the two men were talking above his head, and that the comment was directed at Morcar, not Godwin.

'I could not leave him to Eadric. He would not last the week.'

'It would have been better if you had stayed quiet.'

Morcar put his hand to Godwin's shoulder and gave it a squeeze, but it did little to reassure. That night he did not sleep, but tossed and turned, his ears pricking at every sound. Footsteps set his heart racing; the sound of someone trying the latch made his palms sweat; and when he heard a door creak open, he sat straight up – and found himself in a morning hall and for a moment he was confused. Serving women piled the previous night's embers with tightly twisted bundles of kindling. The kindling was slow to catch and for a long while – as long as it takes a man to saddle an unwilling horse – there were no flames, just smoke billowing silently up in great swirling clouds. The smoke swirled up between the raw oak rafters where hams and fish and sides of bacon hung. All his courage had departed. He felt cold and naked and he pulled the blankets about him. A distant cock crowed, almost inaudible through the thick wattle-and-daub walls.

On the hearth, flames began to appear, small and tentative as primroses; then suddenly fire sprang up, young and fresh and eager, and the cook nudged her freckle-faced helper. 'Hurry!' she said. 'Fetch that pot!'

Someone shouted. Outside, men were talking in loud and excited voices. Fear prickled Godwin's skin. The door burst open. Violent men strode in.

'Where is he?' one of them said. It was Brihtric.

Godwin wanted to run, but his legs shook and he was too terrified to move or squeal.

'There he is!' Brihtric said, and rushed forward and grabbed him.

Morcar was just rising, and he rushed at Brihtric. 'What do you mean by this? This boy is in my care, on the king's orders!'

'And the king has ordered him brought to his hall.'

Morcar seemed dumbfounded by this news.

'Don't pretend you were not in on this,' Brihtric said.

'What?'

Brihtric stopped, and Godwin tried to pull away, but got a

clip round the ear for his troubles. Brihtric's hand clasped tight about his arm till it hurt so much Godwin paled and bit his teeth to stop himself from crying.

'This morning twenty ships are missing. Wulfnoth has stolen them and fled to the Danes. The king is sorely displeased. I wouldn't like to be this imp when the king vents his fury!'

'So you are the traitor's child?' the man, grasped Godwin and his fingers were like claws. 'Don't give me any shit and I won't give you any, but try and escape and I'll set my dogs on you as if you were a common thief. Understand?'

A wave of foul breath washed over Godwin and he refused to answer.

'Understand?'

Godwin nodded, though he didn't know why the man should even ask him such a thing.

Gort, the king's hounds-man, stepped forward and slapped his cheek. 'Bastard!' he said. 'You'd better do as you're told. You've not long left, little laddie! Brihtric's taken a hundred ships. He's going to catch your father. He'll bring him to justice.' The pleasure with which the man said 'justice' made Godwin shiver, but the stench from his mouth was fouler than a July midden. Gort leered down at him. 'And if he doesn't return . . .' Gort winked at Godwin and gestured to the beasts that were chained up outside.

One was an enormous hound, with a neck as thick as a bull's and a ridge of bristling brown fur along its spine. It had a vicious look and ugly scars across its short snout. As its keeper spoke, it stood full-square and growled menacingly.

'See that one!' he asked.

Godwin nodded. There was only one to see.

'That's Fenris. The king's best pit-fighter!'

Gort growled at the beast and its lip curled in response. There was a horrible intelligence in those pebble-hard brown eyes. The mouth was more terrifying than any befanged Mouth of Hell Godwin had seen painted on church walls. It was real and hungry, and he was the next likely target.

Gort seemed pleased as he turned back to Godwin and Godwin flinched again at the stink of his breath.

'If your father does not return, little laddie, I'll feed you to him!'

Gort locked Godwin in the kennel next to Fenris and as soon as Gort had turned his back Fenris bit and clawed and tried to find a way through the wattle walls.

'Not yet!' Gort chuckled. 'Not quite yet.'

Godwin waited till the monster had closed its eyes, but as soon as he moved it sat up and peered at him, ears alert. That afternoon was a long ordeal. The chained beast slept with eyes half lidded, and even when it twitched and growled and its lip curled in its violent and bone-crushing dreams, Godwin did not dare move or shut his eyes or do anything.

Only when the cloak of darkness had fallen did he dare to draw his eating knife and prise the wattle apart. He tugged for dear life. One of the hazel rods snapped. Hope rose in Godwin as he sawed and tugged.

I will make it, he told himself. I will flee.

The sound of the chain gave Godwin just enough warning to pull his fingers back through the small hole he had made – but only just, for Fenris's bite tore the flesh on Godwin's finger. The blood ran down his palm and the inside of his wrist. It enraged the dog.

Godwin sucked the blood away, but it was too late. A lantern swung out into the darkness, and Gort's voice called out, 'Don't eat him yet, my laddie! You can feast on fresh marrow bones tomorrow!'

That night Godwin prayed. He prayed for his father, prayed the hundred ships that Brihtric had taken in pursuit would not catch him. Prayed that when the end came it would be quick.

CHAPTER SEVEN

The Wolf Unfettered

Ethelred was livid at Wulfnoth's escape. The king's hall shook as he vented himself. It was not so much the missing ships, it was the temerity – the audacity – the insolence of a man he had honoured with arm-rings at the feast!

Brihtric took a hundred ships: their crews heaved their craft down the pale and rattling shingle, pushed them into the lapping water. They raised the masts and unfurled the square sails that stiffened to the breeze.

Wulfnoth saw the ships pushing off. 'So the king thinks he has a better seaman than Wulfnoth Cild!'

Beorn clambered up the rigging, hooked a foot into the cleats at the bottom of the sail, and made a foothold for himself, and shielded his eyes. 'At their head is a great ship with a blue cross on a while sail.'

'That's the *St Hilda*, King Ethelred's own ship,' Wulfnoth said. 'She's a great beast. She'll never catch us.'

One man had the sense to keep his eyes on the weather.

'Look!' Caerl called out. 'Behind us!'

Dark and looming against the horizon, the storm came like a

sea beast crawling forward on tentacles of black rain, blotting out sea and sky, sent from the End Times to sweep away mankind in a torrent of flame and rain and thunder and lightning. It was easier for Wulfnoth to believe that right and reason had departed this world. How else could he have left his son behind, he berated himself. Shame battled with pride. Damn them to hell, he swore. Each coward who refused to stand for him.

Wulfnoth had gone from camp to camp, but no one wanted to risk themselves on his behalf. 'I did what you all asked!' Wulfnoth cursed them. They did not look him in the eye.

'You went too far,' one man spoke out. 'You set yourself against Eadric.'

'I went too far! You *begged* me to go to the king. We sat together and you all begged me!'

Wulfnoth looked through the crowd and saw fearful men. They had spoken bravely when the ale was flowing, now they were much less brave than their words. Who were they to say he had overreached himself, he swore. He was Wulfnoth Cild!

Wulfnoth Cild did not fear death, but he would not be dragged off in chains, like a convict, to be butchered like a slave. When the king's men came for him he fought them off. He did not think. It was instinctive. He drew his sword and drove them off, seized horses and galloped to the ships. He expected to be cut down in the attempt. To find armed may waylaying him, his ships seized, a desperate fight on the shoreline where he was killed with his men.

But the way lay open, the eager ships bobbing in the shallows, the wide seas promising freedom. Bravery was a fine thing, but not when it left the weak to suffer. He had not thought, and he had survived and now he looked to shore and the realisation of what he had done stunned him. It was like a dagger thrust into his gut. He clutched the rigging and cursed God as he wept. He had left his son to suffer while he sailed free. He would find a way, he told himself, his son would be taken care of.

Wulfnoth prayed as he had never prayed: desperately and silently.

He would explain, he thought. He would beg for forgiveness. He would be revenged on the king who had driven him to this end.

In an hour the day seemed to change ten times over: from sun and warmth to grey and cold and back again. *Swanneck* plunged into the growing waves. Surf flew like the spittle of thrashing sea monsters and the seas rose so high that the boats plunged down into valleys of dark, shifting and hungry water. A few men cried out in alarm; there was a chorus of voices pleading to the Lord: shouting prayers to St Anthony; making all manner of ostentatious offers of penance and barefooted pilgrimage to the furthest places they could imagine – the Mount of St Michel, Dunholme; Canturburie, even Ierusalem itself – if the Lord of Heaven would bring them safely from this wretched storm.

'Taste it!' Wulfnoth shouted as the salt dried on his skin. 'The old gods are here! Fasten down your sea chests! Hold on to *Swanneck*'s precious timbers! Strike down our foes! Make peace with your Maker, this is the last sailing of Wulfnoth Cild.'

The rain lashed in great sheets that soaked Godwin to the skin. Fenris stood with his paws planted firmly in the mud, tail towards the storm, occasionally blinking the rain from his eyes as he stared at his charge.

If Godwin so much as moved, Fenris began to growl.

'That's it!' Gort shouted through the rain. 'Keep your eyes on that little lob! Hush your barking! I'll feed him to you in the morning.'

When morning came, it was clear and still, and the sky was a pale scrubbed blue. Fenris was sound asleep. Godwin moved towards the hole he had worked on and the dog did not move. It snored gently, twitched a paw, snarled in his sleep.

Godwin hurriedly pulled out his eating knife. He sawed desperately at the hazel rods. His knife was too blunt. The wattle was too fresh and green and swollen with damp; it frayed like rope into pale fibres. He scrabbled at them with his hands, which were wet and numb from the night's chill, and the skin split sooner than the rods did. His finger began to bleed again. Fenris growled and Godwin looked over his shoulder. The animal still slept. Godwin sucked the blood from his finger, and was more careful now. He worked as methodically as he could keeping his finger curled into his palm, lest the scent of fresh blood wake the hogbacked hound.

It took half an hour for Godwin to make a hole big enough to get his arm through. His heart began to beat with hope and excitement. He kept looking over his shoulder; Fenris still slept.

You'll do it! a voice inside his head said, and he became giddy with hope. When his arm was through, he could unravel the woven strands. They whipped his face, sprang back into place. Almost through! Godwin thought. Almost there!

Suddenly the hole went dark.

Godwin froze, but it was not Fenris; it was a smaller yard dog, which had wandered over sniffing for food. It licked its lips, stuck its nose into the hole.

'Heh!' Godwin said, in what was his friendly-to-dogs voice. 'Heh now, little laddie.'

The dog was brown and short-furred, with long whiskers. Its nose was black and wet. Godwin put his good hand up. The nose sniffed; a nervous sniff.

'Hush!' Godwin said. 'Hush.'

The dog sniffed again. Warily this time. The nose pulled back and the dog barked. A short, shart yap.

'Hush!' Godwin hissed, but the dog barked again.

Fenris was awake in moments. He saw Godwin, pushed his head through the hole and bristled with anger. He nipped the tail of the other dog, which fled before him, thrust his thick snout further into the hole, pushed as far as the wattle would allow and strained to catch Godwin.

Godwin was pressed against the far wall of the kennel as the thick neck finally reached the limits of the hole. Fenris's fangs were just inches from Godwin's face. Hot and fetid breath warmed his cheeks. Godwin shrank back. Fenris snapped and his teeth grazed Godwin's cheek.

Godwin cursed his luck. Footsteps came closer and Fenris pulled back from the hole. Gort's face peered in.

'You!' he shouted. 'You're wanted.'

Godwin feet squelched as he hurried after the houndsman. All the faces seemed hostile now – the whole world was hostile, and the door ward was not Gamal this time but one of the king's Danish mercenaries: a tall, freckled man with red-blond beard and hair.

'So this is the traitor's child,' he said.

There was little love lost between English and Danish mercenaries and the man waved Gort through without a second glance.

Ethelred was a little drunk and laughed when Godwin came in. Godwin saw what he was laughing at: a bear that could dance to the sound of the pipe. Godwin drew himself up. He stood and shivered as the bear – held by a chain about its neck – stepped lightly on its brown paws.

Godwin was conscious of the grime on his clothes, and the

lack of any members of the council. There were a few of the king's retainers, and one of Eadric's brothers.

At long last Ethelred turned to him. His drunkenness and arrogance and good looks made his manner more threatening. 'Wulfnothson, your father has taken twenty of my ships!' he said.

Godwin spoke bravely. 'My father will return.'

'He will. I've sent Brihtric after him. He will return and he will pay.'

Godwin started to speak, but Gort struck him and Godwin felt a chill on him and turned.

Eadric walked into the room. In a moment he took in the scene before him.

'We have his son,' Ethelred said.

'So I see,' Eadric said.

They all looked at the boy.

'Your father has betrayed us,' Eadric said, and strolled towards him.

Eadric filled his vision. Godwin stared stonily ahead. A hand took him by the chin and lifted his head, but Godwin turned his eyes away.

'It is a shame for all of us,' Eadric said. He spoke softly, almost gently. 'Look at me. Look at me, child.'

He fixed his gaze on the corner of the rafters.

'Look at me!' Eadric said.

Godwin looked, and instantaneously felt as if he had let himself down.

'Your father is in league with the Danes.'

'I do not believe it,' Godwin said, and tried to look away but Eadric still held him by the chin, and then abruptly let go.

'Deal with him,' Ethelred said.

Eadric nodded. 'Bring him outside!'

At the door the two men stopped.

Eadric looked sadly at the boy.

'How are your hounds?' he asked Gort.

'Well, master,' the houndsman replied. 'Feeling the need for a little sport.'

Eadric nodded. 'Do they have enough fresh meat?'

'It's been a little lacking since we came here.'

Gort took hold of Godwin's shoulder.

'His father is a traitor,' Eadric said. 'Deal with him.'

Gort turned away from the manor, out towards the fields. They left the servants and stables behind. Gort walked a few paces behind Godwin, with Fenris pulling at his chain. The beast began to snarl.

'Where are we going?'

'Over there,' Gort said.

'Where?'

'Never you mind.'

Gort kicked him. 'That way,' he said and pointed to a copse of trees a hundred and fifty yards across the unharvested field of barley. The king's hall was already a few minutes behind them.

The corn was just starting to turn from green to gold. The nodding barley had a bleak and ominous feel.

Godwin stopped. Gort shoved him. 'Get on with you!'

Godwin saw nothing for him but a gruesome death. He shook his head. Gort shook Fenris's chain and the pit-fighter lowered his head, ears and lips pulled back, his body ready to spring.

'Get on with you or I'll let Fenris go!'

Godwin's mouth was dry. He drew in a slow breath, but his legs shook violently and refused to move.

Gort grinned. This was good sport.

'You'd better run,' he said, 'before I let Fenris go.'

'Don't,' Godwin said.

'Start running!'

'Please don't!' Godwin said, backing away.

He could never outrun the hound, but he could not die where he stood. The barley corns whipped across his legs as he turned and ran.

Fenris strained at the chain as Gort struggled to undo the collar.

'Hold!' a voice shouted.

Gort spun round. An armed warrior was striding towards him.

'Who are you?' Gort demanded.

The man was tall and strong, and his blue eyes smouldered as he took in the scene before him. 'I am Hemming, and this boy is my charge. Stand aside. Stand aside!' he said.

'Hemming! How came you here?' Godwin shouted, and looked for his father, but there was no one else. Only Hemming, Gort, Fenris and himself.

'I came for you,' Hemming shouted. 'But run!'

Godwin saw the dog dragging at the chain. He turned and ran and did not look back. His lungs heaved, his fingers bled as he thrashed over a hedge, and the brambles clung to him like grasping hands.

'Run!' Hemming shouted again, but all Godwin could hear was Fenris snarling.

Godwin raced desperately towards the copse. He might clamber up a tree or hide in a hole or a hollow trunk. He could hear the hound behind him, and in his terror Godwin tripped and fell.

Hemming strode towards Gort like the Angel of Death. Gort ran off in terror, letting go of Fenris's chain. Hemming did not give him a second glance. But instead of charging the armed warrior, the dog leapt after the fleeing boy, chain trailing like a convict that has escaped the slave market.

Fenris was gaining on Godwin and there was no way Hemming could reach him in time. Fenris was the king's finest pit-fighter, trained to stand his ground and lock his jaws upon his opponent, and crunch bone and life from his prey. He weighed as much as a full-grown man, could take down a deer unaided.

Hemming lost his sword in the scramble to catch the dog's chain snaking through the barley. He hurled his spear. It was a good throw and arced towards the animal. The blade did not strike true, and Fenris let out a furious yowl, half surprise and half anger.

Godwin risked a glimpse over his shoulder. 'Fly!' Hemming shouted. 'To the woods!'

Just then, Fenris turned on Hemming and there was pure evil in his eyes.

'I cannot leave you!' Godwin cried, but Hemming again shouted at him, 'Fly!'

Hemming crouched down. He glanced behind and knew he could not hope to reach his sword in time. Fenris turned upon him. King Ethelred's hound was like a demon in dog's shape. Hemming did not flinch.

Fenris leapt. Hemming pushed the first jump back, but Fenris was a fighting dog: pure and terrible and simple. A second bound knocked the man back, the third made him stumble and then Fenris was upon him. He tore off Hemming's ear and cheek, clamped the crown of his head in a vicious vice. His neck muscles bulged as his jaw locked and beast shook his head.

Hemming did not cry out, but he let out a low groan, as a brave man will endure his pain. Godwin ran then and Hemming's muffled moans followed after.

The terrible noise stopped when the copse was still thirty feet off. Godwin turned and saw with horror that Fenris powered towards him. At the same moment horsemen appeared from the edge of the wood. They had falcons with them. Godwin heaved in great breaths as he ran on a few more steps, even though there was no chance of escape. He did not care about capture now so much as saving himself from Hemming's fate.

'It's a fugitive!' he heard one of them say. 'You!' the same voice said as Godwin stumbled forward. 'You – come here!'

Godwin turned away from riders and hound and made futilely for the trees.

'Hold!' the voice shouted, and the horse was kicked forward. Godwin could feel the hooves pounding towards him. A blow knocked him to the ground and the rider swung down. 'Stand up!'

Godwin acted stupid and kept his head down.

'Lift your head!'

Godwin lifted his head, but kept his eyes down.

'It's you, isn't it?'

Godwin said nothing.

'It's him. Wulfnoth's son. Hold that dog back!'

Prince Edmund held out a friendly hand to Godwin and smiled. 'Greetings, Godwin. Do you still play football?'

Edmund and Athelstan were cocky, arrogant and impatient for power. They held a rival court around their grandmother's manor of Athelingedean, in Sudsexe, and spirited Godwin away, gave him fine calfskin shoes, a lambswool kirtle with an embroidered hem, and a brass and silver brooch to clasp his cloak tight about his shoulders.

In her youth, their grandmother, King Ethelred's mother, had been the most beautiful woman in England. She had bewitched the old king, and tales were told of how the old man put his first wife aside for her. But her hair was rime-white now, her cheeks were hairy, and she had a slight hunch and a stoop to her shoulders, but otherwise Godwin thought of her as a stern and handsome lady, and she took him in without question.

The old lady had a weakness for honey cakes. They were piled up on a wooden platter. She shared them with 'the boys', shamelessly spoilt her grandsons as she listened to their tales of Ethelred and Eadric, and the ruin of the fleet.

'And now Father has returned to Lundenburh and sent the fleet home,' Athelstan said.

The old lady took another honey cake and held it between her fingers. She paused, mid-bite, shook her head and looked up at Heaven, in both a gesture of despair and witness, as if checking Christ had noticed the foolishness of her son. 'And this is Wulfnoth's son?' she said.

Godwin bowed and the lady scrutinised him with clear and hard blue eyes.

'I have heard of your father,' she said, and she seemed satisfied with what she saw. 'He has escaped Brihtric, I have heard.'

'Has he? I am glad.'

'You are glad? Why? That's ridiculous. He abandoned you, child.'

'He did not. My father would not do that.'

She turned full on him. 'No?'

'He sent one of his men for me.'

'Did he? One man? And where is he now?'

'The king's bandog killed him.'

She raised her eyes in an exasperated look as if that explained everything. She did not approve of bear-baiting, had seen too much of the world to believe in goodness. Did not believe in being contradicted.

'He abandoned you, child. Men these days are obsessed with power. They think of nothing more than themselves. It is an evil I have seen too many times. Your father escapes, Brihtric loses a hundred ships in the storm, and now my son has sent the rest of the fleet home. Even now he returns to Lundenburh, and what a farce has been played out for all men's vanities. What sense is there in that? My husband, Edgar, would never have tolerated it. In those days men were more stern. They imposed peace on the nobles. In those days kings were real kings!'

A month after the English fleet had departed in dribs and drabs to their homes, a new fleet landed. The ships were sleek, the accents harsh; the feet landed with a heavy tread.

England had spent her last reserves of hope on the ships of the navy, and with the fleet's destruction and dispersal there was no will to resist. They did not even look to their king any more, but each to their own safety. The Danish Army marched on Canturburie, and the men of Cantware paid them three thousand pounds of silver for peace, then the Army passed on into Sudsexe and Hamtunscir and Berroscire and burnt and pillaged, and no one stood against them.

At Athelingedean the princes spoke treachery against their own father. Their grandmother encouraged them. 'Raise a banner and declare yourselves kings. Your grandfather had to fight his own brother for the throne. Men thanked him for it. "Edgar the Peaceful", they named him. And not because he was a meek or gentle man, but because he was tough and ruthless and he imposed peace on the land. Peace and law and order!'

Edmund was all for civil war but Athelstan was against it. 'I will not go against the king,' he said, 'but I will fight. Send word out that I will lead men against the Danes. It is time men had faith in the prowess of the royal line.'

The princes and their comitatus – their armed companions – were wolf-hungry for battle. The princes gathered steady coursers from the land about. They were stout horses that could cover vast distances without tiring. There was much excitement as young men gathered. They named themselves 'the Wild Hunt'.

'We'll show those old bastards!' Edmund said as he gave Godwin one of his horses. It was a magnificent bay born of the mare Freya by the stallion West Wind. Godwin named it Strider. He loved that horse. It was steady and reliable, and snorted with pleasure each morning they swung up into the saddle. They slept in royal manors, devoured all the ale and meat, and rode again next morning, looking for their quarry.

A year later, on Godwin's twelfth birthday, he waited in the eaves of a beech wood in Oxenefordscire, watched a Danish party dismount at a village of four longhouses. Shouts of alarm drifted across the open and harvested strip fields. The buzz of a bumblebee drew slowly louder and then faded as it passed by. One of the horses snorted and pawed the earth. The sun came out for a moment as the clouds passed overhead. The shadow crossed over them and drifted towards the hills in the distance.

'There are ten of them,' Edmund whispered. It was good odds. Three to one. The Danes were a poor band, such as tagged along after great warlords like carrion. There were two thin men with scraggly beards, a couple of young lads who must have been on their first trip to England, a one-handed man and a fat Dane who had stripped to the waist. He had a hairy back, striped with old whip scars.

'Look at them,' Edmund spat. 'They don't even bother looking for armed men.'

'The fat one, he's the leader,' Athelstan said.

The fat man was first into the largest longhouse. He came out a few minutes later dragging a girl by the shoulder.

'He is mine.' Athelstan turned so that all of them knew.

'I'll take the redhead,' Edmund said.

There were three lads to each Dane and more. The raiders did not stand a chance. Godwin knew his job. It was to ride behind Edmund and protect him with his own body, if necessary.

At Athelstan's waist was the ancient sword of King Offa. For two hundred years each eldest son had carried it in battle. It gleamed as Athelstan drew it and kicked his horse forward.

Edmund carried a silver worked horn. He put it to his lips and blew a great blast as they kicked their horses forward.

The Danes looked up. They turned in surprise. A thunder of hooves broke from the autumn forest. Anger turned to horror as the Danes saw the furious faces riding down on them. They showed themselves to be cowards and craven as they screamed and turned and ran.

The princes and their company were hunters; their prey were the Danes, and any who helped them. Their number was too few to oppose the Danes openly, but they fought secretly against them and destroyed foragers who strayed too far from the main trail. It was dangerous and exciting, sleeping in woods, eating berries and fresh meat, going for weeks in the field. They were tireless and determined, arrogant as well – and after each trip they swaggered into court and the halls of the older thegns with ill-disguised contempt.

'They disgust me!' Edmund said. 'These grey beards and fat-guts who roll over for the Danes.'

For the next three years the world was simple. Edmund was his one and only lord. Eadric and his wife, Queen Emma, their enemy. They hunted and sparred by day, listened to tales of murder and vengeance, and learnt to hold a gutful of beer. At night keen falcons swooped between the rafters, swift horses stamped in the yard outside, and Edmund's grandmother encouraged them by asking the tale-tellers to put on fabulous tales of the elder days. They passed the harp from hand to hand. They sang of matchless heroes and their greatest deeds, glad voices laughing in the hall; the giver of gold on the benches before them. They were young and angry. When Ethelred died Eadric would be the first to hang from their gibbet.

Edmund flaunted his followers, even took Godwin to court. 'No one will touch you,' he said to Godwin. 'You are my man now.'

And it was true.

Eadric twitched at the sight; Ethelred seemed oblivious and irritated Edmund by saying nothing; it was only Queen Emma who drew attention to the fact.

'What is *he* doing here?' she asked.

No one answered.

'He is a traitor.'

'I am no traitor,' Godwin told her.

The queen's cheeks coloured.

'Will no one send this traitor's son away?'

The men looked at her but did not move. Her mouth opened and then closed without making a noise.

He was Edmund's man. Who could contradict the king's second son except the king himself? They all looked to Ethelred. He laughed at them. 'Look at my warlike little boys! You cannot wait for me to die!'

'Your time is coming,' the princes' grandmother reassured them, but each autumn they kicked through the piles of fallen leaves and cursed the king and his council, and brooded.

More young men arrived at Athelingedean. One of them was a handsome young boy who stood a little apart: unsure and nervous and bewildered. He caught Godwin's attention. It seemed that he must have once looked like that.

When they rode out that morning, Godwin made sure the boy had a gentle mount. As they set off, the boy rode at the back. Godwin pulled his horse to the side and fell in with him.

'My name is Godwin,' he said.

'Blecca,' the boy said. 'I am from Defenascir.'

'I am from Sudsexe.'

Godwin and Blecca shook hands.

Blecca seemed overawed to be talking to Godwin Wulfnothson.

'What does your father think of you coming with the prince?' Godwin asked.

The boy's face fell. 'Oh, he is dead.'

'I'm sorry.'

Blecca did not smile. 'My father failed to pay the taxes and our neighbour paid the tax for him and took all our land and live-stock.'

Godwin listened to the boy tell his tale. It was a common enough story, for the taxes had done as much damage as the Danes. 'My father killed the man who had taken our land and the man's three sons set on my father one day in the field.'

There was something in the way that Blecca spoke. 'Were you there?' Godwin asked.

Blecca nodded.

'I bet you feel guilty,' he said.

'I *tried* to help.'

Godwin drew in a deep breath. He turned and looked over the fields until he could compose himself.

'My father gave me as hostage,' Godwin explained. 'Then he fled and left me to the king's dogs.'

Blecca didn't know what to say.

'I do not know what I did to be left like that.'

Blecca was stumped. He looked up at Godwin and he seemed old and hard and angry.

'Where is he now?'

'In exile.' Godwin looked at Blecca. 'Listen, we are your family now.'

In those years Eadric grew only stronger; England more weak. The princes guarded their power against the day the king died. They seemed idyllic times to Godwin. When Edmund gave his word, he did not break it. Edmund was the rock upon which the drowning man clambers, and wind or storm will not shake his grip.

But he also learnt love of a different kind, for Blecca was like a little brother. He looked up to Godwin and at first Godwin felt uncomfortable with the responsibility.

'He wants to be like you,' Edmund said.

Godwin laughed at the idea.

'What? Look at you. You are a good and brave man. And loyal. And how many men can say that these days?'

The words surprised Godwin, because like many men, his own qualities were less clear to him than his weaknesses.

'You are Edmund's closest friend,' Blecca said to him.

'I do not think so,' Godwin said, but Blecca nodded.

'I have watched. In council he always waits until you have spoken.'

Godwin laughed. Perhaps it was true. He did not know. He did not care so much. He was Edmund's man. And that was enough.

One day word came from the south that Gytha, wife of Wulfnoth, had died.

Edmund broke the news to Godwin, and it came to him like an echo from long ago. My mother is dead, he told himself, but he could not feel it. He was numb, like the man who stands too long in the cold. My mother is dead.

Everyone knew when Godwin strode into the hall, but only Blecca came to sit with him. Godwin sat by the fire and Blecca drew up a three-legged stool.

'I heard,' he said.

Godwin said nothing.

Blecca put a hand on Godwin's arm.

Godwin did not show any emotion, but at long last he looked up and Blecca saw that tears were brimming in his eyes.

'What did I do to deserve this?' Godwin said. 'What did I do that they would abandon me like this?'

Blecca didn't know. He had no answers that day.

'She went back to her people when my father was exiled. I could have gone to her.' Godwin stopped speaking, and Blecca sat for a long time.

'Shall I leave?'

'No,' Godwin said, and stood abruptly up. 'Come – shall we ride? I feel the need for the wind on my face. I cannot stay inside all day.'

It seemed news of Gytha's death had reached Godwin's father, for not long after that a messenger came to Athelingedean. 'The man who arrived this morning at first watch,' Blecca said, 'brings word from your father.'

Godwin looked across the fire. The light of the flames was on his face and flickered in his dark eyes. 'And what did he say?'

'I do not know. He spoke to Edmund.'

Edmund walked in. His face was serious, and he stood behind Blecca and looked at Godwin. 'He wants you to go back to him.'

'Does he?' Godwin laughed. 'Where is he?'

'Dyflin.'

Godwin laughed again, but that laughter masked much.

'He asked for news of you.'

'And what did you tell him?'

'Nothing,' Edmund said. He knew Godwin's mind and Godwin nodded.

'Good,' he said.

'He also brought news,' Edmund said. 'Blecca, go and check on the horses.'

Blecca understood and ran outside. Godwin caught the note in Edmund's voice and waited till the prince sat down. 'Swein Forkbeard is gathering another Army.'

Another Army: battle, death, tax, famine, disgrace. The thought made Godwin feel ill, but his expression did not change, and he made no visible reaction.

'This time,' Edmund said, 'he claims he will take the throne itself.'

'Does your father know?'

Edmund nodded. 'But he will not do anything.'

'I will not leave you,' Godwin said.

'And I will not leave England.'

'We will fight?'

Edmund nodded. 'And die if necessary. Men will sing of Edmund Atheling and how he met the Danes in battle and did not flee.'

They were young and ambitious and a glorious death seemed a fine thing to them both.

CHAPTER EIGHT

Forkbeard

In the summer of 1013 Swein Forkbeard, King of Danemark, sailed into the wide mouth of the Hymbre. It was the largest fleet that anyone could remember.

'Where is your king?' Swein demanded. 'Where is your feeble king? Is there no one in this country who will fight me!'

Swein landed only fifteen miles from Morcar's hall.

Sigeferth burst into Morcar's hall, but Morcar had already heard of the arrival of the Army on his doorstep and he paced up and down like a trapped wolf.

'If we welcome Swein, Ethelred will call me a traitor. If we do not, then Swein will burn us out of hall and home.'

The men argued back and forth, but there was no clear answer. At last it was Morcar's wife who intervened. 'Do not worry about Ethelred. He is an old man. He will soon be dead.'

'But what about the king's sons?'

'They are sound men,' she told him. 'They will understand. Welcome Swein, but do not help him too much. That way, you can plead that you acted under duress. And an oath under duress is no oath.'

Morcar feasted the Danish king, but secretly he looked to the south and prayed for help. When news finally came, Morcar's heart was heavy. 'Ethelred hides in Lundenburh. There is no fyrd gathering. Our own king has betrayed us. He is no longer our protector.'

The men who still believed in Ethelred would not fight unless the he summoned them, but he had lost faith in his own people. They looked and waited for news, or for the war arrow to summon them to honour their oaths, but there was nothing.

'If only the king would come,' Old Athelmar, alderman of Sumersæton, said by way of apology when Edmund's armed company rested their horses in Bade.

'Then follow me,' Edmund said. 'If you follow me, we can persuade Athelstan to raise his banner. Will you take him as your king?'

'You ask me to betray my king in order to crown his son?'

'Yes,' Edmund said.

Old Athelmar thought long. It was a hard thing to ask an old man who cherished his family's long loyalty. 'I would,' he said at last, 'if the Wise were agreed.'

'Damn the Wise,' Edmund cursed under his breath. They were slow and stupid and senile.

Edmund and Athelstan rode about the country attempting to find men who would fight, but it was the same everywhere they stopped. If only the king would come, then they would follow him; if only the Wise would make Athelstan king.

Within weeks the whole country had fallen to Swein's Army and Edmund turned from defiant to despondent. Many young men had joined his company, but almost as many had slipped quietly away.

'Let us ride against Swein,' he said.

'A hundred against four thousand?'

Edmund was fired up with the thought of a glorious death. 'Men will sing our names. We shall shame the country by our deaths. The finest hundred men that England could find, mauled by Danish spears, prepared to fight when no one else did.'

Godwin let Edmund talk, but his eyes wandered over the faces of their companions. He did not want to throw his life away, nor those of men who were dear to him.

That night Godwin took Edmund aside. 'You are the lord of all these young men. If you died, what would become of them? The wolves would descend on them. It would be like Herod and the babes. All those boys like Blecca. Eadric and the queen would snuff them out. We need you, Edmund; your life is very precious to us and to the country. Do not throw it away in anger or despair.'

They made their way to Lundenburh, where the rump of the English court cowered about their king. Blecca acted like Godwin's shield-bearer. He held his horse as Godwin mounted, carried his spears and made way for him on the benches. He was also a good talker, and made Godwin laugh.

One night that September, as they filed into the village where they planned to rest, Edmund called for Godwin. Godwin left Blecca to polish his sword.

When Godwin returned the two of them sat in silence for a long time, and then Godwin stood up and stretched.

'I would not be a king of men.'

'Nor I,' Blecca said.

'Edmund is a fine man. He is the only man I know who never let me down. Even my brother let me down.'

Godwin had told Blecca about his brother a while ago: a vague tale of him dying in a famine. He did not know how he had let Godwin down, and did not ask.

Godwin smiled. 'You have finished the sword?'

Blecca nodded.

'Good,' Godwin said. 'We shall be in Lundenburh tomorrow. Get a good night's rest. It will be an early morning.'

Edmund and his company arrived in Lundenburh at first light. Athelstan had looked for their coming and came down and greeted them at the city gates. A crowd had gathered on the walls above the gates. Their faces were despondent. As Edmund dismounted and embraced his brother, Godwin heard men asking each other, 'Will they fight? Will the king's sons fight?'

Godwin found the faces of the men who were talking and spoke to them. 'Yes. Do not fear. The king's sons will fight.'

His words stilled the murmurs and a few men cheered as they rode through the gates, but when Edmund got to the hall, he was furious with his brother.

They had barely entered the hall when their voices began to rise. Blecca looked to Godwin in alarm, and Godwin tried to hide his concern.

'Look at what has happened,' Edmund's voice carried into the yard. 'If you had raised the banner a year ago, we could have gathered a host of war-eager warriors.'

'There would have been murder!'

'Better murder than this!'

'I told you then and I tell you now, I will not come to the throne like that!' Athelstan shouted.

'Then you will not come to the throne at all,' Edmund said.

'Edmund, I had thought better of you. It is not the time for this.'

Edmund was shouting now. 'Then when? Swein will not be content until we are dead. Where will we run? You want to go to Normandig with Queen Emma? She will poison us both rather than let us live. We are between the viper and the serpent and all because you are a coward!'

'I am no coward!'

'Then take the throne!'

'I will not!' Athelstan roared, and as the two men drew daggers, their retainers jumped up and pulled them apart.

Edmund shut himself in his room. There was a dreadful air in the palace. The newer lads like Blecca stood in uncomfortable groups. More than ever they needed calming. Godwin tried to cheer the others, but the mood was like a funeral. When the door was unbolted, they all stood back for Godwin to go in.

He caught Blecca's eye and walked in alone.

Edmund was pacing under the window. He turned quickly, saw Godwin, and stopped.

'The coward!' Edmund cursed. 'Athelstan's a coward! I told him to seize the throne and he would not. He thought he could just sit and wait for our father to die. And look what has happened now! We have lost everything!'

The angrier Edmund became, the calmer Godwin was. He closed the door behind him and signalled for Edmund to speak more quietly.

Edmund let out a long sigh and buried his head in his hands. 'You know, you are lucky your father is not here to shame you. I wish my father was dead. I cannot bear what he has done.'

Godwin drew in a deep breath.

At last he said, 'Your brother would not go against your father, and you would not go against your brother.'

There was a long pause. Edmund understood he was being gently reproached. He drew in a deep breath. 'I know,' he said eventually. 'I know. You are right. Honour has hobbled us. Look at our enemy. They are like savages. Swein's deposed his own father and set the old man to begging. Should we have done that? Would God have looked more kindly on us?'

'God moves in mysterious ways,' Godwin said. It was what religious men always said.

'Don't you start!' Edmund said, and punched him.

Godwin laughed. 'He does,' he said. 'Bloody mysterious ways.'

'Oh, how he does.' Edmund drew in a deep breath. 'So what do we do now?'

'Fight the Danes.'

'They are closing in?'

Godwin nodded. 'Swein is only three days away.'

'I feel like a boar,' Edmund said, 'as the hounds bring him to ground. He butts and gores, but he is surrounded by a circle of baying dogs and is doomed.'

Godwin was calm and certain. Platitudes were all he had. 'We're not dead yet,' he said. 'Where there's life there's hope.'

'Is there?' Edmund said. 'I do not feel hope. How come you feel hope?'

Godwin laughed. He did not know. He just felt it. 'Well,' Godwin said, 'life has been good to me.'

'Has it?'

'Of course. You took me in. That was a generous act. You have given me food and fire and honour. You have taken us all in. What more can we ask but an honourable lord and a chance to strike against our foe?'

'You are a good man, Godwin Wulfnothson. I envy you. I wish I shared your optimism.'

'You will,' Godwin said.

Edmund half smiled. He stood up and straightened his clothes. 'Where are the men?'

'In the hall.'

'Are they ashamed of me?'

'No, of course not. They love you. You are their lord.'

Edmund didn't seem to believe him, but at last he relented. 'Where is my brother?'

'In the hall.'

'I should go and apologise.'

Godwin nodded.

'Come with me,' Edmund said.

It was a chill September morning when Swein's Army arrived outside Lundenburh's stone walls. A sea of Temese mist lapped against the foot of the walls and the world seemed muffled under a coat of dull dew droplets as the first Danes began to pitch tents in the sloping fields that rose from the river valley. For three days more and more men arrived, until the camp stretched as far as the forests where once they had hunted deer. They sat about and mocked the defenders, bathed naked in the river, feasted on the grass and practised with weapons.

Soon they sent messengers demanding Ethelred come out and fight.

'Bastards!' Edmund cursed the messengers. 'Who are you to tell my father when he should fight!'

Edmund took a hunting bow and shot at them and the messengers hurried away before one of them was feathered.

Godwin and Edmund were up with the next dawn. Blecca came with them.

They had spent all night rolling from side to side, listening to the Danish singing and the strange laughter. Confidence oozed from the Danish camp.

'Will battle come?' Blecca asked Godwin.

Godwin was not sure. 'I think so,' he said.

'Can I stand with you?'

'No,' Godwin said, but he thought of himself at that age, how he was hunting Danes, and relented. 'As long as you stay behind me.'

Godwin, Blecca, Edmund and all the company able to fight took their appointed places on the walls among the strange mix of townsfolk, retainers, grooms and mercenaries who strengthened the defence at the gateways and key points of the line. Two of the king's retainers sat on their shields and played dice.

They laughed and joked as Edmund and Godwin watched the Danes take their places and then dress their lines and move down into the mist between them.

So it has come to battle, Godwin thought as the war horns sang and the Danes' spear tips came forward at a fast walk.

'I always imagined my first battle would be a glorious thing,' Blecca said, 'but somehow this struggle feels doomed. We're here to fight for an unwanted king. This is not glorious or heroic; we are dead men.'

'We are not,' Godwin said to him. 'This is not the end.'

'No?'

'No,' Godwin laughed. 'This is just the beginning!'

Godwin caught Blecca's eye, and Blecca grinned and hefted his shield.

'Remember your father,' Godwin told him. 'Take revenge for his death.'

For three days the Danes attacked, continually testing the strength of the defenders. To the south they tested the wooden palisade that linked Crepelgate to the river wall. To the east they probed the tumbledown walls about Ældgate.

Edmund paced impatiently as the sounds of battle drifted from left and right. He was being cheated of glory. 'Godwin!

We are wasted here. Take a horse and see if they need our help.'

Blecca made to follow, but Godwin waved him back.

'Stay with the prince,' he said.

Godwin half ran, half hurried across the city. He grabbed the first saddled horse – an unruly courser with a butter-brown mane – and clattered down to the main thoroughfare, which crossed the city, thundering across the sturdy wooden bridge over the Fleot River.

'How goes the battle?' Godwin shouted to the commander there, a Danish mercenary, rumoured to be a man that Swein had exiled from his homeland.

The man was dressed in a coat of dark mail, with a boar helmet on his head. He had fine moustaches that reached down to his chest, and he rested his arms on a great bearded war axe.

'Well!' he shouted back. 'They are only playing here. They fight without conviction and have fallen back to eat their lunch.'

Godwin turned the courser back towards the bridge. A waste of time, he thought, cursed the waiting.

Godwin was warm and sweaty as he climbed up the steps to where he had left Edmund on the gatehouse above Crepelgate, but neither Edmund nor Blecca nor any of their war party was there. Godwin did not know the men he saw sitting at the top of the tower. For a moment he thought he had climbed the wrong staircase and turned and looked about, but this was the tower, he was sure.

The men squatted against the wall, their shields drawn up to their knees. They were citizen levy, without mail or swords.

'Where is the prince?' Godwin demanded. 'Where is Prince Edmund?'

One of the men waved a hand southwards, towards the river, from where the din of battle was growing ever louder.

'They're throwing all their strength against the West Gate.'

Damn, Godwin thought, and leapt down the wall. Edmund was in the thick of it, and he was not with him.

He started to panic as he grabbed the courser again and kicked him forward. The West Gate led straight to St Paul's Cathedral, and the heavyset Romanesque church looked dark and gloomy as it overshadowed the longhouse thatched roofs.

Godwin kicked the horse towards St Forster's Church and the closer he got, the louder the din. The city's stone walls had been broken down to build the church, so the walls were weak there. Only a ditch spanned the gap, with a steep bank and palisade that reached high over any man on the other side. He was hoping to catch Edmund up, but either he had taken another route or he had not come this way at all.

'I'm looking for Prince Edmund!' he shouted at the men who were stumbling in the other direction, but their faces were streaked with blood and they stood stunned.

'It's over,' one man told him, and Godwin kicked past him.

Blecca has my shield, he thought, and turned the corner and saw no sign of Edmund. But the sight before him chilled his heart. Just to the north of the West Gate, Danes had stormed the walls. They were leaping down from the palisade and landing among the houses and dashing into the street, running amok, like foxes in a chicken coop, chopping and slashing and grabbing and burning.

Godwin jumped from the horse, grabbed a shield from the ground and pulled it on to his arm. He felt both terrified and brave as he was knocked back by the men stumbling from the battle.

'Fight!' Godwin shouted at them. 'Fight!' he commanded, but his voice was shrill and their spirit was gone. 'Fight!' Godwin shouted, laying about him with the back of his sword. 'Are you English men or no!'

One man used his spear like a walking stick, collapsed against the church walls and slid slowly to the ground, then pitched on to his face; another stared at his half-severed hand; a youth looked about in amazement as if to check that he really was carrying his guts in his arms. A Danish sword-swing ended the poor lad's astonishment. He seemed to suddenly jump forward, head swinging round, blood splattering in an arc. He hung in the air for what seemed an impossibly long time before gracefully falling with the silent slowness of a goose feather.

Then the Dane turned. His eyes fixed on Godwin, as the hawk's hard eyes fix on the startled hare. The world became as bright and sharp and vivid as a stained-glass window. Godwin could see every movement of the man's face; the shock-ripples across the man's cheek, each drop of blood, every stone and pothole in the road before him, each weave of hazel in the wattle wall. Godwin saw the half-week stubble on the Dane's chin, grey mixed in with the black of each crooked tooth, the charging Dane's grimace; heard the grunt as the Dane thrust his spear at Godwin's throat.

It happened with the paralysing speed of a nightmare. Godwin tried to move, his limbs were unresponsive. He saw the grain of the spear haft; the rough finish on the spear blade – the point freshly ground with a rough whetstone; the smear of red – another man's blood – gleaming for a moment as Godwin knew he was about to die.

Godwin threw his sword up, blood and gore showered his face. He screamed and fell back. Something crashed on top of him and pinned him to the floor and he prayed to God to save him this day.

Blecca kept hold of Godwin's shield and stood near to Edmund and tried to keep calm. Two of the king's retainers were ostentatiously playing dice when word had come of a large Danish attack on the palisade at St Forster's Church.

'Up!' Edmund said.

Blecca jumped up. He did not want to go into battle without Godwin, could not quite believe he was about to fight. I'm only a boy, he thought. I ought to stay here on the tower. Yet part of him leapt at the chance to see battle close up.

'Up!' Edmund shouted, and Blecca's feet barely touched the stairs, and then he was jogging down the street.

'St Forster's!' the cry went up, and Blecca swallowed back his fear and chuckled as he thought of his mother seeing him.

He thought of Godwin coming to the tower and finding him gone.

'Where were you?' he imagined Godwin saying. 'What do you mean, you saw battle! You better have looked after Edmund!'

Blecca was approaching the street now, and the men about him were slowing to a fast walk. Men were shouting, 'Here! Look smart! The Danes will be upon us in a moment!'

Blecca lost sight of Edmund, but he saw his banner a little to his left and tried to push closer. He ended up behind the two men who had been playing dice. They were big and strong and wore mail shirts, and he thought that he could shelter behind them if necessary. They crowded up on to the bank. There was a broad level area at the top that had been strewn with a fresh layer of straw to provide the defenders with good footing. Mercenaries and king's men began to arrive and fill the gaps between them. Blecca found himself pushed to the front and he stood there between the two great mail-shirted men.

The Danes came on with terrifying speed and determination, their war chief at the front, his banner-bearer behind him, leading his men on like the head of a boar. Blecca's sword grip was slick with sweat. He wiped it on his thigh, rolled his shoulders to warm them up, the way he'd seen grown men do. And then the arrows and spears began to fly.

Blecca heard a dull thud and a grunt of pain. He looked down and saw an arrow sticking out of his chest. He had not felt it hit him and he looked with amazement to the men on either side of him, as if to ask if they had seen it coming, but instead of words, a trickle of blood came from his left nostril, and then a great gout came out of his mouth, and Blecca fell backwards against the knees of the men behind him and rolled to the left and lay astonished, with his face pressed up against the bed of freshly laid straw, and wished Godwin was there to hold him and tell him that he was going to be all right.

Cross-gartered legs were all about him and he thought someone was going to step on him, but then he felt hands under his armpits, felt himself being dragged backwards through the ranks. 'Mother,' he bubbled as blood filled his mouth. 'Oh, Mother.'

All across the city word spread that the Danes had broken through the wall by St Forster's Church. The king sent his best troops galloping off, the bells of St Paul's began to ring, and the townsfolk gathered in furious bands. They armed themselves with hammer and pitchfork, spear and cudgel, and ran through gardens and alleyways, houses and workshops so that the Danes did not know from where the enemy would come, and in this way, with numbers and ferocity, the English drove the intruders back.

Godwin wiped the gore from his face, and realised it was not his, but that of the dead Dane that lay atop him, his skull staved in by an axe. He wriggled free of the body, somehow managed to drag himself back through the stamping and shoving feet. He found a shield and courage and kept to the back of the fighting. He parried every blow that came his way, did not dare to strike out. But Fate did not spare the fearful man, and Godwin was quickly caught up in the ferocious fighting. It was very different from hunting outnumbered and ill-prepared Danish foragers and Godwin expected to be cut down at any moment. When the last Danes had been surrounded and butchered, Godwin began to ask for Edmund.

It was an hour before he found the company, and he almost wept for joy when he saw Edmund, unhelmeted, running his hands through his sweat-soaked hair.

'Where were you?' Edmund laughed.

Godwin was splattered with other men's blood, his mail shirt had been snagged by a spear point, and his right arm had been so badly bruised it hurt to clench his fingers.

'Fighting,' Godwin said.

Men slapped backs and laughed and bragged as they watched the Danes retreat to their camp.

'Did you kill any?' Edmund asked.

'I think so,' Godwin said, but the details that had once been so clear were now blurred and muddled. He had killed many, or rather he had been part of the mob that had surrounded the stranded Danes.

'I got an axeman!' Edmund said. 'He thought to steal my sword pommel.'

Godwin looked around. 'Where's Blecca?'

Blecca was dead and already cooling by the time Godwin found him in an untidy heap of arms and legs, open mouths and lolling heads that had been stacked up against the churchyard wall. Someone had stolen Blecca's garnet-studded dagger hilt. They had stripped off his red wool trousers and silver belt buckle, and it was the slim white foot that caught Godwin's eye, unmistakably that of a boy among the large and hairy feet of men.

Godwin's bruised arm was numb. He worked one-handed to

roll the other bodies clear. They were heavy and unwilling and seemed to resist his every effort. Godwin rolled the top bodies away. Some of the dead men seemed to stare at him. The open and blank full-moon eyes were terrible to look upon. They watched unblinking as he moved the bodies. One man had a piece of his head missing. Another's guts were beginning to spill out: pink and sausage-like and slippery, and Godwin clenched his jaw shut and yanked Blecca free. The boy's front was dark and wet with blood, and his mouth lolled open, and his eyes were open still – but they death-stared at Godwin without expression or recognition.

'Blecca! You idiot,' Godwin said, as he lifted the body over his shoulder, as if he might have done if his friend was still living, and carried him away from the unclaimed dead.

Godwin sat the body up against the church wall, set the young man's head straight, closed his lids so he would not have to look into those dead eyes, and fetched water to wash the congealing blood from his chin and nose. He rearranged his clothes to hide his naked legs, touched the end of the broken arrow shaft gingerly, as if it might still pain the dead, and felt like St Thomas touching Christ's wounds. 'You idiot!' he said again. 'Hold your shield high till the battle-play begins.'

Blecca did not respond. Godwin was stunned with battle-shock. He grabbed and held the young man's body close to him, felt Blecca's head on his shoulder, and wept.

As night fell monks came with hooded lanterns and began to dig a mass grave for the dead.

'Hello?' one said when he caught sight of Godwin. 'One is living over here.'

Godwin stumbled to his feet and blinked against the light. He was smeared in Blecca's blood and they thought for a moment that he was wounded, for many men stumbled from the battle in shock, or crawled away, like a winged bird or wounded hart, and found some dark place to die.

'Come! Are you hale, lad?' the man said. 'Why it's a miracle! There's not a scratch on him.'

The monks gathered round and all of them touched Godwin as if he were a holy relic. 'Not a mark on him,' they agreed. 'We thought you were dead, child. Christ be praised! Victory against the Danes!'

The monks were not unkind, but there were many men to bury that night and they worked quickly, passing bodies down and stacking them like sacks of oats. Godwin stood to the side and thought silent words for his friend's soul as it drifted into Heaven's harbour. Godwin laid him out with his arms crossed over his chest, but as the other dead were thrown into the hole, Blecca was quickly hidden from view.

The monks carried the lanterns to light the way for men bringing more bodies and Godwin was left staring down into a deep black hole that smelt of blood and sweat and unwashed feet. He remembered a monk one night entertaining them with tales from former days, when Rome ruled Middle Earth and men raised beautiful buildings of stone and mortar. He had recited poems of a man named Horace who sang how great it was to die for your fatherland, while in battle he dropped his shield and ran away. Wulfnoth had guffawed at that. The Romans could recite poems, but they forgot how to fight.

Godwin felt he had passed a test. At least I did not run, he thought, and held out a hand to the grave in a final farewell, then turned away and started wearily home.

It was a weary and silent band who sat about the fire that night. The mood at the benches was grim. Godwin sat alone away from the fireside. He began to shiver uncontrollably.

'Where's Blecca?' one of Edmund's men asked.

'Dead,' Godwin said.

'Oswald too. And Baldred and Cole.'

Godwin could hear the songs and taunts and jeers coming from the Danes outside the walls. He limped, even though it was his arm that was hurt. He limped and was jealous of the men who had more obvious wounds, for he felt like a fraud.

Edmund's mood had improved markedly. Along his stretch of wall the Danish attack had been repelled and he had helped to drive the Danes back over the wall. All across the city men were talking of Edmund with awe.

'Cheer up – you're still alive,' Edmund said to Godwin as he moved along the benches, slapped him on the back.

'Still alive,' Godwin said.

Edmund seemed to revel in the battle-name he had earnt, and many sat round him and set a full horn of ale at his side. One night they sat with a sweaty deacon who claimed to have been on the last ship into Lundenburh before the Danes closed off the river.

Edmund clapped Godwin's back, put his arm round his shoulder and cheerfully accepted a horn of ale. 'This is my bravest companion, Godwin Wulfnothson,' Edmund told the deacon. 'Son of Wulfnoth Cild, no less!'

'Wulfnoth Cild,' he replied. 'Well, well, well, that's some heritage. He was a good man. He stood up to the Danes, didn't he?'

'He did,' Godwin said. 'And will do, I'm sure.'

There was a moment of silence and the deacon gave Godwin an odd look. He cocked his head; began to laugh nervously.

What? Edmund's face asked.

'You're both jesting,' the deacon said.

'He's jesting!' the deacon said to the others.

The crowd looked unsure. They didn't think he was jesting. Godwin didn't understand.

The deacon's cheeks turned purple. 'You mean you did not know?'

Godwin shook his head.

'Oh,' the deacon said. 'Two knorrs from Dyflin brought the news. A week hence. Bound for Flandran.'

'What news?'

'About your father.'

'He's back?' Godwin said.

The deacon shook his head.

'He's dead.'

The deacon told the tale that he'd been told. At midwinter, in Dyflin. Wulfnoth Cild's allotted hour had come and he had passed into the keeping of the Lord. Godwin listened, but he missed almost all that was said. He sat very still and felt the eyes of all upon him. It was at moments like these that a man's character was judged.

Godwin nodded, thanked the men for their kind words, didn't know what to do or say or think. Some men clapped him on the shoulder; others gave him a solemn nod. Edmund refilled his horn with thick, dark ale.

'Here!' one man with grey in his beard said, and Godwin held his empty horn out for more. He was old enough to take strong ale; would drink it all down tonight – damn the morning.

Open doth stand the gap of a son. Godwin remembered. *Woeful the breach where grief floods in.*

Godwin woke with fur in his mouth and a head that spun. He did not know where he was for a moment, did not remember the night before, sat up wondering what and how and why and when. He started unsteadily to his feet and the memory hit him.

Godwin reeled under the impact. He staggered erratically between laughter and tears. The only release was sleep – deep and sound and dreamless – but however long he slept, morning came, insistent as a leprous beggar tugging at his sleeve.

His father's life had been cut short. Godwin picked at the roughly shorn ends: the fantasy where his father came home laughing; sent word to arm and meet him with retainers; when they ran towards each other and his father lifted him off the floor in a fierce embrace. When all was forgiven and forgotten, and amends had been made. When the future lay before them: ordered, peaceful, prosperous and calm and the time when they did not need to talk about the past any more.

The shorn possibilities stunned him.

No man's handshake, no chance to forgive, no last words, no moment when they sat alone by the fire and his father looked at him and saw that he had grown into a man, with stubble on his cheeks, and broad shoulders, and showed his appreciation with a brief pat on the back. 'Well done, son!'

Wulfnoth and Blecca, Godwin thought, and reeled under the loss. There was little time for grieving, though grief was commonplace with so many dying of battle-wounds or the sickness that had broken out in the damp riverside hovels south of Knightridestrete. Spear or sword or sickness. Death hemmed them in.

Godwin began to believe he would never leave this dirty city and he railed against that fate. If I am to die, at least let my bones rest in Contone, he thought, and determined that he would escape somehow the doom that was drawing about them.

The Danes spent another week probing the English defenders. Sickness spread as far as the abbey about St Paul's and many of the monks fell ill.

At last the burghers of Lundenburh came to Ethelred and begged him to leave before the city was forced and the Army poured into the city, or before hunger and plague consumed them all. The king had no choice. Edmund and Athelstan stood in shocked silence.

'You hoped for my death,' Ethelred said, 'and instead you all have to flee into exile with me.'

For once they said nothing. The boats waited.

'We are all exiles,' Edmund said with forced jollity as Godwin stepped down from the gangplank.

Godwin said nothing. Godwin Wulfnothson was no exile. Exile meant treachery to him. Betrayal, oath-breaking, like the broken promises a father made to his son.

They spent two miserable weeks on Wiht, stood and stamped their feet against the cold as they watched ships cross over from Boseham as all that could be salvaged from the Wincestre treasury was shipped across the Soluente.

Edmund said: 'In the spring father will hire mercenaries and return.'

The irony escaped neither of them: the good king did not pay men to fight; he rewarded them after victory.

It was midwinter 1013; lazy cocks crowed; Godwin was up early to split wood. After a long pause Godwin wiped the sweat from his brow. He was about to start chopping again when he spied a horseman riding up from the boats along the shore. His horse went slowly, picking a careful way along the frozen ruts. The rider was a man with a scarlet cloak and hood.

'What news from the mainland?' Godwin called.

The horseman stopped and nodded towards the hall where Godwin had slept. 'Swein is in Wincestre and he is crowned king,' the man said. His voice was loud in the still morning; his words steamed about his head.

'And what business have you here?' Godwin asked. 'You have come with the king's treasury?'

The man heeled the horse forward a few steps. 'I have,' he said. 'You ask of the mainland. It is not good. Swein has conquered all. And now he is raising a tax to send his war chiefs home.'

It was a bitter fate: many would die this winter, from cold or starvation or the depredations of Danes.

On the last night Godwin and Edmund stood on the headland as brisk waves heaved themselves against the shore, and the surf crashed and hissed back down the pebbles.

Neither of them spoke.

'You do not have to come with me,' Edmund said.

Godwin didn't answer.

'You do not have to come with me,' Edmund said again.

Godwin could not bring himself to speak. His sleep had been troubled, his waking hours even more so. His ancestors had been given Contone by King Alfred himself. That land was his as much as he was its. He was the lord and shepherd of those people.

'I swore myself to you,' Godwin said. 'And I will hold to that.'

'You shall indeed. For I shall return. There is a long road ahead of us. But you are old enough to make your way in the world,' Edmund said. 'They are your people. Go – save them!'

Godwin started to argue but Edmund put up his hand.

'Athelstan and I need men who will spread word that the sons of Ethelred are worthy of the name of king. Go! Take back your land and prepare against the day when we return to drive the Danes from England. Go and protect your people.'

Next day they waited for the tide. No one spoke much. Their minds divided on the separate paths that lay ahead of them. When the moment came for the princes to sail, the men who were staying lined up to embrace them. Athelstan embraced Godwin; when it was Edmund's turn, the two held each other hard.

Godwin watched their ship depart and felt lonelier than the boy who stood to watch his father walk from the king's hall.

He walked back to the abandoned camp. The isle was cold and deserted. The fields were empty. The tents blown over. The bright faces gone.

There was nothing but two watching ravens, sitting on a lone hedgethorn, that stared at him with black twinkling eyes.

Woden, whom heathens worshipped, kept two ravens named Hugin and Munin. They brought him news of battle and slaughter, but there was no battle here, just an abandoned camp and a coward king who would not fight.

'Tell him the English have failed,' Godwin called out.

The two birds listened and then flapped away together, low over the field and Godwin turned his back on defeat and despair.

CHAPTER NINE

The Return of Wulfnothson

It was ten miles due north from the port of Boseham to the manor of Contone. At the side of a flooded field Godwin brought his horse to a halt. These lands had now been given to Eadric's brother Brihtric. Godwin felt a prickle of fear across his skin.

There was rain in the hills and the river before him had flooded to a swollen and bloated brown and tugging torrent. It was usually a shallow ford, but today it filled half the field before him, and only the line of naked trees in the middle of the brown water showed where the riverbed lay.

The flood was a warning, or a bad omen. Do not go further, the land seemed to tell him. Godwin took a deep breath. Only fools thought to live for ever, he reminded himself as he led his mare into the shallows. She paused at the brink. The dark water swirled with turf and twigs and a scum of yellow foam, and she shied and snorted.

Godwin swore he would do this or die in the attempt. He kicked her forward and the horse plunged up to her neck. She whinnied and her hooves kicked against brown water, not ground. Godwin was powerless. He urged his horse onward and she swam desperately. The current pushed them towards a tangle of submerged thickets. We shall be snared and drowned, Godwin realised.

'Come!' he urged, and paddled with his hands. 'Come!'

The horse's legs thrashed. Her eyes were wild with fear. The water swirled hungrily around. The yellow foam was the spittle of bridge trolls. Godwin saw brown serpents in the churning water, a thrashing of eels twining about them, and just when he thought his time on earth would end here in the swirling river water, his horse's hooves found something solid and she scrambled forward and the brown water clung to her haunches as she strode up into the flooded field-shallows on the far side.

They were both bedraggled and chilled to the bone marrow. Godwin looked back. No bridge-troll shall take me! he thought defiantly, and the water swirled and writhed as it swept past him.

Godwin remembered his maxims:

Water from the mountain shall flood-grey tumble;
field water shall slow and spread its banks wide;
wide estuary water meanders to the sea.

The sound of his own voice reassured him. He soothed the horse and she snorted in reply.

'Come – no flood shall hold Godwin Wulfnothson from home!'

Edmund's grandmother had filled Godwin's head with tales of how England used to be when a good king ruled. He had spent many years imagining what he would do when he returned home and he saw himself as a thegn or a shire-reeve, imposing good order upon the land. Law and order. They were simple things, easily misplaced, like a comb or coin, but when they went missing chaos reigned; might became right.

The evidence was all about him: houses stood empty; thatched roofs had fallen in; only the graveyards were busy. There were pitifully few livestock in the wattle enclosures, and when he passed by – hurrying on lest he be recognised and reported to Brihtric – wary faces watched him from doorways and under dripping hoods, pale and pinched and snotty. At one point he saw below him the black and jagged outline of a derelict hall, once bustling and busy with harp music and laughter. But now there were overgrown fields and crow-haunted homestead, a row of old graves where the grass bent in the breeze. Waste and bones, like the ruin of a dragon.

At another hall, a cart was being loaded with sacks and hams. It was the tax, Godwin guessed, being sent to Swein. A woman's voice rose in a long slow wail, and when Godwin was a bowshot away a thegn came out of the longhouse door and stood and watched. He wore a red cloak and a blue felt hat, and carried a spear. The man's manner was dark and unfriendly; he gesticulated that Godwin should stay away.

'See what defeat has done,' Godwin said to his horse. 'We are a cowering and timid breed of men.'

The midwinter light quickly failed. The bitter north wind puffed out his cheeks and the air whistled through the black twig hedges and flat winter furrows, turned Godwin's knuckles red, brought sparkling droplets to hang from the end of his nose. He considered stopping at a ruin, but it looked haunted, so he pressed on and spied a wood to the right with a stream running through it.

'That will make a good and sheltered spot,' Godwin told his horse. 'Let us rest there.'

Solitude weighed on Godwin. He was not used to being alone like this, and he had not quite got the thought of trolls from his mind. His imagination teased him. He gritted his teeth against fear. Fear motivated too many men. The shadows haunted with watching eyes – kobolds and gogmagogs and all kind of skin-prickling night spirits.

Godwin screwed up his courage and hummed to himself as he saw to the horse. He pulled a pack of sodden oats from the saddle, filled the nosebag and hung it over her ears. She seemed content. Her flanks were warm and damp with sweat. Godwin stroked them, partly to warm his hands, partly to reassure himself, then walked out into the burnt field-stubble.

He was halfway into the Downs. He looked behind and down, saw a patchwork of brown and green fields, clumps of black trees, the occasional rooftop, and saw how far he had come. Godwin's spirits were raised.

'Contone lies high up in the next valley,' he told the horse as she chomped and lifted her tail, and out tumbled a steaming pile of droppings. 'We will rest here for the night. On the morrow we shall see my home!'

The horse chewed and nodded and snorted the cold from her nostrils.

'I'll see if I can get a fire going,' Godwin said, but even though he dried his flint against his skin, his fingers were numb, the kindling too wet, and he was unable to produce more than a spark.

Lone horses were wary; they did not lie down to sleep. Godwin brought the mare to her knees and hobbled her so he could lie down next to her and warm himself. It was the best he could do. He kept his sword and shield close. As the darkness grew the stars began to shine and Godwin called out in a clear and stirring voice, 'Éala Éärendel, engla beorhtast ofer Middangeard, monnum sended!'

Éärendel was the Archangel Gabriel, war chief of the Angelic

Host. He was the Evenstar, and singing brought hope to Godwin's heart, warmth when there was none.

Godwin slept fitfully. He stood up long before dawn and rubbed his hands together. Dawn brightened the eastern sky, silhouetting the trees and fields and morning rooks, he found a low mound upon which was set an old stone that had been carved with a cross. The stone stood at a weary angle, half hidden by the tall pale winter grass.

Godwin suddenly realised he had been here with his father. This was the stone of the Hundred Court. It was Ælle's Stone – High King of the Seven English Kingdoms – before the English were united. It was on monuments like these that the heathens used to swear oaths.

The horse waited for a long time and flicked her tail, stamped a hoof.

When Godwin came back down the hill he had a frog in his throat. Saddling the horse was a long job with fingers stiff with cold.

'Come!' he said when the task was done. 'Let us go on.'

An ancient oak marked the beginning of the Contone estate. Old offerings of food and clothing hung in the branches, wind-bleached and rustling, or were nailed to the deep and craggy bark. To either side were meadows, lush in summer, where Wulfnoth had once driven his cattle to fatten. Ahead was a small, glistening stream. Godwin stopped and drew in a deep breath. He looked up the valley for a glimpse of his father's hall, but it was obscured by a copse of oak and hornbeam, and only the shingled roof of the chapel bell tower was visible, peeping through the tangle of bare tree branches.

Fate had brought him here, but now his stomach yawned

empty and unsure. He tried to swallow his fear but his mouth seemed full of saliva and in the end he hawked and spat and spat again. This was the land that had nurtured him through childhood. He had played here with Leofwine. Before the Army came. Hope flickered within him, a giddy and excited hope, as if Godwin expected to find his childhood – or happiness – before him.

His brave thoughts lifted him up and bore him forward as a great sea-swell will lift a ship and bear it on. Godwin drew his sword and held it high, pale and cold, gleaming like ice, crossed the stream in a shower of sparkles.

Filibrok – the month of full streams – was the time of year horned oxen were limbered to the plough and fields sown with the first crop of barley. Freemen were already out, leading their teams of four oxen along the furrows, while churls carefully carried seed corn from the winter stores.

Of the great events in the rest of the kingdom they had heard much. By trial of battle their king had been found wanting. Doom! the hedgerow priests called out, for what was Swein but the Antichrist, sent by God as a forerunner of the Apocalypse.

> Out of the North an evil shall break forth upon all the
> inhabitants of the land, and power was given to him that
> sat thereon to take peace from the earth; that they
> should kill with sword, and with hunger, and with
> death, and with the beasts of the earth.

That morning was a Monday. The Sunday sermon was fresh in the people's heads – a long and harrowing homily about death and pestilence and terrible horsemen, delivered by the wandering monk at the field-side stone cross.

Men in the lower fields saw a lone horseman riding up the lane with sword drawn and they screamed and dropped their baskets – seeds and all.

'Danes!' they yelled, and the men in the fields let go of the oxen and fled.

'Danes!' the shout went up the valley, from field to field, and even the oxen panicked and started down the slope, the half-hitched plough snagging in a patch of brambles a furlong away from the path, drawing them up short. The lead ox stretched out its neck; Danes! its mournful bellow seemed to say, Daaanes! and shouts and screams of freemen and churls came back in reply. 'Forgive us our sins! The End of the World is come!'

A few of the villagers rushed out to the lane with any weapons they had to hand. They stood across the lane, crossing themselves and praying to God Almighty to grant them courage as they prepared to sell their lives. At their head stood Agnes the Alewife, pudgy fingers gripping the shaft of her pitchfork. She clutched her charm of woven straw and led the men forward. Her husband had died and her son Godmaer – a chubby lad with a club foot – stood close behind her. Even though she had little enough to lose, she prepared to sell it dearly.

The Dane rounded the lone hawthorn bush and Agnes fiercely brandished her pitchfork. 'Man or devil, come not here!' she shouted, and they prodded forward with rake and pitchfork. 'Back!' she shouted. 'Back!'

Godwin opened his mouth to speak, but the woman almost speared his horse and his terrified animal started in surprise. 'I am Godwin!' he shouted as he batted her thrust away, but she was too angry to hear and thrust at him again, shouting, 'Demon and devil!'

'I'm Godwin Wulfnothson!' Godwin told her, and she was about to spear him when his words and language finally registered and she batted down the weapons of the men around her. 'He's no Dane!' she said. 'Look! He's no Dane. He speaks like an Englishman!'

'I'm Godwin, son of Wulfnoth!' Godwin called down again.

'Lord Wulfnoth's son?'

'Yes!' Godwin said.

'Bless my barrel,' she said, and put up a hand to wipe the sweat from her brow, 'it's Wulfnoth's son or I'm a cat!'

A few men lowered their weapons and peered up at him, not sure if they should spear him or touch their caps.

'I am Godwin, son of Wulfnoth!' Godwin said, and laughed. 'I am Godwin.'

'Wulfnoth's son!' they said in surprise and relief. 'Look – it's Lord Wulfnoth's son!'

More men came running ready to fight; when they came upon the scene it took a moment for them to understand what had happened. They threw down their weapons in shame and embarrassment and pressed around Godwin's horse, grabbing his hands and waving to him and telling him that he should have sent word that he was returning.

'Where's Wulfnoth?' the question came faster and faster.

Godwin crossed himself.

'With Christ,' he said. 'He passed away before Christmastide.' The words seemed too abrupt and he added, as if here of all places he did not quite believe it, 'So the seafarers say.'

Lyftehal – the high hall – was hidden by a long, low hump of land and a thicket of birch. The excited crowd pushed Godwin forward and he was almost fearful of what he might see. The hall was slowly revealed to him as he walked towards it.

It had an unkempt look, the barley thatch was thick with grass and stands of bracken, and a small bush grew at one end, as if it were an ancient ruin. It was lower and smaller than Godwin remembered. He looked around to get his bearings, but the landmarks seemed out of place, shorter than his mind's eye had it. A man came out of the hall, still buttoning up his trousers. A girl hurried off behind him. She had a beaten look about her. Godwin recognised the redhead as one of the daughters of his father's freemen. They think so little of my people, he thought.

The man, Ulf, had not noticed him. He was the sour-faced steward of Godwin's enemy. His lord was Brihtric, and his job was to squeeze every shilling from Contone.

Hands on hips, he looked out at the excited peasants with irritation. 'Who's ploughing the fields?' he shouted. 'What is that team doing in the hedge? I want that acre finished by nightfall!' When he saw Godwin he pulled himself up a little taller, but he did not recognise this young lad, and not knowing was not liking. 'Greetings, stranger,' he said in an unwelcoming way. 'Are you stopping my men working? This is Brihtric's manor. There's no alms to be found here, so if begging is your business then pass along!'

'I am no beggar,' Godwin replied, 'and these are not your men. They are not Brihtric's men, nor yours. They are my men, and I am their rightful lord!'

'Are you now?' Ulf laughed, and looked about him to draw others into his insults. 'Look at this! I've shat bigger turds in the pot at night. Who is this bum-fluffed bairn standing at my hall?'

'I am Godwin, son of Wulfnoth. I have come through fire and sword and battle. Across sea and land, through oath-breaking and injustice, and I am here to right those wrongs. My father was Wulfnoth Cild, Lord of Contone and Marshal of the Southern Shore. Good men remember him well. Who are you to stand in my hall and order my folk?'

Ulf laughed. He was the bastard son of a farthing-a-frolic camp whore, the ugly face of Eadric's brother Brihtric, sent to bully tax or labour from unwilling slaves and churls. His name was English, but his blood could have been Irish or Walsh or Scottish or Danish or Norwegian or Norman or Frankish – any of the mercenary mix who had camped that night, thirty-three years ago, outside the stone and stake walls of Canturburie. Ulf liked to pick the nation that suited his mood. This morning he was feeling Scottish: wild and hairy and angry about something.

He lifted one buttock to let out a fart. 'Your father was an oath-breaker and a coward. This is now the land of Alderman Brihtric,' he said, 'not any Godwin Wulfnothson! Get ye gone before I whip your baby backside.'

'This is no land of Brihtric.'

'No? The king says so.'

'Which king?'

'King Ethelred!'

Godwin smiled. 'And you speak for him?'

'I am Ulf Edwinson, steward of this manor,' Ulf said quickly, 'given to Brihtric by royal writ.'

'Show me!'

Ulf laughed. Of course he would not.

'Have you not heard, Ulf Edwinson? Ethelred is king no longer! I come from the ruin of Lundenburh. I saw Ethelred sail for Normandig, his ships weighed down with English silver. This manor was given to my family by Alfred King in the elder days! It is mine and mine alone. Stand aside and no harm shall come to you!' Godwin spoke fiercely and passionately.

Both men read the situation in an instant. Ulf was a grown man, Godwin young.

'Then let us fight!' Ulf said.

'Why spill blood so close to Lent?' asked one of the onlookers, a timid farmer named Deor. 'Christ will not forgive any of us. Surely there can be parley.'

Ulf laughed at parley. 'I stand aside for no traitor's brat.'

'It is the mark of an unworthy man who speaks ill of the dead.'

Ulf hawked and spat. 'That's for your father – living or dead!'

Repay friends with friendship, gift with gift, betrayal with treachery, insults with an axe. 'I am glad you are a foul-mouthed braggart, Ulf Whoreson. I shall make Sudsexe one nithing lighter when I kill you. Let us find a clear space and settle the issue there.'

So it was decided.

Godwin spoke. 'I call on the Lord Almighty, Maker of Heaven and Middle Earth, to bear witness to this duel.'

Ulf laughed. 'I'll tan your backside before I kill you and send your head to Eadric so that he knows one more enemy is dead.'

Godwin laughed. 'You are welcome to my head if you can remove it from my shoulders.'

A space was found at the foot of a pollarded ash, recently harvested for spear shafts. The boundary of the circle was marked with pieces of hazel rod like a pagan ritual.

'Let all of you hear and keep to my word, even if I should die,' Godwin called out. 'I came here of my own free will and challenged Ulf to battle. If God finds me lacking, I ask only that my body be buried here in the hallowed ground with my forefathers.'

Ulf drew his sword and swung his arms about his head to warm his shoulders. up. 'Can you fight as well as you talk?' he shouted. 'Should I spank you and send you home to your mother!'

'Let him be!' the crowd urged Godwin. 'The man's a fool and a coward.'

Godwin kept his mouth closed and breathed deeply. He was tougher and more worldly than any guessed. He was as still and calm as an evening tarn. Just fifteen years old. His eyes bored into the older man's face. Ulf hefted his shield and stepped into the ring as the morning sun broke through the clouds and bathed the frozen turf in a cold yellow light. Godwin stood still and graven like a warrior of old, with gold in his hair and on his sword and shield rim.

'I do not fear you or your father,' Ulf called out, but his words came to Godwin as if from a great distance.

His jaw was set. He heard the breeze whistling in his ears and dried his hand on his thigh, felt the weave of the wool on his skin, felt the sweat on his hands and the nerves coursing through his arms. This is the moment all the poems spoke of: the sport of points, the banter of spears, the hailstorm of hatred, the truest test of men. Just get it over with, he told himself, and lifted his shield as he stepped towards the challenge.

Ulf was large and strong. He had a fearsome swing and tried to batter his opponent down with mighty blows that sent shivers down Godwin's shield arm. Godwin kept on his toes. Keep your eyes on the enemy; be aware of what his weapon is doing. Godwin began to get the feel of his opponent. Swordsmen strike with their right foot forward, he remembered learning in his stable-yard sparring. Watch the opponent's eyes, for they tell you where the next blow will fall. Ulf was a typical barnyard bruiser. His eyes signalled his next attack like a battlefield trumpet.

Godwin began to hope. Strike towards the face to disorientate a man, then strike under his shield.

Damn! You could have had him there! Godwin told himself as he risked a moment to wipe sweat from his brow. The more Godwin held his ground, the more Ulf circled, backed off and circled. Godwin saw the fear in Ulf's eyes, saw white knuckles clutching the sword hilt.

Yes, I am no child to kill in combat, Godwin smiled.

As Ulf swaggered, Godwin's confidence grew. He strained to keep it back, like a snapping dog. This is yours for the taking, he told himself. Yours for the losing. He threatened Ulf's face. Ulf lifted his shield and Godwin saw his opportunity come again – and let it pass.

I fought at Lundenburh, Godwin's look said. Fate fortuned me.

He threatened Ulf's face again and almost laughed – it was too easy. When your shield is high, you are blind to the enemy's weapon. Always keep the weapon in view, Godwin thought, and stepped forward again, made as if to swing high and Ulf's shield went up again, but this time Godwin stepped to the side and swung his sword hard.

It was a wild swing, but it caught Ulf a glancing blow behind his ear. It was hard to tell who was more excited or surprised, Ulf or the onlookers.

There was a gasp as Godwin ducked back from Ulf's return blow, which missed and spun him off his feet. Godwin paused for a moment, thinking Ulf would swing again, but instead he half fell and let out a dull grunt of shock and pain. The blow had stunned him. But if Godwin thought the battle was over, Ulf shocked him by pushing himself up and charging like a wounded boar, seeking to smash Godwin back with the boss of his shield.

Godwin sprang to the side. He smashed the boss of his own shield into the side of Ulf's head, knocked out his teeth and stunned him. This time Godwin kept on top of him. He stabbed his sword point over the edge of Ulf's shield and drove it through cloth and skin; jammed against bone.

A surer man would have slain Ulf then, but Godwin was still young and the blow did not strike true enough. Ulf started to crawl to safety. Godwin was over him. He put his foot on the small of Ulf's back to hold him steady.

Ulf's hands clutched at his knees. 'Mercy,' he begged.

'Do not fear. I shall make it quick,' Godwin said, drove the blunt sword point into the gap between collarbone and neck. Ulf spasmed with the death blow. Blood ran from his mouth and nose and the corner of his eye, like a red tear.

Godwin pulled the sword free and it came out with a great gout of hot gore.

God had judged. Godwin was right.

As news of the manslaying spread, doubting villagers crept out. Their faces were cold and pinched, hope almost extinguished. They held out their hands as if a single touch could heal the memories of the past five years. 'Where have you been? And where is your father? We heard that he had died. It is a terrible shame. We remember him fondly. How could you leave us to the likes of Ulf? Brihtric is greedier than the fattest sow! Lord help us, it was not right of your father to do this to us!'

It was hard to answer, but it wasn't answers they wanted as much as a chance to tell someone of their plight and their five years of suffering. At last they ran out of complaints and began to laugh and chatter, and Godwin shook hands and promised to right all the wrongs that had been done.

They pushed him forward like a groom at his wedding.

'Godwin, son of Wulfnoth, come and take back your father's hall!' a voice rang out. Under the old doorposts Arnbjorn, his father's faithful steward, waited with a bowl of ale in his hands. The old man's eyes were rheumy with age, but it was not age he wiped from his cheeks. 'Wes tu hal!' he said and presented the mead-bowl. 'Thrice welcome, son of Wulfnoth! For no man is dearer to us than our own natural lord.'

'In!' the crowd urged him. 'Come!'

But he paused at the threshold and patted the heavy cob wall, as a man might pat a favourite horse's neck. 'So the old hall's still standing, then.'

Everyone laughed. They laughed at anything, they were so happy – and Godwin realised he was laughing too, and was surprised at the sound, because he had not remembered how happy life had once been. He looked at the faces around him: Agnes the ale-wife, Grond the bee-master, Dudoc the blacksmith, Hareth's daughter – married now with a boy at the breast – and lads he used to kick around with in the yard. The last five years seemed to lie so lightly on them. It was a bittersweet moment. He envied them.

They mistook Godwin's delay for fear or modesty or indecision and they laid hold of him and pushed him over the sill and into the room.

'Come, lord!' Arnbjorn said.

Godwin had dreamt of home for five long years, and as he stepped into the earth-floored hall, he stared in wonder. There lay the hearth; there was the place his father's carved chair stood; there was where he had played with the hall cat; there was his seat for the feasting; the rafter where his banner of the Fighting Man used to hang. But a pair of old hams hung there now; in place of the chair an empty space; silence where his family used to talk. His family home stood empty and forgetful – like an old warrior who sits by the fire unable to remember his name.

On that first night home after the killing of Ulf, Godwin left the drinking men and went to lie down in his old bed closet, a simple timber enclosure along the far side of the hall. It had been hung with old tapestries and cushioned with the finest hay mattress, but it smelt as if it had been used for drying bacon for the last five years; a smoky meat scent clung to the wood.

Agnes had laid some fresh rye straw down and thrown a length of clean home-spun over the top of it and he wriggled back and forth till he made himself comfortable. He lay on his back and tried to remember the last night he had slept here. He lay and listened to the laughter of men in the hall, and the crackle of the fire slowly dying, and the plank-chinks of hall light grew thinner and paler. Godwin was dog-tired. Warm, sheltered and safe at last, in an instant he was asleep, and about him men lay down to their hall rest.

Outside the hall a fox sniffed the air, and a distant owl screeched. A voice whispered in Godwin's ear, very soft and gentle, and he ignored it at first, but it was soft and gentle and insistent. 'Godwin! Wulfnothson! Awake!'

Godwin turned and murmured in his sleep.

'Keep not your oaths,' the voice said, very distant but clear. 'Follow not the House of Ethelred. Great you shall be when the Dane is king!'

Those last words were like cold water and they shocked Godwin awake. Light showed through the cracks of the closet. It was morning.

The manor of Contone ran to seasonal routines, to laws older and more immutable than those of Alfred or Ethelred, more ancient even than the coming of the English. The fields were ploughed in spring; livestock slaughtered in autumn; sheep were sheared at Lammastide. At Easter they gave their lord two ewes and two lambs; they delivered six large buckets of ale to their lord's hall at Michaelmas, four cartloads of split firewood into his barns. One week in three they worked for their lord, and on nights of the full moon Agnes the Alewife still took food up to the unploughed elf mound for the night spirits to eat.

Godwin and his father's steward, Arnbjorn, found the pile of food, half-eaten by foxes. It was a high spot where the tall, dry grass whistled with wind. They paused their horses, looked out towards the sea, the breeze lifting their hair from their shoulders.

Below them, Godmaer limped out to the fields with fresh oat-cakes for the men. His club foot ached today, and his mother had promised to fetch more holy water. He gave the food to the men, and they sat and rested and saw Godwin silhouetted against the grey sky. They stared for a long time, and the man next to him put down his hoe and nodded in approval as he munched his oatcake.

'Look! Our rightful lord has returned,' he said, and Godmaer looked. He had come of age during Wulfnoth's exile, a time of tumult and strange lights in the sky, weird faces in the clouds, but now at last it seemed that order was returning.

In the abbey of Burne a roll of yellowed vellum recorded the bounds of Contone in the thin and angular minuscule writing of Alfred's court scribe. The abbey kept all Wulfnoth's charters safe from king and Dane and other religious establishments.

Ego Alfred rex Anglorum huius donationis . . . the land-grant began. *Ad nomen optimates* . . .

Godwin had only seen the charter three or four times, but he knew enough letters to know the standard form and he and every man in Contone knew the bounds of the manor, for they had had them beaten into them when they were children. From the ancient oak to the ploughed headland, along fallow strip-marker stones to the ferny mound, where a giant was buried in former days. At the giant's mound the boundaries followed a hedgerow and it was there they found Grond the Old, with both his teeth, lifting the ferny thatch to inspect his beehives. He put down the hive he was cleaning and sheltered his face, and grinned both teeth at them as he touched his forelock.

'It's a cold day to be working.'

'That it is,' Grond said. 'But a bit of chill never killed, and it makes the home fire blaze so much warmer afterwards.'

Grond and Godwin traded news; Grond had seen a fox bitch up here two mornings running. 'And I'll bet she's thinking of a way to get into the dovecot. You'll have to get the hounds out. Ulf was a braggart and a coward, and the dogs would not hunt for him. Nothing worse than a fox in a dovecot! It would be all right if they just took what they ate, but they make a terrible mess. They took a sheep last week, ripped her up from tail to ears. Foxes don't kill nicely, that is for sure.'

'How are your hives?' Godwin asked, once Grond paused for a moment to wet his lips.

'Bah!' he said, and looked at the hive at his feet. 'All right,' he said. 'Though the bees did not produce for Brihtric as they did for your father.'

'Well, make sure they know that I am returned.'

The blacksmith's hammer was ringing joyfully out as Godwin and Arnbjorn made their way back down to the hall. A file of villagers waited outside: a stray cow had broken into a field of fresh oats and ruined the crop; sheep had been stolen; a dog had mauled another man's lambs. Godwin gave judgement, but after an hour of long-winded accounts he found his attention wandering. He should have a mass said for the soul of his father, a coat of mail, a new sword, a helmet and a bright new shield.

Godwin poured himself a cup of warm buttermilk and let out a long sigh. Soon Brihtric would hear of his return. Godwin looked at the motley collection of farmhands and freemen sitting on the benches. He stared at them and tried to imagine them in mail and helm; the image was farcical.

Godwin finished his buttermilk and set the bowl on the table. He did not need farmers; he needed a war band.

CHAPTER TEN

The Feast of Candlemas

It was a foul February night as a horseman picked his way along the road to Selesie. Sheets of rain lashed in from the sea, the road ran with water like a stream, and his cloak had long since stopped repelling the wet.

Brihtric was staying in a small hall, outside the town, away from the tanners' stink and the cattle market. At the hall, the door wards were tardy in opening the gates, but as soon as they heard, they brought the man straight into the hall where Brihtric sat, like a toad, in his carved wooden chair.

'Who are you?' Brihtric demanded. His single eye glared out with all the malevolence of two.

The messenger gave his name, his birthplace and the names of his kin, and the alderman nodded.

'From Peteorde, are you?'

'I am, lord. I bring news of a manslaying at one of your manors.'

'A manslaying?' the alderman said, but in truth he was not that interested. 'Well, report it to the Hundred Court and they will deal with it.'

'I would, sir, but I fear the Hundred Court would not deal

177

fairly with this question, for in this hundred live the friends and kinsfolk of the man who did the slaying.'

'Do they?' Alderman Brihtric said. 'Who is this man?'

'It is the son of Wulfnoth Cild,' the messenger announced.

Brihtric choked on his ale. 'Wulfnoth Oath-Breaker's son has returned?'

A droplet of water ran down the man's matted hair. He nodded glumly.

'To Boseham?'

'No, lord. Contone.'

Brihtric nodded, but he was not a local man, and even though he had married a girl from Leomynstre, the Sudsexe men did not look kindly on him. 'So the wolf's cub has been set free,' he whispered to himself, and his red cheeks were ugly and grease-smeared as he broadcast his laughter about the room. 'Why is this news to disturb our feasting? A lad sneaks back to his robber lair. Does the hunter fear the cub when the sire is feathered? What would you have me do, flee back to Sciropescire? Ha! He is a thief and a son of a thief. They're used to reavers up in the Downs – tell the shepherds to set a guard on their flocks, and send to Boseham for gibbet-timber. It's been too long since a good hanging.'

The long benches rang out with mocking laughter, but later, when the beer had stopped talking, Brihtric brooded on the old names the news had brought back to mind, five years unfor-gotten.

In the hall the men were still laughing, but Brihtric's mistress, a buxom Mercian girl he had brought south with him, said, 'Have you seen the lad?'

'I have,' Brihtric said. 'He was at court.'

'Is he dangerous?'

'Any son of Wulfnoth is dangerous,' Brihtric said, and wondered on all that the messenger had told him, magnified Godwin from an inconvenience to a threat, a boy to a warrior and a leader of men.

'Who was this Ulf that he slew?'

Brihtric shrugged. What did he care.

The girl said nothing. She looked at the confused lines of her palm and shook her head. If Wulfnoth's son was like this when he was still green, what would he be like when he was seasoned?

'Come,' she said, and poured a little more hot water into the bowl to wash her master's hairy white feet. 'Kill him. A man does good work when he rids himself of shit,' she told him, but that night as he lay in his bed, his girl under him, he remembered that morning when Wulfnoth's twenty ship crews had come upon the moored ships at dawn.

'What's wrong?' his girl asked, but he rolled away from her.

'Nothing,' he said, but he could not regain his ardour. 'I am tired,' he said at last, and pushed her hands away from him.

The image, like the shame, was not easily exorcised: a long line of charred wrecks moored along the strand, greedy tongues of flame chewing their painted timbers, the dark columns of smoke rising high into the Heavens.

Forty days after Christ's birth came the Feast of Candlemas. Brihtric declared that he would spend the feast in Selesie and leave the day after to deal with this Wulfnothson.

The morning of the feast dawned clear and damp and unseasonably warm. The hall thatch steamed and through the walrus-snores of his men came the high sound of lambs bleating. Brihtric woke rested and calm. He dressed in his finest clothes, and all his retainers accompanied him to Cicestre Cathedral, an ancient building with foundations of great slabs of dressed stone.

The church dated from Roman times. It had once been a temple to Jupiter Imperator, but four hundred years of Christianity obscured that pagan past. Banks of reed lights guttered with each draught of cathedral air, and the statues of holy men, graven in stone, stared with painted eyes. Christ adorned the brightly painted rood screen while the whale mouth of Hell swallowed the sinful.

Brihtric closed his eyes and tried to erase all the tension. A dog pissed against a church column. One of Brihtric's men shooed it out. Brihtric tried to ignore them. He imagined slow, brown river water; the ordered herb gardens of a monastery cloister; summer daybreak; first smoke rising from a hall chimney.

'Kyrie,' the hidden monks sang from behind the rood screen. 'Kyrie eleison.'

The moment came and Brihtric spoke the single word, 'Amen.'

He knew the Selesie crowd were gathering outside in the sea breeze, their pinched and hungry faces looking on with despair. Tax had ruined many of them; Fate had been cruel. Their hopelessness pricked Brihtric's conscience for a moment, but he had more pressing worries upon him: the tax that he had to deliver to the Danish king, the oaths he had sworn and broken, the sense that Fate had offered him a choice of hands, all bad.

Eadric would know what to do, he told himself as he knelt down to pray.

The monks' voices rose in the Magnificat. Brihtric had made his appearance and strode out of the church. *Et exsultavit spiritus meus, in Deo salvatore meo, quia respexit humilitatem ancillæ suæ.* Brihtric paused at the cathedral steps and the expectant crowd shuffled forward.

> *My spirit rejoices in God my Saviour*
> *He has put down the mighty from their thrones,*
> *and exalted those of low degree.*

He has filled the hungry with good things;
and the rich He has sent empty away.

Among those who watched Brihtric's company leave the cathedral were a few men who wore their hoods low over their faces. They caught Brihtric's attention for a moment, but there were other things to worry about, and he set his men to distribute bread and curds to the poor and soon forgot them.

But the hooded men did not forget. They had broad shoulders, sharp blades and long memories. Brihtric, it was, who had sworn the oaths that had Wulfnoth exiled. And he was the hated brother of their hated foe.

They waited until darkness fell, donned their steel-knit war shirts, remembered the many nights that they had boasted with ale, crossed themselves before mounting their horses, their hooves muffled with knotted rags, and they rode to where Brihtric's hall stood, a little way from the north gates.

Brihtric's men had drunk a great brew of barley beer and slept deeply among the bones and the dogs, slept through unquiet dreams as the gibbous moon rose and began to set again. They slept as the horsemen dismounted and left their horses half a mile off, tethered among the low bushes of a copse, their noses deep in bags of oats. There were fifteen or more, but it was hard to tell in the darkness, and they passed like shades under the low hunting night clouds. The moon saw them scale the palisade and land softly inside. A cloud drew a veil across her face, as if she had turned away, like God, from the sinful.

Dogs barked.

For a while, before falling silent.

Stillness fell.

The world held its breath.

Brihtric and his men all snored. Fate whispered reassuring nothings into their ears, gave no warning.

Brihtric's hall was a fine building, with well-tarred timbers and a thatch of reeds that had grown in the river shallows. There was richly carved wainscoting where the men drank, and around the hearth stood gold-worked mead benches and tables for feasting.

'Burn it,' a voice said, and a light was unhooded. A stealthy fire started under the eaves, where the timber was driest. The flames quickly caught and leapt up from wall to roof and rafter.

It reflected in the eyes of the waiting men, and they stood with blades drawn and shouldered shields. They waited as a voice inside the hall shouted out in alarm. They gripped their sword hilts tighter. Wet their lips. Waited for the hall doors to open.

The first man out of the doors was a young lad with blond hair and a blue cloak. He did not see the blade that killed him, nor the man who dealt the blow. The second fell almost as quickly, hacked by three blades. The third was a serving man, and he was wiping tears and smoke from his eyes when he saw the attackers; he had barely a moment to shout a warning before a blade shaved off the top of his skull. It flew into the air and landed six feet from where the rest of his body lay. The next was a woman, who screamed as she came.

'Let her go,' a voice ordered, and the women and children and old men and thralls were seized and dragged out of the way, while every man and boy of fighting age was struck down, even as they rushed out for air. Some were serving men and some were stable boys. Almost at the last, whimpering, came Brihtric, clinging to his whore.

'Who are you?' he pleaded. 'I will do you great honour!'

But the sword blades struck again and again, cutting Brihtric and whore down together, sending them to the Lord in sin without hope of forgiveness.

The moon set. Godwin tossed and turned in his sleep, found himself lying under a cloak in a windswept autumn field. Many hands were holding him down and a spear was being raised to run him through. The blade glinted in the moonlight and he woke with a start.

The room was silent, the fire low.

He calmed himself, felt his heartbeat slow, but it took a long time for Godwin to get back to sleep. A night terror, that is all. Calm yourself.

Just as he was dropping off there were sounds outside the hall. Nothing, Godwin told himself. Calm yourself. But there it was again! The stamp of a hoof, a horse snorting in the night air.

Godwin stiffened. His ears strained the night. He reached for his sword. There were horses in the yard, he was sure, horses and men's voices. Horse thieves, Godwin thought at first, thought of Brihtric and his hand scrambled over the sleeping bodies next to him.

'Get weapons!' he whispered. 'Foes are upon us.' Godwin drew a warped yellow linden shield from the hall wall. 'Quick!' Godwin said, and kicked the sleepers. 'Up!'

Someone tried the latch; under the door jamb he could see the light of flames; there were muffled voices.

'Who comes to my hall stealthily and at night like outlaws?' Godwin shouted but then the doors flew open and silhouetted against the setting moon was a crowd of cloaked men, swords shining pale in their hands.

'It's him,' one of the cloaked men said.

'Come out!' another ordered.

Godwin's hand shook. 'I shall not!'

Godwin spoke with a courage he did not feel. He knew he was cornered. The tale of Wulfnoth's son was about to end here, in his home.

You should have stayed away, he told himself. Gone to exile in Normandig.

Godwin laughed, but there was no humour. 'I am Godwin Wulfnothson! This is my hall and I shall kill any man who steps inside or seeks to do me or my people harm!'

There was a moment of silence.

'Godwin?'

The cloaked men moved towards him. Godwin braced to strike.

'Godwin, is that you?'

'Do your worst.'

'Godwin?' another voice said. 'Christ's bones! Godwin! Is that you?'

'One more step and I shall cut you down!'

A lantern was unhooded and the pale yellow light blinded Godwin for a moment. 'Godwin,' a voice said, 'it's me!'

'Who?'

'Me!' the first voice said. The lantern was held up: it lit his face. 'Caerl.'

'You betrayed me?' Godwin said, as if this was a final twist of irony.

'No,' Caerl laughed. 'We've come back! Put away your spears – it's Godwin!'

Godwin didn't believe him until he had lifted the lantern and touched Caerl's face. 'It is you.'

'Of course!'

Beorn stepped forward and embraced Godwin. 'Why it's him!' he said. 'We've been looking for you in every damned port between here and Dovere, and where do we find you but snug as a bug at home!'

Godwin was shocked and confused and amazed to see his father's men standing before him with grey in their hair and lines on their salt-tanned faces.

'We've found you,' Caerl said.

'He's grown!' Beorn said. The men laughed. They spoke about him with an authority they did not have. Their manner pricked Godwin's irritation.

'So this is a fine way for you to return,' Godwin said. 'Creeping at night. Do not come here demanding a hall. Last time I saw you all, you left me a boy in Ethelred's care.'

There was an embarrassed silence. The silence was as annoying as the laughter.

'Tell me, why should I welcome you?'

'We have come to help,' one man said.

'I do not need the help of turncoats and cowards.'

The night chill flooded in through the open hall doors.

'We swore to protect you.'

'I am no milk sop. I need no wet nurse. You were not here when I killed Ulf in battle.'

The men said nothing. They hadn't expected this.

Beorn stepped forward. 'We are glad to see you hale and hearty. If you want us to leave, we shall. But we have gifts and tokens to give you first. From your father.'

'We have news,' Caerl said, and the men about him lowered their hoods. 'He has passed into Christ's care. We buried him five weeks before, on a headland above the city of Dyflin, under an ancient yew tree. We piled stones over his grave so that the dogs might not trouble his bones and so that he might look back towards the land of his birth.'

'Your news is no news,' Godwin said. 'I heard it three weeks past, born on the back of the seas. Show me the gifts.'

They brought forward a number of objects that his father

had carried, and a chest of silver pennies that made Godwin rich.

'More than a thegn's weregeld,' Caerl said.

Godwin did not smile. 'Am I only worth a thegn's price?' But men saw that his mood had mellowed. Nevertheless he still felt uneasy at the manner of their return. 'How is it that you come to this manor with weapons, and in the dark, like murderers?'

'That is because we have murdered,' Beorn said. He smiled. His teeth were as crooked as ever.

'And who have you murdered?'

'Ask Brihtric.'

Godwin was angry. 'Enough of the play. Tell me plainly what crime you have upon you.'

'We have avenged your father. Brihtric is dead. His men are slain. His hall now burns.'

Godwin's face grew darker. 'I swore to kill him,' he said. 'Killing after dark is murder, and I do not condone murder. This is not a good deed. You did not tell me that you came with blood on your hands!'

He fell suddenly silent. He had accepted their gifts. If he sheltered them, he would bring their crime upon his own head. If he sent them away, men would talk badly of him. He was tired and confused and paused before he spoke.

A girl stepped forward. 'If Wulfnoth was here today, he would kneel before you and beg your forgiveness. He cannot, so I beg for him, and for these men who cared and protected and loved him.'

'You come to my hall with too much confidence, too much pride and too much gold upon your arms,' Godwin said.

'It is true,' Caerl said, 'that we have prospered in exile. But from what we have heard about Godwin Wulfnothson, you – through honesty and loyalty – have prospered too.'

'Do not lecture me,' Godwin said.

Caerl spoke gently. 'I do not mean to lecture you. But Kendra is right. If Wulfnoth was here, he would kneel before you and ask for forgiveness. And even though we followed our oaths when we went with your father, it was not right that he fled and left you in Ethelred's care.'

Caerl knelt before Godwin. One by one those who had murdered Brihtric and his men bent at the knee. Only Beorn stood.

Godwin looked at him. 'I remember you, Beorn. You were kind to me when I was a boy. But are you my man or Wulfnoth's?'

Beorn wavered. He briefly grinned. Godwin was no longer the snotty-nosed boy he had known. It was hard accepting such a young man as lord, but he looked at Godwin, stern and hard and decided. His smile flashed briefly. 'If all of you kneel, then how can I stand alone?'

As Beorn fell to his knees, Godwin looked at the men before him. 'I will be a lord worthy of you all.' He pulled Caerl and Beorn to their feet. 'But I spoke in anger. I will take you all into my care and defend you at court or at battle. For it was not your choice to leave me in the bonds of a hostage. And you have been loyal. Stand! Stand, all of you. Contone is your home as well as mine and you should be welcome. No man shall say that Godwin Wulfnothson was not a generous lord.'

They ate and drank a simple but hearty meal of bread and ale. At the end Caerl brought in a bundle of tightly bound sheepskins and set them upon the top table. He drew his table knife and cut the thongs and the stiff petals of sheepskin fell open. Inside was a fine red cloak edged with silver embroidery and a brooch with three dogs with eyes of blue jewels. Godwin remembered the brooch clearly, but one of the eye-settings was empty. He put it aside. The dark eye socket watched as Caerl shook the folds of the cloak, as if he could shake the memories out, and threw it over Godwin's shoulders. It smelt of the sea and old peat smoke. Round his waist he tied Wulfnoth's belt of silver links, and at the end he took out Wulfnoth's sword and presented it to Godwin.

Godwin looked at the hilt and thought of all the great moments in tales when heroes took swords. It was the sight of his father's sword that stung one of the Heathobards to vengeance, when he saw it dangling from the belt of his erstwhile enemy at the bridal feast. One of the old veterans saw it and remembered the day the Shieldings defeated them. He cursed the young warriors till he was barbed to action, and blood flowed again and the feud rekindled. Beowulf's sword Næling broke in the dragon-slaying and brought his death. Sigmund was the only man strong enough to pull his sword from the tree in which it was embedded. It was a magic blade that broke all before him, but Wodin shattered Sigmund's sword and the great hero died. The shards were handed to Sigmund's son Sigurd and, reforged, they slew the dragon Fafnir.

Heirloom swords were a mixed blessing. Godwin looked at it. There was a long silence. Fate hung, taut as a harp string. The fire crackled and over them the hall hunched dark and eager. Godwin felt the hairs on his nape rise, as if the Three Wyrd Sisters had set their spindle and shears.

Godwin reached out and grasped the sword hilt – as Sigmund grasped the blade that no other man could pull – and the blade slid free of the scabbard. The war-thirsty blade glimmered as if in recognition. Ruddy firelight played along its surface and Godwin felt a shiver run down his spine, a shiver not of cold but of power, as a man might feel when he beds his first girl, or kills his first enemy.

'Too long have we cowered,' Godwin said. 'Too long have we

bowed to unjust rulers.' His eyes gleamed as he lifted the blade and laughed. That laughter came from long ago and it brought back a lightness and a joy that he had not felt for many winters. He spoke loud enough for the Wyrd Sisters to hear. 'Næling!' He called the sword by name and the blade answered with a sudden gleam of reflected flames, as if filled with the strange spells of the smith. 'Hear me and bear witness!' His voice filled the hall-shadows. 'You are Godwin's sword now and we have many wrongs to right!'

One of Wulfnoth's men had been killed at the burning of Brihtric's hall. Another had been fatally wounded. Brand was his name. He cried over and over, and when the end came, the silence was a relief. Wulfnoth's men were already digging the graves, and Godwin stood outside the hall, a lone figure with his father's sword heavy on his belt.

Kendra came out of the hall, blood on her apron, and walked some way away, kept her back to the hall.

'He is dead?'

She nodded.

'Then he will be at peace.'

Kendra used her forearm to wipe the hair from her face. She looked out from the high vantage point, over a winter landscape, and wondered what this year would bring.

'You're not English,' Godwin said after a long silence.

'Is that a question?'

'Yes,' he said.

'No. Your father bought me in Dyflin. He bought Brunstan too. There were a few others as well, before my time. He often bought people who were from his county.'

There was a lightness about her that Godwin liked. She had been a hostage to Fate as well. 'What's your name?' he said.

'Kendra.'

'No, your real name.'

'Gruoch.'

'Kendra sounds better.'

'It does,' she said.

Far below, they could see a boy on an empty haywain driving the oxen up the slope. His shouts and whistles came faint over the distance as the four oxen tugged and laboured.

'So where are you from?'

'The north,' she said. 'An island that we called Ila, but I do not know what you would call it in your tongue. It means the Isle of Yula. But who Yula was, I don't know.' She went quiet for a moment. The past suppressed unimportant details. Yes, I lived in the northern sea, she thought, on a rocky island above a sheer black cliff in a beehive hut. Until the Norsemen came.

Godwin followed her gaze out and away from where they stood. After a while he tossed a stone towards the field edge. 'We've a lot in common, you and I.'

'Do we?'

'Of course.'

She laughed at him.

Godwin felt awkward. 'Yesterday morning I dreamt of my father. It was at the forging of my brother's sword. His name was Leofwine. He was very tall and strong and handsome. My father loved him dearly. He was the first-born. I was eight or nine.'

'How old are you now?'

'Fifteen,' Godwin said. 'You?'

'Not sure,' Kendra said. 'Fourteen?'

Kendra took out a fine horn comb. She stood behind him and took a lock of his hair in her hands. 'Your hair's as knotted as brambles. Head back!' she said, and began to tease out the knots and snags. She fetched a bowl of water, and after each stroke she rinsed the comb in the bowl and left a wriggling scum of lice squirming on the surface.

'I did this for your father,' she said. It struck her then that the last time she had used the comb was on Wulfnoth's head, as she prepared him for the grave.

Godwin felt her falter and opened one eye. 'What is it?'

'Nothing,' she said and coughed to clear her throat, as if that was what had diverted her, kept combing.

Kendra felt an urge to put her arms around Godwin and hold him safe. She rinsed his hair and he let it hang down and drip between his legs; handed him a cloth to wrap his hair in. It was good to see Godwin at home. Home, Kendra thought, and savoured the word: a bitter flavour. Her keenest regret was her mother's face as her daughters were loaded into the Norsemen's ship. The warriors waded through the surf as they pushed their craft back into the waters. Her mother had been left behind with twenty other folk too old or weak or ugly to be of use. Kendra and her sisters had formed one cold and shivering bundle at the longship's gunwales, noses dripping and white frightened faces peering over the side of the boat as their mother splashed into the waves, her arms outstretched, her face was distorted, her voice incoherent with grief. That moment came back so vividly that a shiver ran through Kendra. But when she closed her eyes, all she saw was her mother's strangely shaped mouth; all she heard was the call of gulls.

Kendra was silent for a long time. A skylark sang. Her fingers worked his scalp through the cloth, then vigorously rubbed his head, and left his hair sticking up with damp. 'Your hair is paler than your father's.'

There was a long pause before Godwin spoke.

'My mother was blond.'

They looked back to the land and spotted the hunched figures of Wulfnoth's crew climbing up the slope, hogsheads on their shoulders.

Godwin watched them come almost within a bowshot. 'Tell me,' he said quite suddenly, 'were you my father's girl?'

Kendra blushed despite herself. 'Yes, I was,' she said.

'Did you give him children?'

'None.'

Godwin didn't look at her, and she felt she ought to say something more, but the men were almost upon them and he stood up and went out to greet them.

The men who had been killed at the fight at Brihtric's hall were wrapped in plain woollen shrouds, the ends tied up with leather thongs: giant knotted socks loaded on to the back of an ox-drawn cart. The cart was driven by a short blond lad who switched his team so abruptly forward that a body half slid off the cart.

Caerl knocked the lad's leather cap off his head. 'Show some respect!' he said.

The procession made a strange silhouette against the dull, cloudy skyline: four men and two bodies, like the eight-legged horse of Odin who carried souls to Valhalla.

After the killings at Brihtric's hall there were many law cases to settle the deaths at Cicestre. Godwin was meticulous in dealing with each one. He rode to see each man who had lost family at the burning, paid over the odds and swore an oath of peace.

The last of the Sudsexe thegns to settle was an old warlord named Wiglaf the Red, who had lost his son in the killings. 'He would rather feud than settle,' Beorn said, and patted his sword. 'Let him feud. He will end up worse.'

Godwin was irritated. 'No,' he said. 'I will not feud, except with Eadric, and he is far away. No feud. Why waste English lives when it is the Danes who we have a quarrel with?'

Godwin made numerous approaches to Wiglaf, but he refused a reconciliation. Godwin armed his men and rode into Cicestre with all his company. They were a magnificent band, all mailed and helmeted and armed with spear and sword and shield. Each man had two horses, and they each had gold arm-bands that they had won in battle. With them rode Kendra, in a dress of fine linen and a cloak lined with fur.

Men stopped and stared.

'Let them carry word to Wiglaf,' Godwin muttered, 'and see just who he is pitting himself against.'

The Hundred Court met each month at Ælle's Stone. But this was a special moot, and a fire was lit to signal that the court would meet on the morrow, and from all the villages men looked and saw and made their way along the byways and lanes. Godwin and all his men came dressed in their finest. They were first to arrive. Godwin strode alone to the top of the stone, still cold and hard and silent. The crowd was eager to see Wulfnoth's son for themselves. They regarded his men, both worn and elevated with the experience of exile, with curiosity and admiration.

Godwin did not contest the case but paid the silver over, without a penny missing, and when the scales balanced he tossed another lump of hack-silver on to tip them in Wiglaf's favour.

'Bear your grief, lord,' men in poems said. 'We all leave our life on this earth and your son now sleeps in Our Father's eternal embrace!' But poetry was not life, and the embrace of the grave was cold and damp and unfriendly, and grief was a heavy load to bear on any man's shoulders – the grief for a son heaviest of all. So heavy that old Wiglaf could barely look at Godwin, and when at last he lifted his face Godwin saw hatred, furious and unhappy hatred.

'Shake hands!' the shire-reeve told them, but the older man's handshake was hard and resolute, like two men about to duel.

I can duel, Godwin's look said, and he took the old man's grip without flinching, returned it knuckle crunch for knuckle crunch.

'This was not my deed and has cost me dear,' Godwin said in a low voice. 'So let us be an example to our men. Let this be an end to the matter. Keep a tight rein on yours and I shall do the same, but if any of your men trouble me I shall repay violence with violence, killing with killing.'

Wiglaf sneered and Godwin gripped him tight.

'Do not doubt me, greybeard! If you had courage to fight, you should have showed it when the Army came to plunder.'

The handshake continued for a few moments more and then both let go, though they held the other's gaze as if they did not want to be the first to turn away.

Godwin watched him leave and let out a long sigh. That is over, he thought, and turned and looked at his father's men. They were a grim and warlike band, dearly bought.

'Come,' he called out, 'let us ride home. The matter is settled at last, and only Brihtric's death remains unpaid for.'

'Let him come and beg for justice,' Beorn laughed.

'Eadric owes me much,' Godwin said, 'but he owes the country more and only his death will repay his debt to us all.'

The weather was grim the rest of that week, but a few days after Candlemas a warm front blew in from the south-west and men woke not to frost and ice but a misty morning, with dew dripping from the trees.

It was still dark when the first blackbirds began to sing and their song roused the sleeping farmers out to the fields, to harrow and sow, each in their allotted place. They were resting the teams of oxen when men in the lower meads shouted up that horsemen were coming up the road from Cicestre. The men ran to fetch their weapons, and Godwin strode out of the hall door Kendra ran out behind him. Godwin buckled on his sword and stood at the hall doors, the wind fretting his cloak hems.

'I see three horsemen,' Beorn called out. 'There is a monk and a mule with many packs upon its back. It's a lady!' he said a few moments later. 'She's wearing a red cloak and a white wimple.'

Godwin rushed forward. It took mere moments for him to recognise her. He started laughing. 'Christ's blood!' he said, and told his men to put away their weapons. 'Look smart! Prepare the welcome. That's King Ethelred's mother!'

Edmund's grandmother gave Godwin's hall a cursory inspection: the thatch on Lyftehal was so thick with grass and bracken that it looked more like a hummock than a hall. It was as crude as she remembered. Windswept and godforsaken. She had been here when Wulfnoth was young, when Edgar the Peaceful was king and she was queen, and the country was good. She walked her horse forward to the hall doors, let Godwin take the reins, but stayed in the saddle.

'Lady,' he said. 'Welcome! What honour is this.'

'Well met, Godwin Wulfnothson,' she said. 'Thank you.'

She had a bad hip and it took a long while for her to slide down from the saddle on to the stool. Godwin helped lower her down, and then she stood and straightened her robes.

'I thought you might have come,' she said. 'I have been fretting about my sons and grandsons. Men say you were at Lundenburh and that you sailed to Wiht with them. Come! Have you a fire? Good. I am an old lady. Sixty-two!' she said. 'Tell me, Godwin, don't you think it's time you knocked this barn down and built yourself a fitting hall?'

'Was it a good journey, lady?' Godwin asked as he gave her his arm.

'In winter? In these times? Don't be a fool,' Edmund's grandmother said, and thought of chat was cut dramatically short.

Kendra brought the bowl of warm water and Edmund's grandmother rinsed her hands, took the linen cloth and dried them. Her fingers were as fine and pale as whalebone, and just as hard.

'You should not have come here.' Godwin said. 'You should have sent word and I would have ridden straight over.'

'I am not so old I cannot ride a horse,' she said, and then took in a deep and irritated breath as she sat on the seat of honour and arranged her gowns. 'I was sick of the sight of the inside of my hall. This winter was too long and tiresome. I always ride once Candlemas is done, and when I heard that Wulfnoth's son had taken back his father's manor I resolved to come and seek news of my menfolk. You were with them in Lundenburh. You saw them leave. What were their plans? Why did they not fight?'

In her lap she held a tiny soapstone carving of the Baptism of Christ. She turned it over in her hands like prayer beads, and Godwin stood and picked out two good pieces of split oak from a wicker basket by the hearth and put them on the fire, and told all he knew.

'And they have sailed for Normandig?' she said at last, when Godwin had finished his tale. 'They should not have left,' she said. 'They should have come to me. I would have sheltered them. They would be here now to seize the chance.

'And your father has died, I hear? A slaver. Alas for Wulfnoth Cild! Your father would have risen high if my son was a better king.' She let out a long sigh. 'When Athelstan is king, you will do better, won't you?'

Godwin nodded. 'I will,' he said, and she held his gaze long as if testing his resolve.

Her eyes twinkled. 'I think you had better prepare for that moment. I have more news to tell. You have not heard, I think.'

'Heard what?'

She was delighted with herself. 'The whole country is so excited by the news. I think it will not be long before you see dear Edmund and Athelstan again.'

Godwin leapt to his feet. 'They have returned? I have much to tell! I have my own war bands now and silver to equip them with the best armour. When he raises his banner I shall be there.'

The old lady's eyes sparkled with her secret. 'No, I think, not yet. But as soon as he hears I am sure he will return.'

'Why?'

The old lady smiled and her wrinkles were dark in the fading light. 'Gaudete!' she sang a song of thanks.

Godwin didn't understand.

She sat forward and touched his arm and spelled it out in simple words that he could understand. 'Our new king is dead,' she said.

Godwin choked.

'Swein is dead?'

'Yes!' she said, and clapped her hands. 'Swein Forkbeard is dead and the Army have declared his son Knut king. But who is this Knut? He is a boy not much older than yourself!'

'He is only a boy! Will he be able to bridle his father's proud warhorses? I think not. They are wild and lawless. They need a stronger master. Prepare your men, Godwin Wulfnothson! Edmund shall have need of you. Your time has come at last.'

CHAPTER ELEVEN

Ethelred Returns

In Snotingeham, Morcar sat in his hall chair and his face went pale when he heard the news.

'Swein is dead?' he whispered.

He listened to the whole story in a fearful silence. When the tale had been told in full, and all Morcar's questions had been answered, he seemed unable to speak.

Swein had left his eldest son, Harald, as regent in Danemark, but he had brought his youngest son, Knut, to England, and Swein had picked Alderman Elfhelm's daughter, the fair and fierce Edith, as Knut's wife.

The betrothal feast had been memorable. Knut and Edith had been wed at the Yuletide feast, and Morcar had gloated. How Eadric would quake!

Morcar shut the doors on his retainers, knelt down as if in prayer and put his head in his hands. How he would be punished if Ethelred returned. How Fate could spin on its wheel. He had taken offerings to Elfhelm's grave and promised his old friend that he would be avenged on Eadric.

'No,' he whispered. 'No Lord, this cannot be!'

But it was, for in Euruic that very day the great and the good lined the street all the way down the slope from Mykelgate, across the bridge, to the gates of St Peter's Minster, where Alderman Uhtred bowed before the dead king's shrouded body.

Swein was laid in a prime spot near the altar, between the archbishops and the men of the ancient Northymbrian dynasty. Knut stood grim and stiff. Swein's war chiefs stood behind him, as wild and shaggy as mountain wolves.

Ethelred had been in Normandig for five weeks when the tidings came. He choked on his morning posset of spiced wine and threatened to have the man whipped if he was jesting.

'It's true! Bring any relic for me to swear on,' the messenger said. 'I was at the minster and saw Swein laid out for his eternal rest. Uhtred sent me in his fastest ship. Your enemy is dead.'

Ethelred jumped to his feet and took a gold ring from his finger and pressed it into the man's hand. 'Bless you!' he said. 'Alleluia! Where are my ships? Have them ready to sail!'

Edmund and Athelstan had sailed to Flandran and had taken a merchant warehouse as their hall.

They heard the news three days after Ethelred, and they also heard that their half-brother Edward had been sent on behalf of their father to negotiate with the Witan.

'He has sent that spotty, gangly lad to the Witan,' Edmund cursed. 'We should have been there first! If *we* were there, then they would be making you king!'

'Hush,' Athelstan said. 'Calm. Swein is dead! Let Edward have his moment of fame. Once people see how weak he is, no man will think he can succeed.'

'He cannot succeed,' Edmund said. 'We shall never defeat the Danes with a weakling as king. What men can we muster? There will be war, Athelstan. We should send out word to all who are loyal to us. They should bring their companions. We shall have to fight for our throne.'

February gave way to March, and little by little the days began to lengthen. Birdsong returned in the morning and evening, Godwin rode home along the Meredone lane, rich with the scent of wild garlic, saw snowdrops bright against the wood shadows. Lent was coming, and even though the news of Swein's death overshadowed the tidings of Brihtric's murder, the thought of Eadric was much on Godwin's mind.

Eadric had remained in England and had no doubt heard by now of his brother's murder. He would be in Lundenburh, where Ethelred had called a court, and Wulfnoth's men were unhappy about the planned trip there: it was like walking into the wolf's lair. But men did not mention Eadric's name. He was the shadow in the room, unseen but watching.

Beorn stamped and blustered. 'Why go to Lundenburh?' he said. 'It's a godforsaken place. Why leave Sudsexe? We have spent years wandering the seas. I feel the need for hard ground beneath my feet, the ground of home.'

There were many who agreed with Beorn. All of them had dreamt of Contone. They had family here, and some had wives and children, and if they did not, they wanted them – and now they had enough money to settle down comfortably.

But Godwin needed them, and for days he did not know how to order them. He wished that Brihtric had not been killed at this moment.

'You should have waited to kill him,' he lectured Beorn, and Beorn shrugged.

'Well, he's dead now.'

Godwin became increasingly tense and frustrated. One night on the benches as they sat and talked, Godwin cut through the bickering. 'We go to Lundenburh because Prince Edmund shall be there. We go because Ethelred shall return and the Wise will make him king. And it is important that we go there and witness that event.'

'I will not go,' Beorn said. 'Let Ethelred stick his crown in his nose for all I care.'

Godwin stood up. 'Has the sea turned you timid, Beorn Rolfson! You killed Brihtric, not I! I took you in and paid off each man and you refuse to come with me to Lundenburh! Where is your shame? You were bold when you cut that one-eyed monster down. I am Godwin Wulfnothson. Eadric shall not dictate where I ride or do not ride. I am a free man. This is my country!

'I tell you, if you sit here, fear will move every shadow till it appears to be one of Eadric's killers. You shall end up fearful to leave your house. And one day the killer will step inside and you will fall down dead with fright.'

Godwin stormed outside and slammed the door behind him in fury. The night was dark and clouded. He felt foolish for losing his temper and foolish for walking out. He drew in a deep breath. The shadows of the past lay heavy on them all.

Godwin stopped at the door, let out a sigh and strode inside.

He expected laughter, or sneering looks, but the men's eyes were sympathetic. Beorn rose. He had a guilty look on his face. He opened his arms to Godwin and hugged him. 'I will come,' he said. 'And even face Eadric, if need be.'

The day before Godwin was to leave for Lundenburh, Kendra waited while the men laid out mattresses on the floor and shook out their blankets. She crossed the hall to where Godwin sat whetting his sword. There was a compulsive manner about him. The scrape-scrape-scrape set her nerves on edge.

'So,' she said.

'So what?'

Godwin put the whetstone down, took out a piece of uncured sheepskin, and rubbed it along the sword till it gleamed with the wool oils.

'Is it your father?'

'No.'

She waited.

He held the sword towards the firelight and used the red reflection to check the edge, which was notched but hard and keen and true.

'You will see Edmund again.'

Godwin looked at her.

'It is hot in here. I think I will go outside. I feel the need for fresh air on my face.'

Kendra stood up. 'Do you mind if I walk with you?'

Godwin looked at her. Her skin was pale, even in firelight. Only her freckles were dark, a small constellation about her nose.

'As you wish,' he said.

The outside air was chill. It took a moment for their night-sight to come. Kendra stumbled and he held out his arm for her to take. They paused at the paddock. The horses snorted in the chill and one of them made water; the piss steamed in the starlight.

Orion had risen high above the horizon, big and bright and ready for war.

'So Ethelred has called a court in Lundenburh.'

'He has,' Godwin said.

'Will Eadric be there?'

'I am sure.'

'What is he like?'

'Didn't my father tell you?'

'A little.'

'Do you fear for me?'

She looked at him and half smiled. 'Of course,' she said. 'I fear for all of you.'

They walked on a little further. The sky had been clouded all day but now that night had fallen and the chill had descended, the sky was clear. It was good to walk under the stars. Godwin let out a long sigh.

'It seems that every time I climb one hill, another peak rises before me.'

'What do you mean?'

He paused. 'Once, I thought that I needed a lord, and I found one, but I could not rest. I was not born to be a serving man. I am a thegn's son and my family were given this land. Then I thought that I would be happy when I took this place back, and yet when I took it I began to fear that someone would take it from me.'

'And now?'

'Now I have men to fill my benches and yet there is another peak. And each one is more precipitous than before, and if I fall I lose everything.'

Like my father, went unsaid.

Kendra leant on his arm as they walked a little further. He followed no plan, but found his steps turning towards the path that led down to the chapel. The bell tower was tall and dark above them. A bat flitted overhead and Kendra ducked.

'I always thought my mother and father would lie here. But neither of them does,' Godwin said.

They stopped at the lychgate. The grass was damp with dew. It gleamed white in the moonlight. Godwin turned and rested his back against the wattle fence and they looked back up the slope to where the hall stood, ghostly in the moonlight.

'Most men build their churches above the hall,' Kendra said.

Godwin laughed. 'My grandfather wanted to keep the clerics in their place,' he said.

There was a long pause. Their backs were to the chapel. The air was fresh on their faces.

'We have fallen far,' Godwin said. 'The English, I mean. There was a great king named Alfred in the time of my father's grandfather. He defeated the Danes and imposed law on the whole country. He had his laws written down and all men had to read them. Even the old greybeards had to struggle with their hornbooks. And the country prospered.'

'So?' Kendra said. 'What will you do when you are the king's friend?'

'I will bring back respect for the law.'

'Is respect enough?'

'No. I will enforce the law.'

There was a glint in her eyes and he saw that she was teasing him.

He smiled, but he was tired. 'It is late. I think I shall sleep.'

She turned to go, then paused. The dew soaked the hem of her dress and penetrated her shoes through to her toes.

Kendra slept in the brew house, Godwin in the hall. Their paths diverged at the water trough.

'Good night,' Godwin said.

'Good night,' she said. 'God bless you.'

Godwin watched her walk away from him. He waited until she was safe inside and the door latch had fallen, then took a deep breath and turned his gaze back to the Heavens. From horizon to horizon ten thousand stars gleamed. Some were so small you could barely make them out; others burnt with such a cold white ferocity that their light blotted out the rest. From eastern sky to western wood stretched a bright path of stars – Wæcelinga Stræt – the path of heroes. That night the Swordsman of the Sky, the three stars of his belt gleaming bright, had taken up the challenge and strode high and triumphant across the winter heavens.

Next morning Godwin looked for Kendra in the grey light of dawn, but she was not there. The horses steamed in gentle rain, leaf-buds dripped under fat-bellied rain clouds, and a mournful raven flapped past; Godwin was not sure it was a good omen.

He suddenly had a flashback of his mother looking very small and futile. He did not know if she was a figment of his imagination, or a spirit sent to warn him. Her hair was bound and covered from the weather, and she clutched her rosary in her hard cold fingers. 'God speed, my son,' she called out. 'Do not forget that your father was Wulfnoth Cild, and that your mother is of the House of Hasta!'

The image froze Godwin and about him the mounts milled in a tight and eager circle.

Kendra appeared at the door of the brew house.

'Look after yourselves,' she called out, but her eyes were on Godwin.

In reply Godwin blew on his horn, and heel-kicked his horse down the hill.

Kendra watched him leave with a mixture of emotions. Godwin was so young and eager and full of expectation.

She did not wave but stood for a long time, a dark figure against the skyline, hair blowing in the wind.

They crossed the country by safe paths. The country about them was quiet and watchful. The men were quiet. As they came down into the Temese Valley, Godwin's last trip to Lundenburh was much in his mind. Then, he had been with Edmund and Blecca, impossibly naive and innocent. He wished he had known what would happen to Blecca. He would have done something, Godwin told himself.

The closer they drew, the worse Godwin's mood. There was no place he wanted to see less. He disliked the place – every stone and midden-pit and pothole. There was no place he less wanted to arrive, no faces he wanted to see less than the court: the men who had condemned Wulfnoth. But that was where Edmund was to sail, where the king would petition to be taken back, so that was where he had to go.

Chingestune was bustling with excitement, and Godwin was hailed by Edmund's younger brother, Eadwig.

Shit! Godwin thought, when he saw the young prince hurrying towards him. He was thin and a little stupid-looking, with a strange intensity about his narrow gaze.

Eadwig was a year younger than Godwin, but he had the air of a spoilt and irritating child. 'Father wants him to go into the Church,' Edmund had told Godwin, but the truth was they all wanted him to go into the Church, and to Rome, and save them all the trouble of dealing with him.

It was Eadwig's misfortune to be the third son of Ethelred, and to be the younger brother of more worthy princes. He latched on to Godwin like a leech.

'Godwin! I am glad to see you. What chance! I am going to Lundenburh. Do you think Father will return?'

'I am sure,' Godwin said.

'He has sent Prince Edward,' Eadwig said, and his tone said everything. Spotty, gangly, uneasy Prince Edward. 'Athelstan will take the throne.'

'Really?' Godwin said in a noncommittal way. 'Let us wait till we start to gossip. I shall save my counsel till then,' he said.

Eadwig looked at him and grinned. 'You're funny,' he said.

When Godwin saw the stone walls of Lundenburh a wave of hatred rose in him. He rode towards them with the eye of an invader, looking for the weak spots, the place where he had stood, the place where Blecca had died.

Eadwig babbled and Godwin ignored him. At the palace at Crepelgate, men were battling to control the jostling crowd. Godwin shoved his way to the front and greeted the door wards warmly.

'Hey there, you! Let him pass! Christ's blood, Godwin, it's good to see you. You did not come to Normandig.'

'My father had died. I wanted to take my own land back,' Godwin said.

'And did you?'

'Of course.' Godwin grinned.

'Good! But half England wants to see the princes. The rats all have an eye to the succession now. I hear the queen has promised money to any who support her sons.'

Godwin laughed at the idea. 'Let her sit on her twig and spin her webs,' he said as he pulled his men through into the hallway. 'I promised I would bring soldiers, and here I have them.'

The man gave his retainers a nod. 'We'll need stout fellows like you. All the men we can get. Pass on!'

Athelstan greeted Godwin equally warmly. Godwin looked and saw Edmund and paused, but as soon as Edmund had greeted Eadwig, he hurried forward and hugged Godwin.

'I am glad to see you!' he said as they held each other's shoulders. 'God, I am glad to be back. Let me see you.' Edmund held Godwin at arm's length. 'You've grown,' he said.

'I have?'

'Yes! Are these your men? They're a fearsome-looking company! Can they fight?'

'Ask Brihtric,' Beorn shouted, and Edmund put his head back and laughed.

'Well spoken! Let me shake your hands. Any enemy of Eadric is thrice welcome! Now the hour has come. It is long past time to teach the Danes the strength of English arms! Fate is spinning on its wheel. It is turning our way at last!'

There was some talk of Athelstan taking the throne, but Edmund quickly spoke against it. Decisions had been made in their brief exile in Flandran. The brothers wanted Ethelred king, and they wanted battle, for the princes knew that the battlefield would give them the perfect stage upon which to stake their claim to the throne.

'Let us think of unity,' Edmund said. 'The Army is still in the north, sitting in our friend Morcar's hall. Now is the time to thank God for His help in taking Swein. We will earn no favour by inciting civil war.'

'When does the king come?' Godwin said.

No one knew. They turned to Athelstan. It seemed that the princes knew a lot more than they were saying. Godwin watched them closely.

'Our father is at Tanet,' Athelstan said. 'He is waiting for all the Wise to gather; then he will arrive.'

The Wise were fluid, hard to define, but it was clear to all men present who among them were entitled to attend, and stand by and be accountable for the decisions they made.

'I think we are all here now Eadwig is come.' Athelstan paused a moment, but kept a straight face. 'And the king sent word that he will arrive on the morrow, on the first tide.'

*

After the meeting Edmund called Godwin to one side.

'Eadric is here,' he said.

'I have heard,' Godwin said.

'He will try and take his revenge.'

'I know.'

'We need unity now,' Edmund said. Godwin began to feel panic, as if he was being thrown to the dogs again, but Edmund put his hand to his shoulder. 'Keep your men in order,' he said. 'I do not want anything that will provoke Eadric.'

'I shall not provoke him.'

'Good. And that warrior of yours.'

'Beorn?'

'Yes. Shut him up.' The words came out in a tone that seemed too sharp. 'We shall need him when the battle comes. I would not waste him in a knife fight with one of Eadric's thegns.' Edmund stopped. 'Sorry. I am delighted to see you again, and my heart is warmed to hear that you have taken your father's land back. Do not worry. There is much at stake here, but I have not forgotten your loyalty.'

Eadric was at the wharf the next morning with a great troop and went from company to company greeting the chief men. He even came to Athelstan and shook his hand.

'Greetings, lord. It is welcome beyond measure to see you safely returned.'

Athelstan returned the greeting cordially.

'Greetings, Alderman Eadric. I hear you feasted with King Swein while we were away.'

Other men would have paled, but Eadric did not pause for a second.

'I did, my lord, for what else could we do? Each night we prayed for his death and lo! the Lord heard us. And He answered our prayers by bringing you back again.' Eadric turned to the men about him. 'We prayed for their return, did we not?'

Yes! They all nodded and agreed.

Edmund admired Eadric's boldness. Brazen, he thought, and smiled back, reminded himself how they had boasted that Eadric would be the first to swing from the gibbet tree when his brother was made king.

The tidal bore had begun to turn back up the river and it was not long before Ethelred appeared at the front of his gaily painted boat, with trumpets blowing, and a great company of fine men.

'Ah look,' Eadric said, and stayed with the princes, at the head of the royal wharf, as if it was his place, 'your father!'

The crowds of common people cheered as soon as they saw Ethelred return. The queen stood beside him, Edward at her side.

'With her hand up his arse,' Edmund whispered to Eadwig as they headed the welcoming committee.

The queen waved. There was a smattering of Norman clerics behind her; they stood out with their strange shaved heads.

'She used half the king's money to stock a divine war chest of relics,' Athelstan muttered to Edmund. 'She's now added the heads of St Ouen and St Augustine to her haul, as well as the tooth of St Bridget, which wards off thunderstorms.'

There was a sudden rush as men tried to be first to greet Ethelred. Edmund and Eadwig stepped in front of Eadric and blocked his way, while Athelstan strode forward to kneel before his father.

Edmund and Eadwig struggled to keep the nervous crowd back. Some thegns slipped and fell into the Temese mud; others were shoved out of the way. Edmund remembered their faces. They had guilty consciences all.

*

Godwin was not at the wharf. He took his men out hunting in the woods beyond Iseldone, about two miles from Crepelgate. They climbed the hill and passed beyond the strip fields into a wild landscape, where there were bears and wild hogs. They did not find anything worth killing. At one point they heard the sound of distant cheers carried up from the river and they turned and looked. So Ethelred has returned, Godwin thought, and felt a strange mixture of emotions: joy and despair in equal measure, for the old order had been restored, and yet it had failed before and would fail again, and yet would not go without a fight.

The Wise of England gathered.

There was no specific place for them to meet, but to add ceremony and gravitas to the occasion, it was decided that it would be held this time in St Paul's Cathedral. The streets all about were overwhelmed with horses and retainers, and there was a crush at the door as the door wards sorted those who were eligible and those who were not.

The cathedral was a massive building with heavy, round arches and high, small windows where God peeped in. The meeting started with a mass of thanks for removing them of their Danish oppressor.

At the altar sat Archbishop Wulfstan of York, his grim face glowering at the shifting crowd. Ethelred sat on a lower step, and a less richly decorated throne, but his robes were as richly ornamented with jewels and gold and the finest furs. He sat with a look of stern kindliness on his face.

Ethelred knelt to receive the water and wine from the archbishop's own hands, a golden plate beneath his chin, like a gleaming buttercup, to catch any crumbs of Christ's body. Incense was burnt. More men pushed inside. Some men tried to bring their horses in; a fat noblewoman from Exsessa was crushed and had to be carried out for air. Morcar and all his folk were missing, so too were those from Northymbria and their warlike alderman, Uhtred. They were too close to the Danes to risk coming, so the meeting of the Wise was stuffed with all the prominent men and families and Church establishments from Wessex and those parts of Mercia free from the Danish.

Then the Witena Gemot began, and quickly turned tense and ill-tempered. Ethelred took his place again on the throne, and there was a murmur of displeasure: he is not yet king, it seemed to say. He presumes too much.

Ethelred began the meeting gracious and understanding, but as men's complaints continued and became increasingly personal, it was clear that they were quite happy to put Ethelred back on his ship and return him to Normandig if he did not agree to rule them better.

Ethelred tried threats, appeals and sulking, but the English were in an unusually unruly mood, and Ethelred's impatience turned to irritation and then anger. 'What do you mean, I should keep the laws better than before?' he blustered. 'God has spoken.'

Yes, the bench silence seemed to say, but what has He said?

Godwin did not go with Edmund to West Minster. His memories of that place were too vivid. He and his men rode to the wharf where the king's ships lay, safely moored to the shore. They watched the heavy gold-rimmed caskets being carried from the ships. They were travelling caskets, with pitched lids, like the roof of a house, so that the rain would wash off and not damage the holy contents.

'Queen Emma's reliquaries,' Godwin said to Caerl.

Caerl had never seen so much wealth and sanctity combined. He mistrusted it.

Beorn scoffed. 'Can you buy God?' he asked.

Godwin laughed. 'The days that follow shall show,' he said.

That afternoon they rode out to hunt again. Godwin was glad to be riding in the fields rather than standing in that unhappy crowd in the cathedral, but as the day stretched on, and the evening bench-talk was all of things that one man or the other had said, he began to feel that he should be there. The second day he went hunting again, caught a mangy old fox and flung her to the dogs. On the third day Godwin decided he would go.

'Once I was just a boy, but I am a thegn now,' he said to Edmund. 'I have a stake now. I have people to protect. I am accountable to my folk.'

Edmund did not argue. 'Then come. I will not stop you, but remember to keep your men in check.'

Godwin left Beorn and the other loudmouths behind, but Caerl came with him.

'You do not need mail,' Godwin said to his men as they began to arm themselves. 'This is a peaceful meeting. I will not have fighting.'

Godwin was stiff in the saddle as they followed Edmund down the muddy street towards the cathedral. As they entered the square before the abbey gates, his eyes flicked from face to face and party to party, looking for his foe.

He did not see Eadric, though he looked all about him.

'Do you see him?' he said to Caerl.

'I do not,' Caerl said, and paused and looked again. 'Maybe he is inside.'

That morning Eadric sat on a horse at the cathedral doors and greeted each man in turn. He was like a lord of men, high above them all. When Godwin saw him it was too late to turn away.

'Stand next to me,' Edmund said as they dismounted.

Godwin nodded. He steeled himself, turned to check his men were with him. The crush pressed in. It would be easy for a knife-man to come close and thrust a dagger into his gut. Godwin looked about. Caerl and the others stepped closer. Godwin felt them, a living shield in the crush. Godwin tried to ignore Eadric as Edmund shuffled forward and he followed close behind.

Edmund took the side furthest from Eadric, Godwin kept his gaze fixed on the doors before him, and it seemed that he would pass by without being noticed when Eadwig – who had been wait-ing by Eadric's side – spotted them and called out across the heads of the crowd, 'Edmund! Godwin! Ah, Godwin, you have come!'

Eadwig pushed towards Edmund, and Edmund had to stop and embrace his brother. The name Godwin seemed to carry over the crowd, and men saw Eadric and heard that name and turned to see. All knew who had killed Eadric's brother. Godwin smiled faintly as Eadwig came up, his eyes boring into Godwin.

'Where have you been? I heard you went hunting. You should have taken me as well.'

'I will,' Godwin tried to say, but his voice stuck in his throat. His ears burnt red. He could feel the crowd watching him. He was sure Eadric had seen him as well.

'What?' Eadwig said. Godwin could have throttled him.

'Nothing,' Edmund said, but took hold of Eadwig's hand, and Eadwig winced.

'Ow!' he said. 'What?'

A voice called out, 'Godwin!'

Godwin kept his jaw shut and hurried after Edmund.

'Godwin!'

The crowd turned to look at him, and Godwin stopped.

Eadric had seen him. He pushed his horse towards them. 'Godwin Wulfnothson.'

The words and that voice fixed Godwin to the spot.

Eadric bent from the saddle towards him and Godwin flinched, and hated himself, for Eadric sat up and spoke to the crowd. 'Don't shy away from me, lad. If you were big enough to kill my brother, you should at least do me the honour of coming to court and settling the issue. You do yourself and your father's memory no good by running like an outlaw.'

Godwin answered him, but he was standing in the crowd and Eadric was in plain view on his horse, so it was his words that carried, while Godwin's were muffled by the people about him.

'It is true my brother was a rough man, but he was a good and law-abiding man who paid his tithes to the Church, and more. You did a wrong deed when you came on him at night and burnt all his folk and cut down those who tried to escape.'

'I did not kill them,' Godwin said, but his voice sounded weak and shrill.

Eadric laughed at the statement. 'No. You sent men to do the killing for you. That is an even baser deed.'

The crowd began to turn against Godwin, and many of Eadric's retainers were eager to fight. Two of them drew daggers and began to shove towards Godwin.

Edmund saw the danger. In a moment he was at Godwin's side. He stood tall so that his face could be seen.

'I am Edmund, prince! This is a council of peace. There is no feud to be brought into the minster this day.'

The mood of the crowd hung in balance.

'Eadric, let us meet at the law court, where Godwin shall pay proper recompense to your family for the death of your kin. And brothers, put past wrongs from your mind. The Army is just five days' march north! Bear that in mind. Let it focus your thoughts.'

Godwin's hand shook as he took his place by Edmund. He held it with his other hand and took in a deep, slow breath. Athelstan strode down the altar steps. It was clear that he had heard what had happened. From Eadwig's manner it seemed he had taken the blame for it all. He sulked as Athelstan took Edmund's arm and they moved a short distance away. The two men exchanged serious looks.

'It was close,' Edmund said.

'He should not have come.'

Godwin realised they were talking about him and he stood like stone as he listened.

'He has as much right as any.'

'Edmund! There is too much at stake here.'

'I told him. He did not bring the hotheads.'

'Look at Eadric. He's playing the wronged man. It's disgusting!'

'Let him gloat. We need Father made king, and we need him to declare war.'

'He will declare,' Athelstan said.

'Then there is nothing to worry about.' Edmund turned and saw Godwin standing nearby. 'There is nothing to worry about, is there, Godwin?'

'No, lord.'

Athelstan looked at them both. He pursed his lips and sighed.

Eadwig came forward and Athelstan took his arm and led him away. 'Listen,' he started, 'I need you . . .'

Edmund raised his eyebrows and winked at Godwin.

Godwin felt like a piece of unwanted baggage. It was hard to say, but he had to say something and looked at Edmund. 'Sorry,' he said.

'Don't be foolish,' Edmund said. 'Remember, who hangs first?'

Godwin laughed. 'Eadric,' he said.

On the third day Ethelred capitulated. A great jewelled cross was brought forward. It was a Roman cross, heavy with gold, blue lapis lazuli and red garnets. Inside was a piece of the True Cross, upon which Christ hung. God bore witness to the compact of king and people.

Godwin kept looking towards Eadric, but his foe did not look his way. His eyes were on the king and the bishop as Ethelred swore a weighty oath.

'I shall forgive all crimes against my person,' Ethelred said. 'I shall forgive all those men who swore false oaths and all those who broke their oath to me as their king. I shall enforce the laws on all my subjects.'

'And let God bear witness to these words!' Archbishop Wulfstan called out, and the sun shone brighter; then the clouds returned and the cathedral was plunged back into gloom.

And so full friendship was established, in word and in deed and in compact, on either side and the Danish king was declared an outlaw for ever.

The next day Ethelred held a feast at his hall in West Minster to announce that he would call a great fyrd, at last, against the Danes. The place was abuzz. Men were delighted to be united. They would drive the Danes from England with great slaughter. Peace would return when the Danes were gone. The possibilities thrilled them.

Godwin arrived as the beer and wine were being poured and water passed round for men to wash their hands. He and his men dismounted. Their footsteps were heavy in the mud outside. The cold clung to their cloaks as they greeted the door wards, left their swords at the porch and strode inside.

Godwin threw back his hood. His eyes were bright with anger when he strode inside and saw Eadric sitting next to the king.

'Shall I come with you?' Edmund said.

Godwin shook his head. His manner was serious. 'No. I shall do this.'

Godwin strode between the benches. The hall fell silent. King Ethelred was in a fine mood. The light of many candles reflected in his eyes. They twinkled with mischievous delight as he saw the killer of Eadric's brother coming towards him. He nudged Eadric and pointed. 'Look!' he said. 'Eadric – it's Wulfnoth's lad.'

Eadric looked. His eyes glittered too. Like a watching snake, or the wolf in the shadows that watches the sheep in the high shieling.

Many a night Godwin had lain awake and imagined meeting face to face with Eadric. He had pictured himself meeting accidentally on a hunt, alone in a clearing with the man he had most reason to kill; or he had imagined walking round some insignificant hall corner and finding himself trapped with Eadric's men before and behind, daggers drawn. Of course he had even imagined himself stepping close to Eadric, ramming three feet of steel straight into the bastard's gut. Stepping so close he could smell the other man's last breaths.

As he strode down the hall before the chief men of the kingdom, he felt his chest swell out, his spine lengthen and his feet boom proudly on the hall timbers. Godwin walked straight up to the high table. Eadric's retainers stepped in front of their lord. Their hands were on their hilts and they towered over Godwin, big and mean and ugly. One of them, a red-haired man with blond eyebrows, stepped right into Godwin's path, but something about the look in Godwin's eye made him falter for a second.

'Let him pass,' came a voice. It was Ethelred.

The king's cheeks shone with wine.

Godwin stopped and bowed, then turned to Eadric. He called

out in a loud voice, 'Greetings Alderman Eadric, Lord and Protector of the March and chief among the Mercians. I am Godwin, son of Wulfnoth Cild, of the South Saxons. All know of the enmity that lies between our families. This is a time that all Englishmen, of whatever family, should bury their differences so that we can present a united front to the foe. I offer you silver for your brother's life.'

Caerl and Beorn hurried forward, with a small chest weighing their shoulders down. They set it on the table before Eadric.

It made a dull thud. The table timbers creaked and bowed beneath its weight.

Godwin stepped forward and threw the chest lid open. Silver coins skittered and fell from the pile within.

Eadric seemed briefly taken aback. He caught the look in Caerl's eye and lost his train of thought for a moment, but quickly rose and bowed to the king.

Nothing troubled Ethelred. A month earlier he was an unwelcome exile in the Norman court and now he was king again and full of bonhomie. He shoved the chest towards Eadric.

'There!' he said to Eadric. 'Make peace. Let's have this feud done.'

Eadric started to speak, but Godwin took the gold ring from his arm and tossed it on to the pile.

'Take this gift from me, Lord Eadric.'

Godwin stretched out a hand, open, to shake on their peace. There was little Eadric could do. He smiled. 'You are a brave lad coming here to me,' he said, but his hands remained by his sides.

'Lord, it is the duty of every boy like me to come along and learn from his elders and betters. Take my hand, lord. Let us promise peace between our families!'

Godwin's hand remained outstretched.

Eadric ignored it and prepared to speak.

'Take my hand, lord,' Godwin repeated. The whole hall listened.

Eadric paused. He did not like to be spoken over.

'Take my hand, lord!' Godwin said once more. 'Show all the good folk here that there is peace between our families and war between us and the Danes.'

'Take his hand,' Ethelred said, and slapped Eadric's back. 'Shake his hand and have done.' The king directed him, and the room – great men all – willed it.

Godwin felt they were with him. Eadric felt it too. He moved slowly. Despite the smile and the easy manner, Eadric's hand extended, Godwin read reluctance in his every movement and expression. The two palms met, the fingers gripped, and if Godwin had expected another bone-breaking tussle, he had misread his enemy, for Eadric knew how to play the pleasant courtier.

'You speak bravely,' Eadric smiled. 'Just like your father.'

'Thank you, lord,' Godwin said. 'But I do not wish to be judged by my words, only by my actions.'

'I will be there to watch.'

'Right behind me, or shoulder to shoulder?'

'Shoulder to shoulder, of course.'

'Then who could stand against us?' Godwin turned to the assembled worthies. 'Witness all of you here how Eadric and I have put aside our feud for the sake of the country. May this be a sign that better things are to come to England.'

Eadric waited. 'Here!' he said, and took a gold arm-band twice as large as the one Godwin had given him and fixed it about Godwin's arm.

There was a murmur of approval. Eadric's band was a princely gift for a young man. There was a flutter of applause; hands slapped the trenchers before them.

Godwin bowed.

'Thank you, lord,' he said, and bowed to the king. 'Lord King, your reign has started well. Pray God this will continue!'

On the way back from West Minster Godwin took the golden arm-band from his arm and held it up. It was a wreath of three cords of twisted gold, each as thick as his thumb, with wolf-head ends with eyes of jet.

Clouds were drifting slowly north, but between them the stars were clear and the moon was setting in the west, and lighting the undersides with white. It glimmered on the reed beds, and on the slow rippling water, that was ebbing as the tide flowed out. Godwin took the arm-band and flung it far out into the water. It was dark against the sky as it writhed in the air and then fell with a dull splash and disappeared.

CHAPTER TWELVE

The Great Fyrd

The Great Fyrd of 1014 drew men from all the shires of Wessex and Mercia that were free of the Army, and Ethelred sent word for them to gather at Oxeneford.

Athelstan, Edmund and Eadwig went by separate routes to Oxeneford, shaking hands, kissing babies, laying hands on the sick. In this way man by man they rekindled old loyalties, reforging the ties between ruler and ruled.

Godwin was sent ahead as harbinger, to gather provisions against their coming.

'It will keep you out of danger,' Edmund said.

Spring was the leanest time, and whilst the men could skip meals, the horses could not, and last summer had not been good for hay so Godwin and his men planned to do some old-fashioned provisioning, riding about the larger farms to beg, threaten or cajole meat and bread, oats and ale. But when they heard the king was finally taking to the field, the people were willing to give. 'Anything is better than the Danes' Rule,' they said, and 'Danes' Rule' remained a byword for many years after for circumstances too harsh to bear.

The princes shared a fine stone hall in Oxeneford, set among a warren of narrow and puddled alleyways. They had many men with them, all jostling for attention and favour, so there was no room for Godwin's war band, and rather than be separated from them, he elected to join the other thegns in the camp that stretched all along Portemeadowe, from the Priory of St Frideswide to the ford.

'Set your tent there, by the crouched willow,' Ordulf, king-thegn, told them. 'Oh, and put peace bonds on your swords,' one of the sword-thegns said, and pointed to where the men of Sudsexe had their camp.

Godwin's men pitched camp, but Godwin was unhappy. 'It does not seem right that we are sent to the fields when all those cowards feast in Edmund's hall.'

'You know why they feast those other men?' Caerl said. 'Because they are disloyal. We are in the mud because Edmund trusts you.'

'You think so?'

'Of course. I see it as plain as the nose on your face.'

'Thank you, Caerl,' Godwin said later.

'For what?'

'Clearing my mind,' he said. His confrontation with Eadric had shaken him.

Caerl put his hand to Godwin's shoulder. 'I was proud of you. You did well.'

'You were?'

Caerl nodded. His father's sea captain was a dour fellow, and Godwin could not remember him speaking so kindly before.

'I always thought you didn't like me,' he said.

'I didn't,' Caerl said. 'You were a spoilt child.'

Godwin laughed. 'And now?'

'You're no longer a child,' he said, and gave Godwin a reassuring slap on the back.

Beorn had opinions about all the various peoples of England, and they were well represented here. Sudsexe men were, of course, the best of the best: stout and brave, and not so stupid they did not know when a battle was lost. Sudsexe women he approved of, even though they were not the most beautiful in the country. The most beautiful were from Dyflin, but they were the worst dressed women in Christendom, and they did not wash more than twice in their lives – when they were born and when they were laid out for the winding sheet.

East Anglians were there with their war chief, Ulfcytel, who carried the scars of his long battle with the Danes. They camped about his banner, which flapped at the door of his tent, a blue banner with a gold crown, in honour of St Edmund the Martyr. Beorn went over to swap stories with Ulfcytel's retainers. They were too thick to realise a battle was lost and thought nothing better than turning themselves into noble and heroic corpses.

'There are no old men among the East Engleas as a result,' he said confidently that evening as the Sudsexe men cooked simple cakes of bread on the hot hearth stones. 'While Cantebrigiescir is full of greybeards who left each battle faster than a hound could run.'

Next morning, once he had finished his morning piss, Beorn looked across the river and swore. 'Oh Jesus wept, look at that lot!'

A war band was pitching their camp about a hundred yards down the hill. They were short and dark, with stout and shaggy piebald ponies, round shields slung on their backs, spears in their hands.

'Walsh!' he said. 'They stink worse than an unwashed

hermit! God knows why Ethelred insists on taking their oaths. They'd steal a brass button from a toothless beggar. Count how many horses they have. I'll bet you they have twice as many by morning.'

They waited for two weeks, eating beans and roots as the fyrd gathered from all the lanes and byways of free England. By the end of Lent Portemeadow was crammed with war bands and they were ready to ride before the Danes could escape.

Good Friday was dull as puddle-water, with prayer and fasting and endless readings from the gospels of Mark, Luke and John.

Caerl put his hand to Godwin's shoulder. 'Your father would be so proud if he could see you here.'

'Really?' Godwin said, but he did not feel like listening to stories about his father yet. There was little point in picking at scabs. He had done that as a child and had learnt that picked scabs bleed.

That evening Prince Athelstan gathered the young men of the Wild Hunt for a sacred and private mass. They were glad to see each other again and renew their friendship. There were many tales to tell as they shared loaf and titled jug, and hall joy shone on their faces. As they broke the day's fast, Athelstan gave out fifty pewter badges with his personal symbol: the stag. They were like the relic badges you could buy in Canturburie from St Hilda's shrine, but they marked them out as the princes' men.

'Many years ago we decided to fight against the Danes. We were the pebble that began to roll. This great fyrd happened because of you, brave brothers. We fought before anyone else dared to stand up. Rise! Drink! The Wild Hunt shall ride again!' he called out.

Edmund declared that each badge-bearer should make an oath.

'I swear that I shall drive out the Danes or die in the attempt,' Athelstan swore.

Edmund was next. 'I swear that if Knut comes within a spear's throw of me, I shall strike him dead. And if I come toe to toe with him, I shall kill him in combat.'

Most of the oaths were about killing Danes and got a little repetitive by the end, so when it was Godwin's turn he put his hand on his sword and waited for silence before declaring, 'I swear that I will uphold the laws of England against any Dane!'

He silently added an addendum between him and God: and I shall see Eadric dead.

Later that night white-robed monks went from war band to war band carrying enormous books with pictures of astonishing blues and greens that gleamed with leaf of gold. The books had a magical aura to them. The monks read passages from the gospels. Overhead, the sky darkened. The low clouds were brooding and foreboding, and the monks' chanting was heavy with the thousand-year-old suffering of their Lord. Fervent prayers they sent Heavenward. Godwin prayed, and in Contone Kendra prayed fervently too.

As twilight fell, thunder rolled in the Chiltern Hills. Doom! it struck, and sharp lightning, as jagged as an upturned tree, smote the high peaks. Doom! it rolled, and through the camp a man flogged himself with knotted cord, calling on them to smite the Antichrist. Behind him a madwoman raved that the Great Tribulation was come, the 'Days of Vengeance' of which Christ had spoken. 'Now from the sixth hour there was darkness over all the land unto the ninth hour. And about the ninth hour Jesus cried with a loud voice, saying, "*Eli, Eli, lama sabachthani?*" My God, my God, why hast thou forsaken me?'

At evensong no bells were rung, no voices sang, and a deep gloom spread over the land as the light slipped quickly from the grasp of the overcast day. Church altars were stripped of cross and candlesticks and embroidered cloths. Night fell, final and complete, and campfires were lit against the dark. As though in answer, the stars began to glimmer in the Heavens and Godwin clenched his right hand and felt power and fury surge though him, as if he was one of the Angels of Vengeance.

Hard they rode through Holy Saturday, but always ahead of them flew the king's banner, a White Dragon on a field of scarlet. Harder yet went the messengers of the king, bidding provisions, horses and reinforcements be made ready for his coming.

Gamal, the king's door ward, was one of them. 'Make ready,' he bade the men he passed. 'The king means to come against the Danes with great speed and force.'

At Northantone Godwin camped with Alderman Ulfcytel and his grim company of axe- and swordsmen, each one mailed in a dull coat of grey links. The English slept as soundly as the carven images in the cathedral chapels, but in the churches of Northantone dark-cowled monks did not sleep. In the hours of deepest darkness, a single candle was lit and seemed to float uncarried into the unlit church. '*Lumen Christi!*' the choirs sang as glowing tapers went from candle to candle till the yellow light blazed and the monks lifted their voices: '*Exultet iam angelica turba caelorum . . .*'

> *Rejoice, heavenly powers! Sing, choirs of angels! Exult, all*
> *creation!*
> *Jesus Christ, our king is risen!*

Sound the trumpet of salvation! Christ has conquered!
Glory fills you!
Darkness vanishes for ever!

The monks were still singing joyfully when again in darkness Godwin's men saddled fresh mounts, took the street known as Wæcelinga – an ancient way, broad and hard and well tended, so wide that twenty men could ride abreast.

Here, in the eastern part of Mercia, the Danish influence was still strong in language and manner and custom. Here men ate cake, not buns; walked on legs, not shanks; washed their faces in becks, not brooks; and in the morning when the hens were laying, they ate eggs, not eyren.

They reached Liguera Ceastre on the third day. Black storm clouds thundered over the great mass of the blue and far-off Bredon Hill. The bells were ringing for evensong as they clattered through the ancient gates; abbey monks were chanting in clear and joyous voices, '*Deus, in adjutorium meum intende. Domine, ad adjuvandum me festina*' – O God, come to my assistance. O Lord, make haste to help me.

The Saxon mint town still huddled within the square Roman ditch and walls that King Edgar the Peaceful had strengthened, but to the north and east sprawled the unplanned Danish town, and it was there that Morcar greeted Ethelred with much pomp and ceremony and as many fresh mounts as his people could gather. Comb-makers went from table to table selling their wares, and young girls gave out sprigs of borage for courage, while the leadsmiths had smelted the little bronze St Cuthbert pendants that the men of Danelaw loved to wear and a heap of simple pewter crosses for the southerners. Morcar spoke for all his people, as honestly as he could, and begged forgiveness.

Ethelred put his hand on Morcar's head. 'Do not fear, good thegn. We have all been tested and found lacking. Will you ride with me and strike a blow against our Danish tormentors?'

Morcar could barely believe his ears. 'I will, lord.'

'Good. Then welcome, for we have all suffered tribulations, and God has been gracious to me, so I have pardoned all crimes against me.'

Godwin watched the exchange with incredulity, then shook Morcar's hand and made him welcome.

That night they rested in Alderman Elfhelm's hall, and Godwin walked around and remembered the kind man who had sat him on his knee, long ago, when he was young. He looked up at the smoke-stained rafters, where threads of soot wafted above the fire, and took in all that had happened, and all who were missing. He brought them back to mind: his father and mother, Leofwine, of course, Blecca and Hemming and all those who had lost their way. He gathered them round him, as a man will gather friends, and held them close. Their ghosts stood over him as he slept that night. And watched. And waited, lest danger come creeping.

In the morning the air was bright and damp from night showers.

'Eadric is here,' Caerl said as they filed out of the gates on to the road north.

Godwin could see Eadric's banner, but he refused to look at the man.

'Has he seen us?'

They couldn't tell.

'Maybe we should hang well back,' Beorn said.

'I will not,' Caerl said and Godwin rode with him.

North they pressed, but the Danes would not give battle.

The princes rode at the head of the English host, and there were many places where they crested a ridge or rounded a wood and expected to see the Army drawn up across the road, but each time they saw nothing, and the fastest riders came back with no news of the Danes, except the ruin of their passing.

'They've ridden past us,' Caerl said that night with grim laughter. 'They'll be burning Wincestre before the week is out. Contone will see Danes long before us.'

Men began to look behind them, and a pessimistic air spread, as if they feared that they would be caught up in another of Ethelred's great defeats. Godwin's exultation began to dip into worry and despair, and he lay under a hedge that night and slept fitfully.

Next morning he woke to the sound of horses. Scouts were coming in and Godwin leapt up to hear their news.

'Gainesburg is burning! The Danes are retreating to their ships with all the speed they can manage.'

Edmund blew his horn to wake the men. 'Up!' he shouted. 'Ride. Before Knut escapes!'

By that evening they had ridden more than thirty miles, north and east, hoping to catch the Danes before they could slip out of the Hymbre. A dusty haze hung in the air, and the evening light lingered as they drew their exhausted mounts onto a ridge of the wolds and looked all about them.

There were fine views to either side. On the right, green salt marshes gave way to the deep-blue North Sea. On the left, the view stretched all the way across the Vale of Lincolia to the Pennines, and between the foothills lay a flat patchwork of long strip fields, curving gently at either end. Before them the wolds fell gently away to the flat coastal plains. Evening shadows stretched across the land, and the last light of the day caught for a moment on the church tower at Bereton.

Godwin's knowledge north of Wæcelinga Stræt was patchy indeed, but Morcar pointed north-west, to where the land faded into haze. 'Half a day's ride ahead, the Liguera Ceastre and Lincolia roads meet at a town named Donecastre. All the land between Donecastre and Eurvic is impenetrable marsh, so the road loops far to the west, following the foothills of the Pennines. It's a wild place of dales and rivers, but there is shelter for travellers at Tatescastre.'

'And where is Eurvic?'

'It is a day's ride from Tatecastre, which is three days' ride from here.'

Godwin stared in silence. He had never thought to travel so far north, and now none of it made much sense to him.

'And what is that?' he said, pointing straight ahead.

'That is the great firth of the Hymbre.'

The water was dark and flat. It was approximately five leagues distant. Between them and it, the land was flat and featureless, except for a brief patch of trees and houses. Godwin looked from west to east and saw no Army, but kept his mouth shut.

They all stopped and looked. And saw nothing.

'Where are they?' Edmund said.

Athelstan had barely spoken the entire day's ride, except to drive them forward. No man wanted to say it before him, and Godwin looked from west to east and back again three times before Athelstan said anything.

'I do not see them,' he said.

Everyone waited.

It was Edmund who spoke. 'Two horses have died already, and we do not have spare mounts.'

Athelstan nodded.

'I think we should rest and push on to the Hymbre. Perhaps

we can catch the Danes before they make the open sea,' Edmund said.

Athelstan nodded again. His voice was dry with dust. 'Let us rest for a few hours and then ride again,' he said, and coughed. 'If we let the damned Danes escape, then all this will have been for nothing.'

They rode quickly down through the sloping pastures and made a brief camp in the first village on the flat. Godwin was asleep before his head touched his rolled-up cloak, but heavy clouds passed over them, hurrying in from the west, and sprinkled them with rain.

They were not there more than three hours before Athelstan had his men up again. Godwin felt as if he had put his head on the pillow and then sat straight back up. A ruddy crescent moon rose over the sea in the east. He yawned and rubbed gritty sleep from his eyes, and leapt up into his saddle.

All the lanes about led inexorably towards the ferry crossing of Bereton, where the stone church tower stood high above the spring trees. Their horses milled around at the muddy shoreline, as if they wanted to ride out over the waves and chase the Danes all the way back across the sea.

The ferry-master ran out to greet them with a branch of may buds in his hands as a sign of peace. 'You have come,' he said. 'Bless you all. You have come!'

'Where are the Danes?' Edmund demanded. 'The king has brought the whole country out. A mighty fyrd rides behind us. We are here for battle.'

The man's face fell. 'You are too late, lords. The Danes came down the river two days past. It took two days for their fleet to pass. They have gone with all their ships, back out to sea.'

'Which way did they sail?' Athelstan said.

'South,' the man said.

South. The word fell heavily among them. They had ridden north, and the Danes had sailed south.

Athelstan said nothing, but you could tell from the way he sat in the saddle that he was broken by the news: humbled and furious and broken.

News came slowly to Contone. Without the menfolk the place seemed to lose its direction, though the routines continued in a dull and predictable way. Kendra kept herself busy, and each afternoon she put her stool outside the door of the hall, so she could look out for men who might bear tidings.

At the end of April, news came that the king had ridden north from Oxeneford to fight the Danes. But then there was nothing. No news filled each day. Newslessness provoked their imaginations: the Danes had won; the English had been routed; Godwin had been slain.

It was four days after the first full moon of May that tidings finally came. At Contone the ale-wife was chewing on a crust of bread when Kendra burst into the brew house. 'We've beaten them!' she said, and it took a moment for the words to register.

'Have we?' Agnes said. 'Are you sure?'

'Two monks are in the hall now,' Kendra said. 'They come from Wincestre. They say that the king has driven the Danes from the north. The Army has fled before the king.'

The Alewife was all in a fluster. They'd beaten the Danes! she thought, and wrung her pudgy fingers with delight and anticipation. Victory meant feasting, and there hadn't been a grand feast in Contone since she was a little girl. She remembered those days with nostalgic delight. 'Well, they'll need ale, if I know anything of men!'

At Athelingedean, Edmund's grandmother lay on her death bed and heard the news with a sigh of relief. She had a special gift sent to the monks at Leomynstre of a hundred and twenty fresh Ethelred pennies, their minted edges sharp and clear. They had ETHELRED REX ANGLO on one side, EDPINE MO GRAN on the other, with the words 'To the good monks at Burne, to pray to the Lord, and express our gratitude for our victory.'

The old lady consoled herself that she had schooled her grandsons, and it seemed as if all her labours had paid off. Her days were short and she closed her eyes and crossed herself and thanked God personally, as if He had done this just for her, so that she could depart this world in peace.

The money was taken and prayers were added, and in Heaven Christ and his Father heard. But victory was measured in the numbers of enemy slain, and there were few Danish corpses buried that spring who had not died of flux or ague.

In the May fields at Contone the corn grew knee-high. The first crop of hay was cut. The king had turned south. Kendra settled back into the routine of sewing and spinning, eating and praying.

'Don't you wish you'd ridden north?' Kendra said to Brunstan.

'Bah!' he said. 'No. I couldn't ride so hard. A day's ride is far enough for me.'

'They have won,' she said.

'Good. I am glad for them. I look forward to hearing their tales. I bet they'll have grown with the telling.'

Kendra smiled. She was brim full of expectation and kept herself busy imagining what they would say and the great deeds they would have done.

'Mistress Agnes has you working?' Kendra said.

'That she does.'

'Where today?'

'Brooms,' he said. 'From the hazel thickets in the top fields.'

Brunstan took the sickle and the twine with him, with a pot of ale. There were many hazel coppices in the high fields. He worked hard that day, was happy to have been left behind at Contone. He had never been a warrior, and had never been much of a seaman either. He liked woods and fields and good hard earth beneath his feet. There was work and company about the manor, constant food in the hall, warmth and conversation and shoulders to rub up against.

The next day he climbed further up into the high fields with a scythe to cut the late hay. Agnes's son, Godmaer, followed him with a long piece of grass in his mouth, and his hands in his pockets. He went slowly with his twisted foot.

'Come on, you lazy bugger!' Brunstan said.

Godmaer grinned and hurried to catch up.

The sun was hot that morning. Brunstan wiped the sweat from his eyes on the back of his sleeve and straightened his stiff back.

Godmaer was supposed to be raking the hay out to dry, but Brunstan turned and couldn't see him.

'Oi!' he shouted. 'Club foot never stopped a man working with his hands.'

Godmaer appeared over the bank that kept livestock from the forest. He was still chewing his grass stem. Brunstan didn't know why he had to have this battle with him.

'Are you going to do an ounce of work today?'

The boy chewed his grass and strolled towards him.

That morning armoured men rode through the Weald. Their harnesses jangled. They carried spears and shields, had violence in their hearts. They were not king's men, and any who saw them stopped and felt a prickle of fear, but the alarm faded as it was apparent that the horsemen were passing them by.

A milkmaid sat on the paddock fence in a high stead and saw the riders passing beneath, spurring their horses down towards Contone. A shepherd stood in the high fields, where he was herding sheep for the first shearing, saw the riders and thought for a moment that it was Godwin returned. But they did not see him and passed on, taking the path through the high pastures that led to the hall. Through the field where Brunstan scythed.

Brunstan's back was damp with sweat and he paused when he felt the thunder of hooves through the dry earth. He looked up. His eyesight was not good. He leant on his scythe and put up his hand to shield it from the sun.

'Greetings,' he called out. 'This is Godwin's land. There is no hunting here.'

'We've not come hunting,' the lead man said. He pulled his horse up as he approached. It stamped sideways, slowing to a trot, biting its bridle and tossing its head. The rider was a thick-necked man with bright orange hair and freckles. He was the ugliest man Brunstan had seen.

'No?'

'No.' The orange-haired man drew his sword. He kicked his horse, drove her straight at Brunstan. Brunstan ducked, but he was no warrior and ducked too late. The yard of steel broke his skull as if it were as fragile as a hen's egg. He was dead before he hit the ground with a sickening thud.

Godmaer finished his crap and wiped himself with moss from the tree trunk next to him. He stepped away from the smell and hauled up his trousers, tied the cord that knotted them and walked out into the field.

He was just in time to see the horsemen ride up towards Brunstan. He spat the chewed grass stalk from his mouth, and sauntered forward. Steel flashed in the sunlight. Brunstan fell dead, and then the horsemen looked up and Godmaer realised they were looking at him.

Shit! he thought, and turned and hobbled desperately down the hill as the horses thundered after.

Two of the farm men saw Godmaer as they rested under a shady tree and ate a meal of bread and cheese. He was hurtling down the hill, arms flailing as he leapt through stubble and fence and stone. The two men had been sharpening shears. They were slow-thinking. They saw the horsemen and they saw the boy and they stood up and scratched their heads.

They'd never seen him run so fast.

'That's Agnes's son,' one of the men said.

'He's being chased,' said the other.

'That he is.'

'What's he done now?'

They shook their heads and tutted. The two men hung for a moment in indecision, but chasing a lame boy, however lazy, with spear and sword went against their sense of right and wrong and they scowled.

'He's not going to make it,' one of the men observed. And it was true. The horsemen rode up to and over God-maer. Once they had passed, his body lay still among the cut grass

And then the horsemen saw them and the two men realised that they were next.

*

Kendra was sitting in the herb garden when Agnes ran around the side of the hall, her skirts hitched up, like a terrified hen.

'Reavers have come! Hide!' she said. 'Do not come out! You have no idea what heathen men will do!'

Kendra ran into the brew house and hid herself behind a barrel of ale. She smeared her face with dirt from the floor. She felt the horsemen ride into the cobbled yard, felt her heart beating and heard her breath coming in quick gasps.

'Who are you!' she heard Agnes shout, but then there was a slap and Agnes screamed.

Kendra burrowed lower. She wished she'd found a better hiding place. Moments passed. She heard voices outside. The brew-house door banged open. She held her breath, crouched lower. A grinning face leered over her, and a hairy hand reached out to grasp her. He took a handful of hair and dragged her out.

'Look here!' he said.

Kendra gritted her teeth. She kicked and thrashed and tried to bite the man, and he shook her violently and threw her through the doorway. She banged her elbow and the pain ricocheted up her arm as she fell to the ground. He grabbed her hair again and swung her into the yard.

Men laughed. Another hand grasped her arm and pulled her to her feet. He tore her clothes, and when she tried to push his hands away, he hit her, and she went limp with shock.

'Have you no shame?' Agnes demanded. It was all a blur but Agnes was there and so it was all right. Agnes pulled the man away. She grabbed Kendra and Kendra fell against her. 'Touching a girl who has been promised to Christ! The Devil must have got into you. Have you no shame?'

Kendra tried to look like a girl about to take oaths. The man laughed and spat as if Kendra was not worth his attention and Agnes bundled her away from the confusion as the men swirled about, seizing anything of value.

'Hurry!' Agnes's hands shoved Kendra away. Her hands said it all: Hurry, hurry, hide!

'Heh!' a voice shouted.

Agnes kept shoving. They were running towards the chapel. The chapel bell was ringing alarm. It stopped abruptly. Someone must have killed the bell man.

Agnes kept shoving.

'You!'

The orange-haired man grabbed Kendra's arm.

Agnes stood between them. He threw her to the side, pulled Kendra away. 'Here's one!' he said.

He dragged Kendra to the brew-house and threw her on to the table. Kendra kicked and struggled, but he was too strong for her. He pulled her towards him and tugged at his trousers. Then she stopped looking at him. She stared at the wall. The board where spoons and knives hung. She thought for a moment of reaching for a knife, but the man was huge and this had happened before and she knew the best thing was to lie still and pray for it all to be over.

The orange-haired man finished with a grunt.

'That's for Brihtric,' he said, and slapped her so hard she fell off the table. She spat blood from her mouth, pretended to be dead.

'Let her be, you beast!' Agnes said. 'Off with you now. You've done your worst.'

The man looked around as if wondering if he had really done his worst and decided not.

'Orc!' he shouted. 'Orm!'

Agnes and Kendra did not wait to see who these men were.

Kendra pulled her clothes round her and ran barefoot over the stone and ruts, Agnes ran with her.

They reached the chapel with a sigh of relief and fell in a hot heap on the chapel floor.

Christ watched with his bold painted eyes. His face was stony and impassive. Stern or alarmed, it was hard to tell. Or deeply compassionate and caring.

'Beasts!' Agnes said. 'Bastards!'

Kendra let her talk. She was exhausted, and relieved to still be alive.

She dabbed the back of her hand to her lip. It had split, and her cheek felt swollen. She refused to sit down. She got up and spat out her blood, stood and waited with the other womenfolk, watched with horror as the men put Godwin's hall to flame. Someone had brought Godmaer down from the field. He was alive, but only just. Agnes took her son and cradled his bloody head in her lap, laid him out on the altar.

'Godmaer!' she whispered in his ear as she felt for his pulse and her skirts became sticky with his blood. 'Do not go, my child.'

Agnes promised many things, as she had on nights when he was a child tormented by fever, or haunted by night spirits, but the cut in his head was deep and the blood flowed faster than Kendra could wipe. They all stood around and looked on as his skin grew paler and paler and his pulse weakened. Soon it was clear that he had gone.

The horsemen did their worst.

It was a long while before the women dared to come out. Serving men lay dead. They gathered the bodies up, laid them down gently, as if putting them to sleep.

They were still alive. They were the lucky ones. They comforted each other, watched in horror as Wulfnoth's hall was devoured by red and yellow flames. The fire was too far gone to stop. All they could do was stand and watch as it burned. It had been a dreadful day. They all began to weep and cry and mourn, and Heaven swallowed the bitter smoke.

BOOK II

CHAPTER ONE

Overmod

It was July before Godwin arrived back at Contone. Summer had reached its peak and the woods and fields were dressed in deepest green, the sheep lay in the shade of trees, the meadows were bright with insects and flowers. His apple-brown stallion walked firmly forward.

Godwin had grown. He looked older and bigger. Two thick gold bands clung to his arm, and he wore a silver belt about his waist. His blue eyes were hard as clenched fists as he looked at the ruin of his father's hall: briars and singed grass, a charred square where home had been.

Godwin came alone. There was no one there to greet him. No kind words or gentle hands, none of the faces he had hoped to see. Inside the hall, the hearth was overhung with ember-scarred beams, the horn-curved gables were charred ruins. Wind whistled where men once sang; pale ash smothered the benches and high table where the gold-giver sat, and men passed the harp from hand to hand. Walls that once enclosed brave warriors, bright with gold and the joy of victory, now lay in blackened mounds.

Fate had broken it. A fool he had been to fare north without leaving protection for his folk. Godwin heard a door open. It came from the direction of the brew-house. He turned to see Kendra walking over to greet him, barefoot with her shawl pulled over her head and shoulders. She stopped ten feet away from where his stallion stood, shaded her eyes and looked up at him.

'You have returned,' she said.

'Greetings,' Godwin said. He slid from the saddle. His throat was tight with fury, his face set hard.

Kendra's hair was unbound. The wind caught a lock and threw it across her face. With a single finger she pushed it back behind her ear. 'You have heard,' she said.

Godwin nodded. He turned back to the branded square. He had more than heard; he had seen.

Godwin's men stayed at the lower hall in Harditone. Many families had moved lower down the valley, but a few brave souls had remained, Kendra and Agnes among them.

'Who would look after your father's hall?' Agnes said later, but it seemed to Godwin that she was staying to look after Kendra, who refused to leave.

'This is a good place,' Kendra said, and felt a wave of emotion at the thought of leaving. 'I wandered long before I found it. I will not be driven away.'

That evening they sat in the barn. A low blaze smouldered. Agnes threw kitchen scraps on; the smoke was harsh and acrid. Anger burnt within Godwin. Shame and fury entwined like rods of steel and iron. Look what happened while you laughed and feasted at the victor's table!

Overmod, the poets called it: hubris.

Kendra told the tale. 'They came in daylight,' she said, 'like king's men. A big man led them. No one came to help us, not from Meredone or Harditone. They fled. All who stood against them were cut down.'

Godwin nodded. His anger glowed like a well-blasted fire, the coals turning from grey to a baleful red, like a dragon's eye, now orange and yellow, till they glowed almost white with rage. 'Tell me who is left.'

Kendra listed the dead instead: Brunstan, Godmaer, Deor, Hareth . . . It was a long list.

'Anything else?'

Kendra paused. 'They were led by a man with orange hair.'

Godwin caught the look in her eye. 'A big man?'

She nodded. 'Ugly. Brutal. He was their leader. He was one of Eadric's men.'

Godwin knew the man.

'He said "This is for Brihtric."'

'Did he?'

Godwin remembered when he was a boy and had hidden in the Weald. A baby had been born nine months later and drowned in the beck, sent to Christ blameless.

'Anything else?' he said.

Kendra shook her head. 'No.'

There were new notches on Næling's edge. Godwin ground them out with long rasping strokes. He worked out every nick and dent, oiled the blade till it gleamed red with firelight. They had come from the Weald. Men must have aided them. He imagined his foe waiting in the dark, haunted forest, planning their revenge.

Heroes laughed at moments like these, but Godwin was no hero. He took this personally. It cut to the quick, like a well-honed knife that butchers flesh from bone. His folk had sworn him service and protection, and now they lay dead or in the arms of his enemies. His men sat around. He had told them the tale and their hearts burnt with fury.

'They could be anywhere,' Caerl said.

Godwin called all the bereaved men together at the stone cross at Hiddeswrthe. He climbed to the top of the stone and put his hands out for silence. The crowd waited expectantly. Godwin's face was humourless. He did not mention Eadric, but addressed what was common among them all.

'For too long we have suffered. We have suffered under a cowardly king. We have suffered under the Danes. We have suffered under unfair taxes, which have been raised too late, when all the damage has been done. And now brigands and lawless men have set upon our homes while our fighting men rode north against the Danes. Can we trust Ethelred? No! There is no law unless we impose it. Let us take spear and fire into the Weald and rid ourselves of this den of thieves.'

Men knew the names of Orc and Orm. They were two brothers, a thegn's sons, who had turned outlaw years before and had earnt an evil name among the people of the Weald. The iron-smelters – honest but wary folk – were glad to help. They pointed deep into the forest.

'They are cruel men. They have many camps, but they were staying at Grim's Ring a week ago.'

'And where is that?'

They pointed. 'Yonder. A summer's day's ride.'

Godwin rode hard. His men galloped behind him. They spotted the ring of trees from miles off. It was a bald dome that peeped over the forest. The huts of the rough reaver camp were all roofed with turf to stop raiders burning them in their sleep. The place was deserted, but the horse dung still steamed.

'There has been a hasty departure,' Caerl said. 'They cannot be far off. Look – these footprints are still filling with water.'

In the main house, a low fire burnt in the hearth.

The brothers fled from Sudsexe into Sudrie, Sudsexe again and then Cantware. Godwin followed them from camp to camp, relentless as a starving wolf.

At the end of a frustrating fortnight they caught the reavers red-handed, in a camp deep within the Weald. There were seventeen of them. A pitiful bunch, like servants tricked out in armour, no match for Godwin's mailed and mounted and murderous retainers. There had been an argument and the two brothers had come to blows. Orm lay dead, but Orc was there. He was a short, thin man with dark hair and clear blue eyes. He had been wounded in the fight, and his face was pale, his arm cradled against his ribs, the sling stained with fresh blood.

Towards him strode Godwin. He was as grim as the Archangel Gabriel. He stood over the man and glared down at him.

'You burnt my hall. Who put you to this evil work?' he demanded.

'No one,' the bastard spat.

Godwin struck him.

'Who put you to this?'

'No one,' the man said.

Godwin gripped his bleeding arm and his thumb dug in, as the nails had dug into Christ's palms and fixed him to the wooden cross.

Orc ground his teeth in agony.

'Is this Eadric's work?'

'Eadric who?'

'Who was the flame-haired man?'

'There was no flame-haired man.'

Godwin had no time for treacherous liars. He unsheathed his sword, grasped the man's head and struck it from his shoulders, tossed it into the thicket, where it caught and snagged and hung: a gruesome witness.

Næling was bare and bloodied as Godwin walked towards Orc's men. He was breathing heavily. The summer leaves were a wall of green behind his back. Gnats swirled in the air above his head.

He spoke in a quiet voice. 'Tell me what have I done to you that you should bereave me so? Who put you up to this? Was it Eadric? Who was the man with the red hair?'

The men said that they had nothing to do with any of them. Godwin kicked one of the cringing men and lifted his face to look him in the eye.

'You choose to bereave me?' he demanded, but the man shrank back and clawed at his legs.

Another man blabbed, 'I do not know of Eadric, but the red-haired man was named Offa.'

Godwin fixed that name in his heart. He let the man go and turned away.

'Mercy! We were honest men once!' they wept.

But they were outlaws and murderers and thieves, and he had no mercy. Honest men indeed!

'And whores were virgins once!' Godwin said, and spat into the ground and turned his back. 'Hang the lot of them,' he said in disgust. 'Let Christ sort out the guilty.'

When Godwin returned to Contone, his mind was troubled. He walked down to the streamside, stripped off and waded into the blurred and stony pool.

It was a quiet spot with an overhanging oak tree and a wattle fence to keep the cattle from trampling the water, which fell clear and light over the stones. It was chill to the touch. Godwin's skin seemed to shrink about him, like loving arms. He shut his eyes, put his head back and let it float lightly on the water, his hair caught by the currents that flowed between the rocks, trailing downstream like yellow weeds.

Godwin looked up through the green oak leaves to where the sun shone in the blue sky. He and his brother had come here to spy on the girls on their bathing day. They'd got a beating for their troubles, but they'd come again.

It struck Godwin as strange. He had always imagined Leofwine older and wiser and more knowledgeable than himself, but Leofwine had only been twelve when he had died and Godwin was seventeen now and he felt notched and gnarled, as tough as old roots.

Godwin lay still on his back. Summer sunlight dappled green light all about him. His skin carried scars, and he was proud of each one, could name the moment he received them, and the moment he had dealt a blow in return. As the breeze whispered through the boughs, a few beams fell straight through the canopy and he shut his eyes against their light, ducked down under the water, came up refreshed.

Godwin's clothes hung on a low gorse bush, waiting for him to give them shape. He looked at them. They were fine garments. The clothes a prince might wear: with silk and silver embroidery around the hems and cuffs, and the finest calfskin shoes. When his skin was clean he strode out. His broad shoulders and narrow waist shed droplets of water. He sat on the grass and dried himself before dressing and returning to the hall.

'Edmund thinks I should marry,' Godwin said to Kendra that evening.

It was hard to read from her reaction what she thought.

'And do you want to marry?'

'Of course,' he said, as if it was as obvious as buying a sword or a prize stallion. 'It is just a matter of when.'

'Does he have someone in mind for you?'

'I doubt it,' Godwin said. 'The virtuous daughter of some grand family, with wide hips and broad shoulders. She'll have to give good strong sons.'

Godwin had been unusually glum since he had returned, so she was glad to see the glimmer of humour in his eyes.

'His grandmother died,' she said.

'I know.'

'It was good she died before she heard.'

Neither of them spoke for a long time.

'So,' Kendra asked after a while, 'what happened in the north?'

Godwin sighed. He was tired of telling the tale. The whole country had mourned when they had heard that Athelstan, the king's eldest son, had died; Ethelred's children were an unlucky lot.

'Were you there?'

Godwin nodded.

'He knew he was dying. He made his peace with God. He spoke well to all of us and charged us with defending England should the Danes come again. He petitioned the king to return my father's lands. I had the charter sent to Cicestre.'

'And the Danes?'

Godwin drew in a deep breath. 'Well, there was no great battle. The Danes would not fight.' Godwin started to say something else, but then he stopped. 'We stood on the banks of the Hymbre and they escaped.'

'They landed at Sandwice.'

Godwin nodded. He had heard. Knut had landed at

Sandwice, demanded a tax, cut the hands and noses and ears off all the hostages that men had given him, and then sailed home. Good riddance, he thought. He hoped it was the last he would hear of him.

'I never thought men could be so difficult. We crossed the whole country. We were eager for battle. And then there was no battle, and everyone began to complain about the plunder. How could they reward their followers? Men brawled before the king!'

Godwin shook his head. 'Eadric wanted Ethelred to punish Morcar's folk for sheltering the Danes, but Edmund and Athelstan prevailed. Ethelred had forgiven all crimes, and sworn a heavy oath, and he did not forget it. But the people of Lindesi in Lincoliascir were not so lucky. It was said that they were planning to ride out with the Danes. They were like the scrap of meat that stops starving dogs from eating each other. So we ravaged the land.'

'Ravaging is always the price of weakness,' Kendra said.

Godwin paused. He missed the meaning in Kendra's words. 'It is true. The fyrd needed to fight and loot and the Danes robbed us even of that. It was during the ravaging,' Godwin said with a heavy sigh, 'that Athelstan was wounded.'

Kendra looked at him now.

Godwin shrugged. 'His horse shied from a burning house, he landed badly and the next morning he took ill.'

'It's a strange chance,' Kendra said. 'Athelstan dies and then your hall is burnt.'

Godwin shrugged. Such was the world: a spinning wheel of chance and ill and cruelties.

'So Edmund is now heir?'

'Well, certainly not Eadwig!' Godwin laughed. 'But Edward is fourteen now. The queen spent the whole time dressing him up in weapons and armour and parading him about the court, saying that he was almost a man.'

Godwin seemed strangely unaffected. But if it was so, it was because he was numb. Men he loved died too quickly. It made him wary of feeling for the pain it brought.

'If there had been something I could have done, I would have done it. It was chance and a fire and a skittish horse. Athelstan took three days to die. He met his end bravely. He gathered us all round and spoke to us. He returned my father's lands. He raised me up.'

'Maybe he saw something in you that he admired.'

Godwin laughed at the idea but Kendra was serious, and Godwin laughed at her.

'What would a prince admire in me?'

'Much,' she said, but he did not feel it.

'No,' he said, and lay down with the other men in an open area along the side of the barn. And slept.

Despite the gloom about Athelstan's death, Ethelred was not short of sons and the mood in the country was good, for Swein was dead and the Danes had been driven off and there was peace in the land at last.

Swein's family had a reputation for internecine fighting and they all hoped that Swein's two sons would waste their strength in a vicious civil war and leave England in peace.

Peace. Prosperity. Hope. They were strange emotions, and men were not quite sure of what to do with them at first. They regarded them with curiosity and wonder, and for the first time that Godwin could remember, men began to look to the future. Beorn found a young girl from the bottom of the valley and rode to her father to ask to be betrothed. He tried not to smile, in case he frightened her. His cheeks were red, and his tongue licked the front of his teeth as he rubbed his hands together. Her father agreed to the marriage.

His betrothed had large breasts and fine haunches. He sat her on his knee on their wedding night, and when he was drunk he put his head back and laughed loudly, and then carried her off to the closet. He came out naked when he had done the deed, drank a horn of ale in one go, before he went back in and slammed the closet door behind him.

Godwin was laughing, but his mind was already turning to the work that needed to be done.

Kendra was not there the night of the wedding. She had started to keep to herself and it was Agnes who noticed, as she saw Kendra standing before the doorway to the brew-house: the shape of her stomach was unmistakable.

Agnes sat down and stood up, then sat back down again.

Kendra turned in confusion, saw the look in Agnes's face.

'You didn't tell me,' Agnes said.

Kendra folded her arms. She was not in the mood for being reproached.

'Oh Kendra,' Agnes said, 'what will you do?'

Kendra shrugged. She looked away and bit her lip to focus the pain.

'Does he know?'

'Godwin?'

Agnes nodded. 'About him?'

The orange-haired man.

'No,' Kendra said. 'You must not tell him.'

Agnes didn't understand.

'He is one of Eadric's men. If Godwin knew, he would try to take revenge.'

'He will take revenge anyway,' Agnes said.

'Good. I shall be glad. But I am his father's girl. If he knew, he would ride and Eadric would kill him.'

'So what will you do?'

Kendra didn't know. She had hoped to miscarry, but fortune had failed her.

'There are herbs,' Agnes said, 'that could rid you of it.'

Kendra put her hand to her belly. She did not think she could do that, but then she thought of a red-haired babe and felt a wave of nausea rise.

July was the name the monks gave to the seventh month, but in the country folk still called it Maedmonath, the month of the flowering meadows. That July was still and hot and uneventful. Godwin wasted no time in setting out the marks in the earth for a new raftered hall, larger than any men about had seen, with wide gables and steep eaves.

Workmen came, staked out the floor plan and started digging the holes into which the great wall timbers would be set. There were twenty great columns, and rooms within rooms, and enough space to sleep a hundred retainers. The size of the hall amazed people and it was like the day when Godwin was a boy and Wulfnoth had brought the great copper bell to the village chapel. Men came from three valleys away to marvel at what Godwin planned.

Mikelhal, they named it, even before it had been raised to the sky, the Great Hall.

Edmund and his royal retinue arrived at Contone late one evening as the sky slowly paled and the clouds began to darken. The men were dusty and thirsty. They drained the place of buttermilk and started on the ale before the oatcakes could be baked.

Everyone came to see Edmund Atheling. He was shorter than Kendra had imagined, but he had a roguish smile and he was a well-built youth, with a blond moustache and locks hanging down to his shoulders, in the manner of the Danes.

'So, brigands burnt Wulfnoth's hall,' he said, and he strode to where Godwin had set his new foundations.

It was on higher ground than the old, and the frame had already been raised and blessed by the priest. The journeymen were now plastering the wattle with a double layer of daub: a mix of sand and muck and straw.

'You'll rival the king's own,' Edmund teased, but he liked Godwin's ambition. 'I shall send the best carvers from Wincestre,' he said. 'Let them carve the pillars for you. Why, this shall be the finest hall in all Sudsexe! And if the hunting is half as good as you promised, we shall be regular visitors here.'

That evening Kendra carried the mead bowl and it was clear that the prince was as smitten as a daisy. His eyes followed her around the room, and when they were all deep into their ale, he leant in towards Godwin and said, 'Who is that girl?'

'She was with my father,' Godwin said.

'Was she indeed?'

'You should hear her sing,' Godwin said. 'Kendra!' he called out, 'I've been telling Prince Edmund what a fine singer you are.'

It was the first time Godwin had addressed her so directly, and Kendra paused before she answered. 'Have you?'

'Yes. Honour us, lady,' Edmund said.

Kendra smiled at Edmund and her eyes turned to him as she sang, and Godwin was jealous.

'She's a fine lass,' Edmund slurred, and Godwin agreed.

He laughed at himself and ignored the voice that whispered in his head, but when bedtime came Godwin looked for Kendra but she was nowhere to be seen, and his jealousy flared.

But there was Edmund, passed out, alone, among his retainers. Godwin had never seen a more welcome sight.

He stumbled out into the night and pissed into the darkness, looked around for her, as if he thought she might be sitting and staring at the stars. When he tried the latch of the women's bowyer, he found the door had been bolted.

'Kendra,' he slurred. 'Kendra, it is Godwin.'

He knocked and called in a gently rising voice, but there was no answer, and the door remained locked and silent. He fell into his bed and slept like a stone.

Loose skirts could no longer hide Kendra's condition and the very next morning Agnes took her by the arm and led her to one side.

'It is the Devil's bastard inside you,' she said. 'No man will want you if you give birth to a bastard. The bastard of one of Eadric's men, no less.'

She gave Kendra a brew of green water that stank of dandelion.

'Drink it!'

Kendra looked at the bowl, held her nose and tilted downed it in one go.

'And the dregs,' Agnes said.

Kendra grimaced as she finished the last drops.

Agnes looked at her as if she expected the bleeding to start there and then.

'How do you feel?'

'Sick,' Kendra said.

'Good,' she said, and gave her another.

Next morning Godwin came to the brew house. Agnes opened the door and he was a little surprised not to see Kendra.

'I am leaving,' he said.

'So suddenly?'

He nodded. 'Edmund wants me to go with him to meet the worthies of Sudsexe. Where is Kendra?'

'She's sleeping,' Agnes said.

'Ah, well, bid her farewell.'

Everyone wanted to talk to Godwin, seeing how close he was to the king's eldest living son, and Godwin never knew he had so many men who were related, however distantly, to his kin. After the meeting in Sudsexe, there was another meeting, and then Edmund learnt that the queen was holding a great Lammas Day Feast to mark Edward's coming of age.

'She's a bitch,' Edmund said. 'But we can play her game. How about we ride west and visit all the great men? Will you come with me?' he asked.

'Of course,' Godwin said, but he really wanted to be back home. He wanted to see the seasons change, and the woods fill with the golden light of autumn. He wanted to ride without care through the landscape of his youth.

A while later he said to Edmund, 'I have a better idea. How about we go to the queen's feast ourselves? She will not be able to refuse you, and what better way of stealing her thunder?'

So they rode to Exonia, where the queen greeted them with exaggerated pomp while her eyes flamed with fury.

The feast was a great success for Edmund and Godwin, and they took advantage of the occasion to visit all the great families of the far west. They crossed Dertemora, and the vast, heaving hills of Defenascir, which rolled away into the blue horizon, till they reached the meandering Tamar Valley and looked across the twists and turns into Cornwalia.

It was a handsome and sheltered valley, the dark green leaves just starting to dry and turn to yellow. Great flocks of migrating birds began to gather in the air and Edmund was delighted.

'There is excellent hunting here,' he said. 'We are just in time.'

Godwin had left men in charge of the hall's construction and promised to send word whenever he could, but news came irregularly. The manor was like a living thing; time healed it of the wounds that the reavers had caused. Lives went on. The seasons did not stop; the routines kept them all moving steadily forward. The harvest was brought in. Men married and died, children were born, and after Yuletide Kendra gave birth to a red-haired boy.

She suckled him with an odd mix of emotions, while Agnes stood over her and fretted.

'He looks well,' Agnes said. Her disappointment was palpable. 'Shall I take him away?'

Kendra nodded. Her gaze lingered on the red hair as the baby was wrapped tight in the swaddling cloth. Agnes picked him up and could not resist stroking his little nose as she paused at the door, babe in her arm, and looked back at Kendra.

'Rest!' she instructed. 'Sleep. I will be back before morning.'

'Where are you taking him?' Kendra said, but Agnes was gone and the door creaked shut. Kendra lay still but her stomach ached.

Next morning Agnes returned with cold on her skin and dew on her eyebrows and her whiskery cheeks and upper lip.

'He's gone,' she said. 'He has a good home. Don't you fret yourself.'

Godwin did not come home for there was so much to do, and Edmund was a driven man, preparing for the day when Ethelred died. Godwin sat on fine benches all across the country. He drank good wine and ale; listened to fabulous tales; sat shoulder to shoulder with great men; saw the most beautiful girls that England offered; and yet his thoughts turned more and more to Contone, and Kendra.

When he did finally come home it was an unexpected visit. The new hall had been raised, but the roof had not yet been laid across the rafters and the building site had a bleak and deserted air. Godwin looked at it, a lone figure on horseback. The new hall was surrounded by the tents of the carvers who had come in to replace the timber-cutters.

Godwin tethered the horse to a post, swung casually down and strode towards the hall doorway, where the boards opened on to a raw timber-framed structure of wattle and daub walls with a high gabled roof. It was bright and airy. Dry sawdust covered the floor, scented with oak and elm timbers.

The foreman wiped the grime from his hands as he went to greet him.

'You must be Lord Godwin,' he said. 'I knew your father. In fact I think I met you when I worked on his boat. You or your brother. You were just a nipper then.'

Godwin laughed. He remembered the day well. 'It was me,' he said and looked up at the roof. 'So this is like boat-building?'

'Ah,' the man said, and craned his neck, 'just like it, only upside down.'

They walked around and the man watched Godwin's reaction to all that he saw.

Godwin seemed pleased. 'And is all well?'

The man sniffed and looked at his work and sniffed in a manner that said, Yes, all very well indeed.

A few men glanced up and nodded as Godwin strode along the carvings. 'It looks very well indeed,' he said.

'And we'll be done by winter,' the foreman told him.

'Good,' Godwin said. 'Yes, it must be done by next Christmastide. I will throw a great feast. You and your men are welcome to come.'

Through the sound of adze and saw, and the plank-splitting hammer, Godwin heard a woman's voice. He turned to the doorway and saw Kendra. She looked thinner and paler than he remembered, and yet more womanly, as if there were a fuller curve to her hips and breasts.

She saw his silhouette and for a moment she thought she was looking at Wulfnoth as he was in his younger days. Then the man turned and it was Godwin.

He smiled and held out a hand. 'Greetings,' he said. 'You look quite the lady of the manor.'

Kendra put her hands to the keys hanging at her belt.

'Greetings,' she said. 'It is long since we saw you here. What news?'

Godwin let out a groan. He had had enough of news and gossip and speculation.

'Too much to tell,' he said. 'But the hall is looking fine.'

They walked outside to admire the workmanship. It was the largest hall in the Downs, larger even than the alderman's hall at Cicestre. Once they had completed a full circuit, there was a pause. Godwin had done what he had come for, but he wasn't quite ready to leave. He felt a little odd, being here without Edmund or the company of many young men.

Kendra watched with a smile on her face.

'Are you hungry?' she asked.

'I am.'

'Come, I have some fresh-brewed ale inside. Agnes's finest.'

They sat and drank and Godwin put his feet up on the brewhouse table and his shoulders relaxed. He sat there as evening fell.

'You should be off,' Kendra said, 'if you want to get to Wincestre before dark.'

Godwin smiled. 'I think Edmund can do without me. And I do not think I would make it by nightfall.'

There was a lengthy pause.

'So,' he said, 'tell me what has been happening this year.'

Kendra felt Agnes throw her a warning look, but she kept her eyes on Godwin.

'Well,' she said, and retold the year's happenings without mention of her child.

Godwin kept his feet up on the table and watched Kendra. She sat with a candle at her shoulder that threw a stark yellow light across her face. It had been a long time since he had been with a girl and as he watched her he felt a new kind of yearning: as much familial as it was sexual. He was drawn towards her; but the strength of his desire made him hesitant.

'You seem happy here,' he said.

'I am.'

'If any of the workmen gives you trouble, you must tell me, understand?'

'Thank you, Godwin,' Kendra said.

Agnes made herself scarce. The two were alone. They sat and talked until they ran out of things to say. Godwin was almost too attracted to her to speak of his feelings. The more charged the air between them, the more trivial their conversation. It petered out into the small details of the manor. They fell silent.

The silence grew. Godwin saw the fire reflected in her eyes, the shimmer of flames on her black hair and the rosy glow on her white cheeks. His mouth went dry as he watched her sit and look into the flames.

Godwin reached suddenly across and took hold of her hand.

His fingers were rough with calluses. Hers were as smooth as calf-skin.

'You're drunk,' she said.

'I am,' he said.

She pulled her hand away. 'I cannot,' she said.

'Why not?'

'Godwin,' she said and let out a great sigh. 'I wish I could, but I cannot.'

Godwin was not used to this. 'Am I beneath you?'

'No,' she said.

'Is it because of my father?'

'No,' she said.

'Then why?'

'People will talk,' she said.

'I do not care.'

'No. You don't understand.'

Godwin knelt at her feet. He was young and passionate and determined to understand.

She kept her eyes on him. 'When the men came . . .' Kendra began, then looked away and almost changed her mind. 'No, the reavers.' She paused, and that pause said a lot.

'Tell me,' he said. His voice was light and gentle.

'Well,' Kendra said. She was wary of telling, for the truth was a sharp blade. 'The red-haired man . . .' She paused again. 'There was a child.' She looked to see his reaction. 'It lived. As far as I know.' Godwin stroked her shoulder. 'Agnes took it away.'

At the end Godwin took a deep breath. He remained kneeling by Kendra's feet. He wished that she had told him before. 'You have weighed down my heart,' he said, 'for this was my fault. I should have left men to guard you all. I am sorry,' he said. 'Can you forgive me?'

Kendra started crying. She laughed at the same time. 'Forgive you?'

He nodded.

She hugged him. 'Of course I forgive you. I thought that you would hate me. I did not think that you would kneel and ask me to forgive you!'

'You will?' Godwin said. It pleased him more than he could say to see her smile and cry all at the same time.

'Come,' he said, and lifted her up. She was light in his arms as he carried her to the bed. Godwin lay down next to her in front of the dimming fire.

'Hush!' he whispered in her ear. 'Do not fear.'

And he gently loosened her girdle.

That year, 1014, ended peacefully. By Yuleide the hall at Contone was finished and was a wonder to behold. The cauldron chain, which hung from the high roof timbers, was twenty yards long. Men had never seen such a long link before. The beer vats could cheer a war band with prodigious thirst, the copper mash-pot could sit ten men inside, and the kitchen house was larger than most men's homes. Godwin was justifiably proud.

He stood as the walls were being whitewashed and imagined them ringing to the sound of the bravest war band a thegn ever led. He pictured the fairest maids in all the kingdom, the finest feasts, the best tales ever sung. He had spared no expense on the tapestries that hung over the wainscoting, and Prince Edmund had been true to his word: the carved pillars now writhed with living figures, birds, beasts and the divine jewel-work of twig and leaf.

The onset of winter was a time for staying inside, feasting and taletelling, and the crescent moon was still hanging in the morning sky when the guests arrived in all their finery on their finest steeds to celebrate the completion of the hall. There was white bread and butter, and though there was little meat, there was fish aplenty and pickled oysters. The fires were lit, the benches were adorned with laughing faces, and Godwin welcomed all the people from miles about to come and feast. Kendra was with him, with keys at her belt and ivy in her hair, and there was joy on both their faces.

CHAPTER TWO

The Red Road to Malmesberie

Two years passed in unfamiliar peace and prosperity. A new order returned. The land grew fat again with wool and trade and lawfulness. Bishops died and were replaced; fields were sown; April rained and in the ploughed strip fields new green shoots shimmered with hope and promise of full stomachs and a bounteous year.

Godwin turned eighteen and then nineteen. He was a good and well-respected lord, was generous with alms and at the Christmas feast. He was as strict with freemen as he was with thegns, men respected him for that: that he imposed the law on all, whether they were great or small.

Whenever Godwin returned from seeing the prince he brought gifts for Kendra: a necklace of polished amber beads, a gilt brooch, a belt of bright colours, rings of silver and a Celtic cross necklace he bought from some Norse traders in Cicestre.

One day he came back with a broad-chested bay mare. 'She is the gentlest creature in Christendom!' he said.

'Why do I need a horse?' Kendra asked.

'Because!'

'Because why?'

'Because I am away so much, while you are at home, and I thought you should see more of this country.'

Kendra was not keen. 'It was a long and cold journey that brought me to Contone. I think if I never left this place, I would remain content.'

But Godwin was used to getting his own way these days and did not take no for an answer. 'You shall come with me. There are places I want to show you, people I want you to meet.'

So Kendra travelled with Godwin and Edmund as they toured the country, but each time she returned to Contone the place seemed to have grown even more beautiful.

In the autumn of 1015 Godwin took Kendra to the coast. The larger the sky grew, the flatter the land, and Kendra looked up to the high shoulders of the Downs with a mixture of longing and wonder.

'Where are we heading?' she asked.

'This way,' Godwin said, and turned his horse towards the low, windswept headland, that thrust far out into the choppy grey waters.

Selsie lay a mile or so off to their left, still inside its square of pale grey Roman walls. The wind whipped Godwin's cloak and hair. He stopped his horse and looked out to sea. Kendra saw a scrap of driftwood – a piece of ship's planking, she guessed – and remembered when she had drifted about in the waves. She thanked God for bringing her to a good resting place.

Godwin led her to the end of the spit of land. The grassy dunes turned to sand, then shingle, and then shallow beach and finally to the restless slate-grey water. The waves swirled with gulls, and flecks of rain flew into their faces, and broad bladed grasses battled in tufts. To the right, a gannet stood on a hump of tussocky grass and spread its wings to the sea breeze – a Christ-like silhouette, crucified against the bright sky. A curlew called out. It made the wind bite more coldly. Godwin took no notice, but pointed into the water. His voice was thick with memory.

'Out there, at low tide, there are sandbanks. My father took me out one day to stand on them. We were knee-deep in water. "This is Cymen's shore," he told me.'

Godwin turned to look at her. His eyes were veiled. 'Cymen was the son of Ælle. This headland used to extend far out into the sea. I don't know why he took us there. I was only five years old, my brother a few years older. My father was proud of the place. Proud to set his feet where the old heroes stood. But it seems sad to me. Look!' he said and turned back to the shifting waters. 'The sea has taken the land from us, just as we took it from the Walsh.'

He stretched out a hand to her. 'This has been a blessed time,' he said. 'And if I died now, then I would be happy.'

'Why are you talking like this?'

Godwin smiled sadly. 'There is news,' he said. 'Knut and Harald have made peace. The Danish king has let it be known that in the spring he will lead a fyrd to England. They mean to drive Ethelred out.'

Kendra did not like the tone in his voice. 'Good. You have prepared for this for two years. Are you ready for them?'

'Yes,' he said. 'We are ready.'

Kendra's blue eyes were hard. 'Look at you! You are no boy now. If Knut returns, he will have a shock when he meets Edmund and Godwin in the battle play.'

Ethelred called for an Easter moot at Oxeneford in 1016. A gruff Euruic trader, in Russian fur cap, gave a complete account of the Danish preparations, which were well underway. Ethelred's health had not been good and he was tired and irritable, and sat sulkily.

269

'If they come we shall march against them,' he said.

Eadric was at his shoulder. 'Lord, how can we repel the enemy when there are traitors in our midst?'

'What traitors?'

Eadric did not like to point the finger. 'Well, there are some here who are related by marriage to Knut.'

Morcar was furious. 'And there are some of us who swore oaths to Knut,' he said. 'If you had a daughter, you would have married her to Swein's son faster than a cat in heat. I was there that day when our dear Ethelred had fled, and Swein was in my hall, and you came crawling on your belly like a worm, begging to be let in and allowed to swear your oath to Swein. And I buried the feud between our families and let you in! And how have you repaid my generosity? By continually spreading rumour and lies about me and my folk.'

Eadric said nothing. Rumours had their own life. They were difficult to kill, and their poison was as slow and sure as the inexorable decline of age.

'Swear your loyalty to King Ethelred, then,' Eadric said.

'Why should I?' Morcar said.

'To show that you are loyal.'

'I am loyal. I have sworn an oath. Why should the finger always be pointed at me?'

'You will not swear.'

'I will not do anything that you tell me to do, Eadric the Cursed.'

The queen spoke. She was still a young woman, only twenty-eight years old, but her voice had become deeper, Godwin noticed, as if she wanted men to take her more seriously. 'Morcar, all men should be prepared to swear an oath, and if we are to repel our enemy, then you will have to fight side by side with Eadric.'

'I will not stand next to him,' Morcar said.

'You will,' Ethelred said. His temper was short and his voice was stern. 'Eadric is your alderman. You will stand with him in battle if I command it.'

Morcar's bald pate began to sweat.

Godwin felt for the man. He remembered the day that he had stood with his father, before the whole court, and knew how alone that felt.

Godwin stepped forward. 'No man doubts Morcar's loyalty.' His voice carried through the silence, but it did not break the tension. 'Morcar, words do not wear out loyalty. I would gladly swear an oath to King Ethelred. Stand with me and let us swear.'

Morcar and Eadric clashed again, accusing each other of stealing land or sheep or breaking the peace oaths, and one day Eadric brought into the hall to swear a large, ugly man with red hair.

Godwin's heart skipped a beat. He tensed at the sight of the man, waited to hear his name.

'This is Offa Fox,' Eadric said to the king.

The ginger man's eyes sought out Godwin and he smiled a crooked smile. Anger flashed in Godwin like a swiftly drawn sword. He felt hot in his kirtle and clenched his jaw as he breathed through his nose, trying to calm his fury.

'Enough!' Ethelred suddenly shouted. 'Is this how the kingdom of Alfred and Edgar has fallen? Bickering thegns in an Oxeneford barn? If Knut triumphs, his men will seize your widows; take your daughters as common slaves without price or honour or recompense; sleep in your beds; and take your halls and your herds as their own! I am sick of you all. You will ride and fight, and that is it!'

That evening Ethelred summoned Morcar and his cousin Sigeferth to his hall. 'The king wishes you would join him at his prayers this evening,' the messenger said, 'and he would like to feast you afterwards.'

'Thank the king,' Morcar said, and sent him away. But Sigeferth and Morcar were concerned that they use this opportunity to impress upon Ethelred their loyalty.

'Perhaps he has changed his mind about Eadric,' Sigeferth said.

Morcar shook his head. 'He is too stubborn for that. How can he admit that? He would have to admit his guilt in Elfhelm's murder. No. Ethelred will not do it until he is on his death bed.' Morcar wished that his wife were there. 'I miss her sense,' he said. 'She would know what to do.'

'Well, what would she tell you to do?' Sigeferth asked.

Morcar put a hand to his bald scalp and scratched it.

There was grey in Sigeferth's beard. It gave him a handsome and war-fierce look. Morcar was glad that Sigeferth was with him because their mothers were sisters and they had grown up together like brothers.

'She would tell me not to go,' Morcar said, and laughed. 'But she told me not to come in the first place.'

Sigeferth nodded. 'What else?'

'To repeat my oath. "Swear whatever he wants," she'd tell me, "and let God be your witness."'

Sigeferth crossed himself. 'So,' he said, 'we go and pray with the king. And let your good wife be our guide. Let us do that.'

Morcar and Sigeferth washed and dressed for the mass that evening. They wore their best and came ready with fine gifts for the king; each brought twenty retainers, as the king had said.

Their retainers were all the men of their family. There were longbeards and young men and everyone in between. For some this was their first glimpse of the king's hall. Others had ridden with Elfhelm long ago and had sat in Wulfnoth's hall when they had more teeth and stronger grips.

There was a buzz among them as they rode through the muddy Oxeneford streets and entered the king's manor there. Stable boys led their horses away. The men waited for Sigeferth and Morcar to straighten their clothes. Morcar tightened his belt and adjusted his kirtle over his stomach.

'Let us swear anything,' he repeated to Sigeferth. Sigeferth nodded. They were loyal to the king. They would do what he said. They would take holy mass and feast, and if Eadric was there as well, then they would refuse to rise to any of his barbs.

Sigeferth and Morcar and all their kinsmen and retainers, young man and old, left their weapons at the door. They strode into the king's hall and the hall doors were hastily shut behind them. Morcar paused and looked about. The room was empty. The king's chair stood at the head of the room, but the benches had been put away to the side, fresh rushes had been spread, and in the long hearth an old fire had crumbled to ashes and smoked lazily. The tapestries rippled in cold drafts. Morcar looked about him and rubbed his hands together. His men stood and waited.

Morcar appeared unruffled by the moment. 'It's chilly,' he said.

Sigeferth nodded.

'I suppose we'll be going to mass first.'

A door opened at the far end of the hall. It was the door that led from the king's robing room and they turned towards it with expectation.

But the king did not step through it. A single man walked into the room. It was the little figure of Eadric, not the king. Morcar noticed Eadric's paunch and noted how they had both grown old and stout during the long feud between their families.

He drew in a deep breath. 'Greetings, Eadric.'

Sigeferth gave Eadric a curt nod.

Eadric walked to the back of the king's chair. 'Greetings, Morcar and Sigeferth,' he said. 'You are waiting for the king?'

'That we are,' Morcar said. 'Are you taking mass as well?'

'As well? I do not know. I shall certainly be taking mass.'

Morcar nodded. He had no intention of entering into a play of words and half turned to his men and gave them a cheerful and jolly smile. 'Good,' he said to Eadric. 'Good.'

Morcar took a few more steps. The door into the king's robing room remained open, but the king did not come through. Morcar started whistling to himself. It was a thin tune that quickly faded. When Morcar turned, he could see that Eadric had not moved. He was watching Morcar, and there was a bright light in his eyes.

'I do not know that tune,' Eadric said.

'No?'

'No. Whistle it to me again.'

Morcar almost started to whistle again, but Sigeferth was tired of this. 'We are not songbirds,' he said. 'We have come here to see the king.'

'Whistle,' Eadric said.

Morcar was irritated too. 'I shall not. Where is the king?'

One of the men tried the doors behind them. 'The doors have been bolted!' he cried.

Eadric smiled. 'Yes,' he said, 'they have.'

Morcar turned on him, but at that moment armed men poured into the room, at their head was a large, red-haired man. Offa Fox. From behind the tapestries, more men appeared.

Eadric grinned. 'I am sorry to say that the king is not coming,' he said, 'and will not have the pleasure of seeing this.'

'What?'

Eadric's retainers drew their swords.

'How we deal with treachery.'

Sigeferth and Morcar and their men had nothing but eating knives with them, knives and bare hands and righteous fury. Once they saw that they had been tricked, they charged at their hated foe.

Offa stepped before Eadric and his sword came back as Morcar rushed towards him with knife raised. Come to me, his posture said, and the sword stroke fell.

It was a brief and bloody business. The last sword strokes were unnecessary as the steel-gored bodies fell. Morcar's fat corpse was almost unrecognisable. Sigeferth's grey-bearded head had been cut from the body and kicked across the room. The forty men of their families had been dealt with without distinction. They all lay dead.

Ethelred was in Christ Church Cathedral. He heard the church bells ringing the hour, knew that the deed had been done, said three paternosters, then crossed himself and rose stiffly from the prayer cushion.

It was a hard job, being king, taking tough decisions for the good of the people, and sometimes he had to break his own word if it aided the country. He had organised it all. The hall would be washed of blood, the bodies handed over to the Church. Fifty armed retainers were already riding hard to the dead men's halls to stop this feud from spreading. They would seize hostages, take them far away from their kin and lock them safe in Malmesberie. It would stop any man from rousing his people against the king, cut off the angry head of dissent.

The news of the murders spread through Oxeneford with wild lamentations. As soon as the washerwomen and mistresses and travelling women of Morcar's company heard of the treacherous crime they hurried to the scene and tore at their hair and clothes and bewailed the loss of their proud and handsome men. Eadric's men tried to keep them away, but they grabbed at mementos and clothes, and dipped them in the pools of blood, so that they could take them back to their people as tokens to remind them of the blood-debt that Eadric owed them all.

As soon as he heard the sound of grief, Edmund summoned his door wards. 'What is that noise?'

A moment's hope sparked and he imagined that his father had been struck down with elf-shot and had died at his cups or collapsed in prayer. You will be king, the thrill of hope ran through his veins, but when the door wards ran back into the room, Edmund saw their faces and his hope was crushed.

'Morcar and Sigeferth and all their retainers have been foully slain in the king's own hall.'

Godwin was with Edmund as they strode into the king's chapel. Gamal, the king's door ward, now had shots of grey at his temples. He put his hands up, to try and stop them entering. 'No swords!' Gamal said. 'No weapons in the king's presence.'

Edmund pushed past them. 'I shall never enter his presence without a sword.'

Ethelred was kneeling on his prayer cushion.

Edmund stood over him. 'What have you done?' he demanded.

Ethelred put up his hand so that his chaplain would stop reading.

'What have you done?' Edmund's voice rose, but Ethelred did not like any man standing over him.

'Do not question me!' he said.

Father and son glared at each other.

'The wrong men died tonight.'

'I did not kill men,' Ethelred said.

'Do not hide behind Eadric like a naughty child who hides behind his mother's skirts. At least have the courage to accept what you have done.'

'I lanced a boil,' Ethelred said.

Edmund turned away from his father in disgust. Godwin paused in the doorway, not as certain as Edmund of entering the chapel with a drawn sword.

'I once counselled Athelstan to rise against you,' Edmund said in a trembling voice, 'and to his eternal shame he did not. I shall not make the same mistake.'

'Go!' Ethelred raged. 'I have other sons!'

Edmund strode from the hall and paused for a moment on the stone threshold, as if to consider – or consign those words to memory, to stoke his anger long after. 'You have no sons like me,' he said, and slammed the door behind him.

Edmund's household were riding out of Oxeneford within the hour. Their horses clattered on the polished cobbles, passed out of the south gate and crossed the ford in a shower of cold water. Godwin looked about, as if he expected to see armed men sent to hinder their escape. They did not know which way to ride and Edmund drew them to a halt about a mile from Oxeneford. His hand was shaking.

'I have done it,' he said. His face looked terrible. 'Oh Godwin, what have I done?'

Godwin was as shocked as the prince. He tried to sound enthusiastic, but he did not know yet if this was a good thing. 'You have done it,' Godwin said. 'You will take the throne.'

Edmund's knuckles were white as he gripped his reins. He

turned to Godwin, hurt in his eyes. 'I have done it,' he said, in barely a whisper. 'God forgive me, I have done it.' After a moment's pause he said, 'Will God forgive me?'

'Of course,' Godwin reassured him. 'Keep Him in your heart. Do what He thinks is right. Think of the oaths a king must swear when he takes the throne: to protect the Church, protect the people and uphold the law.'

Edmund crossed himself and said a paternoster. Godwin joined him and soon the whole company had come to a halt and they were reciting the paternoster together.

> *Panem nostrum cotidianum da nobis hodie;*
> *et dimitte nobis debita nostra . . .*
> Amen.

'War!' Edmund said. 'He has brought it upon us. What else can we do? The country is doomed. God has long turned his face away from us. If Ethelred was still favoured by God, then He would have been able to heal my brother. I can see it all now. We are being punished for this dreadful man. He is a blight on us all. No wonder God keeps killing my brothers. His will is against him. This is all my father's doing. It is his fault. From now on there shall be war between us.'

It was a dull May evening in Malmesberie, two weeks since the murders. Gnats were beginning to rise with the river mists, and the gates of St Aldhelm's Abbey were shut against the world.

Godwin drew his horse to a halt. 'Open the gates!' he shouted.

The abbey walls stood silent. A swan paddled out into the dark evening water, spread wide-spreading ripples.

Godwin took a deep breath and called out, 'Open the gates! In the name of Edmund Atheling!'

A monk's head appeared. 'We cannot.'

'I give orders from Prince Edmund,' Godwin shouted.

'And ours come from the king.'

It was an odd standoff because neither side wanted to kill other Englishmen.

The leader of the king's troops was his door ward Gamal. Inside they held prominent members of Morcar's and Sigeferth's families hostage.

'You saved my life once,' Godwin called up. 'I would spare yours.'

But Gamal had sworn to Ethelred just as Godwin had sworn to Edmund: to flee not a foot space, nor weaken in war; to defend folk and fold; to man the shieldburg about my lord, and follow him in the fight as long as I can hold war board.

'The king has entrusted me with his hostages,' Gamal shouted back, 'and Ethelred is still king. These hostages are Morcar's kin. I cannot allow his hostages to escape, for they will raise war against Eadric and Mercia will go down in flames at this moment when all Englishmen should come together.'

'You are right,' Godwin said, 'but Ethelred cannot unite them.'

'And you think Edmund can?'

'Of course. Gamal, you have seen him as well as I. He can fight as well as any man. Gamal, you seem to be a sensible man. Open the gates and let us in. I would not have Ethelred's soul charged with your blood as well as those of Morcar and Sigeferth.'

But Gamal would not.

Godwin was grim. 'It will be sad if we have to kill him and all his men, but I will do it if I have to.'

That evening a young monk by the name of Elmer opened a side door and waved to the guards.

'If you promise to spill no blood within the abbey precincts, I will open this gate when the king's men are at table.'

Elmer met them that evening with a horn lantern.

'Remember – no bloodshed!' he told them.

'No bloodshed,' Godwin assured the man behind the candle, but as soon as the door was opened, he and his men pushed past him into the courtyard, swords drawn. They found the king's men and far outnumbered them. Godwin did not have to speak. They could see that there was nothing they could do. Gamal drew his sword.

'Put it down, Gamal!' Godwin shouted, but even as he spoke one of the hotheads struck. A single blow to Gamal's head and he went down like a stunned ox. Red blood mixed into his year-grey hair.

'Put your swords away,' Godwin shouted. 'Leave him. You! Take this man to the leech-master and pray for his soul for he was a good and honest man. If this man should die his soul will be added to Ethelred's guilt. Now where are the hostages?'

They were taken to a room full of women. Most of them were short and stout and well-thighed.

'I am looking for Sigeferth's widow, Ealdgyth!' he called.

'I am here,' a voice said.

A lady appeared at the top of the stairs. A young woman: small and dark and very pretty, with a turned-up nose and long, dark lashes. 'You are Godwin, son of Wulfnoth. We have met before,' she said, and lifted her skirts to come down the stairs, 'In better days. You came to my hall.'

Sigeferth's widow was Alderman Elfhelm's niece. Ealdgyth was chief among the hostages that Ethelred had seized. After the death of so many of their menfolk, her people looked to the daughters and wives to lead them. She was fierce and determined, and vengeful, but at that moment she saw Godwin and smiled pleasantly.

Godwin bowed. 'I bear tidings from Prince Edmund,' Godwin said. 'The prince says, "Greetings to the Lady of Lincolia. Bid her come to my wedding."'

'He is getting married?' Ealdgyth said sweetly.

'He is.'

'Oh. Who is the lucky girl?'

Godwin smiled. 'Why, you.'

The betrothal feast was a boisterous affair. The women of Morcar's people were large and loud and angry, and there was a rowdy air as they all rode to the church door to be blessed, then hurried off to the feast hall, where the companies mixed: woman and warrior on the benches together.

Some of the women felt they would be better taking sides with the Danes. 'Knut is married to one of our own, a girl who sat at the loom with us. She was our sister. If Knut becomes king then Eadric will never have a good night's sleep. We will hunt him down and castrate the bastard before we kill him, and all his women and children, and all those dearest to him.'

The women were bloodthirsty and their oaths were furious and cruel. In the end Ealdgyth stood and called for silence. 'Hush,' she told them. 'The fool chatters who talks too much and lets the ale-jug unveil his mind. Why take Danish rule back? When Knut is king he will need to pay his father's men to go home. How big a tax will they raise? How much can you pluck from your children's mouths before you regret your words here tonight? Yes, he is married to one of our own. But I am now married to Prince Edmund. And tonight, perhaps, he will plant in my womb the son that will seal our hopes together.'

*

Edmund galloped north and unfurled his banner in Lincolia. All of Morcar's folk came to his side. They were burning with anger against the king and Eadric.

'Will he be able to control them?' one of the men said.

Was this wise? Godwin did not know. But he said 'Yes. What else can he do? If he did not take their oaths, they would have supported Knut. Now at least they will fight on our side.'

At Oxeneford the rump of the king's court went home with the agreement that each man would go back to their shires and stock and ensure that the fyrd was ready to ride at a day's notice and so bring all the strength of the kingdom to one battlefield. But after the murders of Morcar and Sigeferth the men would have agreed to anything just for the chance to leave their treacherous king and wash their hands of him.

Ethelred banned any mention of Edmund's name. He gathered Queen Emma and her sons about him and rode south, to his favourite manor of Cosham in Hamtunscir.

Away from the raging puddle of thegns and clergy, life continued much the same. The harvest was half cut, sheaves of wheat stood in the lower fields. Kendra walked up the hillside and saw a flicker of light leap out against the gathering evening. She dismissed it at first as the twinkling of a star or a firefly, but as darkness fell, the light grew stronger and brighter till it was a flickering dot glowing brightly on the southern horizon at the spot where the beacon on Blackdown stood.

The Danes had returned.

CHAPTER THREE

The Rough Wooing

Edmund called on men to abandon the king and come to his side.

No one came. The camp remained deserted.

'Where are they?' Edmund demanded as the stared at the empty roads.

'Give them another week,' Godwin suggested, but he had a growing sense that Edmund had been wrong to declare against his father. The Danes were here. England should be united, not descending into civil war. The people would scarcely rally to help the next shire from slaughter; they would never rally to fight a futile civil war.

The sense grew stronger and stronger, and by the end of the week Godwin had to speak. He found Edmund outside the hall, once more staring at the deserted roads.

'Your father was wrong, but you have only strengthened the case of Eadric and the queen. She must be rubbing her hands with glee. This is what she wanted all along. Who knows, maybe she and Eadric conspired against Morcar.' Edmund had his back to Godwin and did not turn around. 'We should be fighting the Danes!' Godwin's voice rose as he spoke, and the last word was a furious shout that surprised everyone, Godwin most of all. He had put a name to his anger and he stopped abruptly.

Edmund did not like being shouted at.

Godwin had nothing more to say.

Edmund kept his back turned.

Godwin waited. He did not see the point of standing here like a naughty child.

'Shall I go?' he said.

Edmund kept his back turned. He simply nodded. Godwin left. He stood at the hall door, ran his hands through his hair and puffed out his cheeks, shut the doorway behind him.

The whole room watched his face. They knew what he had gone to say, and the sound of Godwin shouting had alarmed them all.

'How went it?' Caerl asked.

'Well,' Godwin said, but to be honest he wasn't sure yet. 'I said my piece, and he listened.'

No one dared confront Edmund after that. They sat and watched the rain dripping from the thatch and the puddles grow wider. The horses trampled the turf to a sticky mire; each day Edmund's cause sank deeper into the mud. Each day they waited for warriors who were not coming. Occasionally news came to them, like scraps tossed to starving men: Ethelred had ridden south to conduct the defence of the kingdom; Eadric had raised his war bands and followed him.

Edmund's cause remained deserted. The rain did not stop. They tramped the mud into the hall till it was everywhere.

Men spoke less because they could not speak without going against Edmund and they increasingly ran out of words to say, except the bland and the weather-related. It was hard to talk about the rain – save to comment on how long it had gone on for.

'Good news,' Edmund exclaimed one morning, and men sat up to listen. 'My wife is with child.'

There was a muted reaction. It wasn't the good news they had hoped for.

Edmund threw a feast that night, and Godwin got drunk as a monk as the storm outside grew to a downpour, deeply and joylessly and determinedly drunk. He drank to swamp his despair, but in the morning the despair was waiting, with an awful hangover as well.

Three days later Edmund strode into the hall, where the men sat silently.

'So,' he said. 'It seems the fyrds are not coming.'

No one said anything.

'It seems not,' Godwin said, just to break the silence.

'When will this rain stop?' Edmund said.

No one spoke.

'Well, we're not much use to England sitting in this hole.'

Again, no one said anything. Edmund raised his eyebrows.

'So,' he said.

So, they thought.

'What should we do?'

Godwin was irritated, because he had already said what to do and saw no point in being ignored again, but no one else spoke and everyone looked at him. 'Well, I have spoken already,' he said.

They all nodded.

'What do the rest of you think?' Edmund said.

One by one – and in many different ways – they supported what Godwin had said. 'No one wants civil war. The people want a king who will defend them and impose the law.'

'I am he,' Edmund broke in, but he could see that they did not agree.

'You are he,' Godwin said, 'and we all know it, but the rest of the country – the men of far-off Dornsætum or Tanet or Cestre – they do not know you from Eadwig or Edward. What do they know of you, other than that you are Ethelred's son? And no doubt they are so sick of your father they have started to wonder if it isn't time for a change of royal family. Revolution is in their hearts. They are tired of failure.'

Edmund was silent, but this time he listened and heard and the words sank in.

'But we have always fought against the Danes.'

'Yes, we hunted ravagers. But no doubt for each Dane we killed as boys, they killed five Englishmen in return. Let us be honest. It is a lot to ask for men to trust their futures with us. They wouldn't even trust us with their daughters.'

Men started to smile. Godwin had caught the mood and pricked the gloom with a delicate stab of humour.

Edmund nodded. He had not understood before.

'So,' he said at the end of a long discussion, 'what should we do now?'

Godwin was exhausted. His head hurt. 'Don't look at me!' he said, but they were already. 'What do we do? Well, we raise Morcar's folk and we ride south and make peace with your father and devote ourselves to his cause. There are two months before harvest. We could have the Danes beaten before Lammas Day, and then men will take you seriously. Oh, how they will flock to your banner!'

Edmund rode south at the head of five hundred of Morcar's folk.

People were curious when they saw Edmund riding at the head of a mounted warhost.

'They're not used to seeing a royal heading warriors,' Godwin said. 'Next morning, let all of us don mail and spear and shield, and we shall impress upon them that we are a warlike company and that you are a warlike prince.'

Next morning they did as Godwin said. It was hot and heavy. The chain mail clinked as it weighed on their shoulders, but men in the fields put down their hoes and scythes and baskets and stared in astonishment.

'Who are you?' they called out.

'I am Edmund Atheling,' Edmund replied, 'and we ride to fight the Danes!'

'Not so few,' one man said.

'No, with all the country! Come, fellow, will you follow us?'

The man laughed. 'No, not yet, but beat the Danes and yes, I will gladly follow you.'

The king was still at Cosham. Edmund sent out messengers offering peace to Ethelred. One of them was Caerl.

He gave Caerl a golden ring that was large enough to fit upon his middle finger.

'Take my greetings to my father,' Edmund said, 'and tell him that I have five hundred fierce warriors to fight on his behalf.'

Caerl took a short-legged courser and arrived at the king's manor two days later.

Cosham lay a few miles from Portsea Isle, on the fringes of the Soluente. It had broad fields, thick with tall, green corn, a high stone hall and a well-paved road leading to the shore, where the king's men gathered all manner of shellfish. There Ethelred kept his fleet on the sand flats within the sheltered bay of the Port River. There were thirty warships, all that remained of the fleet he had raised seven years earlier, lying on their sides like lazy cows.

Ethelred welcomed Caerl with gruff words, but Caerl spoke

carefully and honestly, and talked more of the Danes and how they were the foe of all Englishmen than he did of Edmund.

'How can we trust Edmund?' Queen Emma said.

'What would he gain by any violence against his old father? None. His enemy is the Danes, who oppress us all. He regrets speaking with haste. He has charged me with these words.'

When Caerl came back to Edmund, they all stood around to hear what he would say.

'Well,' Caerl said, 'Eadric and the queen questioned me closely and spoke vehemently against the king granting you mercy. They accused you of all kinds of evil and treachery.'

Edmund seemed almost gleeful to hear news of his father. 'There is no one to rein them in, and when men may do as they wish, they do as they are.'

'I spoke my best,' Caerl said, 'though I do not know if it is enough. You will have to see the king in person.'

Edmund's men made camp a short day's ride north of Cosham. He was careful to keep his men well away from where Eadric's men were camped. Godwin was not sure what would happen. The only armed men available to the king were mortal enemies.

That afternoon they decided to go and see the king.

They spent the morning bathing in a pool overhung with willow branches. The little arrowhead leaves floated curiously about them. They pushed the duckweed away and lay back in the water.

They sat naked on the grass to dry themselves, and then threw their cloaks on and strode back to the hall, where they combed their hair and beards, and dressed in fine clothes.

'Bring your swords,' Godwin reminded them all, 'and do not put them aside.'

*

A feast was held that night. A war feast. All men sat with their swords by their sides; the mood was formal and guarded.

On the high table sat the queen, with Ethelred at her side. Eadric and Edmund's men were drawn up on the tables opposite each other, like armies on the battlefield.

Godwin sat on the right flank. The ginger-haired man was opposite him. He winked at Godwin. Godwin did not look away this time, but held the man's gaze, unblinking, so long that it became a test of wills.

The ginger-haired man looked away first with a sneer. Godwin felt the thrill of victory and took a deep breath to calm his fast-beating heart. You burnt my hall, he thought, I shall see you dead.

Ethelred cleared his throat and the room went quiet as everyone turned to look. 'So,' the king, Protector of the People, said. 'the Danes are in Cantware. What should we do to drive them off?'

'Call out the fyrd,' Edmund told him.

Eadric was not keen on such a move. He was weighing greater matters in his mind. The old king paused, as the goldsmith waits for the scales to balance.

Eadric spoke more directly than was his wont. 'Lord,' he said. He did not like to have to defend his honour. 'I have been your loyal servant for many years. We have laboured in so many ways against the Danes, but we have constantly been undermined by them within our borders. Your son has thrown his lot in with their camp and married the widow of one of the traitors. It weighs my heart to see this. How can a country stand firm on the battlefield when we have traitors so close to the heart of our nation?'

Edmund let Eadric talk. He did not trust himself to speak.

Godwin admired Edmund's reserve. They had spent the

whole trip south reminding themselves that the goal was the kingship. Our goal is the kingship. Our goal is defeating the Danes. He hoped that the people of Morcar would remember.

When Eadric had stopped talking, Godwin could not resist answering. He sensed a weakness and was almost falling off his bench in his eagerness. 'Lord King, we are all your loyal servants. It is an odd chance that all men who stand against Alderman Eadric are named traitors and turncoats. My father was one among them. He killed Danish pirates and took their treasure and gave it to the monks at the Old Minster, to give thanks to God. He was named Wulfnoth Cild until he crossed Eadric's path. Then Eadric discovered he was a traitor and he was sent into exile.

'Lord King, if the alderman was right our cause would have grown stronger and more worthy, and England would have gone from strength to strength. Instead, with each traitor whose name he blackens, the weaker we become. I have never heard your name connected with any action against the Danes, Alderman Eadric. Perhaps there is only one traitor among us, only one man who undermines our cause.'

Godwin stopped there.

It was better to let the listener do a little work himself.

Ethelred reminded them that they had sworn peace towards each other. 'And all your followers!' Ethelred said, and banged his open palm against the table. 'I will have no fighting.'

Edmund congratulated Godwin later that evening. 'You should have seen Eadric's face,' he said. 'I was proud of you. You have a fine tongue, Godwin Wulfnothson, and a good speaker is worth a hundred swords.'

They slept in one of the guest halls of the king's manor, and Godwin posted watchmen to keep an eye on the hall where Eadric's men slept.

The night passed peacefully, but when Ethelred suggested a hunt the next day, no one was keen. The next day news came that the Army had taken to their ships and were sailing from Cantware towards the king's manor.

'I shall bring my men here,' Edmund said, 'to defend you, lord!'

Eadric looked sourly at them all. Godwin found it hard to ignore the big red-headed man, but he was bullish and confident. It was clear that the people favoured a reunion of Ethelred and Edmund over any alliance with Eadric.

Ethelred brought Eadric and Edmund into a council. 'For Eadric is still my most loyal subject,' Ethelred said.

Eadric smiled but said nothing, and that worried Godwin, for Eadric did not work in the open, but by secret murder and slaughter.

At the end Eadric asked to be allowed to go to his people. 'There is much that I must tell them.'

They let him go. It had taken a few days for the chill between Ethelred and Edmund to thaw.

'How is your wife?' Ethelred said.

'She is well.'

'You could have asked.'

'I could have,' Edmund said, and then stopped.

A messenger had arrived. 'The Army landed in Dornsætum last night,' he told them. 'Their fleet landed at the mouth of the River Froom'

Ethelred looked concerned. The Froom. Their horsemen could be here in two days.

'I will send a hundred men to strengthen the men at the burg of Werham,' Edmund said. 'I have told the alderman of Dornsætum to gather his war bands.'

Ethelred stopped and turned to him. 'It is not your part to order my men. You are not king yet. You cannot just summon men to battle willy-nilly. There are ways of doing this. Believe me, I know – I was made king when I was twelve.'

Edmund had to clench his fists. He had heard this for years and had stopped believing it long before. It was all he could do to hold his tongue.

Knut's berserkers stormed the burg at Werham and all the men inside were put to the sword. The Danes took horses and rode all about Dornsætum, Wiltunscir and Sumersæton, burning, pillaging and seizing supplies against the coming winter.

Messengers were sent out, but the response to the call was poor. Edmund took it personally. Godwin understood a little better. 'Well, the men who have been pillaged have little left to lose, and the men yet to be pillaged would rather pay a tax than lose another battle.'

'They will not come unless we fight, and we cannot fight without armed men.'

The days turned to a week, a week into a fortnight, and as harvest approached many thegns lost heart and began to ride to Knut's camp and swear loyalty to him. They went singly at first, and then in threes and fours, and eventually whole companies of sword-thegns in the full light of day, dwindling into the distance.

'Our old king cannot protect us. We will give you our oaths if you will stop ravaging our land.'

Knut's Army swelled; the men loyal to Ethelred and Edmund dwindled.

'All he has to do is sit in Wessex,' Godwin said, 'and demonstrate that the king cannot and will not protect the people against him and the country will go against us all.'

Godwin's words seemed prophetic when news came that the prominent Dornsætum and Hamtunscir families had ridden to Knut's camp to offer him their support.

Edmund was furious. 'I know those men,' he said. 'We have sat at their bench and shared food. How can they turn their backs on us?' He raged and ranted and then calmed himself down. 'I am sorry. Godwin, don't look at me like that. I know why they have done this, but it angers me.'

Caerl brought even more sobering news: 'Eadric has ridden west.'

It was clear that he was going to Knut's camp.

Edmund acted as if he was delighted, but there was nothing to celebrate. Eadric's defection was the final insult.

The men's mood was grim. They had been in the field all summer and were keen to get home and set their farms and halls in order for the long winter.

'Eadric has gone to Knut's side. Who is left to us?' Beorn said.

Caerl said nothing. Godwin rubbed sleep from his eyes and yawned. 'Eadric is no loss, but the other aldermen, they were men who were loyal in the spring.'

'Why should Eadric flee now?' Beorn said.

'Because Ethelred is doomed,' Caerl said.

Godwin felt gloomy. 'Or he thinks that if he has to choose between them, Ethelred will favour Edmund over him.'

'Both are probably true,' Edmund said as he strode up.

They straightened themselves and felt abashed to have been discussing this.

'But there is worse,' Edmund continued. 'Eadric has told Knut how weak we are. The Danes have started riding towards us.'

'Shall we give battle?' Godwin said.

Edmund hoped so. 'Let us see the king.'

Ethelred collapsed when he heard of Eadric's flight. He had to be revived with hartshorn salt. Since then he had been in a strangely humorous mood. It unnerved everyone, even the queen, who came out to meet them, falling over herself to welcome Edmund.

Godwin studied her as she spoke. He did not feel like gloating. They were all in the shit, he thought. And the queen was more alone than any of them. She had pinned her fortunes on Eadric.

'Your son is here,' she said to Ethelred.

The king was sitting in a chair by the fire, with blankets over his knees and an untouched bowl of warmed ale sitting on a stool by his side. Ethelred heard and closed his eyes.

Emma turned and whispered, 'He is not himself. Be gentle with him.'

Edmund and his men pulled up benches and stools. Edmund sat next to his father. He waited till he could see that Ethelred was listening. 'Knut is coming here. All over England men are calling for Knut to be made king. We must think of all the kings of Wessex. Think how they laboured and fought. Tell the people that you need their service in battle. We could fight shoulder to shoulder. Father and son, our companions mixed together! The finest of England's strength. No man could stand against us. Father, call out a great fyrd.'

Ethelred's mood swung from elation to gloom. He massaged his temples with his fingertips. 'What makes you think they will come?' he said.

'They will come if you ask them.'

Ethelred waved a hand at him. 'You will be king soon enough.'

'Father, if you would but come out, then men would know that you lead them and they will fight.'

Ethelred agreed, but when the thegns were drawn up, word came from the groomsmen that the king had changed his mind and would stay abed.

'He has taken ill with aches and pains in his head,' the queen said.

Edmund again went to his side 'Father—' he began.

Ethelred put up his hand. 'I will, I will, later,' he promised again, but still he did not come.

That night Edmund bent one knee and knelt by his father's side and clutched the old man's hand and pleaded with him. 'If you cannot show yourself, then give me command and I will drive the Danes from England.' Edmund's words came out almost like a prayer.

Ethelred waved a hand. He was bewildered, but Edmund saw a strange light in his eyes that belied his illness. 'Why?' the king said.

'Why what?'

'Why did you do that to me?'

'What?' Edmund said, and let his hand go.

Ethelred fell against the pillows. 'Marry that woman,' Ethelred said. 'Did you want me to look like a fool?'

'No, Father.'

'She is a witch.'

'Father, she hates you because you murdered her uncle, and then murdered her husband.'

'I did not murder him.'

Edmund laughed. 'Eadric murdered them.'

'It was a feud.'

'And did you punish him?'

Ethelred looked away. 'Don't shout so,' he said, waved a hand in self-indulgent pity. 'I am dying.'

'Father, Knut's riders are not more than fifteen miles off.'

'So? Why trouble me?'

Edmund gave up. 'I am leaving you.'

'To be killed by Knut?'

Edmund paused at the hall door. 'No, to see if there are any loyal men left in England.'

Edmund remembered himself and walked back to his father. Ethelred winced as if recoiling from a blow, but Edmund bent and kissed the old man's brow. 'Farewell, Father. May God have mercy upon your soul.'

Godwin remained leaning against a carved column. Edmund had left him with clear instructions. He imagined squeezing the breath from him, as a child might flatten an inflated bladder. It would only take moments and it would be over at last. Ethelred looked up. He saw the look in Godwin's face.

His voice was frightened. 'Who are you?'

'I am Godwin Wulfnothson, whom men called the Cild.'

Ethelred panicked. 'Where is my son?'

'He is gone.'

'Are you to kill me?'

Godwin smiled. He could smell the corruption in the old man's soul. It would be better for the kingdom, Godwin told himself. He bent down, arranged the bed sheets, put his mouth next to Ethelred's ear and whispered, 'I will not charge my soul with the sin of killing my king. But you, my lord, should use every minute left to you to pray to the Lord God of Heaven for forgiveness.'

Godwin brought Ethelred's hands together and laid them on his chest, as if in prayer.

'Where has my son gone?' Ethelred said.

'He has gone to Lundenburh.'

'No!' Ethelred waved his hand in irritation. The name took a long time to come up, like an anchor dredged up from the Soluente mud. 'Ath-elstan,' he said at last. 'Where is Athelstan?'

'Athelstan?'

The old man nodded.

'Dead.'

'Dead?'

'Three years past.'

'It cannot be.'

Godwin nodded. 'It is.'

The old man fell back against the pillows. It was the strangest thing. He crumpled before Godwin's eyes.

'How?' he said at last.

'He fell from his horse.'

'Dead? My own beautiful son?'

Godwin nodded again and Ethelred wept – harsh, croaking sounds, like quartz stones splitting. He was crying as much for himself as his son.

'I cannot go. I am sick,' he said, in a voice like a child's. 'They have not fed me. Where have they gone? My servants and my retainers?'

'Fled,' Godwin said. He brought a hunk of bread, dipped it in a cup of stale wine and held it up to Ethelred's lips.

'My wife?'

'Gone to Lundenburh.'

'Well, I cannot go. I am sick.'

Godwin shrugged. 'Well, it's stay here and wait for Knut or come with us.'

Ethelred's eyes looked pleading. 'You will take me there?'

Godwin lifted the grey head up gently so that the king could drink.

'I will take you,' he said.

The king smelt of urine, but there was no time for a bath and he would not have his nightshirt taken from him. His chaplain sprinkled him with rosewater, and Godwin helped him dress as best he could, in a hunting kirtle of lambswool, a thick overcoat lined with mink, a pair of trews and fur-lined boots.

Godwin put his own fur cap on the king's head. His grey hair was stiff with grease. It stuck out about his ears. Godwin gave it a rough comb and tugged at his beard as well. Ethelred stood like a dumb horse.

Godwin laughed. 'Well, I never thought I'd be combing the king's beard. Here, you do it,' he said, and gave his comb to the chaplain.

The man finished the job, hung a nosegay of cloves and cinnamon under Ethelred's chin. 'Come,' Godwin said, 'your guard awaits.'

The chaplain led the old king towards the door. Godwin waited for him, and took the aged king by the wrist so that his heart might have no fear as the doors were thrown open and they stepped out into the yard. Ethelred took his hand away from Godwin's. It was as if he wanted to see if he would fall or not. He swayed for a moment and then steadied himself.

'I am well,' Ethelred said. 'Look – I can walk!'

'Indeed,' Godwin said.

If Ethelred had expected a fine troop, he was disappointed. These men had been in the field for weeks. Their clothes were weather-stained, their hands were dirty, and they had a hard, frostbitten look in their eyes as they sat in their saddles or squatted against the wall. Their horses' breath steamed in the yard, and behind them a heavy dew still dripped from eaves and leaves and gable.

'Where is Dunmane?' Ethelred called, looking about for his finest mare.

'There are no horses here,' Godwin said. There was little left now that the king's servants had ransacked the place.

A gentle dun mare was led forward.

Godwin spoke quickly. 'Ah, look! Here she is,' he said.

The old man patted her and took a shaky hold on the reins. 'Ah, Dunmane!' he said, and Godwin helped the old man swing up into the saddle.

CHAPTER FOUR

The Half-Hundred

They kept a steady pace along the quiet lanes heading ever north and east. They avoided Wincestre and let it pass along their left-hand side at a safe distance. Ethelred complained bitterly about the cold and begged to be taken to his palace there, but Godwin took the reins from his hand.

'There is no good welcome for you there,' Godwin told him. 'Come, we will be in Sudsexe soon. I will take you to my hall and we will sleep safely among my people.'

They reached Contone on the second evening. Kendra ran out as soon as she learnt that Godwin had returned.

'We heard the fyrd would not march,' she said, as she hurried down the hill, 'and that no one will fight!'

'Hush!' Godwin said. 'I have the king with me.'

Kendra took a moment to understand what he was saying, but she followed his gaze. She put her hand to her mouth. She had heard so much about Ethelred, but here was a scrawny and unwashed old man, with Godwin's cap pulled tight on his head, with a long scarf knotted about his neck.

'That is the king?' she said.

*

Since Contone had first been given to Godwin's family, no king had ever visited. The fact did not escape Godwin as he helped Ethelred down and led him into the hall. It was late in the day. Most had long since sought their household fires. The weakening light failed as the troop dismounted, stretched their stiff limbs and filed into the hall.

Serving men were busy stacking the fire, and although the hearth flames were already licking the air, the hall was still cold.

'It is the king,' men said, and the cauldron of broth had hardly boiled before people began to appear like shadows in the night. Even though Ethelred's name had been a byword for stupidity and cruelty and injustice, the common folk of Contone greeted him with wonder and respect.

They took away his dirty clothes and the women set water to warm. 'Come,' they said, 'we'll warm your marrow in the vat. Nothing is so warming as a bath.'

Ethelred was unwilling, but Agnes and Kendra led him to the side chamber, where men were emptying the last of the hot water into the tub. Godwin came in to check on the king. He sat like a Bible saint – grey hair plastered to his unhappy head – as Agnes and Kendra washed and scrubbed him.

'How is he?' Godwin asked.

'He is better now,' Kendra said. Her sleeves were rolled up, her skirts wet.

'How are you?'

The brightness of her smile surprised him. 'I am well,' she said. 'Much better for seeing you. We have worried so. We were all worried. It has been weeks since the beacons were lit, and we feared that Knut would ride over the hill at any time. I buried everything, as you said. The boys have been set to watch, and I've brought the livestock into the lower fields.'

Godwin put his hand to her cheek. 'You have done well,' he said.

She took his wrist in her hand and winced. Dirt was engrained in his skin. 'When he is done, you shall be next!'

And as she washed him, Kendra laughed. 'I would never have thought – such dark days and you appear! I am overjoyed to see you again, Godwin.'

But later, as he dried and dressed, and the fact that he was soon to leave again sunk in, she frowned.

'Are you sure you should take the king to Lundenburh tomorrow?'

'Yes,' Godwin said. 'Why?'

She didn't like to say.

'Why?' he said, as he buttoned his kirtle.

She seemed to clench up, as if to force the words out.

'Godwin, the king's cause is doomed. All men say so.'

'Who?'

She half laughed. 'All men.'

Godwin stood up. 'I do not fight for the king. I fight for Edmund.'

'And how can Edmund succeed where his father has not?'

'He will fight!'

Kendra's eyes were sad. She held her words back, but her eyes were imploring. Godwin held her gaze for a long time. 'I have to go to Lundenburh,' he said, as she helped him with his brooch. 'I have sworn to him. I swore an oath, and it is more than that. It is something I said of Eadric. I am who I am. I cannot be other. I have made my choices, and if it is God's will to go against us, then what can we do against the Almighty?'

She paused for a long while, unconvinced.

'Go,' she said. 'Your men are waiting.'

Godwin kissed her. She seemed a little cheered.

'To each his own way of earning fame,' he said.

She smiled, though he thought there were tears in her eyes, gleaming with candlelight. 'You have made your choice,' she said.

'We have made our choices,' he told her.

Later that evening all of the men who wanted took turns in the bath water. It was black by the time they were finished and Agnes tipped it out on to the herb garden. Ethelred's humour rose as he sat by the fire. The blaze put colour in his cheeks and the hall was crammed with people who had hurried through the gloom to see him, as if he were a saint.

'You are my good and loyal subjects,' he told them. 'I am blessed to see you all. If only I had so many good men in my court, then things would not have gone so badly.'

As the night darkened, more and more astonished locals came to see their king, and it wasn't long before the sick appeared, begging for the king to heal them. They were a pathetic lot: a woman with a growth on her neck, a boy with a twisted leg, a shepherd who had been bitten by an adder, and whose foot had swollen up to twice its normal size, and an old man whose legs were covered in running sores. They crept to the door and waited silently.

Godwin did not have the heart to let them wait in vain. 'My brothers,' he said, 'the king is ill and old. Go home and pray and the Lord will have mercy upon you all.'

'No!' Ethelred called. 'No, let them in. Come, my children. Do not be shy. I am your anointed king, Ethelred Edgarson.'

Ethelred insisted on seeing them. They waited patiently as he laid hands on their wounds and prayed to God on their behalf.

Godwin looked around and caught Kendra's eye.

See, her look seemed to say, he is curing them.

The devotion of the sick did more to heal Ethelred than anything else. As each one sat and shuddered at the king's touch, he seemed to draw extra life out of them, and that evening as he drank his posset he was in better spirits than Godwin could remember.

Godwin slept like a stone and Kendra lay next to him, her head on his chest and her arm about him as she listened to his heart beating. It was slow and steady. She kissed his side and lay for a long time as the hall timbers creaked over their heads, and the hall fire crumbled and cooled to low-burning embers, red in the darkness.

'They stand unnoticed who stand dry in a storm,' her mother used to say, and Kendra had never quite worked out what she meant. But that night she willed that for Godwin the storm might pass over him and leave him dry.

Godwin and his company were away with the dawn. He said farewell to Kendra at the door. 'I will send word,' he said, and squeezed her hand one last time.

The people of Contone gathered in the damp morning to watch the king depart. Ethelred sat straight and proud in his saddle, put his hands on them and they looked up at him with awe and love and loyalty.

'God speed!' they called out, man, woman and snotty-nosed child. They stood, immovable, it seemed, like figures carved from stone, and watched their king depart – a fugitive among his own people.

Godwin led the company across the North Downs. The first night at the fireside Ethelred's mood was bewildered, as if he had stumbled from another world, and aged from twelve to fifty in the blink of an eye. 'They murdered my brother, and made me king. In my youth I was wayward,' he said and there was a long pause. 'Bad men led me astray, and they took much land from the Church. But good men came to my aid. My mother, Ethelmar; Ordulf and Wulfric. We made amends. Restored lands to the Church. And Byrthnoth was a good man. He should not have died the way he did.'

'Why did you not fight?' Godwin said.

The old man looked at him as if bewildered.

'Why did you never fight? I grew up in terror of the Danes, and all men wanted was for you to lead the English to battle. But you never did.'

Ethelred stared at him. His expression changed from anger to irritation, to a wicked light, as if he was thinking of punishing Godwin for this question.

Godwin sat and stared at him. It was hard trying to resist the urge to be cruel, but Ethelred pulled his cloak over his head. It was the gesture a child might make, who refuses to talk any more.

On the third day they descended into the prosperous farmlands along the banks of the meandering Temese. On the fourth day they came to Chingestune, the ancient seat of the Wessex kings.

When they reached the king's hall, Godwin spoke gently to the old king, supported his arm as they entered. It had been looted and ravaged. Tapestries had been ripped from the walls. Grain stores had been smashed as men searched for gold, and holes had been dug in the floor and walls.

'This was a fine hall once,' Ethelred said as he looked at the destruction.

Godwin pitied the old man. 'Why should men do this?'

Godwin picked through the shattered benches and tables. He had nothing to say. The destruction was senseless, and it had been done by English.

'Set a guard on the walls. Find some servants. Let's get a fire started,' he told his men.

They found unbroken benches and fed the rest to the hearth flames. Just then the sound of shouting came from outside.

Godwin strode out. It was not so much a delegation as an angry mob.

Their leader was a local monk, a fat and worked-up man with striking blue eyes and a curiously smooth-skinned face. 'The people have asked me to come,' he said. The crowd jeered in support. 'We do not want the king here!'

Godwin let him speak. His eyes roamed over the crowd. They were cold and pinched. He could feel their mood wavering between fear and anger, terror and violence. He let the monk have his say; having someone listen to him seemed to calm the man.

'We shall leave,' Godwin said, 'but not because you come here to demand it.'

There were jeers and insults but Godwin faced them down, and as he picked out the troublemakers, they fell silent.

'Tomorrow we shall take boats to Lundenburh. The king intends to make his peace with the Lord at his palace of West Minster. Edmund will raise the fyrds of all the shires. Do not come here and jeer me. I am not your enemy. Knut is your enemy, and his Spear-Danes. Save your jeers for them. Save your anger and your fear for the day you meet them in battle. If you were so brave, you would not come here to berate an old man who will meet the Maker soon enough and pay for his sins in Purgatory, but you would look to the future. When winter passes there will be a great struggle. What would you rather – Danes' Rule again, or the return of a good and honest king?'

'Who would that be?'

'Edmund Atheling, who has hunted Danes for as many years as I have known him!'

The crowd seemed unimpressed. What did they know of Edmund? But Godwin spoke proudly and firmly, and the people listened. He told them what to do and they followed. 'It is a cold and bleak day and no time to be standing in a muddy street. Take word back to your homes and your families and spread the news that Ethelred is dying and that his son stands ready to lead us all. Edmund Atheling! Descended from a long line of kings. Remember your histories! Remember how kings used to act. Edmund is like the kings of old. Come spring, he shall lead the English against our enemies, and he requires the prayers of all the people. Be gone! Good folk, do not trouble your dying king's rest. God will judge him harshly enough.'

Winter set in. Campaigning ended. Knut rode all about Wessex, feasting and distributing the law, as if he was already king.

'He does not have to fight,' Edmund said. 'All he has to do is sit and wait until there's just thee and me to fight for England.'

Edmund and Godwin rode as far north as Tanshelf, on the borders of Northymbria, and found men who said they would ride if others would too. That February was the bleakest that men could remember. Snow fell, sleet lashed the watchmen on the walls, and the weeks seemed to drag slowly as they waited for the campaigning season to begin. Edmund and Godwin crossed the Temese into Cantware and went from hall to hall, but the men hid behind their oaths.

'When Ethelred calls us, we will come,' they said.

Edmund lost his temper with them, and then the real reasons came out. 'I came out for the great fyrd and rode all the way to the Hymbre and we did not see battle, so I came home without so much as a penny or even a goose to give to my men. They are still grumbling about that ride,' one man said.

'I came to the last summons, but no one else did. We were sent home and all my neighbours laughed at me. My wife berated me, and my best men left.'

No battle, no plunder, no hope, no reason to summon men and ride out to war.

Edmund listened in disgust. 'To each his own way of earning fame.'

Meanwhile, the king lay at West Minster, alone with his wife and his chaplain. His favourite hunting hounds lay sprawled along the side of his bed, twitching in their sleep. His time was close. Everyone knew it, waiting in the hall shadows.

Queen Emma opened the psalter to the page with the blue-and-red illumination. She read badly and Ethelred closed his eyes and pretended to doze, but she kept reading the words, stopping at times to ask the chaplain's help.

'*Quadraginta annis proximus fui generationi huic*,' the chaplain read.

Emma tried again, then at last put the book down with a sigh.

He could tell that she was watching him and half opened an eye, as if to check.

'Intercede for us,' she said.

He nodded. 'Wulfric,' he croaked, and the chaplain came forward.

'Mass,' he said.

It was an hour before vespers, but the monk took out his gold-embroidered stole and hung it about his neck, muttered a blessing as he washed and dried his hands, took up the Holy Book, assumed his Holy Book voice and sang the mass.

Wulfric had the sweetest voice of any cleric and Ethelred closed his eyes and almost forgot the world and its millstone cares.

Benedictus! Benedictus Dominus Deus Israel;
    quia visitavit et fecit redemptionem plebis suæ:
Et erexit cornu salutis nobis.

The palace fires burnt themselves hollow, their colour fading to yellow and then red, then black and finally ember grey. Unseen in the darkness; the half-moon rose late in the night, cast a thin light on the rain-pitted river. Dawn came slowly, a sliver of light on the eastern rim, gradually growing to a strange half-light, neither light nor dark: an indecisive start to the Feast of St George. From the king's chamber word spread like ripples to his family and the court, the palace stables and workshops, the fields between West Minster and the palace, quickly along the streets, across the river to the market at Sudwerca, then further afield into the shires: Ethelred was dead.

Two Witans met. One in Hantone. Another in West Minster.

In Hantone Knut was crowned with Alfred's ancient crown: a narrow band of gold with six prongs, each one set with great garnet roundels. There was a vast crowd of Danes and English in all their finery and they were in glad mood at the feast that followed, where Knut presented the abbot of the New Minster with a golden cross.

At West Minster Edmund's coronation was a much more sombre and religious affair. Archbishop Wulfstan led a hastily formed Witan of abbots and aldermen, followed by the assembled warriors and Ethelred's chaplain and his widow, Emma. Edmund knelt in mail and sword and prayed. It was a rushed and shabby coronation, as urgent as the ancient German tribes who met to elect a war chief on the eve of battle.

At the end Edmund was dressed and anointed, and stood before God for the English nation.

'Amen,' sang the monks in quavering voices.

Godwin closed his eyes and crossed himself. 'Amen,' he said.

Two days later Godwin and Edmund stood at the isle of West Minster as the lapping currents recalled another drowned body from the Temese. This one did not drift past, but snagged and stayed, nudging against the evening reed beds as the ebb tide turned. The two men ignored it at first, but it refused to go away. It lay pale and limp in the water, the blond hair rooting it to the anchor of rank weeds.

'Another girl,' Edmund said to Godwin, as one of his retainers splashed into the water and turned the body over. Another girl, naked except for the water and the weeds, and a leech-dark frog that slipped over the pale wet skin. The Danish noose was drawing closed.

Godwin and Edmund stood for a long time, silhouetted against the silver evening river water. A swan pushed out from the far bank. The sweet smell of wet reeds hung in the air. Spring insects were beginning to swarm over the river. A lone fish jumped and broke the glittering surface for a moment.

'This is the hour, Godwin, that we knew would come. Let us see how strong our hand is. Pick your best men. Let us ride out. The loyal take word to the loyal.'

'But who will stay here?'

'Eadwig,' Edmund said, 'and Queen Emma. Her men will put backbone into the defence. And it will keep her out of trouble.'

Godwin picked out ten of his men to come with him, one of whom was Beorn. Godwin had a feeling that he was the kind of big and fearsome man he needed at his shoulder. The rest were to stay behind to repel the Danes. Caerl was chief among them. Godwin did not want to leave him, but he could think of no better man to add heart and courage to all around him.

'Be here when I come back,' Godwin said.

'Come back,' Caerl laughed, 'and I will be here.'

The two men hugged. Neither man wanted to let go.

'Be off with you!' Caerl said, then hugged Beorn. Make sure he comes back, Caerl's look said.

Beorn grinned and winked.

Next morning Edmund left all the men he could spare to hold Lundenburh and rode out with just fifty men. Some rode north and east, but most rode south, to avoid the approach of Knut's army. Half a hundred to raise a war host from a broken nation. The size of the task overawed them all. Few thought they had any chance.

When they reached the borders of Midelsexe, Edmund turned east towards Canturburie and Godwin turned his horse south towards Sudsexe. They paused to say farewell. Godwin held Edmund for a long time.

'Men shall sing of this day when we beat the Danes,' Godwin said.

Edmund grinned but his eyes looked sad and weary. 'I will miss you.'

Godwin turned his horse away.

Snow frosted the crowns of the Downs. The land was dressed in the drab winter garb of mud and twigs.

The hall was shut up. The paddock was empty, the flocks had been sent down to Harditone to escape the freeze. Only the brew house showed signs of habitation. Godwin tethered his horse and walked towards it. This place did not feel like home. Either he had changed or it had. Or both of us have changed, he thought, like young lovers who grow apart and lose their passion.

Kendra was not there and Godwin began to fret.

'Hello?' he called into the brew house. His voice echoed back.

'Hello?' it asked in a quizzical tone.

Godwin found Kendra in the bottom yard, herding the chickens out of their evening coop. She seemed taller and slimmer than before, and beautiful too, in her blue linen skirts. Her ankles were bare, and her shoes damp and muddy, the hems of her skirts worn and faded where she had scrubbed the grime from them.

The chickens ran through her legs and he clapped and laughed.

'Godwin,' she said, looking round and speaking as if he had just been down to the market to sell a cow, 'you are here!'

He smiled broadly as another chicken escaped her.

'Stop it! You're encouraging them!' she told him, but he did not move and he caught the last one in a flurry of feathers and handed it to her.

There was a hand's breadth between Godwin and Kendra as they walked back to the bowyer. When they got to the door, Kendra put her hand on his forearm. Her touch was very light, but it relieved him and his unease settled.

Using Contone as his base, Godwin rode from manor to manor talking to the headmen and trying to gather a war band. They wanted to support Edmund, but they were fearful. 'The chief men have gone over to Knut,' they said. 'They have betrayed us all.'

There was little disagreement, but when Godwin asked if they would ride when the beacons were lit, they were hesitant.

'I cannot,' the headmen said. 'I have wife and children. What would they do if I was killed in battle?'

Godwin felt as though he was ploughing through stony and heavy clay soil.

It was weary and exhausting work.

One night Godwin came home drunk and despondent and he and Kendra held each other under the furs. Godwin lay with his head on her shoulder. If she still doubted the cause she did not let on, but bolstered his resolve.

'If I foreswore Edmund, what would you think of me?'

'You will not foreswear him,' she said.

He nodded and she kissed him again to stop him saying any more and pulled his head back on to her shoulder.

On the night before Godwin was due to leave to rejoin Edmund, he and Kendra made love. First passionately, then desperately, and by the end of the night their lovemaking was tender – and as the night began to pale about them they clung tightly onto each other.

'How go the preparations?' she asked as the men gathered in the pre-dawn gloom.

Godwin forced a smile. 'Well enough,' he said. 'More men have come than are obliged to follow. I could not have hoped for better.'

'Do not waste their lives or their loyalty.'

He resented her words, but took her hands.

'I will not,' he promised.

The stable lads had spent all evening gathering in the horses. There were three for each man: one to ride, one for a change of mount and one to carry the fodder. The horses steamed in a thin and freezing rain, leaf-buds dripped under fat-bellied rain clouds.

Godwin's war companions mounted up. They were quiet and grim and businesslike.

'Is all ready?' Godwin shouted.

'Ready,' Beorn shouted.

Kendra presented Godwin with a bowl of warm mead. 'Do not forget that your father was Wulfnoth Cild,' she called out. 'God speed you all.'

The ground shook as the company heeled their horses towards the lane. Kendra stood for a long time after the silence had returned. She stood alone looking at the empty lane and the trail of churned up hoof prints.

It was past noon, and already the afternoon light was waning. Shadows gathered among the trees and the fading winter fields, the narrow coomb sloped before her to the black sea.

'You'll catch a cold,' Agnes said, and bustled Kendra back inside.

The loom waited in the corner of the bowyer, the threads hanging slack, the pile of combed wool waiting to be spun.

That evening the hall was thoughtfully quiet. The hearth had been swept clean; an unlit fire stacked by the high seat where the Fighting Man would hang when the victorious men returned. The benches were stacked against the far walls; the tapestries were rolled up and wrapped with linen. How briefly it had gleamed, Kendra thought as she turned the hall key, how fleeting the bench-mirth.

Before she shut the place up again, Kendra walked along the hearth and tried to bring her memories back. She sat among the stacked up benches and tried to imagine smiling faces, and the longer she sat, the more she was aware of the new hall creaking and breathing about her. It was like a living thing, soaking up the lives of the people inside, taking on their shape and hopes and character, as a pair of new shoes bends to their wearer's toes. She felt unbearably sad and did not know why, and laughed at herself. Silly girl! she told herself. You are a slave girl. You should be thankful you have a simple life here, safe from war and violence and lawlessness.

Kendra felt tears inside her, and took in a deep breath and stood abruptly up, stepped outside, let the latch drop behind her, left the hall to its dreams.

The cool night air felt good. A frost was falling. She pushed the hair back from her face and drew in a deep breath. Her footsteps took her slowly across the yard. The muddled hoof prints were hard underfoot. A shooting star curved through the eastern sky. She did not have any more wishes to make, and did not know whether this was a good omen or not.

What now? she asked herself as she lay down on her bed. There was no one to share her sheets or pillow her head, and she curled her legs up to keep herself warm.

'Pray,' she imagined her mother telling her, 'and wait.'

'Live, laugh and enjoy!' she imagined Godwin telling her.

It was easy to leave, she thought; harder to be left behind. But when morning dispelled the darkness, she stood and shivered in the damp air. The sky was cloudless and a heavy dew dripped from the eaves. There was life in the tree twigs, just biding its time, and the first sign of shoots in the hedgerows. And despite everything Kendra felt strangely cheered.

Edmund's warriors gathered in a secret spot along rich river meadows in the west of England. Godwin reckoned there were maybe five hundred men. They waited for a week and another three hundred joined them.

Beorn was unimpressed. 'I've killed more men than this. Bugger me, I've slept with more women! And they could probably fight better than this rabble.'

Godwin trudged up to the top of the hill that looked to the south. The flattened grass shivered in the wind; the blades shone silver in the low dawn light. His oxhide soles squelched with grass-damp, his toes numb from the wet and the wind. He paused only to retie his leggings round his sky-blue woollen hose, to unpick his cloak from a patch of briars. His cloak had been torn on the ride and the one he wore now had been taken from a dead Mercian. There was the brown stain of blood on the hood.

Godwin had tears in his eyes. Edmund's force was pitifully small. The country had failed them.

CHAPTER FIVE

The Siege of Lundenburh

Knut left his coronation and moved straight on Lundenburh, as his father had done three years earlier when he had driven Ethelred into exile. His host was vast, bigger than Swein's Army. There were as many Englishmen as Danes. Their camp filled the fields where Edmund and Godwin had raced horses. It stretched all the way up to the distant woods.

'Lord King, there is your prize,' Eadric said to Knut, as if it was his for the giving.

'Ethelred's treasury is there?'

Eadric nodded. The wealth of England – the mint, the royal scribes and chancellery, the crown, the throne, the archbishops of Euruic and Canturburie – were all there.

Memories of past days came to Eadric. Ethelred, you should have used those three years, he thought. His mind was much on the decision he had made to betray Ethelred, but God had clearly deserted the old man, and Eadric's enemies had drawn close about him. It was clear whose side God was on and Eadric had the sense to listen to the Almighty.

Lundenburh was even bigger than Euruic itself.

'How will we take it?' Knut said.

'How do you take any town?'

'Force,' Knut said. Eadric laughed. He knew Knut better than that. 'Or hunger, or trickery.'

Eadric nodded. He didn't have much time for frontal assaults and scaling ladders, and all the sweat and effort of dragging trees from the forests and battering down the gates. 'I have always found,' Eadric said, 'that treachery was the easiest gate to open.'

Knut's men laid siege to the city. They surrounded it with ditches and ramparts of stacked turf, then tied boats across the Temese and closed it to traffic.

Lundenburh would see sense. Knut seemed content. They were on high ground and could look down and survey the city.

'So that is Crepelgate Palace,' he said, as he made out the distinctive square walls of the royal palace. 'And there is the bridge. What is the southern burg called?'

'Sudwerca,' Eadric said.

'Imaginative. That is the weaker of the two?'

'It is, sire. My men will show you where the weak points are.'

'Show?' Knut said.

Eadric nodded.

'You will do more than show,' Knut said. 'You will lead the way.'

Eadric did not sleep well that night. Treachery was the key. Gold would open any gate. He had to prove his loyalty, and he would do it, even if it was with the blood of the Sudwerca men.

At dawn the next morning the Danes entered Sudwerca through an open postern gate. Offa Fox was with them. Eadric watched as they quickly filed inside. It was soundless. No one shouted. No swords rang out. The men lifted the gates from their hinges and let them crash down on to the floor. Eadric blew his horn. The way was clear.

Caerl was with the defenders on the north side of the river who watched with horror as smoke began to pour up into the air from the south side.

Shit! Caerl thought, and grabbed his sword and shield and ran to where the bridge crossed the river.

Edmund had left Eadwig in charge of the defence of the city. The bridge had been readied for this moment, so that they could cast it down if either burg fell.

Men were fleeing back over the bridge. Danes were pointing and shouting. The bridge had to be cut.

'Break the bridge!' Caerl shouted, but the men were in a confusion of panic.

No one seemed to be in charge. No one did anything.

Caerl sprinted towards them. 'Break the bridge!' he shouted, but Danish warriors were already on the far edge.

'Bowmen!' Caerl shouted. 'Where is Eadwig?'

'Fled!'

Caerl cursed. The defenders were simple citizens, standing because they had nowhere to flee to. In their terror they had forgotten themselves and no guard had been set.

'Shoot!' Caerl shouted.

'But our own men!' they said.

'They can swim,' Caerl spat. 'Shoot those Danes!'

They quickly drew bows and there was a zing! as the arrows leapt out towards the enemy. The first flight drove the Danes back. Four of them fell off the bridge and disappeared under the slow brown water.

More Danes charged forward.

Caerl looked about him. Where were the men? he cursed.

Damn Eadwig! Where were the men? Treachery, Caerl thought, and drew his sword with a great flourish.

'Break the bridge!' he shouted again.

The men began to haul on the ropes. The timbers creaked and the bridge began to sway. Caerl ran forward on to the bridge. It wobbled under him. He shouted behind him, 'Pull down the supports!'

The first to be killed was a young Dane with blond hair and a blue cloak. Magnus was his name, and he had come a-viking from the cold villages of Jutland to earn the silver his father had done under Olaf Tryggvason. He lifted his shield and thought to drive Caerl off the bridge. It was the error all young men made. Caerl swung low and his sword bit deep into Magnus's thigh and shattered the bone. Caerl kicked him off the bridge and Magnus drowned in the murky Temese water, and his mother waited for many years and watched the empty straights and wondered what had befallen her dear son.

The second to die was Stenkil, who sailed from Gotaland on Skoglar's thirty-oared ship *Sea Stallion*. Caerl splintered his shield and shattered Stenkil's collarbone. Stenkil fell and Caerl put his foot on his neck to hold him steady, clove in his skull with a single blow. Stenkil died clutching the hilt of his sword, so that he might fight at Ragnorok against the demons of Hell.

The third was an axeman named Skarp-Hedin. Caerl's sword gashed his left shoulder, but Skarp-Hedin was foaming with battle rage and shrugged off the blow. He smashed the butt of his axe into Caerl's face. Caerl staggered back. The Dane was upon him. He knocked Caerl from his feet.

Caerl spat out his shattered front teeth. He groaned as he crawled towards the side of the bridge.

Skarp-Hedin made a great show of repeating the death blow that Caerl had just dealt. He stood over the crawling man, set his foot firmly in the small of Caerl's back and pinned him to the floor. Skarp-Hedin roared with battle joy as he raised his axe. He brandished it in the air, lifted his head and saw men on the river bank stopping to watch. There was terror and horror written on their faces. The world paused for a moment to witness. He understood why they were transfixed.

Caerl did not see the blow that split his skull from crown to teeth. At the moment of his death the last post came free and the bridge timbers hung for a moment, and then crashed into the river.

Eadwig was found by Queen Emma, dressed as a serving woman, hiding in the Palace of Crepelgate.

'Get up!' she hissed. 'Put on your arms. The bridge has been broken and the city is safe. Remember who you are. Get out there and show the people your face.'

There was wailing that night. It would not be long before Knut had taken the whole city. Queen Emma felt fear enter her as she had never felt it before, a cold rod of steel that left her calm and fierce and resolute. She had sons to lose, and if her sons went, so did her future.

Queen Emma called a council of all the important men in the city. She took her seat next to Eadwig. He bumbled and blathered, and all she could think of was him dressed as a girl hiding in Crepelgate. She stood abruptly in the middle of Eadwig's speech.

'Lundenburh will not fall!' she told them. Her voice quavered, like a metal bar vibrates when the smith's hammer strikes. 'Listen to me, all of you. Put fire in your guts, revenge in your fists. King Edmund will bring a forest of spears, bright warriors in their hammer-knit war shirts, men of grim and warlike aspect. Stop this talk of defeat and slaughter. Edmund will bring relief. Alfred, Edward, come and sit with me. Look, Englishmen, the athelings are here. These are Edmund's brothers. He loves them as dearly as life itself. Eadwig, don mail and helm and lead your men. Whose blood runs in your veins? Woden's blood! No! If I was a man I would lead from the front and I would smite these Danes for daring to bend one blade of grass. I would summon rivers and storms to smite their camp. I call on Christ the Saviour to gnash their bones with teeth of plague. Edmund is depending on us to hold this city. He promised us all. Is he a man to swear false oaths? Do not forget that Edmund is king. He will come and he will bring all the brave men of England.'

The assembled council met her assertion with stunned silence. No one dared to contradict her. Emma stood and looked each man in the eye. Few could meet her gaze and not believe her, such was her force.

They strode out that evening as different men. Lundenburh would not fall. Ethelred's widow had made them swear, made them believe it themselves.

The Army camped on the north side of the Temese, on the high ground above the walled city. Spring was come and it felt like summer to the Norsemen. They stripped off and relaxed, and played summer games in the open spaces between the tents and banner poles. They were unwilling to risk their lives if the city could be taken by terror or treachery or the simple statement of overwhelming force. Some men wrestled; others listened to histories and sagas; a pair of braves knelt in the grass as a monk baptised them. Knut took a dim view on any pagans within the Army, and they would get a silver penny that night for converting to the White Christ.

But Lundenburh did not fall. Traitors were hung, the gates remained shut, and a steady stream of men and food found their way in through the leaky siege. Nevertheless the five weeks had taken their toll. No ship had entered the city. No reinforcements came, but Queen Emma paraded round the walls each day. She dressed all in white and rode a magnificent white horse, with golden bridle, and behind her came Alfred, Eadwig and Edward, followed by a procession of monks carrying some of her collection of reliquaries.

Men looked for her coming and cheered as she approached, then fell silent when she spoke, so that her voice carried far over them all. She lauded the defenders, left them in no doubt that God was watching them from the clouds above their heads, and that He expected them to protect this city against the Danish invaders. She gave the men hope and courage, and the jeering defenders bared their bottoms to the Danes and hurled insults and curses. Many of the insults were too obscure for him to understand, but Knut got the tone, and understood the hand gestures.

The defenders raised curse poles – horses' heads stuck on to tall sticks – and turned them towards the Danish camp.

'And they call themselves Christians!' Knut swore.

Next to him loomed Thorkel the Tall. The great warrior said nothing.

They had become as used to the queen's procession as the defenders and Knut enjoyed the spectacle of a beautiful woman dressed in red and white, and the scent of incense that drifted from the city. From far off, he saw a handsome woman, nine years his senior, large-breasted, wide-hipped and with a white wimple pulled tight about her face.

'She's magnificent,' he said.

Thorkel nodded as Queen Emma passed south towards the

river walls, and the English cheers drifted towards them. 'But she's no virgin.'

Thorkel had once served Ethelred as a mercenary. He knew many of the men in court, and had low opinions of the lot. He had taken Ethelred's unclipped coin and kept his mouth shut.

'So why do they fight for Edmund?' Knut asked, turning to the mighty Thorkel.

He shrugged. 'They're fools.'

'How long till we break them?'

Thorkel took a long time answering. 'Well, we do not have any engines of war, and the stone walls are too strong for us to storm.'

Thorkel fell silent and Knut turned to him. 'So?'

'We wait,' Thorkel said, 'and starve them. Or they sue for mercy. Or we threaten to burn and rase the place to the foundation timbers.'

Knut looked round to the other men about him, but none of them wanted to go against Thorkel's opinion. 'Eric?' he said at last.

Eric of Hlathir was the son of Norse kings. He had strawberry-blond hair, freckles and bright blue eyes in a narrow and hawkish face.

Eric half laughed, but he spoke his mind. 'Our ships have cut off the river. We have taken the southern side of the bridge. Once they start to eat their horses, they'll see sense. Either that or disease will drive them out.'

'And what of this princeling hiding out in the woods?'

The whole company laughed. Edmund led a dwindling war band, hated and hunted among his own people like badgers.

'Eadric has caught ten of his men and killed them all. He is drawing in on the rebels. He has promised to bring his head.'

'Can we trust him?'

Thorkel laughed for the first time. 'Eadric? No. But then don't trust any of them. They're English.'

Knut promised a purse of gold to the man who brought him Edmund's head. It was now June and still Queen Emma processed about the walls and still Lundenburh's defenders hurled determined abuse at the Danes. Each time Thorkel was forced to put on mail and helm and lead an assault his men were repulsed more viciously than before and Knut's temper began to wear and fray.

In the end Knut called for a parley. He came forward under peace oaths and saw the English leaders approaching.

'Where is the woman?' he said.

Eadric frowned. 'She's up there.'

Knut squinted towards the walls. He could see a glimpse of white.

'So who are these lot?'

'Eadwig, Edmund's younger brother, and her elder son, Edward.'

Knut lost interest. 'You go and talk to them. Ask them if they're ready to surrender.'

Eadric came back half an hour later. His cheeks were red, and he was breathing quickly.

'What did they say?'

'No,' Eadric edited.

Knut was irritated. 'Next time say we want her to come.'

'She will not come,' the word came back when Knut offered parley a week later.

Knut laughed.

One day Knut was playing chess with Eric. The pieces were made of carved walrus ivory. Knut's king had been surrounded by Eric's warriors and his impatience was growing.

'What is it?' Knut snapped when one of his men interrupted.

'There is a man outside who claims to know how Lundenburh shall fall. He claims to be able to open a gate where our men might break in.'

Knut's father's rise to power had been ruthless and bloody. There were skeletons all over Danemark to prove it and it was almost because of this that Knut disliked treachery of any kind. But traitors had their purposes. He had the man shown in. He was ugly and stooped, with grasping hands and a lisp. He spoke English in a manner that Knut could not understand.

'What is he saying?' Knut demanded.

Thorkel translated. The man's name was Cuthbert and he claimed to be a shoemaker. He said that he knew the commander of one of the gates, who would open it to the Army for a certain weight of gold.

'Hold out your hands,' Knut said, and inspected the man's open palms. They looked like a shoemakers hands. The man smelt of leather. Knut was satisfied. He gave him a purse of silver. 'I shall make you a lord among men if you deliver Lundenburh to me.'

That night Eric led some of his best men along the stream to the culvert nearest to the gate. The signal was given and they made their way forward and were lost to sight.

Thorkel waited with his finest warriors. When the signal was given, they would charge the gate.

'Lundenburh will be yours by dawn,' he promised Knut.

The sound of distant shouts drifted across the fields. The unmistakable clang of steel. An hour later Eric limped into Knut's tent. His arm was bandaged. His mail had been broken in two places and the padded undershirt showed through. His hair was matted, whether with sweat or blood it was too dark to tell. There was a smeared splatter of blood across his right cheek.

'We were discovered,' he said simply, tossed his helmet on to the floor. 'They came at us from all sides. It was a trap. She was there. I lost twenty of my best men. They died bravely.' He touched the broken mail links. 'I killed the lad who did this.'

'So they are not close to surrender,' Knut said.

Eric winced as he sat down and one of the men began to unlace the thongs on his mail.

'Are you sure it was her?'

Eric nodded.

'It might have been a man dressed in white.'

Eric shook his head, and his smile was lopsided. 'I know her voice. It was her. She screamed fury at us.' Eric shuddered. 'No man could stand against such fury.'

Next morning Eric did not get up from his bed. Three ribs were broken, and he came down with fever. He was carried into the war council, where he sweated and winced and said little.

'We sit here while a woman holds Lundenburh against us and that upstart lad rides about the country unopposed,' Knut said. His volume rose as he spoke, as his tension finally broke through. 'And now I hear that Edmund was allowed into Wincestre last week and feted like a conqueror. He should have been caught and bound and brought to me. I am the king!'

With each day the news got worse. Edmund had been in Wincestre and Wilton, Bade and Beiminstre, adding men to his household guards. Knut would hang every man who betrayed him. He decided that it was time to remind the English of their oaths. It would serve as a warning to Dane and Englishman alike.

'How large is his war band?'

Knut had more than eight thousand men.

'Eric,' he said, 'stay here till you are rested, but take

Lundenburh for me. Thorkel, we shall ride and hunt down this Edmund.'

So half the Army remained in Lundenburh with Eric of Hlathir, who had recovered from the fever but until his ribs mended was unfit for hard riding, while the other half rode in search of Knut's rival.

At the head of the Army rode Thorkel, his red wool cloth tight across his broad chest, one enormous hand holding his reins, the other resting on the pommel of his sword.

'Keep him close to you,' Swein had warned Knut before he died. 'He is as unpredictable as a sea wind.'

Knut made Thorkel swear that he would catch Edmund. Thorkel took his oaths seriously and there was no more terrifying man. His long, thin sundial nose had been broken at a sharp angle and veered across his face as the sun moved from east to west – as if finding his way to Edmund.

Thorkel burnt the halls of the Hastingas. He ravaged Leomynstre and Cicestre, and burnt the farms about Wincestre. The longer they plundered, the heavier the baggage train of mules and pack animals that carried the Army's booty. It was rough wooing. The Danes quite enjoyed themselves. No shield-wall met them. No burg of brave warriors were thrown across the path. No man resisted; they cowered in their halls and prayed. The Danes took their pick of livestock, altarpieces, ale, stallions, hack-silver and a glut of slave girls.

'We are here to catch the upstart, not stuff your gut,' Knut told Thorkel one day when his men lay drunk in a hall they had plundered already. 'The whole country is at stake.'

Godwin and Edmund wore out ten horses as they rode about Wessex trying to rally more men. Edmund wore mail and helm and a kingly sword, and Godwin carried the Wessex banner of the

White Dragon. These tokens were like the bones of saints. Men stood about and stared in wonder at the banner that Alfred had carried in battle, and every king after him, from victory to victory. But the shadows of Alfred and Edward, Athelstan and Edgar loomed over the young men like the giants of old.

Edmund and Godwin still found it hard to persuade men to fight. At some halls they came too late, at others too soon, like the ill-timed guest who arrives when the ale is all drunk or yet unserved.

Men and women lined up to bicker with them.

'Why should we fight so our neighbours can steal our lands?' some said.

'Who needs more corpses? We have enough maimed men for our shielings.'

'I want my sons to grow old. I want peace and order, and if that means a Dane as king, then I shall take it.'

Sometimes they managed to tilt men's anger away; other times they were less successful.

'Only fools think that leaving their shield on the wall will save them,' Godwin said as they left another untidy meeting. 'Old age promises no man peace.'

The prominent families welcomed them surreptitiously. The more they had, the more they had to lose. They could not afford to take sides with either king. It was a cleft stick with a sharp edge. They listened and nodded and tugged their beards, and eventually their hearts were heavy and they promised aid: 'No lord is dearer to me than those descended from the House of Cerdic.' They had tears in their eyes. They had suffered so much anguish and despair, but at last they made deadly serious and solemn promises. 'If you can raise the fyrds, I will come to your banner.'

'If we can raise the fyrds!' Edmund cursed when he and

Godwin were alone. 'Why doesn't one of them stick out his dumb neck? If we could raise the fyrds, then we would not have to tramp about the country hiding in trees and begging men to come and fight.'

They sat and shook with frustration.

'Set a date,' Godwin said. 'Set a date and a place and tell them that all their neighbours have pledged their support. They will be too fearful to be left behind, and that way we will gather a great fyrd.'

Throughout June and July the Army followed the rumour of Edmund's path. Knut was restless. The same thegns who had made promises to Edmund lined up to swear their loyalty to Knut. 'You swore oaths to me in Hamtun in March,' Knut told the men kneeling before him. 'No doubt you swore oaths to Edmund as well. Why should I believe you now?'

'Edmund threatened us!' they wailed.

'And I threaten you!' Knut told them. He stuck his chin out and glared at them. 'I threaten you!' he shouted.

They shrank away from him. There was not an honest man left among the English.

'Three years ago your lords gave my father hostages. I took those men and cut the nose and ears and hands off each one. What should I do now to make you keep your oaths? Should I take your wives with me?'

The men's faces went red and the Danish warriors laughed as the womenfolk fell to their knees and started beseeching Christ's mercy.

They talked a lot about Christ and God and saints and angels, but Knut took a long time to calm down.

'I tell you what I shall do,' Knut said at last. 'I shall trust you. Hear me? I shall trust you all to keep to your word, and as God is my witness, He shall judge you when the Doomsday comes. But if you fail me again, I shall let my war hounds loose upon the land and they will ravage and burn as if the Devil himself had come.'

The men bowed and scraped and Knut wanted to kick them.

'Bring me Edmund's head,' he said, 'or woe betide you all.'

Edmund was sly as a fox. Traitors came with word of his whereabouts, but each time the trap was set he managed to slip through. According to reports, his war band had grown, but they kept to byways and tracks, left the straight Roman roads deserted.

Thorkel's frustration grew. The Army became more violent and ruthless as the summer continued. The Devil was not far off. He sat on each Dane's shoulder as they meted out punishments, which became harder and crueller. They were like the farmer who scatters the ploughed field with seed, but the seed the Army sowed was grief and anger, fear and the stark lesson of unfaithful men hanging from gibbet trees.

Men wept as their halls were emptied, their daughters dragged off. 'Forgive us,' they wept, 'for not resisting him. Save us and do not treat us so harshly!' But Thorkel ignored them.

He rode ever at the Army's fore, long shanks dangling down the flanks of his black cob, fingers twitching dangerously. He rode under a continual storm cloud, with ravens and crows around him and smoke at his heels, as if he was bringing the apocalypse – weighing the souls of his men down with sin.

That summer was cold and wet and gloomy. In the woods and field-fringes, the first foxgloves began to bloom. Knut saw meadowsweet by his horse's hooves as it drank from a stream and he thought of a day back in Danemark when he had been falconing with his father and had brought down a giant crane. The bird had been almost as large as Knut himself. He recalled how it had flapped its broken wings, trying to rise into the sky with the falcon's claws embedded in its back. The thought disturbed Knut.

Where was that damned Edmund?

It was like trying to grasp stream water in your fist.

It was just after midsummer's day when Eadric rode into the Danish camp as puffed up as a toad. 'We have him!' he said, and clapped his hands together. 'We have him now!'

Knut looked up from the game of chess he was playing. He did not like Eadric and did not believe him, but Eadric seemed convinced.

'I have a man with Edmund's company. He is just one day ahead of us, riding north and west. He has sent out word that he will raise his banner at Penne.'

'Where is Penne?' Knut growled.

Eadric drew a map on the palm of his hand.

'We are here, and Penne is there.'

'You are sure?'

'Sure.'

Eadric was like a cheap camp-whore, Knut thought, as he let the man speak: alluring, seductive, eager and grasping. 'If we send men behind him here, we can ride up this valley here, then we shall bag him and his men and they'll all be with Christ by the Sabbath.'

Thorkel came forward and the plan was repeated. Then local men came and listened and gave advice and drew a more accurate map in the dirt. Thorkel squatted down to ask which way the land around Penne lay. There were few men with more experience of war and campaigning than him. Eadric answered every question and at last Thorkel was satisfied.

He rose stiffly and nodded. 'Good,' he said, and the shadow from his sundial nose was at eight o'clock. 'We have him now.'

The meeting place for Edmund's war band was set at Cenwealh's Mound, where the men of Sumersæton, Dornsætum and Wiltunscir traditionally met. Edmund brought his men to a rest in the dark shadows of the field-edge trees and waited in hope for loyal warriors to arrive. From the shoulder of the high ridge they had fine views back to the south and the rolling Sumersæton fields. To the west the land fell away to the Adelingi Marshes, and to the east lay the Stour Valley, while the Fosse Way went a little to the north.

Edmund strode to the fringes of the trees and looked about him. Godwin stepped up behind him. This was the moment when all their hope – or fears – would be realised.

Before them lay an empty field. There was no smoke, no sign of smoke, no sign of the warriors they had hoped for. There was simply an empty field, the summer meadow just starting to turn to seed.

'Where are they?' Edmund said.

'Well, they're not here,' Godwin said.

'I can see that.'

Godwin said nothing. Ask a stupid question, he thought, get a stupid answer.

Edmund stalked about the field. They were all saddle-sore. There was no sign of a camp.

'Not one.'

Godwin's skin prickled. It all looked too quiet. His mind was full of possibilities. This was a trap. But to Edmund he said, 'They will come.'

As they dismounted and made a fire, a few lads came out of the tree shadows. They were young men, in threes and fours, with their father's swords, their grandfather's helm and their neighbour's shield. Few of them had mail shirts, though all had spears, whether they were made for hunting or fighting. This was not the great and noble company that Edmund needed.

'They're boys,' Edmund said, when he had welcomed them all.

'Not long ago we were boys,' Godwin said.

On the second day Edmund's men were preparing the night meal when armed warriors rode out of the trees at the bottom of the valley.

Edmund walked forward, thinking they were English, but then he saw the way they wore their hair and the emblems on their shields.

'Danes!' he said in shock.

'The Danes!' someone shouted. 'We are betrayed!'

Someone thrust a bridle into Edmund's hand. 'Flee!' he urged.

Edmund pushed him away. He was tired of constant flight. A sudden calm came over him. He was the anointed king. He had struggled years for this moment and would not be rushed. 'No,' he said. 'I will not fly without striking a blow against the foe.'

Despair made Edmund wild. Godwin ran up and saw the look in Edmund's eye and understood. This was it. This is where it will end, he thought.

'Take the hill ridge,' he ordered. They would die here, but they would die well and with honour.

Godwin took Edmund's banner and drew Wulfnoth's sword and it flashed white and angry in the flat sunlight. Their men were too green, too few in number; only the crowd gave them courage – that and their innocence. It was not the war band they had hoped for, but it would have to do.

'The slope will dull any charge,' Godwin shouted. 'Shoulder

to shoulder. The Last King of England! Let's make a stand worthy of a song!'

Thorkel's men were practised and experienced soldiers. They moved quickly and efficiently as they drew up their shieldwall and hurried up the hill. Edmund's men were still dressing their ranks; some barely knew how to hold a shield. At the back of the camp, confusion reigned. Some men took horse and fled; others were riding back to camp. They milled about, unsure what was happening, and were rushing to get their swords and shields from saddlepack or camp.

It was too late to rally them, Godwin saw. The banner flapped defiantly in the hill breeze. Up the hill, the Danes came, a wall of shields, a thicket of spears, a stack of wood to be split into kindling.

Godwin shouted to the men about him. 'Stand firm! Do not fear the foe. Sons of fame, awake to glory! Remember the great heroes of Wessex!'

A fey fury came over him. Oh, at last! Godwin thought, and all the pent-up frustration surged through him. These were the warriors who had tormented his father, tormented his childhood, brought fear and concern into days that should have been prosperous and peaceful. Leofwine, Godwin promised, I will die today, but at least I shall take some of those bastards with me.

The wind flapped the banner harder, as if the ghosts of England had rallied to Godwin's side, and Edmund felt the chill ruffle his hair. He set his helmet upon his head and the war cry rose: 'England!'

The Danes came within twenty feet. Thorkel hefted his shield, and without even looking round at his companions he let out a great roar and then charged towards the royal banner.

Thorkel gutted the first man, drove his sword hilt into the

mouth of another, and the third was felled by a spear-thrust from behind. Thorkel laughed as he drove his pommel into one lad's mouth and saw his teeth shower the men to his left. His sword was a whirlwind of death about him. He moved towards the English king like a reaper working his way along a row of corn. It was almost too easy.

Edmund's companions fell back before his fury. Their spear points glanced harmlessly off his mail shirt. Thorkel killed Goldwyn the Fair and Rathstan Longbeard. Godwin gripped the banner and set it firmly in the ground and his heart swelled with honour. He saw the sword rise and begin its murderous descent, but against Thorkel came Beorn and all Wulfnoth's men.

Beorn came with all the fury of a terrier as it leaps at the shaggy heath wolf. He grinned his ugliest grin, drove his shield pommel straight at Thorkel's chest. It was not how heroes fought, but it was just enough to throw Thorkel off balance. Thorkel tried to stab again but Beorn drove his spear at him and hit him in the sternum, which knocked the great Danish warrior back on his feet. The men about Godwin surged forward.

Beorn's heart leapt at this opportunity. He would split the old Dane from snout to shin. He laughed and drove his spear at Thorkel's face, but just at that moment a spear grazed Beorn's throat and he pulled his blow. Behind Beorn were all who had gone into exile with Wulfnoth. They were ferocious, hard and effective.

Thorkel had driven too far from his companions. He was hemmed in by a hedge of jabbing thorns. His Danes fought like mad beasts to rescue their lord. Bunna – one of Wulfnoth's men – took a spear straight through the soft flesh of his throat; another lad had a sword drive into his groin, and he groaned as he fell.

'To me!' Godwin called, and held the banner high. Behind him came Edmund and all of his companions.

Fate brought them to make their stand on Cenwealh's Mound that day. A thousand men to stand in battle on behalf of their country. Doomed but determined, anger drove them. They did not care about their lives. All they wanted was to cut down each Dane until there were none left before him. Men who had begun to run paused. They saw the Danish charge had been halted and began to take heart. They called out to the others.

Cenred the Young and his youngest brother, Cynric, who had promised his mother he would not fight, died together, glad that they had each killed a Dane. Ulfkils the Lame had spent the night in prostrate prayer, but his twin sons, Tilwine and Tinwulf, both died at Thorkel's sword. Stigand the Singer fell, a spear in his bladder, and a young thegn's daughter, who had fallen in love with him, would renounce love when she heard of his death and commit her body and soul to the Lord.

The English died where they stood, but more stepped up behind them. Beorn's crooked teeth were red with blood, making his smile even uglier. He grinned at the foe and the foe shrank back. Godwin shrugged off spear blows as if they were slaps. The ferocity of the English was unnerving. The Danes took a step back. The English were upon them, their courage renewed.

Men who had wavered between flight and fight pulled their shields from their backs, drew their swords and charged into the fray. Others crept out of the line of trees and fell upon the Danish rear with spear-thrusts seeking face and neck, bright swords slashing, shield butts punching forward. It was confusing and chaotic. Men roared and shouted as they killed and died.

One voice rose louder than the rest. 'Wulfnoth!' it said. 'Wulfnoth!'

It took a moment before Godwin realised that it was his own – roaring with rage. 'Wulfnoth!' he shouted. 'Wulfnoth!'

From left and right and pushing behind he heard his father's men answering his roars. They carried him forward and he felt like the tip of a spear of men that is thrust into the heart of the enemy. Man for man, the Danes far outstripped the English, but for each English man the Danes killed, three jumped into their place and fury made up the difference in courage or skill. The White Dragon of Wessex began to push the Black Raven back. Edmund blew his war horn and the Danes took another step back. And another. Then suddenly the Danes were three feet away and Godwin could not believe his eyes and did not know whether to thank God or charge.

A more experienced troop would have routed Thorkel's men – pursued them from the field, hacked at their backs as they turned and fled – but the Danish shieldwall bristled with spears. They retreated in good order, dragging their wounded with them.

A few fools ran after them, hoping for a slaughter and were quickly cut down and surrounded.

'Hold!' Edmund was calling.

'Look! More Danes!'

Danish horsemen were rushing up to join Thorkel, but the fierce Spear-Dane had been overconfident; he had reached out to grasp victory before it was his.

The English jeered and booed as he glared up at them, blood-ied and beaten.

Godwin stared in stunned silence at the Army as the setting sun threw long shadows across the slanted battlefield. His hand was stuck to the banner pole by dead men's blood. His helmet had been knocked off somewhere and he stood a slow realisation came over him: they had just met Thorkel the Tall in battle and yet lived and breathed.

'We have won!' someone said, and Godwin turned almost without understanding.

'We have won!' the word was repeated, and it took long moments for the battle rage to fall from Godwin so he could understand: they held the place of slaughter.

Godwin remembered very little of the fight, had only discovered the cuts to his left leg and thigh on the ride from the battle, but he heard Beorn telling how he had wounded Thorkel. Godwin was not there, though he thought he had seen it.

'I've not heard of a legend that was pegged down by truth,' Edmund said that night. 'But what concerns me more was how Thorkel's men found us.'

Two days later the survivors camped at a stinking and run-down manor named Langelete. The traitor was brought out. He was a young Sumersæton thegn named Edwine who had joined the band at Sarum. Godwin had shared bread with him, but Beorn had seen him try to slip away to meet with the Danes. Edwine had been bound and gagged. His face was puffy with beatings.

'Here is the man who would betray us,' Godwin said, and kicked Edwine to the ground. Godwin grabbed Edwine by the hair and dragged him to his knees. He held him bowed forward before his king.

Edmund drew his sword, said a quick prayer in Latin. 'May the Lord God have mercy upon your soul!' Edmund said and then his sword flashed and Edwine's torso fell as his head remained in Godwin's hand. Blood squirted a foot into the air. Edwine's body still struggled for a moment, kicking and twitching as if the trunk did not know that it was dead.

There were no cheers. There was no time to rest. They were the hunted and the hounds had their scent.

Four days later the English drifted into Malmesberie saddle-sore and hungry.

A wondrous sight awaited them. Godwin had to clench his teeth to stop himself from weeping. There, before the gates of the town, were two thousand English warriors. There were grey-beards and veterans and all the banners of the great Wessex families, rank upon rank of mailed men; banners that had been carried at Brunanburgh and Ethandun, Ashdown and Basing; grim faces, sharp spears, men who had remembered their pride. It was as astonishing as the parting of the Red Sea or the columns of flame that brought God's chosen through the desert.

The company lifted their spears and saluted them with a great cheer and a blast of war horns. At the fore rode a woman: Ealdgyth of Lincolia, Edmund's wife, sitting side-saddle, her stomach heavy with child, certainly too heavy for her to be riding.

'I have brought you a fyrd fit for a king, Edmund, son of Ethelred. The English have remembered how to fight.'

That night masses were said for the souls of the dead. Godwin and Edmund knelt before the rood screen. The last words of the *Te Deum* echoed in Godwin's mind.

In te, Domine, speravi:
non confundar in æternum —

O Lord, in thee have I trusted:
let me never be confounded.

CHAPTER SIX

The Battle of Sorestone

Edmund's new war council sat on barrels in the monastery cloisters as Godwin spoke: 'The river and marshes make Malmesberie a fine place to defend, but we need a battle, not a siege.'

The mood of the newcomers was against a battle. 'Let us harry the Danes,' one said. 'Send to Hamtunscir and the South Saxons to bring more men. When we outnumber Knut, we can meet him in battle.'

They all looked to Edmund so that he could decide.

There was a long pause. Edmund's head was lowered. At last he looked up.

'Godwin speaks right,' Edmund said at last. 'One victory can bring us a thousand men. If we fight again, we shall have the whole country with us.'

'But what if we lose?' someone said.

'Or if you are killed?'

'We do not lose,' Godwin said. Someone else tried to speak, but Godwin spoke over him. 'We do not lose.'

Edmund laughed. He looked at anyone to contradict this.

'We fight again and we do not lose.'

*

It was Beorn who found the place of battle, a village a few miles north of the Fosse Way, along which the Danes would come.

'There is a village named Sorestone, about a mile north of the road. The river there has carved a narrow and deep cut through the flat fields. On the north side the cliffs are a man's height. If we make our stand there it will go hard on the Danes, even if they outnumber us. But it will also be a difficult place to leave in reckless pursuit,' Beorn said.

'That is good,' Edmund replied, 'for the Danes could lure us out too easily, as they almost did at Penne.'

Godwin went to look at the place and felt in his bones that this was where they would win the next battle.

'Have the fyrds camp here,' Edmund said simply. 'It will be good to get them away from the alehouses and women. Make our position clear. We shall fight the next battle here!'

It was July. The Army had paused to gather in all its strength. Edmund's scouts trailed them as they moved north along the Fosse Way.

'Knut is so confident he does not care what we see,' the scouts reported. 'He even offered us a meal.'

Edmund didn't like to hear of his enemy's magnanimity. 'How many men has he?'

'Five thousand,' the scouts said, though in reality he had more. 'There are many English banners in his company.'

'I am sure there are,' Edmund said. 'No matter. They are the worst of the country. We shall do ourselves a benefit to thin them out, lest they breed more traitors among us.'

A day's march off, the Army stopped.

Edmund waited for two days. He wanted battle and paced up and down. He even rode out to see the Danes for himself.

'Why does he wait?' Edmund fretted.

Godwin was nervous as well, but he tried to sound calm. 'Do not worry so,' he told him. 'Our strength grows daily.'

'Why does he wait?' Edmund demanded again. 'I fear a trap. Send scouts all about to see if Eadric has brought more of his kinsmen from the north.'

'Don't worry,' Godwin said. 'The Army is weighed down with plunder. They are rich men now. They do not want to risk their wealth in battle. But we have nothing, which will make us strong.'

'What if we win? Will we become fearful?'

Godwin laughed. 'That will be a fine fate. But let us worry about that when the time comes.'

Twilight was falling that evening as the Danish vanguard rode into view on the far fields and began to make camp. Edmund sat on his horse and watched them across the field.

'When I was young,' he said, 'I had to learn the names of my forebears. Edmund, son of Ethelred, son of Edgar, son of Edmund, son of Alfred, son of Ethelwulf, son of Egbert, who married Redburga. We are the oldest royal family in Christendom. Can you believe that? Our ancestor was Woden, whom heathens worshipped as a god. But he was no devil; he was a brave and mighty warrior. Who is Knut that he thinks to take my land from me? He comes from a barbarous people who have long since given up the right rule of kings and submitted themselves to the rule of the strongest sword.'

They watched the Danes light kindling and chop branches off trees to light their watch fires.

'So. There will be battle on the morrow,' Edmund said. 'Is there enough ale for breakfast?'

'Enough to give them courage,' Godwin told him, 'but not so much that they will rush forward and get themselves killed. Do you know what the people are calling you now?'

'Their crippled king?'

'No. They call you Edmund Ironside.'

'Ironside?' Edmund laughed. 'I like that.'

The two men looked at each other, and for a moment they saw themselves as the lads in the yard at West Minster, playing football with Athelstan.

'We have come a long way,' Edmund said. 'And there is just a little thread left to play out.'

That night some men sat quietly, others drank in noisy and cheerful bands, while the few devout warriors knelt and prayed for their souls to pass into Heaven's keeping. Godwin walked to the rampart where they would fight in the morning.

There was a thin trickle of water running through the narrow valley, with steep banks on either side. It was as if a mighty river had once flowed here, or as if giants themselves had carved the ramparts. He tried to picture the Army massing below and felt his breathing speed up as he imagined himself standing here, on the morrow, with sword and shield and helm.

Godwin stood and braced himself and looked up at the stars and prayed for their help in the morning. Penne had been little more than a barnyard slapping match. Tomorrow would be real. He feared the dawn, but he wished it would come and be done with.

'Sleep,' a shadow said.

It was Irwyn, one of Wulfnoth's men.

'Have you said your prayers?'

Irwyn nodded.

'Will you pray with me?'

Later that night Godwin could not sleep. Around him in the dark the campfires had smouldered and sent sparks flying up into the darkness. He felt that this was his very last night on earth. Each sound was as clear as etched glass, each sensation of the uneven ground beneath him, each star that glimmered above his head. He marvelled at the sweetness of the cool night air, watched the sun rise through the blue smoke of Malmesberie and felt tears in his throat.

Kendra's face came back to him as clearly as if she stood before him. He wondered where she was now. He felt unbearably guilty, as if the whole weight of his past wrongs was being measured on the scales. He would give her land and a dowry and she could set herself up as lady of her own land, and find a good thegn who might marry her. He would be good to all, and never speak ill of any man.

He let out a long sigh. 'Hold your shield high until the battle-play begins,' he could remember his father telling him.

Sleep, he reassured himself. Sleep.

Next morning dawn spared none of her glory. She broke over a field of barley that was just starting to turn to gold. The ball of red grew brighter as it rose and its colour changed to orange and then yellow and then became too bright to look upon, spread clear blue skies like wings over the fields.

Edmund drew up his shieldwall at the brink of the bank, with a hedge on the left and a marshy hollow on the right, where the slope ran down towards a fish pond and a mill stream. It was there in the centre that he raised the White Dragon of Wessex, and took off his helm and shook the sweat from his hair so all could see him. Godwin stood next to him. His chain-mail shirt hung heavy on his shoulders, the links repaired where a spear-thrust had been turned.

He felt as though his whole life had been in preparation for this trial. Felt the blood of his ancestors humming in his veins.

'Abbot Wulsy,' Edmund called out, 'will you give mass and bless us all!'

The abbot was a well-born man with a fine accent and thinning hair, a favourite among the fireside riddlers. He knew more and dirtier riddles than any other man alive. That morning, however, he spoke quickly and solemnly, and promised God's aid as surely as if Christ himself was donning heavenly war shirt and spear and standing amongst them.

Godwin took his place while Edmund Ironside rode along the line, pointing and joking and recalling men's names. He greeted each thegn and war leader in turn as the Sumersæton fyrd gathered about their alderman. His name was Elfric the Short, on account of his great height. He was a stunning man with yellow hair that shone almost silver in the sun, and a drooping moustache that reached his belt. There was not a maiden in the whole kingdom who would not give her right hand for such golden hair, Godwin thought, or lashes so long. He found himself staring at the man, for he was both handsome and wild. If he went against Thorkel in mortal combat, then it would be like a tale of old, when the giants fought the gods.

Elfric wore a coat of long mail, hard and hand-wrought, that hung almost to his knees, each link cunningly crafted, and his men were well armoured. They talked quickly and laughed easily, and although the bosses of their shields were of a fashion that Godwin's grandfather might have used, their spears and swords were as finely decorated as any Godwin had seen.

Edmund put them on the left wing, where Thorkel liked to fight.

'Strike hard!' Edmund said to Elfric and his retainers. 'Strike true! Do not give ground. A pound of gold to the man who kills Knut!'

The Sumersæton fyrd cheered and grinned at him, and the

king passed by, Elfric unfurled the banner of Sumersæton: the red dragon on a field of white. He knelt and shook the king's hands with both of his own, put his helmet back on and lifted up his red shield and his men gave three hurrahs.

In the centre, the men of Defenascir were gathering. They were shorter and darker than the Sumersæton men, and few of them had the silver-blond hair of Elfric's house. They carried light throwing spears and short stabbing spears, and stank of cider.

Their alderman was named Ethelsy and was Edmund's cousin. They shared the same lanky build of the House of Cerdic, but Ethelsy was a full-grown man, and his son Ethelward was there.

Along the line of the river bank the fyrds of Hamtunscir and Oxenefordscire were coalescing from the milling crowds to form the right wing. Abbot Wulsy led the men of Hamtunscir. Their alderman, Aylmar the Darling, was noticeably absent.

'He now follows Knut and brings shame on us all,' Wulsy declared. 'Let us make up for his shame by placing ourselves against Knut's best warriors. Each one of us shall fight as three and so make up for the men who failed you!'

Abbot Wulsy had brought St Swithun's clavicle with him from Wincestre. His monks had carried the reliquary through the camp the night before, swinging incense and singing hymns, while Wulsy drank half a hogshead and performed his old party trick of saying the catechism in Latin forwards and then backwards, before bawdy riddling began. His banner was St Swithun's Cross, yellow on blue, flapping proudly between the Red Dragon of Sumersæton and the White Dragon of Wessex.

Next came the men of Oxenefordscire, who had suffered most at the hands of the Danes. They were eager for vengeance and it was in the centre that the battle would be won or lost. There between the two wings Edmund placed his household retainers, against Knut's hersirs.

'Knut's Army is larger than ours, so we'll just have to do without a reserve today,' he said simply as the captains came to share the Eucharist. 'It'll make the men fight harder if they know there is no one behind them, and the main battle will be in the centre, king to king.'

Edmund paused on his horse for a moment and took in the whole battle line as the last men filed into place.

'So, here we are,' he said to Godwin as his horse was led away from the field.

'Here we are.'

'It's going to be a hell of a battle,' Edmund said to his companions and grinned. 'It has been a long road for many of us. Are you ready, brothers?'

They nodded and murmured, and some of them smiled, or looked across to the enemy, or adjusted their shield straps.

Godwin caught Edmund's eye.

Yes, the look in his eye said. Ready.

When the Army had finished drawing themselves up around their banners Knut made a great show of having his horses led well back from the battlefield.

'All the easier to catch him,' Godwin said.

The banter all about was cheery, but the cheerier the men were, the more nervous Godwin felt. He stamped to feel the ground beneath his feet, drew in a deep breath and stepped out to check the lines. The various banners shuffled either forwards or backwards, and the men in the front line prayed as they lifted their shields and overlapped them. Prayers were chanted, songs sung, lucky rhymes and words of bravery and encouragement sounded out all around, and when someone farted, the Sumersæton ranks rippled with laughter.

Between the restless ranks was a broad, lush meadow, a tapestry of rich green embroidered with the reds and blues and yellows of many flowers, buzzing gently with bees and tiny yellow butterflies and the occasional noisy bumblebee. The close-packed Danes started silently across the fields. They trudged towards them like ploughmen going to the furrow, a line of reapers marching towards the corn.

All soldiers pray to God before battle, for even in the company of their fellows, a man is never so alone. The businesslike manner of the enemy made Godwin nervous. He prayed for strength and pride. Prayed that God would bring them victory, as He had brought it to the Israelites. Prayed that it was not the English homes that wept that night. Prayed that it was the Danish widows who waited at the ends of empty lanes and wept.

Remember your boasts, Godwin told himself, felt the mood of the men around him. They joked and laughed and began to mock the Danes for being dull and serious, wild or illiterate. And they all fed off their king's mood too, and Edmund was determined and bloody-minded.

The war cry was 'Ironside!' and Ironside would lead them to victory. They would not die that day. They would be victorious. Godwin felt the courage flow from man to man like a rumour as he stood by the side of Edmund's banner-bearer, a fellow Sudsexe lad named Egbert Halftroll.

Godwin had practically lived in his mail and now he marvelled at how little weight he felt. He crossed himself, wished he had kept every oath he had ever made, wished he had prayed more devoutly, wished he had given money to the Church, wished that he had not killed Ulf in the duel, wished he had not cursed his father's name, wished the damned battle would start.

*

Edmund couldn't have more than two thousand men, Knut thought as he looked up at the English shieldburg perched precariously along the lip of the steep and pebbly bank. He had nearly twice that many, in depth of ten men, with his own English on the left and the Danes and the Norwegians in the centre and the right, where a hedge defined the edge of the battlefield.

It was there that Thorkel would lead the best men. A blunt snout, like a boar spear, driven into the guts of the English. The men who were to lead the charge were warming up now. Jomsvikings and berserkers – big men who butted their helmets against one another, laughed and shouted, swung their axes in big circles to loosen up their shoulders.

Knut thanked Christ he was not facing them. Each man wore long shirts of iron mail. They carried long bearded axes, chased and damascened and lovingly polished, that could cut through helm and head and split a man down to his navel. Shield-bearers protected them from enemy blows, and it would not take long for their ferocity to batter the enemy back. And once their shield-wall was broken, their line divided, the English would break and run, and then the slaughter would begin. It was like watching a wolf seize a lamb and crunch its bones. They'd tear the soft heart out of them.

Knut had seen these berserkers rip open shieldwalls from the Baltic to the Irish Sea. It was a simple ruse, but then it seemed to Knut that battles were simple enough. He had forgotten how many he'd seen in the last four years, fighting Dane and Wendel, Norwegian and English. Some battles were lost before the two sides came to blows. You could sense it in the enemy, how willing they were to stand against you. If both sides wanted to fight, then they beat at each other till one lost heart and courage and ran for the nearest hedge or hollow. This could come quite suddenly and without any obvious reason. The slaughter could go on for miles.

Knut smelt the wind and sensed a new will this morning among the bristling English line. Maybe it would take a little longer than usual, he thought to himself, but all his captains – who had spent most of their lives butchering Englishmen – agreed: the English only had the spirit for a short, stiff fight; then they would break. It had happened more times than they could count. The English fled, and only the companions of a wounded lord – too lame or old to run – would stand about him till they were cut down.

Knut had saddled horses picketed near his reserve so that they could mount up at a moment's notice. His riders had carefully scouted out the land in the last two days and determined not to let fugitives flee to the safety of Malmesberie; instead they would force them into an unfordable reach of the river, where they would either be slaughtered or drowned.

The crucial thing was that Edmund died. When he was dead, no one would dispute God's choice. Knut did not doubt that by the time the evening star rose in the east, Edmund Ironside would be a hacked and stripped corpse. It was a simple fact. He could almost taste it, like a feast that is being prepared on the kitchen table.

Knut led the toughest warriors in Christendom. They strained at the leash like fighting hounds. Knut put his war horn to his lips. His blast was answered from both shieldburgs, and there was a roar like thunder as his dogs charged towards the English.

Godwin gripped his shield as the Danes came forward. The monks paced in front of the lines, hurriedly finishing the last masses and then rushing to safety at the back. Godwin pressed his eyes shut. A sense of guilt and unworthiness pressed down upon him.

Forgive me, Lord, for I have sinned, he prayed as the Danes lined up at the base of the far river bank. Forgive me, Lord, for I am a pitiless sinner.

Godwin could hear them now, make out their faces, smell the leather of their harnesses and the stink of horse that worked its way into any marching host. His hand was shaking violently. He stamped his feet. The man next to him undid the thongs at his crotch and pissed into the ground. Godwin felt the same need and pissed where he stood, lest men think he was trying to seek the safety of the rear. Irwyn was next to him.

'We will win!' he whispered.

Godwin wished he had the same faith.

Edmund stood before the English.

'Can you see them?' someone behind him called forward.

'I can see them and they're a cursed ugly bunch!' Godwin shouted.

They all laughed. A few archers sent deadly barbs thudding into the Danish shields. The Danes paused on the far bank of the defile and slid down into the valley. They redressed their lines, took in the English position with a clinical eye, as if looking for the weakest spot, and then came steadily onwards. The English checked their ranks, checked their shield straps, their sword hilts, wiped the sweat from their sword-palms, checked their footing and their consciences, bit back their fear and waited. Men started to shout and curse. All along the English line men were hurling insults at the Danes.

Whoreson!

Heathen!

Bastards!

Even men who could not see the enemy joined in. The noise swelled from individual voices to a great and voiceless din, filled with fear and hate and anger.

'Ironside!' someone shouted, and the war cry caught. Soon it was a chant, roaring at the Danes who were wading across the narrow water. 'Ironside! Ironside!'

The Danes paused thirty feet away, took a few moments to steady themselves, as the horns bellowed and javelins and arrows flashed through the air.

The Danes let out a great roar and charged. Godwin could feel the thunder of their footfalls, could hear their voices and shouts, could smell the unwashed horde of sea-wolves. The front ranks of the English went silent. Stones rained down, rattling against shield board like thunder. Spears, axes and pieces of wood made a deafening tattoo on the Danish shields.

Edmund led the men to the lip of the bank that the Danes had to climb. The rear ranks pressed too eagerly forward and Godwin pushed against them. 'Back!' he shouted as the first of them began to spill over the lip of the embankment. 'Back!'

The Black Raven banner led the Danish charge. As it reached the bottom of the bank the White Dragon of Wessex surged down to meet it.

'Edmund cannot keep his men in check!' one of the men next to Knut shouted over the din.

Knut stood at the back of his men and he nodded and laughed, for they had given up the height advantage. With the banner came Edmund, at the fore of his household troops, a magnificent warrior in silver armour and a gold-worked shield, blond hair streaming in the wind.

Knut had often wondered where the good men in England were, and it seemed then that they were all with Edmund.

It was a shame that the best of England should die that day, but die they would.

*

Edmund's companions fought like men possessed. They soaked up wounds that would have killed others three times over. They were so eager to kill that many Danish veterans who thought they had dealt a death blow were cut down by the return slash, while others clung to spear or shield with their dead fingers. They were like the ivy that takes a tall, proud building and topples it. The English fought beyond themselves. They fought with a common aim: to kill the Danish king.

Closer and closer they came. Edmund looked over the fray and caught Knut's eye. Edmund shouted at him, but the words were lost in the tumult.

'Kill him!' Knut shouted to his men. 'You crowded my father's benches. Earn your keep! What are afeared of? These are only Englishmen!'

His toughest retainers heard his words and battled back, but the fury of the English onslaught stunned them. There was a furious tumult of spear shafts and helmets and hacking swords, and Knut felt fear.

'There he is!' Edmund shouted, closer now.

Knut drew his sword and hefted his shield, and his bodyguard closed about him, like men preparing for a last stand. Knut had no intention of dying this day. He wiped the sweat from his palms and checked which way his horses were tethered, then readied himself and pushed his retainers forward.

'Kill him!' Knut raged, but the Danes fell back before the English fury.

Ealdgyth could not bear to sit in Malmesberie and wait for news.

'Bring horses!' she told her men.

She and her companions rode cautiously along the Fosse Way, wary of carrion Danes. The fields were quiet, and when the breeze was stilled, all they could hear were birdsong and insects, buzzing in the meadows. The land rose gently before them. A gurgling steam meandered to their right, before them were stands of woodland, the spring green replaced with dark summer green. An aspen flashed its rainy sounding silver leaves as the breeze went through it. A skylark sang somewhere above them.

Ealdgyth could feel her baby kicking. Royal blood flowed in the child's veins, Woden's blood, mixed with her own Danelaw fathers. It was a potent mix, the royal line blended with the new blood of the conquerors, as a sword was forged from iron and steel. Iron for subtlety, steel for the strength and the sharp cutting edge.

In her heart her babe was a boy. 'Soon,' she assured. 'You will see your father's victory soon.'

An open gateway led on to the next field. The passage of the English fyrd was clear in the muddy hoof prints of three thousand horses. They passed through the screen of trees and suddenly they could hear the sounds of battle.

Ealdgyth's horse snorted.

'Hush!' she assured it. It is only battle.

'Only a little further,' one of the women said, and their horses walked to the top of the hill. and the battle sounded suddenly much closer.

Ealdgyth held her breath. Battle!

She had never seen such a sight before. It was two fields wide, a seething and confused mass, gleaming with steel and surging back and forth about the banners while shouts and roars surged up almost like surf on a shore.

'Are we winning?' she asked, but every sinew was tense and eager. 'Surely we are winning!'

One of her retainers came forward. 'Danes have been pushed off the crest of the bank, but the men of Hamtunscir and

Oxenefordscire still hold the lip. See! At their fore flies St Swithun's Cross. That must be Abbot Wulsy!'

Fat Abbot Wulsy had lost his helm, but he was furiously urging his men forward, waving his sword above his head.

'Where is the king?'

'In the centre. See his banner? There he is, in the silver helm.'

Ealdgyth knew the helm, for she had lovingly polished it, and set it, that morning, upon her husband's head. But she was too fearful to judge for herself. 'How goes it there?' she asked.

There was a long pause.

She held her breath and the child in her womb kicked again.

'Edmund's shieldwall has been broken,' the man said at last. His voice was heavy.

Another boy spoke up. 'Both shieldwalls are shattered. The two kings battle towards the other's banner. See! The White Dragon surges forward and against it comes the Black Raven.'

'You have keen eyes. Keep talking,' Ealdgyth told him, but then the boy shuddered.

'It is a terrible press. There is barely room to swing a blade.'

The battle raged for more than an hour without either side retreating or advancing. Both sides pushed and drove and seethed against the other. Many lay sprawled face down in the dust, English and Dane beside one another. At last the sun broke through and Edmund's silver helm shone suddenly out, before it was hidden again among the surging tide of death.

One of the women cried out, 'That is Edmund! The king yet lives!'

Occasionally they could hear a single voice or scream rising amongst the general melee. Sometimes it was an English voice, sometimes Danish. Grief, pain, anger, desperation – the meaning was not lost, though the words were unclear. The women strained to see where their lords' banners were, tried to gauge consolation from the confused and angry crowd.

'They're fleeing!' one woman cried.

'No!' another said. 'No, look – it is just the dying and the wounded being brought back to safety.'

Panic settled, like a startled hen.

'How long have they been fighting?' Ealdgyth asked, but it was hard to tell how quickly time was passing when so alert to the present moment.

'More than an hour,' her chaplain told her.

The abbey bells began to ring back in Malmesberie.

Ealdgyth said the paternoster.

She made a private wish, when she saw the yellow cross of St Alban, which marked out the Mercians with Eadric Streona: in the name of Elfhelm and Morcar and my dead husband, Sigeferth, and all their loyal and fair-hearted retainers, kill Eadric for me, Lord!

Her chaplain was praying out loud as well. 'O God, strike down the Danes,' he intoned. 'Strike the Danes and their kins-men down!'

Men stumbled up the slope towards them. They were weary and bloodied. Some rested on other men's shoulders; some used a spear as a crutch; a few men crawled to safety, or fell down, or were dragged back by the armpits and dumped. One of them crawled a little way and then stopped and lay still.

'Help him!' Ealdgyth wanted to say, but she was rigid with fear. The longer the battle went, the more certain it was that one side would break and flee and be massacred.

Please God, she prayed, please God.

Blood splashed Godwin's cheek as he stabbed straight at the faces of the enemy. He rammed spear through teeth and bone and up

357

through one man's palate, splattered his brain out the back of his head. He caught the next man in the hip socket. The fighter fell to one knee and writhed as Godwin stabbed him in the side, then set his heel upon the man's midriff, wrenched out his ash spear.

The press of men seethed blindly about him and brought up another Dane – a shorter man with freckles, strawberry-blond hair and bright blue eyes – and without a moment's hesitation Godwin thrust the spear into the indent between his collarbone and the base of this throat and heard him scream as the crowds drove them apart.

The spear blade was wrenched from Godwin's fingers and his shield arm was caught between him and the next man. Godwin did not dare reach down with his free hand for his dagger, but kicked and kneed and clawed at Danish faces. He felt the wet softness of eyes and nostrils and mouths, and one man bit his fingers so hard Godwin thought he might lose one of them.

Spear shafts splintered; skulls were shattered; a fragment of bone grazed Godwin's cheek; and a lump of someone's brain hit him in the forehead.

Voices roared with pain and fear and anger. At one moment Godwin was pushing forward with his shield; the next he had room to draw his sword and was slashing and stabbing over a Danish shield. He felt neither pain nor weariness. Just a terror and a joy that surged over each other like angry waves. Then very suddenly a great sigh of exhaustion seemed to pass through both hosts. There was a tremor along the killing line. Both sides gave ground just a little. There was no order, no signal, but the fighting lines stepped back from one another, panted for breath, wiped salt sweat from their brows and stared in exhaustion, just as the stone-quarrier, who spends all day chipping at the cliff face and despairs that a crack will ever appear.

Godwin looked for Edmund. He was there. His helmet was dented in many places and he pulled it off, and pulled off the linen cap and ran his blood-matted fingers through his hair and shook it free.

'Up! Up, you Englishmen!' Edmund called out. 'There are your enemies! Let us at them one more time!'

But he was hoarse and his voice barely carried to where Godwin was standing, and the English were exhausted and had stopped listening to him.

'Have we lost?' one woman asked.

Ealdgyth looked to the monk. He shook his head, not so much as to say no as to express his confusion.

'I cannot tell,' he said.

'They're breaking!' someone shouted, and Ealdgyth bit her lower lip as men on the left of the English shieldwall began to fragment and run.

'Stop!' she shouted as Danes began to pour through the gap, widening it, deepening it. 'Stop! Someone stop them! Where is the reserve? Is there no one who can see the danger?'

For a moment the cohesion of the ranks was lost in swirling combat. They could see individual Englishmen break off and sprint for safety. The Danish rearguard had already mounted their horses. They were fresh and eager, and their spears gleamed with cold sunlight.

'Stop them!' someone was shouting, and Ealdgyth realised it was her voice, and all about her women were lamenting.

'Lady, we must ride to safety!' the monk's voice broke through at last, but she was too shocked to speak. 'The child, my lady, it is the king's babe.'

The babe in her belly kicked again and Ealdgyth wondered if its father still lived.

'Come!' the monk said, and took her reins and led her away. 'When we reach Malmesberie, we'll seek sanctuary,' he kept saying. 'Knut is a Christian; we shall seek sanctuary.'

But Ealdgyth did not know if they would make Malmesberie before the Danes. She wished she had not ridden out like this. Futures appeared before her like a handful of threads in the hands of the weaver. Many were terrible; some hard and short; a few offered hope, which was all she could grasp on to. She put her hands to her stomach and wished her child could see the battle. Battle and struggle would temper her son. You will be a warrior and a king, she promised him. I will make it happen!

'Hurry!' the monk urged her. 'Alas, alas, the day is lost!'

CHAPTER SEVEN

The Ironside

Knut paced up and down the hall where he held court. 'He lives!' he spat. 'Edmund lives! Christ's shit! How the hell did he escape! Where were the riders! We were supposed to kill him today. We were supposed to kill them all!'

His captains were too exhausted to answer. They stood – sweaty, bloody and stunned by the battle they had fought that day – barely able to speak. They did not know whether to stand or sit, did not know what had happened today, only that they had survived, though they felt as though they had been caught between the hammer and the anvil. They had no answers for him. They had done their best. They had not routed. They had battered this new English fyrd. They held the place of slaughter.

Eadric and the other English nobles made much of the wounds they had suffered. Only Thorkel seemed unruffled. He limped towards the girl with the ale-jug and held out his horn. He dwarfed Knut, but Knut held his ground before the huge warrior.

'We had twice their number!' Knut said. 'How can it be that we did not break their line?'

'We did break their line,' Thorkel said, and drank noisily. His clothes were dark with blood or sweat or both. He held out his horn and drank again.

'Yes, but they broke ours!'

Thorkel shrugged. 'Let us line up again tomorrow. I will lead the charge myself. Tomorrow I will kill him. If not, I will surrender all that I have taken from the English.'

That evening the ale flowed and Ottar the Black, an Icelandic skald, chanted a quick poem:

> Great king you grappled
> On the green Sorestone fields
> Bloodshedder of Swedes,
> You laid waste the English.

But Knut was still fuming. He felt that fear, felt that what had previously been assured – a Danish victory over the English – was now in question. 'Damn your poems!' Knut told Otter. 'I want Edmund dead!'

'I should not have listened to you to split the Army,' Knut told Thorkel. 'Brawn could win this battle. We need a man with cunning, like Eric.'

The Danes debated back and forth. Eadric found it hard to hold back his irritation. 'You should not have split the Army! If Eric of Hlathir was here, we would have caught the traitor by now.'

'If Eric was here, we would not have let them slip away at Penne.'

'If Eric would have been here we would have hung Edmund's corpse from a gibbet tree.'

Eadric put his hand to his cheek. A scab was forming, but the flesh all around was sore and throbbing. It had been caused by a stone or an arrow; he didn't know which. It had struck him as the two lines came together, and served as a badge that he had fought bravely, even though he had stayed well back from the front.

Let Abbot Osgodric bludgeon his retainers' shields to kindling. Poor dead Osgodric. Eadric had seen his body, hacked to pieces as the English broke. You might have spoken for God, Eadric had thought as he looked down on the dead cleric, but you chose the wrong king to fight for today.

Indeed, from the dead bodies, it was clear to Eadric that Edmund had paid a heavy price that day. He found many bodies as he stalked along the battle line, where the dead lay three deep. The biggest pile was about the giant handsome body of Alderman Athelsy of Defenascir, Edmund's cousin. His hearth troops lay about them, their sugar-loaf bosses marking them out. Someone had cut off their ears to make a grim necklace. The Defenascir men had served their lord well. They had taken the soldier's wage and were dead. Edmund had lost a strong ally, and the enemies of Eadric had been whittled away.

In the hall that night Eadric watched Knut closely. It was half the skill of knowing what a man wanted to hear before even speaking to him. And to know what he wanted to hear, you had to know his soul.

Knut doubts himself, Eadric thought. His father's shadow is long. He resents these old men. And they, Eadric saw with pleasure, resent him.

Knut turned suddenly and looked at him. 'You have been unnaturally quiet, Earl Eadric. Speak!'

Eadric paused and drew in a slow breath. He was like a virgin, tossed into a pit of hairy Danes, sweaty and unhappy after the indecisive battle, looking for a weakling upon which to strap their shame.

Eadric tasted his own fear, breathed it deep, found it almost exhilarating. He let the pause drag on so long Thorkel began to shuffle uncomfortably.

'Neither side can claim more than the other, but Edmund had more to lose, so God favoured him this day,' Eadric stated. 'He has punished us for our pride, but it is clear that He is still on our side. We should offer prayers.'

'I do not need you to mediate between the Lord and me,' Knut said. 'It is I who was made king, not you, Earl Eadric.'

'Apologies, lord. You know this as well as I. Well, for more mundane advice – bring Edmund to battle once more as soon as you may. Alderman Athelsy died today, and with him the best men that Defenascir could offer. Abbot Osgodric died as well. Edmund has run out of allies. Your Army grows stronger each day. We held the battlefield today. This is a war Edmund cannot win. We all know that. Edmund was lucky, and luck is like love – it has a habit of running out.'

Ealdgyth's horse was led slowly to the end of St John's Bridge as the sun set in the west. She watched as the sky paled and the air grew cool and as the light began to fail the battered and weary English force filed slowly back to town.

A wild-eyed nun stood at the market cross in Malmesberie and called out to the Lord. A random collection of stout matrons and young girls lifted their quivering voices: 'Protect us, Lord, from plundering Danes.'

All the long summer evening wounded and exhausted men streamed into the burg gates. In the shadow of the walls, monks had dug a large pit and were rolling the dead into it like sacks of grain.

'What news of the king?' Ealdgyth called out to one of the stragglers. He was leading a horse on which a wounded man sat, the gash in his thigh bound tight.

'What news of the king?' she repeated but the man shrugged. He did not know. He could not speak.

One man brought news that the local thegn, Jehan Rattlebone, had been killed and a great cry went through the town, for the fighting for his body had been fierce, and they feared that their sons and brothers and husbands had been killed as well.

'What news of the king?' Ealdgyth asked any man she could find.

'Edmund lives,' one man told her. His voice was hoarse, his hair matted to his head.

'Is he wounded?'

'Not last I saw,' the man said, but at that point the figure on the horse groaned and the speaker gave him a quick look. 'Forgive me, mistress, my lord's son is sorely wounded. He needs a priest.'

There were a lot of funerals.

A one-eyed monk sang the Benedictus as some townsfolk hurried to the battlefield to pilfer the dead and others helped the wounded and weary back into the town and gave them drink and bread.

'Come to the abbey!' Ealdgyth's handmaidens begged her, but she refused. Instead she sat like a statue upon her horse, staring out at the straggling survivors.

Her eyes were keen. She saw into the hearts of the men, could tell who had fought bravely and who had shirked. Some of the men were almost dead in their saddles, some swayed with exhaustion, and others tramped on foot, their hacked shields abandoned at the battlefield, their spears over their shoulders, helmets hanging from their belts, mail shirts weighing each footstep down.

The long shadows slipped away after sunset, and the half-light was starting to fail when at last Ealdgyth saw the White Dragon jolt towards her, as if the banner pole itself was striding along the beaten track. She looked for Edmund's face and did not see it. She saw only one of Edmund's retainers, a young, fair man named Wiglaf, helmet hanging at his saddle, his sword wrist bound with cloth.

'A glancing blow,' Wiglaf said.

'Where is the king?' she called out. 'Where are the others?'

The sudden onslaught of questions seemed to stun him. Wiglaf did not know. He had been in battle. He put his hand to his ear and it came away sticky with blood.

'Where is Edmund?' Ealdgyth cried. Wiglaf frowned for a moment. He had been next to the king's banner, had charged into the battle alongside him, but early in the fighting he had been struck with a hammer blow that dented his helmet and knocked him almost senseless. He had been dragged to safety and had lain stunned for the rest of the battle, his ear bleeding and his hand still clutching the broken end of his spear shaft.

'The Danes,' Wiglaf said, and she gave up and pushed on.

By the time Godwin made it back to Malmesberie lanterns had already been lit against the darkness. He was parched and weary, had left Irwyn by the roadside, with promises that he would come back with a horse to bring him to town. When he reached the town, there were people everywhere, shouting and calling and lamenting, and all Godwin wanted was food and drink and a horse.

No one seemed to understand him. It was almost midnight by the time he found a mule and stumbled back the way he had come. He could not find Irwyn or see him among the bodies that had been laid out by the side of the road.

He searched for hours, and thought of Blecca, and that terrible night in Lundenburh what felt like a lifetime before, but he found no one. Godwin stood alone, calling, 'Irwyn! Irwyn! Where are you?' until the day overcame him at last and, he stood, holding the reins of the mule, and started to cry – dry, wrenching sobs that came from his gut and waved, insanely, between tears and laughter.

Eventually Godwin stumbled back to Malmesberie. The moon had already risen and it was as if he had never seen this place before. The streets were unknown; the people and shouts and weeping a confusion of sounds and light and faces. Some men sat and stared into the darkness; others lay and wept; others prayed for their deliverance.

His men were about to come out and search for him by the time he stumbled into the firelit hall.

'Godwin!' they said, and jumped up.

'Irwyn,' he croaked back. 'I have lost Irwyn.'

Two of his men said they would go out, as others pressed a bowl of milk into his hands.

'You're still wearing your mail,' they said, and Godwin winced as his warshirt was unlaced. It fell to the floor in a shapeless heap of knitted steel and Godwin suddenly felt as if he was as light as a feather. But his body ached, and he was tired beyond reckoning.

'Ale!' he said, and drank deeply, then asked, 'What news of the king? Does he yet live?'

The men in the abbey great hall shivered as bowls of broth and meat were passed around. Godwin sat pale and shivering on a seat by the fire.

'Drink,' someone called out, and a jug of small beer was brought. It took three horns full before Godwin could speak. No one had seen Edmund for hours, and some began to fear that he had been mortally wounded, but the abbot came in to assure them that the king was hale and within the queen's chambers.

'I have seen and spoken with him,' the abbot said, 'and it is a blessing from Christ that he is unwounded.'

Men cheered then, but Godwin stayed silent. The last time he had seen Edmund, there had been a look of such desolation in his eyes. Godwin had never known him so exhausted and broken, struggling to keep the tears from his eyes.

The chaplain had a worried look on his face, but he opened the door, let Godwin in.

Edmund did not rise.

'We failed,' he said. 'We were so close and we failed.' Edmund looked up. 'I saw him. He is no older than me. He hid behind his father's warriors, and I knew that if I could bring him within the arc of my sword I would cut him down. I swore that oath long ago. Do you remember?'

'Portemeadow. When Athelstan gave us his pewter badge.'

Edmund nodded. Godwin had been there since the beginning. There were not many others who had. The less of them there were, the more precious the survivors became.

'I felt God within me, like a great wave, and I felt sure we would break them. But I could not. I failed.'

Godwin hung his head. He had no words of comfort. It was not the battle so much as the fact that they had come so close to Knut's banner, had even traded blows with his retainers. When Edmund looked up, there were tears on the young king's cheeks. Godwin put out a hand. Edmund did not speak, but he took it and squeezed it, then looked away at the far hall shadows, which watched and waited and judged.

'We are still alive,' Godwin said.

Edmund nodded.

'We are still alive,' Godwin said.

Edmund looked up. He thought his friend was touched.

Godwin looked at him. 'Edmund. We are still alive. You are still alive. We met the Danes and we almost beat them. You led the English against the Danes! We would never have believed that when we were young.'

It was true. But not helpful. But Godwin had a light in his eye. 'Edmund, Knut came here to kill you and break the English. We bloodied his nose and we are still standing. That is a victory!'

Edmund did not feel it.

Godwin kept talking. He stood up and spoke louder and more passionately. 'Edmund, you proved yourself this day. Those bastards, they have terrorised our childhoods. We met them toe to toe and we shoved them back!'

Godwin's words did just enough to get Edmund to his feet.

Edmund came out of his wife's chambers an hour or so later. He still wore his battle clothes, but the blood and gore had been washed from his cheeks and his hair, and his hands were clean, and even though his eyes still looked haunted, he forced a smile, cleared his throat, called for ale and food and a scop to sing to his warriors.

'I am proud of you all,' he told them as he paced the benches. He did not feel the words. 'Every damned soul here! We bloodied Knut's nose this day, and while we dine in Malmesberie he is still camping out in the fields!'

It was all he could say. He laughed, but his laughter was as humourless as the croak of a rook. 'I am proud of you all,' he said, but his voice faded almost to a whisper.

Godwin summoned lads and young men who had not been in the battle.

They looked clean and uncomfortable as they stood before

him. They were all conscious of the wounds and bruises on his face, and the clean look of theirs. The men had no idea why Godwin Wulfnothson – the name was now spoken with awe and respect – had called them here.

'We are riding out,' Godwin announced. His lips had cracked and as he spoke one of the cracks opened up again. He felt his lip tear and almost enjoyed the brief stab of pain. 'To raise the war bands again. I want you all to take the fastest horses. Take word to the shires. Edmund beat Knut this day.'

The words came out very clearly. He looked each man in the eye.

'Thank God! King Edmund beat the Danes this day.'

It took a moment for them to understand what he was demanding of them.

'You have heard the stories?'

They nodded.

'Good. Tell all the stories of King Edmund's valour. Sing his name!'

They got the message.

Godwin leant against the table and rested. The young men bowed and thanked him and began to leave.

'Have you heard the name that men have given him?' Godwin called.

The men paused at the door. They looked at each other. They shook their heads.

They reminded Godwin of himself when he was their age. 'Men are calling him Edmund Ironside. Spread that name. King Edmund Ironside has beaten the Danes! There will be great booty when the final victory comes.'

Thorkel and Knut rode to the gates of Malmesberie, but the burg was too stoutly defended, and they did not have the skills or the patience for a siege. Men who had arrived too late for the battle clashed with Eadric's men and wounded his banner-bearer, and fearing for their plunder, the Danish war chiefs were wary to move out.

'So Edmund has escaped again,' Knut said as he looked at the God-created burg of Malmesberie, impregnable with its walls of river and stone. As hard as Edmund, Knut felt the weight of failure pressing down on him again. 'And the corn is still wet. We cannot ravage land that we have already picked clean.'

Thorkel did not answer.

'You have nothing to say?'

Thorkel shrugged. 'I am listening, lord.'

Knut did not like the thinly veiled mockery. He had lost too many men at Sorestone, and that night Knut decided that it was no longer safe to keep the Army divided. 'It is not safe for us to split our strength now. The rebels are too many. We will return to Lundenburh and finish the siege.'

When Knut returned to Lundenburh, Eric of Hlathir came out on foot to welcome him. He threw a great feast to celebrate Knut's return. His men ignored the tales of the new English skill in battle and eyed the train of booty that followed Thorkel's men with unreserved envy.

'I give you all that I have taken,' Knut told the unhappy men who followed Eric. 'How is the White Queen?'

'She is still riding, though her horse is no longer white.'

'She's probably eaten it. So no ships have got in?'

Eric was certain. 'None, lord.'

Knut nodded. He liked Eric. He had an honest face and manner, and he had birth and breeding, and a long record of winning battles. 'Bring me the bigger prize of Lundenburh and I shall give you the pick of the plunder.'

*

Eric's men manned the ramparts that the Danes had thrown up about Lundenburh, while the others constantly raided for supplies. At first the farmers had given gladly, but as the siege dragged on without conclusion, the farmers had nothing left they could give without starving, and the Danes had to seize it from them by force. They scoured all the land for two days' ride, and by the time of Knut's return, his men were forced to send hundreds of men in raiding parties deep into the hostile fringes of Midelsexe and Sudrie. Each day ribbons of smoke smeared the trees of the Temese Valley and beyond. The wooing was a rape.

'Still no sign of Edmund. Where is he?' Knut asked Eadric as a raiding party returned.

'Well, he is not in Mercia,' Eadric said. 'I have sealed off the north to him.'

'East Anglia?'

Eadric shook his head. 'He will hole himself up in the marshes of Wessex. When Lundenburh falls, no one will follow him.'

'When Lundenburh falls,' Knut said, and did not bother turning to look at the rebellious city. 'When Lundenburh falls!'

Knut thought of the White Queen. When Lundenburh falls, he thought.

Eadric pursed his lips. 'It cannot be long. The whole country accepts you. The Wincestre mint is already striking coins with your image.' Eadric held out the shining penny. 'Here!' He spun it into the air and Knut caught it. 'Accept this, the first of many.'

Knut weighed the penny in his palm. When he was a boy, picking in wonder over the mismatched and clipped coins from Middle Earth, it was the English ones that had fascinated him. They were the truest coin and one of his earliest memories was climbing on to his mother's knee. She wore a necklace of Ethelred coins, each the same weight and thickness and purity of silver.

I want to be king of that country, he thought to himself. And here he was. His face remained expressionless, but inside he was glad.

Knut put the coin away.

'Make sure the roads are watched,' he said to Eadric and Thorkel that evening.

In the privacy of his bower, Knut took the coin out again. Edmund had already shown more grit and guts and determination than twenty years of English kings and aldermen. Knut felt he was beginning to understand his enemy and, curiously, to like him.

Unbeknown to the Danes, Edmund stayed in Malmesberie to organise the defence of the town and the abbey.

Ealdgyth went into labour three days after the Army had departed. Edmund wanted a sign that he should continue the fight and decided that if God gave him a boy, he still had the Lord's blessing.

Ealdgyth did not shout or curse. The nuns kept up their prayers as she let out a low and tortured moan as the baby slipped out and all the labour pains lifted – as sudden as an unforeseen victory.

Edmund was with his war chiefs when the thin sound of a newborn's crying echoed down the stone cloisters. He caught Godwin's eye, but they all continued as if nothing had happened, but it was hard to concentrate as they heard footsteps hurrying towards them.

A monk entered the room. The messenger faltered.

Edmund snapped at him, 'Wait!'

The meeting went on for another half-hour. The baby's crying stopped. Edmund thanked his captains, and they bowed and left. Only Godwin remained.

It was only when all had been finalised that Edmund turned to the monk. 'Step forward,' he said.

The monk bowed and came forward, his hands clasped together in prayer.

Edmund feared this moment. He spoke in a low and guarded voice. 'Tell me.'

The monk bowed again. 'My lord, England has an heir.'

'Speak plain. It is a boy?'

'It is, my lord.'

Edmund turned to face the tapestry. Tears brimmed in his eyes.

God had spoken!

Edmund's boy was named Edward, 'Happy Guard', after Edward the Elder, son of Alfred, who brought Mercia, Exsessa, East Anglia under his rule, and who defeated the Walsh in battle at Farndon, and the Norwegian kings of Euruic at Wodensfeld. Baby Edward was fat and healthy, and busy suckling at the wet nurse's breast when Edmund first looked on him. Battle shock made his heart heavy, and he looked at the boy and felt – to his surprise – little, other than a deep well of gladness and relief, which bubbled slowly and gently to the surface. When the boy had eaten his fill and slept, the wet nurse carried him to Edmund's arms. It seemed a strange thing to see a king who still wore the scratches of battle holding such a small and tender life in his arms.

The child had a mop of pale hair and his father's face, and strong fat arms. 'Why is he yellow?' Edmund asked.

The wet nurse spoke gently, as if she feared to wake the babe. 'It is so with many. He will plump up soon and take your colour.'

'He would be better to take his mother's,' Edmund said.

Edmund did not seem inclined to move, so Godwin sat down next to him.

The wet nurse swaddled the baby up to the chin. There were thin wisps of blond hair on his head and cheeks.

'He looks strong,' Godwin said.

The two warriors looked down on the boy. Ealdgyth watched them. The shock seemed to pass from their faces, and they smiled and stroked the baby's cheek with the backs of their fingers, touched his button nose, his cleft chin, his flattened brow.

'Let Edward stay here with the wet nurses,' Edmund told his wife later that night. 'I shall ride east with my men, and you should follow us when you are rested. We might need another heir.'

'You will fight him again?' Ealdgyth said.

'Of course.'

'Will the men follow?'

'Of course they will follow!'

But many of the men were reluctant.

'They think of themselves as heroes,' Edmund's wife told him. 'Heroes do not like to be kept in the field after victory. Let them go home and tell their wives all their exploits. What say you, Godwin?'

Godwin did not like to be called upon like this, but it was hard to keep men in the field who have bodies to take home.

'We won at Sorestone, so throw a victory feast,' Godwin said. 'Parade your son to all the warriors and show that God has blessed you. Then let the men return home with news of our victory. They will take word of Edmund Ironside to the folk at home, and when home begins to dull, summon them again and they will bring twice as many men.'

News of the Battle of Sorestone spread; the mood of the whole country changed, like a silver coin that is tossed from heads to cross. Hundred courts met and in their enthusiasm unanimously decided to outlaw Knut from the land for ever.

Edmund and Godwin rode with a great company. They processed through Wessex. They rode openly on the Roman roads without fear of betrayal or detection. They got the same response each place they came to: a tearful admission of disloyalty, a bold declaration of support, a drunken evening.

Edmund accepted them at their word. The English were beginning to remember themselves. He was gracious. He was forgiving. He was their king.

CHAPTER EIGHT

The Battle of Sudwerca

A month after the Battle of Sorestone, Knut sat in the king's hall at West Minster, playing chess with Thorkel.

'Is your king going to lie down and die?' Knut asked, as he removed the last of the guards.

Thorkel moved the last of his king's companions between his king and the warriors of Knut. 'There,' he grunted.

It took two moves for that last companion to die, and two more for Thorkel's king to be surrounded and killed.

Thorkel reached across the cloth mat they were play-ing on and slapped Knut's upper arm. 'Good,' he said. 'Well done!'

Knut had already won the second game that morning. Thorkel was letting him win, which irritated Knut almost as much as when Thorkel beat him.

'I was lucky,' he said.

Their minds were on Edmund, but they had no idea that the English king had gathered a mounted fyrd; that his men had spent three days circling far to the north out of sight of the Danish pickets; that they were at that very moment touching their heels to their horses, their spears gleaming silver with freshly whetted blades, riding slowly towards them.

As the smoke of Danish cooking fires were being stoked for breakfast, Edmund unfurled his banner, the White Dragon on a field of red, and led two thousand English towards the Danish ramparts to the north of the city.

The first Danes to die were walking back to camp after visiting a house where girls could be found. They were cut down and trampled as the sun lifted over the forests. Edmund kept his men going at a brisk pace. The turf was soft and springy. The horses passed swiftly over the dead Danes. They paused in the forest fringes when they saw the Danish ramparts and Edmund Ironside put on his silver helm, took out his hunting horn and blew a single note.

Danes came out half-dressed and bleary-eyed to take their morning toilet.

They barely had time to shout the alarm before Edmund Ironside cut them down.

Knut and Thorkel were setting up a third game when angry shouts disturbed the stillness. Knut ignored them, but Ottar the Black ran in.

'It's Ironside!' Ottar said.

Knut was sick of that name and had banned its mention in his presence, but he let it go and leapt to his feet.

'At last! Where is he?'

'Here!'

'We've found him?'

Ottar's eyebrows met in a frown and he said, with typical Icelandic understatement, 'Well, he's found us.'

Knut ran out and looked in astonishment at the scene

378

before him: English lead riders were already within the camp, hacking and stabbing. They were cutting down Knut's men. The ditches that his men had dug with so much labour were swarming with English riders, who turned their horses' heads straight at him.

One of the English threw a spear at him and it thudded into the wall of the barn.

'I thought you said they would stay at home till after hay-making,' he swore, but Thorkel was nowhere to be seen.

Knut drew his sword. He backed against the door. He feared treachery. Ottar grabbed a bearded axe and strode out into the yard and cut down a rider and horse with one mighty swing.

Suddenly Thorkel reappeared, organising a hasty defence.

He was almost as tall as some of the mounted men. He was a giant of legend, and when he ran, he seemed to lope across the ground.

'To the boats!' Thorkel shouted. 'Fly!'

Knut got his feet wet as he scrambled through the muddy shallows to the Sudwerca banks. He turned and watched in silent fury as Edmund rode in state at the head of his warriors.

The Danes abandoned their plunder and their ramparts, fled across the river after their king, who watched the rout in fury and dismay as the gates of Lundenburh, which had remained closed to him for so long, were thrown open. The city that he had worked so hard to starve was soon supplied with wagons of grain and herds of livestock.

Queen Emma greeted Edmund. She sat on an old bay horse, with Eadwig behind her. They all looked leaner than last time Edmund had seen them.

Godwin and Edmund and all the English looked older and more battle-worn than last time Eadwig had seen them.

379

'Much has happened,' Edmund said.

'We have heard.' It was Queen Emma who spoke. From the reaction of the men about her, Edmund could see who it was who the people looked to for leadership.

Eadwig kicked his horse forward.

Edmund embraced him.

'Thank you all!' he called out. 'Thank you, my people, for your faith and resolution.'

Godwin rode into Lundenburh with an odd mixture of delight and wariness. There were a lot of memories here, and when he heard that Caerl had been killed, he stopped and paused and sat down.

'I am glad he died well,' he said at last.

Godwin got very drunk that night. He and Beorn stripped to the waist and compared scars.

'All in the front!' Beorn declared.

'That one is in the side!' Godwin told him.

Beorn was appalled, before he realised Godwin was jesting.

'All in the front!' Beorn shouted. 'I've never turned my back in battle!'

An hour later Godwin and Beorn were seeing how high they could piss up the hall wall.

'I have a friend to visit,' Godwin said suddenly.

He staggered out into the dark street and stumbled back in to fetch a lantern, then blundered through the dark streets to the Church of St Forster's.

The church stood silent beneath its thick thatch; the windows were shuttered, the doors closed.

Godwin dragged the memory back to mind. It was here, he thought, and stood for a moment to piss again. Yes, he thought. It was here. Godwin wished he had brought wine for a libation, but he knelt down and then lay forward so that he was touching the earth, with his right ear pressed close.

He shut his eyes. The cool earth was soothing.

Blecca, he whispered in his mind, we did it! Was your spirit there? We did it, Blecca! You would have been proud of us.

Godwin's breathing started to slow. He jerked awake. His lantern had gone out. He could hear men cheering one of the poems that were being chanted about the Ironside. He pushed himself up and walked straight towards the sound. He needed more beer.

Godwin woke next morning at dawn with a firm-breasted girl lying next to him. She had blonde hair and nut-brown eyes and freckles, and it took a few moments for her name to come back to him.

Jesu! he thought. Hilda did not look as pretty as she had the night before, and he grabbed his cloak and his trousers and stumbled out into the rain.

The street was still littered with drunken thanes.

What a feast they had had last night. What a welcome from the Lundenburh folk!

Edmund was not seen until nearly midday, and his guards kept Archbishop Wulfstan from his chamber until he had finished. He lay back. His head hurt and he was still a little drunk from the night before. He could hear the archbishop coughing outside. He rubbed his eyes ran his fingers through his hair.

'You take that door,' Edmund said to the girl. He patted her backside as she slipped out of a side door and the archbishop was let in at last. Queen Emma was with him.

Edmund's legs were bare and hairy. He grinned at them.

'What a fine day,' he said. 'Drizzle has never looked so cheerful! Smell the shit. That's Lundenburh!'

The English were like hounds that had the enemy's scent, but the bridge across the Temese to Sudwerca had been broken, and there had been rain in the Oxenefordscire hills and no crossing was fordable before Breguntford. It was late in the afternoon when they finally crossed the Temese. Godwin was among the outriders, searching for the Army.

The forces met again on the second day. The Danes arrayed themselves on a marshy field along the southern banks of the Temese. Both armies were at least twice as strong as the forces that had met at Sorestone, and all the banners of the great men flapped eagerly.

Edmund was as cocky as a barnyard rooster. King Edmund Ironside. He believed in himself, and his cause, and the faith of the country. He knew he could not lose as he rode along the line with his head unhelmeted. He fixed gazes with his eager warriors, ostentatiously dismounted, had his horse led far off, stood for a moment out in front of his men and beheld the great size and glory of his host, drew in a deep breath.

'Dear God,' he prayed, 'give us Your strength. Send St Michael down among us with his revenging blade.'

Then Edmund took his place in the front rank of warriors, where a true king stood, before God and country and his fellow warriors.

Godwin stood next to him. He was a veteran now, felt the weight and responsibility and the thrill as well. The men around him seemed very different from those who had stood on the ridge at Penne or the valley lip at Sorestone. Caerl was dead. Others too, many of whom had shared a cup or a joke under a hedgerow anywhere from Hamtunscir to Defenascir. Men who had ridden alongside Godwin and swapped tales and histories and family tales. Young, brave and glad-hearted men. All dead.

He did not look at men in the same way now.

He will not last in the front of the shieldwall, he would think of one man.

He will last an hour, if he is lucky.

Godwin remembered names, but learnt to forget them quickly as well. At least Beorn was unscathed and Godwin's neighbour, a stocky farmer named Enwulf, had caught up with them and brought fresh mounts and twenty mailed warriors, with grim humour, who were eager to kill Danes.

The sun shone today, and the spear-line was keen for battle. They drew themselves up smartly, and the Danes did likewise. Both lines banged their swords against their shields, shouted war cries, and someone at the back of the English line struck up a war song that made them all laugh. They had the Danes and both sides knew it.

The two shieldwalls formed and strode towards one another. They paused briefly to hurl spears and javelins, insults and stones. Godwin saw a spear curving towards him, laughed as it fell three long strides short. Edmund turned his back to the Danes, slowly put on his helmet, drew his sword, blew his war horn and then waved his father's ancient sword. The English let out a great cheer and marched forwards, the shieldwall firm.

Men on either side quickened the pace and charged. Godwin felt no fear today. The sun was too bright, the air too clear, the omens too good. He exulted in the coming battle. Time slowed about him and he took in the world. It seemed to him that there was a glorious moment of possibility as both warhosts moved towards each other, banners flying and brave hearts, and it seemed almost sad that one side had to lose. Then Godwin saw the man who would come up against him and he fixed his eyes upon him and raised his spear to shoulder height. He saw a gorse bush to his right; it seemed fitting that the bush would be there to witness his stand.

There was a thunderous clash of linden shields. Godwin killed the man, but his shield bent under the force of the spear-thrusts against it. The two hosts hewed at each other over the war linden. Amidst the shouts and the din of sword on helm, there was a low groan. Godwin cursed himself. His shield was too high and he could not see his enemy well. The grass was slippery. Under the trampling feet it turned quickly to mud, which smothered wounded men. Godwin's spear shaft snapped and he thrust the splintered wood into the face of a bearded Dane. He drew his sword and beat down upon the enemy helms. Godwin struck and slashed and found that the roaring he could hear was his own voice, raging. He realised that the shield in his hand had been hacked away and he slammed the boss into the face of the man opposite him.

Godwin fought by the gorse bush for an hour or more. He did not remember taking a single step back or forward. He hacked and stabbed and trampled the wounded underfoot. Suddenly a blow knocked Godwin sideways. He winced as he tried to stab again, but he could hardly lift his arm. He fell to one knee and it was only the crush that kept him from the ground. He thought he would be trampled to death and fought desperately to get back to his feet.

Godwin would have died if it were not for a tremor that went through the Danes and made their lines give just a little ground.

The English followed up. 'After them!' someone shouted. 'Don't let them get away!'

'Hold!' Godwin shouted as he limped after them. 'Hold!' But his side stabbed with every breath.

In front of him, a fat Dane limped after his hurrying fellows. He was set upon by Beorn and his men and there was a sickening sound as the Dane parried the blows with his bare hands and forearms.

In the end one of the men lifted the bottom flap of the Dane's mail and stabbed his sword up into his gut.

'Here's one,' the shout went up, and another Dane was ruthlessly butchered.

Godwin paused and watched as the Danes fell back and groups of pursuers gave chase.

Godwin turned round, pulled off his helmet used his forearm to push back the sweat from his face. Just twenty feet behind him he saw the gorse bush. About him was a field of dead and wounded. The thick green summer grass was trampled and littered with the bodies and weapons of the slain. Men lay like torn sacks in a line across the field, their pink guts spilt over the grass. Others were still moving, hands and legs twitching or waving, scattered voices calling out for help or their mothers. The wounded Danes were being killed. Godwin understood then why men fought for the bodies of their friends. Leave no man behind. Not to this, he thought.

The sun broke through the clouds. A blackbird sang. Godwin saw the face of a man who had been killed. It was ugly and twisted in death. One of his killers had stripped his fingers of rings and taken his heavy purse.

The pursuit might go on for miles. Godwin slumped to the floor. Joy bubbled up. After the long crush the field now seemed empty. A watching raven swooped down to a far hedgethorn, and stared at Godwin with black twinkling eyes.

'Wulfnoth's son fought well today,' Godwin called out. 'The English put the Danes to flight and held the place of slaughter.'

Back in the safety of the hastily erected camp, Godwin ached as if it had been beaten by hammers. His bruises were livid, and as he stripped his mail shirt off he found that he had taken a spear-thrust in his left thigh, just below the mail line.

'Under the shield!' Wulfnoth had taught him. 'That's where the hidden blow will come.'

Well, they got me, Godwin thought as a serving man draped the clotting wound with a spider's web.

'A web and a prayer,' Beorn laughed, and when Enwulf came in he laughed and rubbed Godwin's head.

'How did you come to harm? Tripping up fat Danes?'

'No idea,' Godwin said.

Enwulf bent down to look at the wound and wrinkled his nose. 'My, that is a close blow. He certainly got you, didn't he!'

'I got him back.'

'Really? How do you know?'

'Because I killed every Dane I saw.'

Enwulf slapped Godwin's shoulder. 'Listen to him! Little Godwin. Let's share a cup or two.'

There should have been great merriment that night, but the men who chased the Danes the farthest came back in dribs and drabs, under the guard of Edmund's mounted companions.

Godwin could tell from the way they carried themselves that they had bad news. He used a spear as a crutch, limped out to see what they had to tell. The Danes had pulled away in good order, and many of their pursuers had become overstretched and the Danes had fallen upon the scattered groups of English and cut them down or driven them into the Temese.

'And there they drowned,' the survivors said.

That evening Godwin drank heavily. He woke late in the night in a stable hut and he groaned. His head ached, his body ached and each breath hurt. He shut his eyes and tried to sleep.

386

'Lord,' a voice said, and a hand shook him. 'Lord, are you not well?'

Godwin squinted. It was day and Beorn was standing over him. His body hurt more than before. 'No,' he said. 'I do not feel well.'

Beorn went off to find someone who knew their physic and ended up bringing back the king's own blood-letter, a thin and slightly inebriated monk with liver-spotted head and bushy grey eyebrows and his sharp physic's knife. The monk had not had time to clean himself between each bloodletting and was so blood-splattered he looked as if he'd been in the battle himself.

'This is the one?' the monk asked as he smeared the blood off on his robe front and knelt next to Godwin. He lifted each eyelid, looked into the eyes and tongue and the wound on his leg.

'Where is his urine?'

A bowl was produced.

The monk smelt it. 'It smells of beer.'

'He's been pissing all night. He was at the ale,' Beorn explained, though it was hard to explain when he wasn't sure what the man was looking to learn. 'Can't you just let some blood?'

Godwin's arm had already been bared to the elbow and still the monk insisted on smelling his breath. Beorn had never seen a medical man take so long to decide to let a pint of blood. It took a few more moments for the man to bring his blood-bowl out, and Beorn looked away as the monk said a quick prayer and wiped his knife on his knee. He never liked bloodletting, and this moment took him back to a stinking hall in Dyflin, as Wulfnoth lay on his death bed and he bit his lip and wished there was a Dane he could kill. He would murder him with his bare hands, Beorn thought, rather than watch this again.

'If I die,' Godwin said as the blood flowed into the bowl, 'then have prayers said for me. Care for my people. Have prayers said for my father. Look after her.'

Beorn let Godwin talk, and did not need to ask who 'her' was. Yes, he nodded, yes, and did not look up till the blood had stopped flowing, and Godwin's face had turned ashen and his eyes had fluttered and he had fallen silent.

'I dare not let more,' the monk said, but the men knew too little to question him and they stood around and looked at Godwin and prayed silent prayers, made silent vows, tried not to remember that night in Dyflin when they were made lordless men.

Edmund came unscathed from the battle, but his warhost was as weak as Wulfnoth's son and too many of his best warriors had been drowned. Even Wiglaf, his standard-bearer and the two men who took the White Dragon up after him had been cut down. Edmund's fyrd had lost as many men as the Danes. More, Edmund feared, when he saw how few of Leofwine of Hwicce's men came back to camp that night.

Beorn rode with Edmund to see the Danish camp, and it was twilight as he returned and Éärendel, the even star, glowed bright in the south-eastern sky. The dead had been stripped and they looked very ordinary as they lay in the mud and waited for burial. The Danes had camped where the horsemen had left them, and he could hear them singing their war songs. They seemed in an unusually good mood considering the drubbing they'd been given.

No doubt they'll be singing more of their poems, he said to himself, and wished his own men were singing as well, but there was a strange hush in the English camp, for even though they held the battlefield, all of them knew that they had had a chance to rout the enemy and had let it slip, and that the Eternal Lord might not offer them such battle-fortune again.

That night the captains gathered at Edmund's fire. The flames were red on their faces; some of them had broken noses, swollen eyes or bandaged wounds.

'You were an ugly-looking bunch before the battle, and I do not think it's made you any better,' Edmund said. A few of them laughed, but the laughter was weak and weary. 'So, we've beaten Knut again, but the Army is intact and harvest time is upon us. We must let our men go home.'

Edmund fell silent. He had gambled so much on a quick strike before harvest time came, and he had certainly caught the Danes unawares. Perhaps with five hundred more men he could have tilted the battle from victory to a massacre. Damn it, he thought, but he was still alive and that was a blessing.

At that moment Edmund realised how much he missed Godwin. He was not here and Edmund needed him. Godwin always spoke sense, and even when he was silent, Edmund drew strength and comfort from his presence.

'So,' he asked the companions left to him, 'what should we do?'

There were lots of ideas, but none of them rang true. He listened and the various opinions were like the chisel blows of the minster mason. As he listened and differed, Edmund found his own opinion being revealed from within himself, like the image of a saint inside the squared block of stone.

'No,' he said. 'Today was too close-run and we have lost too many to fight another battle. But we have a whole country to supply us and Knut is far from home. Let's picket the Danes in this corner of England and gather another fyrd. Give out all my share of the plunder. Let the men go home to harvest. Let them tell their neighbours of the victory. Perhaps shame will winkle the fyrdsmen out.'

The English fyrd drifted back to their folds, and Edmund came to see Godwin, but he was feverish and did not understand what Edmund said to him.

'Take him to Lundenburh,' Edmund advised.

Next morning Enwulf and Beorn started to move him, but Godwin pushed them off. 'No. Not Lundenburh. I will die there,' he said. 'Take me home,' he urged. 'Take me back home. Contone! Bury me in Contone.'

'That's a long day's ride,' Beorn hissed.

'Contone!' Godwin said again. 'Take me home!'

Edmund's riders kept a close watch with orders to bring news to him if the enemy so much as stirred. But the Danes shrank like snails back to their holes. Godwin knew none of this. He was not there and his absence was everywhere, especially in victory.

Edmund tried to joke of the days of the Wild Hunt, or playing football on the lawns at West Minster, or stealing honey cakes from his grandmother's kitchens, but there was no one left on the benches about him who knew what he was talking about. These battles had cost Edmund, of those who were close to him, most dearly of all. And now Wulfnothson was gone.

Edmund mourned Godwin as if he were dead. He was heavy with friend-loss.

CHAPTER NINE

Twilight at Contone

The last time Kendra had seen Godwin was in April, just after Edmund had been made king. She felt hollow for want of news.

Not long after he left they had learnt that Lundenburh was surrounded by ditches, the river closed. A few days later they heard that the Danes had taken the burg on the south side of the river and that it could not be long before the north bank fell.

'If Edmund comes, then like as not he'll come too late,' men said. 'Even now the Danes are pulling the noose tight about the city.'

On May Day Arnbjorn, Wulfnoth's faithful steward, dressed as the Green Man and capered about like a fool, before handing out honey-cakes to the excited children. The whole scene seemed oddly detached. Kendra watched the children from the shadows; they left their branches in the yard, their ribbons and clothes got torn and muddied as they tramped off into the fields, and the little ones cried and held their hands out to be picked up.

There was a forced atmosphere to the celebrations, as if the festivity had been put on for the children's sake.

'Do you miss him?' Agnes asked.

'Who?'

'Lord Godwin.'

Kendra nodded. 'I do,' she said.

In early June the first cuckoos were mocking the other birds when news came that Knut was besieging Lundenburh. Men did not sleep well, as if they expected Contone to be one of the places that King Knut might visit. Grond the bee-master's wife had recently replaced the seat of his trousers, and he settled himself comfortably down, chewed on the grass stalk in his mouth and spat loudly as he lowered his backside to the stool and licked his remaining teeth.

'Bah!' Grond said as Arnbjorn did his rounds. 'The bees are not happy. It's too damp. Too little sun.'

'You say that every year.'

'This year's worse. What is this – all these kings? What are we – heathens? It's unholy, it is, and it's affecting the bees. They swarmed twice yesterday, and if you listen to their buzzing you can tell they're unhappy. Their honey'll not be sweet, mark my words!'

'You say that every year.'

'Well, harvest will tell all. Are there two kings or not?'

'Not,' Kendra said, who was listening near by.

'So what happened at Hamtun? You tell me. Godwin has got us into a mighty pickle. We'll pay for his loyalty.'

Kendra grabbed a bucket of water and tipped it over Grond's head.

'You should be ashamed of yourself!' she spat, and marched away.

So the summer dragged, and word was that Edmund and Godwin and a ragged war band were being hunted like a fox throughout the country. As July turned to August Kendra felt that she was being slowly crushed, as if a fist were squeezing out her life. She had unquiet dreams. Her mother came back to her, standing by the boat-side, screaming like a gull. Kendra woke with a start, but the night was dark and still and she lay with her eyes open and remembered the procession that carried Wulfnoth to his grave high on the headlands above Dyflin.

In her dream she lingered with Caerl by the fire but when Kendra looked at Caerl she saw his mouth was full of blood. She shrank back from him. His skull was split, and he reached for her, and she leapt like a gull out from a cliff. She swirled for a moment over a stormy grey sea battering a lonely isle of black rock, swirling on the up-drafts, the waves crashing themselves against the against the stone.

Kendra's dream startled her. She felt the spirits were talking to her, and when word came that a battle had been fought in the far west, and that Edmund – everyone was calling him Ironside now – had been victorious, Kendra questioned the messengers closely, and then ran to her room and sat down suddenly and put her hand to her mouth and dared to hope.

In the following months the crops in the fields grew tall and strong. The wheat corns full and heavy as they swelled with the summer rains, green-gold in the sun. But Kendra was restless. She felt that bad news was coming. It hung on the horizon like a gathering stormclouds that turn from white to grey to bruised, furious black, the dark shape of things ordained.

A party of tired horsemen picked their way through the fields towards the dark shape of the Weald, which reared up like a shadow before them. They were armed and wary, weather-stained and hungry, and moved cautiously under the low branches. It had been a hard and dangerous ride, for there were Danish raiders about the country, and many of the fords were held against them. They were forced to swim the Temese at a grubby little hamlet named Ettone, in the marshes by the river, and much of their food had got wet and spoilt in the crossing.

'Let us find a farmstead to rest,' Beorn said.

He looked pained when he saw Godwin, slumped in his saddle. It was a cleft path before him, and Beorn did not like to make decisions. He scowled. Caerl should have been here. Caerl would know what to do. Why was Beorn having to make decisions by himself?

'Well,' he said. 'It looks as though the ride might kill him. But if we stay here, who knows what Danes are about. Even if we hide our mail and weapons, they will know us from our horses, and are any of you willing to let the horses go and walk?'

They shook their heads.

Beorn paused for a long time. He hawked and spat. No one offered him any advice. Godwin mumbled through his illness, but Beorn had long since stopped trying to find meaning in his words.

Beorn looked about him. 'Right,' he said. 'Listen to me. We rest till evening, and then we ride at night, unless we see raiders.'

They found a farm at the edge of the Weald, and the people there were good-hearted and loyal. They fed the men with fresh-baked barley bread and gave their horses as much hay as they could eat. But they were also suspicious folk, and as soon as they heard that Beorn planned to take Godwin into the forest at night they looked pale.

'Do not go in!' they warned him. 'There are fear-babes in the forest that steal men's souls to Hell!'

Beorn was quiet as he stood and watched his men getting ready. At the end they went in to fetch Godwin. The men here slept sitting up, and Godwin was propped up by pillows, his head lolling to the side. Beorn sniffed. Wulfnoth had died of sickness, and Beorn felt for a moment that this was the fate of all the men of Wulfnoth's family: to be consumed by the fast-burning fires of sickness.

When Godwin was safely mounted, Beorn checked the ropes that tied his master to his saddle. He had done this for Godwin and Leofwine when they were knee-high. Godwin's trousers were warm and wet. They smelt of urine. He ought to change them, but he was eager to be off, patted Godwin's thigh and put this from his mind.

'Let's go,' he said.

Under the heavy summer canopy the forest was dark and sombre and watchful. Beorn crossed himself and touched his swords and went under the dark arch of the evening wood that plunged him into night. It was a path little used by horsemen, with many low branches and trailing brambles. The path was thick with the dry brown mulch of many years of leaves, so the horses went almost without a sound, and it was soft underfoot. There was an eerie stillness, with sudden views down rows of trees or into far glades, where surprised deer started. As darkness gathered its cloaks about the world, strange sounds came from the branches above their heads.

'Turn back!' Beorn imagined voices calling from the shadows. 'Beorn the Brave, do not ride down the road to doom. Turn back!'

But Beorn kept his horse on the path ahead. His hand grew sweaty as he gripped the reins of Godwin's horse, and behind him the men followed.

It was a long, quiet ride. As they grew used to the darkness, and it to them, it no longer seemed hostile or threatening, and there was no danger of Danes so deep in the forest. It was almost a shame to see the light paling the patches of sky above their heads. Beorn yawned. He dropped off and startled himself awake, heard birds beginning their chorus, like forest angels celebrating the return of the sun.

The low fields at Contone were already being harvested. The men stood in line and moved through the corn, slashing it down. Behind them the women and children were bent at the waist, bundling the corn into sheaves, which lay like bodies in the field behind them.

Kendra had her sleeves rolled up to her elbows as she loaded the ox cart with fresh cheese and bread and pots of refreshing ale. The sun had coloured her cheeks and forearms with a blush of brown.

She wiped the sweat from her forehead with the back of her forearm. The men in the fields had stopped working. Horsemen were coming down the hill towards them.

Kendra froze in terror. Oh God, she thought, not again, and was about to turn to run for a pitchfork when she noticed that there was something odd in the way the men were greeting the horsemen. They were running to welcome them. She shaded her eyes. The horses were strange, but some of the men looked familiar. Harder, rougher, leaner perhaps, but familiar as well.

One of the men was slumped in his horse. The harvesters moved in a way that showed concern as well as welcome, and then they began to look to the hall and gesture wildly.

Kendra grabbed the reins of the oxen, and took the goad from it's peg.

'Yah!' she said, and the surprised oxen pitched forward. 'Yah!' she said, and they started to plod along the lane, and the wheels crushed new ruts into the dry-crusted mud.

Kendra was appalled when she saw Godwin: he was pale and feverish, his cheeks were hollow and his eyes bulged.

She was furious with Beorn. 'Look what you have done to him! You should not have brought him. The journey has almost killed him.'

Beorn was tired and irritable. He flashed an ugly smile. 'The filth of Lundenburh would have killed him more certainly.'

'Why not take him to a village?'

'The whole of Cantware is full of raiding parties of Danes and English,' Beorn said. His temper was close to breaking. 'Hush, woman! You will disturb him. I give him to your care. Don't let him die, as you did his father.'

They parted without further words. There was nothing left to say. There was no point arguing. Cattle, like dying men, knew when to come home from the grazing ground.

Kendra had Godwin brought gently down to the hall. As she did, the sun came out from behind a high drifting cloud and the land gleamed with golden light, and Mykelhal seemed thatched with silver as Godwin was carried by four men, eight legs, into the cool shade of the hall.

Mykelhal arched above Kendra. She arranged a bed of fresh straw and blankets and bent over Godwin as she stripped away his clothes.

There were fat swollen ticks on his legs, lice in his hair and rows of brown lice eggs in the hems of his kirtle. Kendra put his clothes aside for boiling. Gently plucked the ticks off, and dropped them into the fire. There was a few seconds of silence before each tick popped. She combed his hair, washed him, and felt his brow. He was burning up.

Kendra looked up and saw Godwin's men standing in the hall door.

'All of you, take off your clothes. Go and wash and comb your-selves. Agnes will boil your clothes. You'll sleep better tonight.'

*

Kendra felt both frustration and relief, and as Godwin did not die that first day the feeling grew. At least Beorn had brought Godwin to her, she thought, so that she could care for him as if no other hands would do.

She sponged his brow, wiped his arms and chest with the damp cloth. Godwin's eyelids fluttered for a moment but he did not speak, just let out a low moan as if he was trapped in a night-mare.

'Hush!' she told him. 'Hush. You are safe at home in the land that raised you. Hush, Godwin son of Wulfnoth, son of England and Contone and the fair Downs of Sudsexe.'

Kendra sat over Godwin day and night. She sang the songs she had learnt as a child, charms against elfshot and witchery and other men's curses, but sickness waged a war within Godwin and no one knew what would help him beyond their prayers and herb lore and the beneficence of Christ.

Agnes sent boys out to find all manner of roots and herbs, and spent long hours by her cauldron, mixing and tasting and prepar-ing poultices to strap to his wound. It was hard and his sickness spread, as if it had taken over his body, battle by battle, province by province, till the will to resist collapsed.

'How is he?' Agnes asked in the first few days, and Kendra would force a smile and say, 'A little better,' or, 'No worse,' or, 'He is fighting it.'

But the days stretched into a week and still Godwin clung to life. An unsure rope, frayed and hanging, that would snap under any weight.

Agnes no longer asked how Godwin was. She stood behind Kendra and looked down on him, and her hand squeezed Kendra's shoulder as if to say, So he is still alive?

'How are you?' she asked. 'You should get some rest.'

Kendra forced a smile. 'I am well, thank you. Now leave me alone.'

But Agnes lingered. 'You should fetch a priest,' she said. 'It never hurt any man to be blessed before he passed into the next world.'

'No,' Kendra said, but she was tired and exhausted and she was not thinking clearly. Godwin's soul and his sins weighed upon her and in the end she relented.

It was Beorn who brought the monk. He was a skinny fellow who had come over from Dyflin with a gift for the minster at Cicestre and stayed on.

'So, this lad is dying, is he?'

Beorn grunted in the affirmative.

'In battle, was he?'

Another grunt.

'Poor soul. It is the end of the world, you know. The signs are everywhere. It is both uplifting and terrifying, is it not? All of us should be ready for his coming. I feel it is near. It is a thousand years since Our Lord Christ departed this world. It is fitting that Christ will return in our own lifetimes.

'I've always been one for a good funeral. The Pope has just declared that a priest must be there to bless a marriage, but I can't see the point myself. Weddings are just for two great families to show off, and when they come to the church door to be blessed, they're all in a hurry and cannot wait to go and get drunk at the wedding feast. But at least at a funeral they stay and listen to the hymns.'

Mass was said, and holy water used to make the sign of the cross upon Godwin's brow.

One of the men waited outside.

'Should we dig a grave?' he said.

Beorn hit him. 'Wait till he's dead!'

*

That evening Grond stood outside the hall and eased his patched backside down on to the wood pile where the other men sat.

'So he's dying,' he said.

'That he is,' another man said.

Grond let out a vague noise. 'So who will be lord next?'

No one knew. Maybe they'd be given as book-land to the Church in return for prayers for Godwin's soul.

'The bees won't make honey for fat old monks. A good lord is in hall, and a good lord is one who will fight against the Danes. Prayers never stopped any Danish axe.'

That night a warm dry gale began to blow. It tossed the trees back and forth, while the hall fire burnt low and Kendra lit a candle to hold off the night. The flame guttered in the draughts. When the wind moaned most loudly, its light shrank back against the wick and seemed many times to almost go out. When the moaning of wild spirits stopped, the flame always sprang back, its small circle of yellow light for all the world defiantly holding back the dark.

Kendra tried to sing, but she could not. Her throat was sore and she had no more heart for singing. Singing had not worked.

Alone, with the dying lad, she sat silently for a long time and urged him to fight. The world is a good and beautiful place. Do not leave so soon, Godwin, son of Wulfnoth, she willed him.

Your father loved you, she told Godwin.

He was a frightened fool that day. Five years the memory tormented him. He loved you more than he could say. You were not guilty. You did nothing wrong, for look how you have prospered. Hearth fellow of your victorious king. Do not let that life slip by now. You have worked and laboured for so long for this. Oh Godwin, do not slip into that great night.

Spirits howled and moaned, and it seemed that Godwin drew

strength from the wild winds and racing clouds that hid the fitful moon, and he did not die. It was as if Leofwine was there, and Wulfnoth also, and all the men who had stood with him at each battle he had fought in.

His ramblings became more lucid. Then they stopped altogether, and rather than fitful tossing and turning, he lay and slept and snored deeply and soundly.

Two days later he opened his eyes abruptly, as if he were waking from a brief nap.

He frowned as he looked about him. 'What are you doing here?' he said to Kendra.

Kendra laughed. 'Looking at you!'

'Where am I?'

'Here!' she said. 'Home!' She could have shaken him, but she was too happy, and he was still too weak and confused. 'They brought you home,' she whispered. 'They thought you would die.'

'Why would I die?' he mumbled, and closed his eyes again, because he was not as strong as he had remembered. The day was too bright, the noises too intense; he had no idea what was happening. 'Where are the Danes?' he said. 'Where is Edmund?'

'Hush!' Kendra said.

'He needs me,' Godwin said, but Kendra held him down to the bed, and it struck her that she was strong enough – or that he was so weak – and his voice faded as he slipped back into sleep, 'There is danger coming. I must stay by his side.'

Hush, Kendra thought, and wiped the sweat from his brow.

Slowly but surely the colour began to return to Godwin's cheeks. Kendra kept him both warm and rested, and after a few days he seemed in much better spirits and laughed when she told him how close to death he had been.

'Oh Kendra All-Knowing,' he teased, 'you have no faith.'

He listened to all that he had missed. He learnt what had happened since the battle in the fields of Sudwerca, where the Danes had been put to flight.

'Edmund has the Danes pinned down on Tanet,' Beorn said. 'When the harvest is over, all the kingdom's men will be brought to bear.'

Godwin laughed. 'Thank God,' he said.

A shadow passed over Beorn's face. 'But there is something I should tell you.'

The tone in Beorn's voice said a lot. Godwin did not feel as recovered as he had ten seconds before. He felt weak and sick and uneasy. 'Is Edmund well?'

'The king is well. All have come to Edmund's banner. All,' he said, with heavy emphasis.

Godwin's mouth hung open. His whole body ached.

'Eadric,' Beorn said, slowing down the syllables, 'has left the Danish camp.'

'No,' Godwin said.

Beorn nodded. 'He begged Edmund to forgive him. Edmund has accepted Eadric's oath.'

The words had a visible effect on Godwin. It was like watching someone hear about a loved one's death. Godwin did not know what to say, was fearful of what had happened whilst he had been sick. Many voices began to speak in his head. A Babel. Godwin stilled them all. Only fools thought that victory came easily. Even victors had to carry their dead home with them.

But fear, like a long and slender blade, slipped into Godwin's side and worked slowly deeper. He could not rest.

'I have to go,' he said. Blind panic built within him. 'Eadric is with Edmund. No good will come of it. I must go to Edmund. The king needs me.'

'The muster is set for three weeks hence.'

'I cannot wait.'

'You are too weak to ride.'

'I cannot wait,' Godwin said.

'Is Edmund a fool?' Beorn said.

'No.'

'Does he know Eadric?'

Godwin nodded. 'Yes, but—'

'But nothing. He knows a snake as well as you. He is the king. He has to unite the country.'

'Beorn,' Godwin said, 'I have to go to him.'

Beorn pushed him back down. 'Rest,' he said. 'Do you want to stand with the king when the last battle comes?'

Of course he did.

'Then rest. When you are fit and well, then we shall all go.'

The last days of that battle summer of 1016 were bright and clear and heartening. Kendra cared for Godwin as if he was the spoilt youngest child. She had lambs slaughtered and roasted each night, and did not spare the cinnamon, but added another pinch to his cup of warm mead, and at night when they both slept, she lay with both arms wrapped tight about him.

Godwin was withdrawn at first. Kendra waited for him. When he came to her, she held him tight, and when night fell and the closet door was shut, they clung to each other through their lovemaking and beyond, as they lay asleep and dreaming.

Autumn was just setting in. Halfway through September they awoke to a thin scattering of frost that lightly dusted the morning slopes of the Downs.

There was a glorious sky that afternoon as a storm blew in from the west. It was time to ride, Godwin thought.

That night they sat in the hall. They listened to the blackbird.

The doors were thrown open, and Godwin stood outside and watched as twilight slowly settled over England.

Kendra stepped up behind him. He felt her step close to his side. She leant her head on his shoulder.

An early fox barked in the far valley. It made Kendra's skin shiver.

'So,' Kendra said, 'the summons has come.'

'It has.'

'Your king has need of you,' she said. 'You had better go.'

On the next morning Kendra stood in the hall doorway and watched them go.

Farewell, Godwin son of Wulfnoth, she thought and stood and watched for a long time but he did not turn and the horsemen disappeared into the fringes of the Weald, and despite everything, Kendra had a feeling low in her gut that she would not see them come again.

CHAPTER TEN

The Battle of Assandune

All England was united and all men answered the summons who could make it to Lundenburh in time.

Godwin had quite a reputation and many wanted to ride with him. They stopped at his tent as soon as they arrived at the muster, and when the day ended, he rode at the head of nearly a hundred mailed warriors who were keen and eager as young pups.

As he looked behind him, Godwin felt strangely hollow, despite the warm words and the friendly greetings and the firm hand's grip. There was an air of things passing. The leaves were turning to yellow, red berries splattered the green hedgerows. And the men about him were gentler folk. There was no need for secrecy; they rode the straightest and most open roads, and every few miles companies of horsemen fell in with them. Many men brought their wives and sons to witness the triumph over the harried Danish remnant. It was as if they were drawn from a different nation: fatter, more complacent, less angry, more cheerful, like the rich pilgrims who set out to St Hilda's Shrine in Wincestre each year.

Godwin yearned to be with Edmund again, riding in his mail.

He felt as though that were the only real life, and that now he was falling asleep again, or that something within him was gently dying. All he wished for were more of the men who had spent the summer eluding Knut's riders, the men whose names he had not known, the dirty and the desperate men, the half-hundred who had lain under hedgerows to sleep, been rained on each night and stood back up with dawn and shared a breakfast of cheerful words and grinning dirty faces. But they lay slain on the many battlefields.

That night at the feast he looked at the confident faces of this new muster and a voice in his head asked, Where were you at Sorestone? Why did you never answer our summons?

Edmund had girdled the Danish camp about with burning and such was the confidence of the new muster that it was hard to get men out of their beds each morning, after the long night's drinking. In the end Godwin left them behind.

'Come! When the battle's over, there'll be time enough to sleep,' he said to Beorn as they waited for men to comb their hair or boil their morning brew. 'Let us ride together and leave these lazy thews behind. I wish to see King Edmund.'

Lundenburh had not changed, but the tents about it were no longer Danish besiegers, but an English host such as had not been seen before.

Godwin rode along the West Minster causeway and hoped to see men he knew on the gateway, but he did recognise them.

'Go away,' the men called. 'The king is busy in council. Camp in the fields like other men and come at the appointed hour.'

Godwin was furious. 'I do not know your face, young warrior, but I am Godwin Wulfnothson, returned from the dead. Open this gate!'

The men were horrified, and Beorn gave them a long, hard stare as they rode through into the palace. There was a sudden shriek and Godwin paused as he handed his reins to one of the stable lads and turned and saw the old peacock strutting out from behind the abbey walls. It cannot be the same, he thought, but as if in a sign, the bird turned its narrow head towards him and opened its fanned tail in a brilliant blue and green and turquoise salute.

At the hall there was a crowd waiting, and Beorn was appalled. 'I was fighting Danes when this lot were still dangling from their mother's tit. Are they here to fight a battle or learn how to ride a horse?'

At least the door wards knew Godwin. They pushed the crowd out of the way and a voice called out, 'Godwin Wulfnothson, King's Thegn of Sudsexe, Banner-Bearer at the Battle of Penne, Companion to the King.'

Godwin's heart swelled to hear this title attached to his name. Surrounded by his men, he strode into King Edmund's hall, heels booming on the well-cut boards.

Edmund jumped up when he saw his friend. The two men hurried to greet each other. They embraced. Edmund crushed Godwin to him; the strength and passion of the greeting surprised him, and the anger and irritation he had felt at the door wards fell from him.

'God Almighty be thanked,' Edmund said. 'My bravest warrior is brought back to me!'

'Yes, lord,' Godwin replied.

Edmund held him again. 'I have missed you, Godwin. Come, sit next to me. Word has come this morn that Knut has broken out of Tanet, but we have him trapped.'

'Are you sure?'

'Sure,' Edmund said. 'Here, sit!'

Many of the men sitting on the king's bench were men that Godwin knew. Ealdgyth was there, and Queen Emma, the White Queen, as men now called her, and Archbishop Wulfstan, of course. And Eadric.

Godwin stopped. 'You are with us again,' he said.

Eadric smiled.

'Find any traitors amongst the Danes?'

Eadric's smile soured.

'We found a traitor, after the battle at Penne,' Godwin said. 'His name was Edwine. He was a young Sumersæton thegn who sold news of us to the Danes. He was one of your men. I remember him clearly. We cut his head off.'

'Then he is surely dead,' Eadric said.

Godwin laughed. 'Yes, that usually does the trick.' His gaze lingered a little longer on Eadric than was normal.

'Sit!' Edmund said. 'We have greater matters afoot. Knut has run out of food and crossed the Temese into Exsessa. Godwin, you are just in time to ride! I have a fleet sailing into the Temese to prevent the Danes' escape. This time Knut cannot flee. He must meet us in battle, and as God is my witness, we shall destroy the invaders.'

The court that sat that day was very different from the rough court the princes had kept. Strangers held places of honour; some men looked at him and wondered who he was.

'I am Godwin,' Godwin told one man who was old and a little blind.

'Oh, you are Godwin,' the old man said, and many in the room turned and stared.

Yes, Godwin's look said. I am Godwin. Who are you?

There was no time to get Edmund alone and so Godwin sat unhappy and brooding as the council went on. Men who had sworn oaths to Knut that summer were now sitting on the same benches as men they had tried to kill.

The sight robbed Godwin of hunger or pleasure.

Godwin had a brief moment in the king's dressing room. Eadwig was there, Edward and Alfred also.

'There have been a lot of changes,' he said to Edmund.

Edmund nodded. He could tell what Godwin was getting at and did not like to have to explain himself. He took Godwin by the arm and led him aside. 'Much has happened since you were last at court, Godwin. There have been many hard choices. I have extended the hand of peace to all honest Englishmen. All of them have relinquished their oaths to Knut. Knut is like a frightened girl now, forever running from us. We have him.' Edmund held his hand open and Godwin saw the scar where they had cut their palms as blood brothers. Edmund's hand closed into a fist. 'We have Knut here. I have not forgotten you, or the oaths we swore when we were young.'

'That Eadric would be the first to hang.'

Edmund gave Godwin a look and spoke in a low voice. 'First the Danes.'

Godwin nodded.

Edmund laughed then raised his voice so that all could hear. 'Listen, tonight you shall sit with me at the feast.'

'I do not need to be honoured in public. Let another man, less trustworthy, take it and I will sit on the lower benches.'

Edmund spoke sincerely. 'No. You have earnt the place more than any other man. I would not have any say that the king does you dishonour when you have worked so hard for my cause.'

*

They ate finely spiced stews and rich platters of crusted bread but the food tasted bland as barley as a procession of traitors took their places at the benches.

First was Aylmar the Darling. He strode in with his two grown sons and sat on Edmund's left. Aylmar talked quickly and laughed too loudly and watched too intently the face of the king, like a hound that searches its master's face as it waits for scraps.

Godwin felt sick as Eadric strode into the hall. I would have him crawl on his belly like a worm. I would string him from the gallows tree, rip his guts from his belly and roast them over an open fire.

Edmund stood and smiled. 'Eadric Alderman, welcome.'

Eadric caught Godwin's eye. A smile played about his lips and Godwin looked away. Father, there is your enemy. Forgive me that I cannot strike him down where he sits, for I am bound by strict oaths of peace within Edmund's halls.

Eadric and Aylmar made pleasant conversation, but it seemed to Godwin that the mood of the majority was heavy. No one could bring cheer to a room so full of feuds and hatred. It was like a wake, Godwin thought, or a purification, and he caught Abbot Wulsy's eye and wondered if he was thinking the same thing.

Godwin excused himself from the hall as soon as he was able, and when he was alone with Beorn he was furious. 'Is this what we fought for! For that bastard to sit in the hall? Why does he allow them to sit at his table? How long has this been going on?' Godwin raged till he was red in the face.

The night outside was foul and wet: it lashed the hall with rain and wind. They stayed up late drinking and laughing and boasted of how they would deal with the Danes, and stumbled late to their beds. Godwin had a gut full of wine, and he bragged how he had stood by the gorse bush, gone toe to toe with

Danemark's finest and cut them down. Godwin bragged till he was sick, put his fingers down his throat to empty his gut and then fell into place on the hall floor, where his war band slept, sword and shield by their side, as he had done in the hedgerows: always ready for war.

That night Godwin slept and Næling slept next to him and dreamt of other battles it had fought, the skulls it had shattered, the storm of spears, the meeting of wounds, the uncaring and unlucky judgement of swords.

Daybreak brought clear skies. Cocks crowed as the morning minster and trees stood silent and still as Edmund Ironside's warhost filed out of Crepelgate, and the sick and crippled reached up to touch the hem of Edmund's kirtle.

'Back!' some of his retainers shouted, but Edmund put up his hand and let them touch him. The hands pawed at him, clutching and grasping and diseased and dirty.

There was a mixture of wonder and disgust and pity on Edmund's face. He was God's anointed now. The father of the nation. A saint or a martyr, singled out by Christ.

'Bless you all,' Edmund said. 'Bless you all! Pray for us. Farewell!'

The way was paved, the stones led the way as they followed Wæcelinga Stræt north, through fields still damp with a light rainfall, that steamed under the bright autumn sun.

Edmund had his best huntsmen riding far ahead, but there was no need to hunt the Danes down. They made no attempt to hide their progress. There was a column of smoke by day, flames by night.

Ulfcytel, alderman of East Anglia, rode south and greeted them and brought his horse into step with theirs. 'Knut dares not ride into the fens,' he said, 'lest my men surprise him. My men saw the English ships enter the Temese two days ago. There is no escape for the Danes this time. He has already turned back to his ships. They lie on the mudflats next to a hilltop village named Carrenduna.'

'How far away is that?' Edmund asked.

'Three days' riding.'

Edmund heeled his horse. 'Then let us do it in two!'

Every reeve and pompous thegn and staller wanted his pound of flesh and Edmund worked to entertain them all.

'Yes,' he said, 'I understand. Let us first destroy the Danes; then we will hold a council and put all these matters to rights.'

Godwin resented all these petitioners.

When Eadric cantered up Godwin found some excuse to let his horse hang back. He could not bear to be around the man, but on the second morning he saw Edmund laughing with Eadric and jealousy flared within him.

What is Edmund promising? a voice in Godwin's head asked.

Fat, brave Abbot Wulsy put a hand to his shoulder. 'You are well named, "God-win" – "Good Friend". The king will not forget. Do not fret so. Edmund is now cyning – of the people. A king must deal out rings in hall.'

Godwin laughed. He knew the maxims as well as any man: rivers flood-grey flow from the mountain; fyrd ride together, a glorious war band, the bear on the heath, old and terrible, God in Heaven, judge of deeds.

Edmund's mounted warriors followed the long, low ridge that ran along the north of the Temese estuary. It was a bleak and wind-blasted place, dwarfed by the emptiness of the flat horizons.

At the end of the ridge was the last hill before the land gave way to salt marshes and wading bird mudflats – unstable and temporary land – and then ten thousand acres of restless and uneasy steel-grey sea.

It was there that Edmund ran the Danes to ground. From the heights of the hills they looked down to the Danish camp, which had a gloomy and trapped air about it. Their camp was on a low hump of land at the point where the Cruc River drained through reeds into the Temese.

The Danish ships were beached on the mudflats.

Between the hill of Assandune and the sandy hump the Danes were sheltering on was a narrow causeway of fields that led through the marsh-green reeds. It was evening on the second day.

'They say that place is named Carrenduna – the Hill of Cana,' Edmund told Godwin.

Edmund held a mass that night, before another feast of hard drinking. He entertained all his chief men and then sent each back to their companions.

That night Edmund gathered all his companions, all stout men who had stood in battle with him and followed him through hedge and marsh. Eadric was not there, and it was like the days of the Wild Hunt. Godwin raised a silent cup to Edmund's grandmother and hoped her soul was watching this moment when the blood of the English kings ran true again.

In the morning Godwin took out sturdy leather shoes. 'No lamb for the lazy wolf,' he could hear his father telling him as he folded his trousers twice in the front and then crisscrossed the thongs up to his knees. He triple-knotted them. Did not want to lose a shoe when battle came. He laced up his padded hauberk over his kirtle and was helped into his steel-knit war shirt by Beorn, felt the weight of it upon his shoulders.

Godwin's footsteps were heavier then; he walked with more gravitas.

My laces are too tight, Godwin thought, and bent to retie his left shoe. He fastened the right, wiped the sweat from his hands on his thighs and buckled Næling to his side, the sword sleeping in her silver-tipped sheath.

When all was done Godwin took his hood of hand-linked mail. He'd stripped it from a Dane at Sorestone. The fine-forged links, woven at the smithy, were lined with calfskin. Godwin thought it lucky. He held it open. The padding smelt of stale sweat and leather. Godwin set his helmet on his head, a single piece of black vaulted steel. Gold-worked boars decorated the cheek-plates, the rim-work embossed with cunningly crafted gold.

The helmet was open faced, but it restricted his view to either side. It was like blinkers on a horse, driving the man ever forwards. It gave him a handsome look as he stood in his bright war shirt, every inch the warrior, hard eyes gleaming beneath the wolf-worked gold rim.

In his left hand Godwin grasped his wide shield of linden boards. In his right hand's grip two fine ash spears, steel-tipped and eager: one to throw into his enemy's face, the other to wield at shoulder height, and thrust into the face of his foe.

All about him men were putting on mail and helm, and lining up in their grim war bands. Beorn was tight-lipped. He had a long bearded axe in his hands, was proud of holding such a magnificent weapon. He rolled his head from side to side, swung the axe to limber up.

Edmund was dressed in a knee-length mail shirt. His hair fell free to his shoulders. He had cut it short in the English fashion.

The bishops came forward and Edmund knelt.

Godwin's gaze strayed to the Danish camp half a mile away in the crook of the Cruc River. He knew how the Danes must be feeling. They were outnumbered, hunted, doomed. It made him uneasy: it was how they had been at Penne. The cornered dog bit hardest. But the Danish camp seemed confident. They were busy readying themselves, with men drawing up around their banners in the flat sloping strip fields before the chapel at Carrenduna.

There was little room for hidden troops or surprises. Toe to toe, he remembered, and Edmund's horse was brought forward. He sat high above the English host, so that all could see him, and led them down the hillside.

A low, smooth ridge of dry land connected them to the fields where the Danes were lining up. The English took up their positions opposite. Thousands upon thousands, as leaves and flowers appear in season; the finest of England arrayed that day. Godwin spoke to many of them as they stood at the front of the battle line; conferred with Edmund, shook hands, patted shoulders, gave the men encouraging words.

Alderman Elfric of Sumersæton greeted Godwin as if they were bench-fellows. 'Wulfnothson! It is a long way from Sorestone, is it not?'

'Yes, lord,' Godwin said.

'The king will remember this, if we come through this alive.'

'I pray we do come through it alive,' Godwin said.

Elfric looked up at the Danish lines and wrinkled his nose. 'Look! Thorkel is in the middle and Eric on the left.'

'It'll be a fine day, Wulfnothson,' Alderman Ulfcytel said as he strode past. 'Chin up. Strike hard. Do not fear the foe!'

As the English began to line up in battle array, Bishop Ednoth said the blessing. He was a fine sight, his purple gown showing beneath his mail, and a helmet with a golden cross worked into a noseguard. He crossed himself and many men crossed themselves as well, took a few brief moments to make peace with the Lord.

Godwin needed to piss. The urge became so strong that he put his shield down for a moment to empty his bladder, but all that came was a few warm drops that fell into his trousers.

Godwin stamped his feet. The knots on his shoes felt too tight one moment, too loose the next. He stamped his feet to calm himself, focused his mind on what he was about to go into, felt suddenly like a novice. 'Fetch a shield,' Caerl had once said to him, and Godwin felt his heart patter just like that day when he wanted to prove himself.

He remembered the day Wulfnoth put a hilt into his hand.

'Here,' his father had said. 'Like this.'

Godwin took in a deep breath and let it out.

Grant us victory this day, Godwin prayed silently. Let me die if you will grant England peace and protect my people. He watched for a sign, but he could not tell if God had heard.

I will give up life, he said again, for an English victory.

But the sun remained clouded, the wind still; no ravens circled in the sky; there was no shape in the clouds that gave a hint of God's intentions.

War bands were still coming along the dry land. They jostled forward, finding their places as Edmund drew up the two wings of his warhost and the reserve he intended to fling into the battle at the critical moment.

Godwin did not like the long wait, no more than he had done when he was a defender. Come on, let's get this bastard battle over with, he thought to himself, but Edmund paused for the monks to sing a psalm, the one that they had sung when Godwin was a boy: 'Arise, O Lord; save me, O my God: for thou hast smitten all mine enemies upon the cheekbone; thou hast broken the teeth of the ungodly.'

When the singing was over Godwin stood at the front of the English and looked up at the Danes, who took the crest of the low slopes. They were tall and well-dressed, and did not look afraid. They looked eager for battle. The sight was sobering.

Do not parry with the sword. Sword on sword will ruin a blade. Do not watch the enemy's blade; watch his body and wait for an opening. Do not end up like Ulf Edwinson, he thought, remembered killing the thug who had claimed Contone, or Caerl, or your father.

Godwin needed to piss again, but there was no time. He took his place at the front of the line and they moved forward and Godwin felt the field slope upwards.

The Army waited, a line of painted shields, quartered with red and white, blue and green, black and yellow. Some were decorated with crosses; the bosses gleamed, the edges of axes and spears and swords had been freshly whetted; they gleamed with a cold white light. The Danes were silent till Edmund dressed the English lines one final time and then led them forward at a slow walking pace. The Army winded their war horns, hurled smooth, round estuary stones and roared their war cries. The English responded enthusiastically.

By the horns of hell, Godwin thought as Edmund led them forward into the hail of deadly darts. Hell, hell, hell, he thought as each step brought the Danes closer. He could now make out faces among the mass of shields and lined himself up.

When they were three spear lengths apart Godwin could smell the sweat and the fear, and he could see the features that made each Dane distinctive from the next. When he was clear which man he would face, Godwin's mouth went dry.

Christ help me, Godwin thought, and felt the sweat on his

417

spear shaft as the distance between them closed to less than a single furlong. That's one big, ugly bastard.

Whenever warriors gathered about a fire, their conversation invariably found its way to battles they had fought in. They spoke with authority and claimed to know how a certain victory came about: the enemy's left wing collapsed; a certain captain ran out of his store of courage; panic ensued and they ran and were cut down with wounds in their backs.

'They're all liars,' Wulfnoth once told Godwin. 'No man can tell what goes on a sword's length from the end of his nose. He is hemmed in by a deathly ring of faces, all angry, snarling, cursing, as terrified as he. They might try and make sense of it later – in fact they must – but only the servants who watch from the horse pickets and baggage have any idea, and they are not fighting men and know much about how to saddle a horse or treat a lame hound, but little of battle.'

On the fields between Carrenduna and Assandune that day, 18 October 1016, King Edmund Ironside met the veteran warriors of Knut of Danemark. Bitter the battle rush as fearsome companions drove against each other. Spittle and blood erupted and they came to a crashing halt and settled down to hew and stab over the war linden.

'To the left!' someone shouted, and Godwin shoved leftwards.

Godwin had his best men all about him, shoulder to shoulder, brothers fighting as one. They did not withhold the blows; they hacked men to pieces, stood firm and resolute, steadfast before the foe; spear-shafts driving forwards; steel took life; the English crowned themselves with glory.

'Kill him!' Beorn hissed to men behind him.

Godwin did not see the blow or the parry, but he heard a man scream and Beorn laughed, 'Good!' and someone else shouted something, and Godwin didn't know who it was or what the hell he was saying, because he was trying to stab a Dane with crooked teeth and pale, staring blue eyes that gleamed over the rim of his shield.

Beorn bared his war grin, a grim rictus, glaring at the enemy. He split the skull of a Dane to Godwin's right. Ufi the dead man's name, father to the twins Jorunn and Jodis, whom he would tickle by the hearth, and who stood on the milk cart to wave to their father on the day he left, and who would never know where their father ended his life.

Beorn's blow was so fierce that one of Ufi's back teeth hit Godwin on the cheek.

'Three!' Beorn counted, and Ufi groaned as he fell and his corpse was trampled as his soul fled the earth's small bounds.

Godwin smiled for an instant, before a leering Dane with a wild blond beard rose suddenly up above the shield line and thrust his spear at Beorn's face. Godwin saw the blow coming and it was his sword point that caught the Dane full in the face, knocking him back with a low grunt of pain. Then a spear point grazed Godwin's helmet and he could hear the frantic shouting: 'Left! Left!'

Godwin had no idea why they were forcing themselves left, but left they went, pushing, hacking and stabbing, and they came up against a younger Danish war band that seemed less well armoured and experienced, and suddenly the killing was easier. Death took them all. Broad arms, a deluge of ghosts, driven grieving from the body.

Godwin's men were an efficient unit and they made quick work of this enemy, isolating the chief warriors and letting Beorn do the rest. He carried no shield himself, but used his long-hafted axe to swing over the shields into the heads of the men who stood against them.

'Strike!'

'Shove their shields apart!'

'Get him! Fill him with holes!'

Godwin's war band talked to each other, working as a team, with Beorn's axe cleaving the heads of the toughest Danes. Even a glancing blow was enough to shatter the bone-frame beneath mail and hauberk. Godwin laughed for the joy of it all. The poets were right: it was a glorious thing to fight in battle. They killed a man and then pushed over his body, pressing ever deeper into the Danish lines, dragging richly bejewelled Danes into their lines, where they were butchered and stripped of arm-rings and armour. These items were then displayed, the Danes taunted with the severed heads of their dead lord.

All about them men were dying. Dead arms were weighed down with twisted gold; dead faces trodden underfoot; Death's blade stropped and buffed as it scythed through the men on that ridge beneath the forested crown of Assandune Hill.

It was not beer talking, Godwin thought, when we swore to drive the Danes from our land. He hacked a young Dane on the spear arm and heard the bone break, saw the lad's face turn white as his arm flapped on a thread of skin. You chose the wrong man to fight this day, Godwin thought, as he broke the lad's skull with a vicious blow from Næling.

Alongside Godwin's war band, Edmund and his men pushed ever deeper into the Army. Godwin paused to see his banner, high above the furious storm of steel. Knut's banner was driven back; Edmund's banner was twenty helmets to Godwin's left. He risked a glance and saw Edmund's silver boar helm gleaming under the flat grey sky. This shirt that shouldered heroes shall not jingle again, Godwin chanted and felt like a hero in the poems:

Wayland wove this, fine-knit battle shirt
Hung from a shoulder that shouldered warriors.

The Danes pulled back, no more than a couple of spear lengths. Godwin held his men back. 'Rest,' he shouted. 'Draw breath.'

The two sides watched each other for a few brief moments before the English line crashed again into the Danes.

'They're too soft here. Let us find their best troops. Beorn!' Godwin shouted. 'Let us follow the king's banner.'

Edmund had still not committed his reserves, for there was a large group of mail-clad men standing in the centre of the battle-field, looking tense and ready.

'Godwin!' a voice shouted, and Godwin turned to see Abbot Wulsy, sweating profusely and wiping his brow with the back of his arm. 'How goes it?'

'Good,' Godwin said. 'Good.'

'You're going to leave some for us?'

'Of course,' Godwin said, and pointed up the low slope, about three furlongs distant, where the gentle ridge formed the spine of the battlefield. 'That's Knut's banner there. Edmund has promised a pound of gold to any man who cuts him down. Fancy your chances?'

'Not I! That's for young men like yourself. But we'll all do our part. By Christ's blood!' Wulsy looked up and screwed up his nose, as if he was considering how many Danes between him and it. 'Well, no sense in delaying,' he said. 'Your father would be proud of you,' he added as a parting shot, before leading his men, all fine warriors, straight into the fray with shouts of 'Ironside! Ironside!'

A while later Godwin paused. His cheek was sticky with blood, but he couldn't remember being hit. 'That Dane's tooth cut me,'

421

he said, and Beorn grinned. Godwin loved that ugly smile. He grinned back.

As far as they could see they were pushing the Danes back all along their side of the battle, but the lines had slowly edged to the left, so that the left wings were now fighting on the other side of the low ridge, and they could only see the tops of the banners, standing still in the battle lines.

It looked good.

'We shall feast tonight,' Beorn said, and slapped Godwin's arm.

'They're pinned back! Once we've driven them to the top of the hill we'll be able to strike down upon them and they are sure to run.'

Then suddenly there was a great shout and the Danish centre seemed to stem their retreat and a new war band charged into where the White Dragon flapped in the wind, and drove a wedge into the English line.

'That is Thorkel the Tall,' Beorn shouted. 'He will cut the king off unless we help him! He escaped me once, not this time. My axe shall split the old giant's ugly head.'

Godwin led his whole company back into the fray as a bleeding thegn stumbled back towards them.

'We met Thorkel the Tall and he and his men were very terrible,' the thegn said, and Godwin rushed past.

He was pushing right behind Edmund's banner. They did not meet Thorkel but some Norman warriors, with shaven lips and cruel eyes and swords of the best Frankish steel. They cursed in a barbarous tongue as Beorn cut them down, and they bled like all men when pierced with steel. One of them seized Beorn's axe head and tried to pull it from him. Another Norman tried to drag the shaft from his hand, but Beorn would not let go, even though they hacked at him. His mail shirt saved him and he shrugged off their blows and laughed as he grasped one by the throat and crushed the life from him.

The battle wavered. At one point it seemed the Danes would break, at another the English. In rushed the men, like grains of wheat pouring into the mill when the sluice gate is opened – ground by the thousand to husks and bone-pale flour.

Godwin saw Abbot Wulsy away to his right – helmet off, wolf-grey hair flying in the air – and realised that the abbot had been cut off and surrounded. 'Help him!' Godwin shouted to no one in particular, but he was far away and it was already too late. An axe caught the abbot on the back of the head and then he was lost from view and all Godwin could see were weapons hacking down in the space where the good monk had once stood.

Suddenly a shiver seemed to run through the English as Thorkel led his berserker axemen in another terrible charge. The great Dane was like a maddened bull; bloody foam fell from his lips, he strode towards Godwin's men, cutting men down with his berserkers all about him.

'Stand firm!' Godwin shouted. 'We held him once. Beorn, is your axe ready!'

'Ready!' Beorn shouted.

Godwin's shield took three blows from Thorkel's sword. The first split the rim; the second shattered the timbers; the third left Godwin with a boss and some splinters, that he rammed at Thorkel's face and drove him back, Beorn swinging his axe with equal ferocity.

Thorkel stepped back and then charged again. Eric of Hlathir charged too.

Knut was terrified. 'Charge!' he told his veteran captains.

Danes stood about Knut and the Black Raven banner and fell without taking a single step backwards. The English pressed to the crest of the hill. The last hill, Godwin thought. Such a small coastal hump, and the crest where Knut stood with his banner was only thirty paces away.

Edmund pressed forward, Godwin with him. Their shieldwall held, and the Danes were like a maddened ram battering its head against the sheep-pen boards. War band after war band beat on the English shieldwall. Again and again the English threw them back, but they were making no headway. They had stalled. Godwin could feel the mood of the English fracturing. He looked suddenly for Edmund and could not see him.

'Is he dead?' someone asked.

'Where is Edmund!'

At that moment Thorkel and his men charged again, bellowing his war cry. It was like watching a weary timber suddenly snap. The English shieldwall broke. Thorkel's men plunged deep into the English. The front ranks of warriors had been worn very thin and Thorkel battered his way through them into the ranks of boys and old men who made up the rear. Thorkel set about him, murdering children and greyheads. The shudder in the English ranks started a panic. Panic turned to terror, terror to flight. Godwin wanted to go back and seal the breach, but Knut saw his opportunity and all his great warriors charged.

The Fates seemed uncertain to whom they should award victory. The English wavered, and Edmund mounted a horse, took off his helm and called out to the English.

'Ironside!' the shout went up. 'Ironside!'

Edmund swung his war sword. It flashed silver and red in the pale white daylight.

The sight of him gave fresh heart to the English. They threw Eric of Hlathir and his Norse companions back upon their dead and wounded. The battle surged back and forth. Both shieldwalls broke. Edmund's banner pushed to the brow of the hill, and Knut trembled behind his hearth companions, who drew themselves up and prepared to sell their lives dearly.

The fighting was terrible. Men fell and screamed and begged for mercy.

'Remember the speeches we made on the benches! Now let us prove who is truly valiant,' Edmund called.

Godwin followed the king deep into the enemy. He could tell he was approaching the brow of the ridge. He was paces from the crest of the hill, Knut was fighting for life.

'Remember your oath!' Godwin shouted, but his voice was hoarse.

'We're winning.' Beorn grinned. 'We're wearing those bastards down.'

It seemed true. Godwin laughed and fought with renewed energy, but suddenly he turned and saw far to the left Englishmen flying from the battle.

Why should they flee?

'Stop!' men shouted. 'See we are winning.'

It was an incredible sight. The battle seemed to stop as the Danes and English looked in wonder at the sight. Who ran from victory? the English thought. What chance was this? Knut wondered, and then saw Eadric's banner leading the flight and laughed out loud, his grin flashing as he swung his sword in the air.

Many Danes ran after Eadric, cutting men down, as wolves snag the deer by the hoof and bring it down. But the veteran Danish war chiefs kept their heads. With a swift strike into the English right flank they could win a glorious victory.

Horns and shouts rang out. The war chiefs came together. They made a shieldwall, swung round like a door on its hinge and swept the exhausted and astonished English right wing before them.

Alderman Elfric was first in line. 'To me!' he cried. 'To me!' and his men leapt to his defence. There was a fierce struggle but the Fates, the three giant maidens, Past, Present and Future, chose that moment to snap Elfric's chin strap. They knocked the silver helmet from his head, left his glorious head exposed, and blows rained down.

Elfric called on his men to not let his body be despoiled by the foe. His words stopped when a sword hit him full in the face. Five steps backward, doomed and dying, he crashed to the ground. His soul fled in terror from the ruin of his body, abandoning the best of life: love and light and laughter.

'Hold on to his corpse!' his retainers called to one another and a savage battle broke out over the dead man. One side tugged his legs while the other cradled his blood-splattered head and called on their ring-giver to make his peace with the Almighty Lord. The time had come that they had all long feared, but had prepared themselves for, and sold their lives dearly.

But they were an island in a stream of men who fled for their lives.

The trickle became a flood. The flood a deluge. In the space of a few minutes the battle was lost. Godwin strode to Edmund's side. His men tightened about the king, a beleaguered knot about which a stream of Danes was beginning to flow.

'Eadric has fled,' Godwin shouted. His words came out in a hoarse whisper. 'That bastard Eadric has fled!'

Edmund was spattered with blood and sweat. He was too stunned to speak, but Beorn kept his head.

'Stand firm, five deep, there on the right. There are Sudsexe men there, but their leader is dead and they're close to running,' he told a group of men standing near him. 'Where are you from?' he asked another man.

'Leomynstre,' the man said. 'But our lord Unferth is lost.'

'Then stand firm and fight in his memory,' Beorn told them. 'We all must leave the earth and this is as good a place as any to die. Cowards' graves are small and mean, while great mounds mark the bones of the brave.'

The band about Edmund retreated slowly. They were a menacing sight: bloody and mailed and determined to sell their lives dearly. Most Danes passed them by, eager for the easier prey, but Knut saw his chance to surround his enemy and kill him. He summoned his best fighters.

'Let us surround Edmund and kill him!' he shouted.

Godwin caught Beorn's eye and pushed to Edmund's side.

Alderman Ulfcytel was shouting at Edmund, 'You must flee. Our lives are nothing, but yours is worth all the world. Lord, the day is lost. Flee! I shall stand here with my companions. Promise me that you will break free and flee from here and raise another fyrd, so that our deaths might not have been in vain.'

Edmund resisted. Ulfcytel grabbed Godwin and shoved him towards the king. 'Talk sense to him,' he shouted. 'Go with the king! Defend him and protect him!'

Edmund would not listen, but there was no time for discussion. Knut's men were beginning to encircle them. Godwin and Beorn took him by his belt and lifted him from the ground.

'With me!' Godwin shouted to his men.

CHAPTER ELEVEN

Isle of Derheste

In Contone Kendra woke with a start. The hall thatch was still and silent; outside a man screamed. She threw back the blankets, ran to the door and opened it a fraction, and the scream came again.

'Agnes,' she whispered, but there was no answer. Kendra clutched the doorframe and smelt pigs and remembered all of a sudden that the herds of swine had been brought down from the beech woods.

It was Bloodmonth, the time of slaughter. The clove-spiced brines were ready; twine had been bought from the market, ready to hang the bacon and hams from the hall rafters. Kendra's stomach lurched. She could not bring herself to go outside to see the killing. She felt queasy enough already, could not sit inside all day and listen to the sounds of the slaughter; saw Dudoc climbing slowly up the hill, crook in hand, and her heart wished for the climb and the broad and sunlit uplands.

The night before, Kendra had dreamt of her mother again. She had not said anything, just stared at her daughter and pointed, and Kendra had wanted to call out to her but found that she could neither move nor speak, even when her mother's ghost reached out an imploring hand.

The feeling clung to Kendra all that day, the sensation of a lost mother who could not be reached and it left her even more unsettled and irritable. The sound of the pigs made her heart beat. She remembered the day the Norsemen came to Yula and killed and murdered. Her heart raced and her palms sweated. She did not understand why the memories of that day should come today. She grabbed her shawl and threw it over her head as she went outside, kept her head turned away from the hanging brown pigs. She lifted her skirts to climb quickly to the top of the ridge, but the sound of the squealing swine carried after her until the exertion and regular pant of her breath and steps drove everything else from her mind.

Edmund fled from battle as Ulfcytel and his East Anglians stood firm to stop Knut's warriors. They knew they were dead men, laughed as they saluted the Heavens, thought this was a fine day to die.

Beorn called his two shield-bearers back. 'Godwin, you go. Go!' he roared. His face had a desperate look. 'Take the king to the horses and make sure he lives.'

Beorn was joined by those few of Wulfnoth's faithful men who still stood.

There was no time for a farewell. The last Godwin saw of Beorn he was striding up to Ulfcytel's band, shouldering his axe and stooping to pick up a fresh shield from a man who lay dead.

The weight of the Danish onslaught fell on the retainers of Ulfcytel. 'Death comes at last,' Beorn smiled. 'I never thought I would live so long.'

Around Edmund there were barely fifty men, but they kept close order and did not turn their backs, and the Danes held back from them, like wary wolves, who trail the pack.

'Make sure he survives,' Beorn had told Godwin, and he thought of nothing else. Save yourself so you can save the king.

At times it seemed that they would never make it through to the king's horses, for Danes and fleeing Englishmen were everywhere: a panicked mob, all streaming round the bottom of Assandune Hill, looking for the fastest and driest route to safety.

Edmund could not talk.

'What happened?' someone asked.

No one knew.

'Eadric.' Godwin named the traitor. 'Eadric led the flight. I saw his banner fleeing from the battle.'

The boys who had been guarding the king's horses lay butchered; the horses had long been stolen.

Godwin grabbed the bridle of a fleeing Defenascir man's horse. The man tried to hit Godwin with his sword, but Godwin caught his arm and dragged him from the saddle and in a moment he was cut down.

'We cannot flee with just one horse!' someone shouted, and Godwin saw the hopelessness of their situation as Knut's men charged the thin shieldwall where Beorn stood.

'Take it!' Godwin said.

Edmund shook his head.

'Take it!' Godwin repeated. 'Take it or I shall kill it now and we shall both die.'

Edmund would not, but Godwin shouted at him, 'If you live, our cause has hope. Save yourself for our sakes.'

Edmund cursed him, but at last he swung himself up into the saddle. They looked about but it was confusion everywhere. Ulfcytel and his shieldwall held – just – but other Danes had picked out Edmund from the chaos. Godwin saw the Danes run down the hill towards them. We are doomed, he thought, but they fought anyone with a horse and did not care if they killed.

In this way Edmund's men gathered twenty horses from flee-ing men, and Godwin ripped the royal banner from its pole, thrust it into another man's hands.

'Take this!' he said. Godwin turned and saw that in that moment almost all of the horses had been taken. 'I will not leave you behind,' Edmund shouted but Godwin whipped Edmund's horse. 'Go!' he shouted.

'No. Come – sit behind me!' Edmund said.

'Go!'

'Not without you. I am your king. I will not leave you here.'

But as Edmund spoke one of the riders grabbed the reins of his horse and they broke into a gallop as Edmund cursed them all.

Godwin was glad to see Edmund escape, glad to the bottom of his heart. He had tears of joy and hope in his eyes, but the rim of his third shield was riven and useless. He tossed it aside and found another abandoned in the autumn grasses. It had not been scratched, and he thought of the thegn who had carried it so far from his home, just to drop it without having struck a blow. Coward, he thought, and exchanged a grin with the men about him as he fitted his arm into the strap.

'Brothers, I am glad to die with you,' he said. 'Let us make a stand worthy of a poem.'

But as the Danes approached the men turned and fled.

Godwin stood alone, terrible in his war gear, covered with other men's blood. He cut the first Danes down and his sword stuck to his hand with congealing gore.

He panted and looked about him. The Danes sized up the lone warrior and let him alone. There were easier pickings: the battlefield was littered with corpses that wore enough gold to make them rich men.

A riderless horse suddenly cut across the field in front of him. It paused for a moment, and Godwin looked around as if expecting someone to have brought it here. The horse slowed in front of him, as if waiting for him to mount up. Godwin did not need a second invitation. He caught its bridle and swung himself up.

Godwin put his heels to the horse's flanks and galloped after the king.

Knut stared at the last war band. Ulfcytel the Bold, the Danes named him.

'Surrender!' he called out, and the old man laughed at him.

The men of East Anglia were the Wuffingas; Dane and East Anglian spoke almost the same tongue. It made their insults easier to understand.

'I will never kneel before a Danish king!' Ulfcytel shouted back. 'There are no pacts of faith between lions and men.'

'I will not ask you again,' Knut said, but the answer was jeering and hooting. 'So you have chosen. Now dogs and birds will devour you all.'

Knut ordered his men into the kill, but they were reluctant to press the attack at first, for Ulfcytel's men were renowned fighters and none wanted to feel their kiss. Beorn was with them, limping now. He stood next to Ulfcytel and heard his words.

'Watch, brothers, no man will fix a spear in my back as I flee.'

Ulfcytel made his last stand there. Battle death took him and all the men he had sat with in hall.

Beorn fought long after the men about him were cut down. He fought till the sword he had picked up shattered against a Danish helm. He used the broken sword. The Danes hacked at him. Beorn parried blows with his left arm till the bone was broken in five places. His grin still made men fearful, but he was cornered by swordsmen. One blade caught his chin and cut as deep as the bone. Another hit him near the eye and filled it with blood. Stunned and blind, a spear-thrust took out the teeth on his right side and came out his other cheek.

Danes stood to see if he would fall, but Beorn swayed and cursed as he spat out blood. An axeman behind him swung a blow at the back of his head. It was a rising blow that lifted Beorn off the ground, shattered the helm and drove deep through mail and skull into his brain.

Beorn fell forward on to his knees and then sprawled on to his face.

The Danes did not wait to see if he was dead; he was clearly not. They were impressed. One used a spear to turn Beorn on to his back.

'Kill him,' the spearman said, and the axe descended full into Beorn's face, cutting through his left eye and his nose and crooked grin, almost cutting his head in twain.

Once Beorn lay still a silence seemed to descend, a weary and exhausted stillness. From the low rise Knut looked out. It was an awesome sight: thousands of brave men breathing their last; the Cruc River choked with the drowned bodies of English lords, strange fish gleaming in their steel scales, floating in the river weeds as the water gently nudged them out to sea.

Knut pushed his helmet back and saw that he had won, and this devastation was named victory.

Twenty of Edmund's company escaped the battle. They rode heedless of direction or destination, through the ruins of the English hope, terrified warriors clogging up the roads and paths.

About three miles from the battle there was a narrow ford, and there was a bottleneck of men all struggling to cross, or splashing into the water and attempting to swim. Some tried to drag their anointed king from his saddle, such was their terror. Edmund's companions cut them down.

It was there Godwin caught them up. 'Out of the way!' he shouted, but the men grasped at him and tried to drag him from his horse. He twisted the angle of his sword and struck one man dead. They were battle-shirkers and traitors.

Once across the river, Edmund's men were out into open ground. They rode hard, passing through the monks from Ely who were busy burying the gold-worked relic cases in terror that the Danes should bespoil the bones of their most treasured saints. Godwin looked back once – and saw that the Danish horsemen had caught the stragglers up at the river crossing, and he could hear the screams and lamentation carrying on the wind, and he turned his back and lashed his horse onwards and long after the place was haunted by the ghosts of men who were slaughtered that day.

That evening Godwin fell off his horse and did not care for anything more than a cupped hand's worth of stream water and a crust of oatcake.

'Godwin!' Edmund said. 'Godwin, how are you here?'

'God sent a horse,' Godwin said.

Edmund half smiled and fell against Godwin in a rough embrace.

'Thanks be to God,' he whispered. 'Godwin. I could not have lost you today. A kingdom, yes, but not a friend.'

Godwin was out of words. He had nothing left to give. They were sitting in a hall that the Danes had looted three days earlier. The people had just returned from the hedgerows and were terrified of the bloodied men.

They sat and some wept; others began to moan with wounds. Godwin shook uncontrollably. Edmund could not speak. He sat with his head in his hands.

'We will raise another war band,' Godwin said once they had drunk ale.

No one said anything. The silence was long and telling.

Edmund's hands dropped.

Still no one spoke.

'Maybe Ulfcytel salvaged a part of our strength,' Edmund said. 'He is a great warrior. He gives heart to fearful men.'

Maybe, Godwin thought. We will go back to the hedgerows, he thought. But immediately he knew they could not carry the country now. Not now God had so clearly spoken.

News of the battle came in shattered fragments. Alderman Elfric's sons had been cut down as they fought their way from the field, and his sister-son, the fair Osgood lay with them. Ethelward the Fair would never return to his father's hall, would never sit his son upon his knee again, nor hold his wife's hand as they knelt at the painted rood screen.

'And Ulfcytel?' Edmund asked a monk who claimed to have buried the bodies.

The monk did not know, but many others did.

'Ulfcytel refused to flee, even when the rest of the English were in flight. He fell and his household fell about him, defending his body.'

And with them are my father's men, Godwin thought. All sons and brothers of his Contone folk. He could not face returning home alive when all he had led to battle had died.

That night they were too grief-stricken to sing songs, even of the dead. Words would not come. As the camp fire divided them all, they sat in stunned silence, numbed by their loss.

'Northymbria?' Godwin suggested when they debated where to flee, but many voices rose up against him, for many did not trust the Northhymbers, as they were Danish in speech and blood.

'No, let us go westwards,' Edmund said. 'They gave the least. We shall shame them into raising another fyrd.'

The night after the battle they set off. They had brought in many stragglers as the day wore on, and by dusk they were a company of a hundred horsemen, picking their way along little-used paths again, riding under the stars through a clear and bitterly cold night. As the moon set it began to rain, and Edmund announced that they would rest.

When he called them to rise again it was still dark and many men refused to get up, and some of them could not for, they were all cold and damp, and many were wounded, and they left them to Christ.

Winter was close. Dawn was as bitter as any Godwin could remember. The north wind rose to a gale and shook the gaunt black trees and skinned the backs of their hands, and it was all Godwin could do to sit in his saddle and stop his teeth from chattering.

They were a sorry sight as they crossed next morning into Oxenefordscire: cold and damp, with hedgerow hair and bedraggled mounts. The sun appeared for a few brief moments, to illuminate the hedgerows, netted with gleaming webs, before the light and the gleam faded, and then the rain returned harder and more determined than before. News had already reached Oxeneford, and the welcome was uncertain and fearful: the king had submitted himself to trial by battle and he had been found wanting.

They passed from Oxenefordscire to Wiltunscir and Sumersæton, and a few men feasted Edmund, but they were glad to see him off the next morning, and wary of what King Knut might do to them.

They even stopped at the hall of Alderman Elfric, where his wife greeted the men with a gaunt face. She bore the news of her husband and sons well.

'Who saw him die?' she asked, and a Defenascir lad who had fought with Elfric stood up.

'I fought beside him in the battle. He killed many of the enemy and stood bravely to the end, when many others fled.'

'How was he?' she asked. 'How were his spirits?'

'Good, lady. He died bravely and with honour.'

She fought back tears and spoke bravely. 'And my sons?'

'They all fought well,' Edmund told her.

'And my brightest son, Acwellen. Was he killed too?'

They nodded solemnly and bowed their heads, and she drew her shawl over her face and sat for a long while in silence.

In the morning Edmund and his companions departed. Three boys trailed after them.

'Ignore them,' Edmund said to Godwin.

But they kept pace with them.

'Perhaps they're spies,' Godwin said.

Edmund stopped his horse. They waited for the boys to catch up. They came within twenty paces and Edmund shouted to them, 'Go back!' But one of the boys pushed his horse forward. He was thirteen, perhaps, with the first down of blond stubble on his chin.

'We want to follow you,' he said.

'Go back,' Edmund told them. 'You have neither mail nor helm, and things are not so dire that we need boys to fight for us.'

The boys did not move. In the end Godwin rode up to them and spoke gently. 'Go back and care for your mother. That is your job now. She has lost too many sons this year. But tell me your names.'

437

The boys announced themselves proudly.

'Well, Egbert, Elfstan and brave little Dunstan, the time will come, I am sure, when it is your turn to step up and defend our country. Save your lives and your strength till then. Listen to the great tales; practise your sword skills; keep your oaths and pray each night before you go to sleep; and remember your father and brothers, and feud against the Danes.'

Godwin smiled, but they did not move.

'I will come back for you when the time is come,' Godwin said gently. 'Do not make a gift of glory to the Danes. Wait till your lives are better spent.'

The boys turned their horses slowly back, labouring under the weight of disappointment.

Each time they arrived at a village, town or hall, the eyes of the women seemed to ask, We have already given you our sons and husband. What else can we give you? Make peace, their sad eyes seemed to say. Make peace and let us live.

Edmund gathered five hundred men. Some of them were those who had come too late for battle; others were wounded men they had left behind; a hundred came from the garrison at Malmesberie.

They camped in the graveyard at Glowcestre and waited for news.

None came.

The country was exhausted and timid.

In the end it was Eadric who rode deep into Wessex to find them. He brought three hundred of his own men and left them outside the burg gates as his horse walked forward. Eadric's men were tellingly hale. There were no wounds on them, or broken limbs. It was as if they had never been on that battlefield.

Edmund would not open the gates. He glared down from the

wooden palisade and Eadric approached as cautiously as a carrion bird that tilts its head, hops sideways towards the carcass.

'Why are you here, fickle traitor?'

'Knut wishes peace,' Eadric said.

'There will be peace when he is gone from this broad kingdom and when you lie dead, throttled with your own guts.'

Eadric was unswayed. 'God has judged you, Ironside,' he
called up. 'It would be well to heed his voice.'

Edmund looked down. 'If your men stood in battle, we would
have won at Assandune.'

Eadric said nothing. The two men stared at each other.

'I will return in three days,' Eadric said at last. 'Knut has said
that he will take Mercia and the old Danelaw. He offers you all
of Wessex as your own.'

'Wessex is not his to offer!' Edmund shouted but Eadric rode
slowly away.

There were burgs and shires that did not send men to
Assandune, so Edmund sent men out to raise more war bands.

'There is time for one last battle before winter sets in,' he said.

Godwin went from hall to hall. The reception ranged from
polite to frosty, but no one wanted more war.

'Make peace!' the women urged. 'If God is against us we
cannot give you more of our sons.'

Godwin came back with barely enough to fill a hall, and he
had done better than most.

'They will not come,' he said.

'They will not come *yet*,' Edmund corrected.

Later, when Godwin and the king were alone, Edmund was less
cocksure. 'What if Knut rides into Wessex? How will we resist
him?'

Godwin frowned. 'We cannot. No doubt Eadric will ride with him. Will your wife's people ride with us?'

Edmund did not know. Fate had spun on its wheel.

'We could take to the hedgerows and byways again,' Godwin said.

'They will not,' Edmund said and their gaze fell on the weary men as they prepared for sleep. 'We left all the best men on the battlefields. They are buried.'

'Maybe, but our greatest kings and heroes walked on the same soil as us, slept under the same sky. What is a little frost and rain?'

Edmund smiled. He loved Godwin.

All through the next days monk and abbot and reeve and thegn battered Edmund with talk of peace. Godwin and Edmund resisted, but at long last Edmund's shoulders sagged lower with each hour, each day that passed and he was persuaded to at least meet with Knut.

Godwin was appalled. It was like a girl being cajoled into an unhappy marriage. But he was as beaten as Edmund.

'What should I do, Wulfnothson?' Edmund asked, but Godwin could see that he had already made up his mind.

'I would fight,' Godwin said. 'Everything Eadric touches is poisoned. But you are king. This is your decision to make.'

The peace-makers cast mistrustful looks at Godwin.

Edmund nodded. He coughed to clear his throat. 'If it gains us time to meet with the Dane, then I will meet him.'

The isle of Derheste in the Vale of Glowcestrescir was chosen as the meeting place. It was a wet green land of many rivers, which drained into the Avon and Severne, crisscrossed with marshes and soggy hollows of watching, stagnant green water, soaking the long tresses of the hanging willows.

It was also a site of ancient religion, where men threw sacred objects and waited for the response of the water-spirit.

Derheste lay in the middle of this mysterious landscape. It was a secluded spot, with the slow brown Severne drifting along the north side, marshes and wetlands on the south. There was a monastery now, built on the flat-topped hump, to tame the wild water-spirits with prayers and devotion.

Edmund came from the south with a hundred retainers, and it was arranged that Knut should come from the north with the same number.

Both kings had sworn oaths on holy relics, and each had given the other twenty men as hostages.

'I want Eadric as a hostage,' Edmund insisted.

When Knut heard, he was glad to agree. 'Tell Edmund that I will give him Eadric and his chief men as well as twenty of my own warriors.'

'What do you think he's like,' Edmund asked Godwin as they prepared to meet their foe, 'this Knut?'

Godwin gave an odd gesture. 'He's a bastard.'

Edmund nodded. 'I find myself looking forward to meeting him.'

They washed and dressed and turned out in the finest clothes they could find or borrow. They were a young and handsome company as they set off that morning. Godwin rode at the front with the king. His skin prickled as the road tipped them gently downwards towards the green and reedy isle. Far off, in the distance, rising above the morning mists, was the humped back of the Malvern Hills. The road descended to the Severne Valley. The dank air was chilling, the dark water impenetrable.

Mist filled the valley, and only the tops of a few tall trees and the monastery tower rose above it, but they were lost to them as they went deeper. Godwin looked down into the flat black water.

It was still and stagnant, and did not bode well. They passed a swineherd driving his charges to the side of the road. His dirty face looked up at Edmund's company as they passed by. The lad caught the eye of Edmund, Godwin and many of the chief men of the kingdom and stared dumbly up at them.

He does not know that he has just seen Edmund Ironside, Godwin thought. He does not know and he does not care as long as he has a gut full of food, and peace enough to marry and raise sons and daughters of his own.

Doubt was rust corrosive.

If he does not know us, then why are we fighting? Godwin wondered, and did not know any more, except that he had sworn oaths to Edmund and that he would never betray his dear lord.

The river was high and many of the lower pastures were flooded, but monks came out with boats to show them the way, and their horses slowly picked a way across the flooded pastures.

'So this is Derheste,' Edmund said as they climbed up the far side. 'Alfege was an oblate here, was he not?'

'He was, my lord king,' the abbot said.

Edmund gave him a bag of silver. 'For your troubles,' he said, and the abbot bowed and thanked the king. Godwin caught an odd tone in his voice and wondered if other monks were addressing Knut the same way. If the same thought crossed Edmund's mind, he did not let on, but dismounted and knelt and crossed himself. His company joined him, a noble congregation, men with much on their minds, and many sins to atone for.

Godwin prayed only reluctantly. The words came slowly and a voice in his head kept accusing God of failing him, failing them all at Assandune. Godwin saw that the abbot was looking at his king and there were tears running down his cheeks, and Godwin understood. The monks wept to see the piety of this bravest of kings.

Edmund rose. 'Is he here?' he said gravely.

They all knew who he was talking about.

'He is, my lord.'

'Then,' Edmund said with weary note in his voice, 'it is time that we should meet.'

Godwin felt uneasy as they all put their weapons aside, but the monks were very thorough.

'It is the same for both sides,' they assured them. Godwin looked at them as if he suspected them of not telling the truth, gave them Næling without words but with much feeling. This was his father's sword, notched with the deaths of many men.

Two bodyguards then led the men to the church door. Edmund went quickly, as if he wanted it to be over. Godwin lengthened his stride to keep up. His footsteps were heavy and solemn on the linden boards. He was Godwin Wulfnothson. He had fought at Sorestone, Sudwerca and Assandune. He had the scars to prove it.

The two bodyguards halted fifty yards apart. Now the two companies stood and stared at each other with frank curiosity.

Knut stepped forward. Godwin had heard much about Swein's second son. He looked small and slender. Though his face was handsome enough, Knut looked no more than eighteen.

'You fought a good battle,' Knut said. His English was heavily accented.

Edmund spoke to him with the Northymbrian accent of his mother.

The two young kings understood each other well. They shared words that Godwin could not quite catch, and then both of them laughed and Godwin found himself laughing as well, and then the whole room was full of laughing men.

'Shall we feast?' Edmund said, and they all filed through to the room the monks had prepared and sat in alternate seats and drank and laughed and were glad to put war and war shirts and weapons aside.

England was divided along the ancient border between Mercia and Wessex, but Lundenburh was to remain inside Wessex, and Euruic under Knut's sway.

Peace felt good to all of them. It was a relief, like standing under a waterfall and letting the torrent wash care from your head. Oaths of fellowship were sworn; then they filed into the church for a solemn mass. Relics were brought out, including a phial of water that St Oswald used to wash pilgrims' feet, and Edmund and Knut renewed their oaths of peace and brotherhood. Edmund agreed to pay the Army a great sum of silver.

'So it is agreed,' the abbot said. 'Knut Sweinson shall rule Danelaw. Edmund, son of Ethelred, known as the Ironside, shall rule the kingdom of Wessex, and peace will remain through the kingdom.'

The two men kissed each other on the cheek, sealed their friendship with gifts in the traditional manner of their ancient ancestors.

'Farewell Edmund, King,' Knut said as they prepared to leave the isle.

'Farewell Knut, King.'

The two men shook hands, holding each other by the wrist. It was a frank and honest handshake. They embraced a final time, and their companies witnessed it and then walked away from each other. Boats carried them back to the far shore, where their weapons were waiting. Godwin strapped his sword to his belt again. They were back in the real world now, and his sword hung heavy.

That night they rode back to Glowcestre in silence.

When they returned the hostages were let go. Eadric rode harder than most.

'He is eager to be gone,' Godwin said.

They watched as Eadric's silhouette faded into the distance.

'How long till Knut breaks the truce?' Edmund asked.

'The Walsh will be keen to test their new neighbour, so give him a season putting them down, and another year to get the recalcitrant in line,' Godwin said.

'So we have a year before war begins again, two at best.'

Godwin and Edmund looked at the future before them, and although it seemed hard and difficult, they did not shirk.

'We shall have to prepare the country for war,' Edmund said. 'But tonight you know what we should do?'

Godwin shook his head.

'The abbot here keeps some good Frankish wines,' Edmund said and turned and looked at him. 'I think we should get very, very drunk.'

CHAPTER TWELVE

Shorn Threads

The news of peace between Edmund and Knut spread throughout the country from the marshes of Cantware to the cliff shores of Cornwalia, to the city of Cestre on the wild borders of the north-west, to the holy coast of Northymbria and even to the parts of Northymbria that paid tribute to the Scottish king Malcolm.

In Lundenburh Queen Emma sat with her sons Alfred and Edward. Both boys were shaken by their first sight of battle and had been safely plucked from the ruin of Assandune and brought back through the Crepelgate gates, which were shut behind them, barred and barricaded against the coming of the Danes.

The Danes passed by and the White Queen stood on the walls and refused to grant them access. Knut rode up. He enjoyed the sight of the White Queen holding the city against him still. She had a chair brought to the gate top and she sat there, with her robes arranged about her, and looked down on him. Emma was a Norman. There was much about her that showed her Danish ancestry. She had a well-shaped face and an upturned nose, her hair was golden, though her eyes were nut brown.

Knut admired her.

'They say men in Normandig still speak Danish,' Knut said to Eric, who was sitting next to him on his horse.

Eric had lost a finger at Assandune and the bandaged stump itched. He rubbed it against his thigh and nodded. 'Along the coast they do,' he said.

Knut cleared his throat and called up in Danish, 'Who is this lady that stands on my city walls?'

There was a long pause, and Knut thought that she did not understand, but after a moment a voice came back. It was deep for a lady, authoritative and clear. Her accent was a little barbaric, such as the country folk on Sealand spoke. Knut found it quite charming.

'Lundenburh was once Mercia.'

'Yes, but the oaths you swore ceded it to Wessex.'

'I shall take it one day,' he said.

'Maybe, but that day is not yet.'

Knut laughed. 'So you will not open the gates to me.'

'No,' Queen Emma told him. 'And not until you are king of all England. Lundenburh is in the realm of Wessex, Edmund Ironside is our king, and there will be peace between us as long as you keep to your oaths, Knut Sweinson. Keep to your oaths, young king, and God will look kindly upon you.'

Edward and Alfred saw their mother step down from the walls.

Edward was an uncomfortable youth and disliked his mother. She disliked him almost as strongly.

Later that night, when Alfred was asleep, Edward sat silent in the corner and listened to Queen Emma talking to her chaplain.

'What will I do with my boys?' she said.

Edward pricked up his ears.

'They have more of their father in them.'

Queen Emma's face turned and saw Edward was listening.

'Edward!' she said sharply. 'It is time for sleep now. Go say your prayers.'

In Contone Kendra had not been able to sleep. She sat that night listening to Dudoc sing a poem about a great warrior doomed to die, as all men must, in the end, however much glory they won in life: 'Wyrd oft nereð unfægne eorl, þonne his ellen deah,' Dudoc said. Fate is often merciful to the brave man.

But poets sang too much of war and glory. What did they know of loss and longing? And next morning, once the chores were done, Kendra felt as though a great weight was pressing down upon her. She sat at home and stared at her loom, with all its hanging threads, and could not bring herself to weave.

All she thought about was the news of Assandune: that the English had been broken after a battle that lasted into the ninth hour of the day, and that the king had escaped, but many of the great men of the English had been slaughtered.

She woke each morning and longed for sight of a horseman, or a band of men, picking their way home, weary and wounded.

Had she cared for Godwin just for him to be hacked to meat by Danish swords? She would not have tended him so gently if she had known.

King Edmund rested in Glowcestre for a week while he set the defence of his people in order. He brought back the old provision that no man should be more than a day's walk from a burg where he might seek shelter from raiders. The whole country was crisscrossed with burg towns, and the maintenance of their defence was put upon the local landowners. The first to be repaired were the burgs along the border of Wessex and Mercia. From Malmesberie, Cracgelade, Oxeneford, Walingeford, Sashes and on to Lundenburh, men deepened the great earthen ditches and renewed the wooden palisades.

By the time King Edmund Ironside reached Oxeneford the repairs to the burg walls were already well underway. Edmund and Godwin rode out to inspect the work on the north gate.

'It's been a hundred and fifty years since the Temese was the line between our kingdoms,' Edmund said. 'Will men remember me as the man who lost England?'

'No,' Godwin said. 'Alfred lost his entire kingdom and ended up taking it all back, and more.'

'Why would God do this?' Edmund asked.

Godwin did not know.

Edmund sent emissaries to the Walsh and Scots, the men of Cumbraland and Ealdseaxum the Flems and Britons. 'Half defence is diplomacy,' his father had told him, and for once Ethelred was not wrong. The people had hope in King Edmund because he had proven himself a great warrior, and his first priority was setting the defence of Wessex in good order.

Godwin and Edmund spent most of November in Oxeneford. On the 20th they celebrated the Feast of St Edmund the Martyr with a mass. The mass had a special significance, and the monks wept as they welcomed the king and his entourage. Outside the abbey gates, a great crowd had arrived to see their young king.

Edmund had tears in his eyes. He trembled as the great crowd stood before him. He remembered the angry men who had shouted at his father but for him there was a hush, then one by one the crowd knelt before him.

'No king ever did more to help his people,' they called out.

Edmund lifted them gently to their feet.

'Will you lay hands on us?' one sick woman called.

Edmund felt God within him. He moved to the woman and stretched out his hand, and she flinched at his touch, just as the man who was possessed by Legion flinched at Christ's hand.

'Thank you, lord,' she said, and Edmund looked Christ-like as he stood and touched the long line of sick people, who limped and crawled and hobbled or were carried towards him.

'Enough!' Godwin said after a long time, but Edmund laid hands on each one, then blessed them.

Edmund was keen to proclaim his law codes and he sent for Archbishop Wulfstan, who knew the laws of all the old kings, and wrote all four codes that Ethelred published. Godwin sat with him and talked of how they would enforce the law.

'Hold courts each time you stay at a manor. Show the people that you will enforce the law on all and sundry. If any resist . . .' Godwin paused. There were many options. He did not feel quite comfortable imposing exile or outlawry, but it was necessary.

Edmund patted him. 'No one will resist. Not for a while at least. When it comes, let us decide what to do.'

Godwin and Edmund decided that the king would hold a great Christmas feast at Wincestre, where he would be enthroned again in peace and proclaim his law code for all the folk of Wessex.

But there were rumours of men seizing the lands of men who had died at Assandune and Edmund took Godwin aside. 'I want this put to an end before Christmastide. Take men, return to Sudsexe and see that all is in order.'

Godwin nodded, but he had a bad feeling about the trip.

'I have no one else, Godwin. But fear not: I will not take Eadric back.'

Edmund smiled. It took Godwin back to a younger, more carefree time.

'It is as you have always told me. I am king now. I need men who will help govern the shires when I am away. I want you to help me. You are loved by all the men in Sudsexe. Set the land in order. Here, take my seal.'

Edmund took the ring from his finger. Godwin weighed it in his palm. It fit his third finger.

'Keep it on,' Edmund said. 'You deserve to wear it.'

Edmund listed all the things he wished to be done and Godwin committed them to memory. Godwin was charged with setting Sudsexe to order and riding to Canturburie and Lundenburh to ensure that Archbishop Wulfstan and Queen Emma were brought safely to the feast.

'Eadwig is already on his way. Make sure Edward and Alfred are brought, by force if need be,' Edmund said. 'Make sure my men are holding the treasury. Who's the mint master there?'

'Godric.'

Edmund nodded. 'He's a good man.'

'Do you think he can resist the White Queen?'

'I don't see Emma marrying a moneyer. She won't sit quiet. We ought to get rid of her somehow. She's no maid, but she's a few child-bearing years left to her. There must be some prince in Saxony we can send her to. She can pour all her ambition into a couple of Saxon whelps.'

Godwin nodded. There was a lot to do, and they could not risk civil war, or Queen Emma trying to take advantage of Edmund's weakness.

It was a gloomy and misty morning when Godwin and his men mounted up. The air was still – the migrating birds had all left – and the thistle heads were white in the fields.

'Ride hard!' Edmund said. 'I shall see you at Wincestre. It will be the most magnificent feast. I shall send the finest huntsmen to start catching hind.'

Godwin paused to lean down from the horse and embrace Edmund. Then he waved and urged his horse to follow the rest of the company, who were already disappearing into the fringes of the winter forest.

Something made Godwin turn to look back. King Edmund Ironside, bravest and most resolute of English kings, stood in his hall door, hand raised in farewell.

As Godwin caught his men up, he saw a fat old hare was sunning itself on a rock. As Godwin approached the hare hopped slowly back into the bushes. If I had hawk or hound, Godwin thought, but the thing was too old to roast.

So Godwin left Edmund, with peace in his heart. He wished for nothing more than a quiet year or two: hunting with hounds; marriage perhaps, to some good catch that Edmund nudged his way. The thought depressed him a little. If Kendra had been a fine-born girl he would have married her. But marriage was political. Love was saved for mistresses.

Godwin would do his best. He would raise a hall in Wincestre, provide for all the families of the men who had died. He could raise children and hunt where Alfred had hunted. He imagined Edmund coming up to Mykelhal. He could see them both sitting in his grand hall, feet stretched out towards the fierce blaze, fine ale in hand, and good meat with plenteous spices, remembering the good days.

The next morning dawned damp and still foggy. No note of bird, no motion, except deep in the thickets, and stillness except for the drip of trees, like tears.

There was rain in the hills and the ford into Hamtunscir was flooded and matted with fallen trees. Godwin and his men found a hall to rest, and Godwin lay down, stretched out, pulled his hood over his face and closed his eyes.

He closed his fingers on the king's gold signet ring and clutched it as he slept.

Edmund woke and stretched both arms over his head. Ealdgyth had arrived that morning with fifty of her family. Their loyalties had been strangely divided, but it seemed an odd irony that Alderman Elfhelm, from beyond the grave, had conspired to have two of his womenfolk – Knut's wife Elfgifu and Edmund's Ealdgyth – married to the kings of a divided England.

'They're delighted,' Ealdgyth said. 'They are falling over themselves. Men take them seriously now. Eadric does not have long. Knut will wring his scrawny neck.'

Edmund laughed. He liked this brusque northern woman with her fair hair and broad shoulders and clear blue eyes. Baby Edward was in fine health. Ealdgyth was pregnant again, five months gone.

'You've a fertile womb,' he told her.

Ealdgyth laughed. 'Sigeferth was married to me for three years and I never bore him a child. I am married to you for barely two years and bang' – she clapped her hands together – 'I bear two children.'

That night the hall was quiet. Edmund sent his men to their beds. He sat with Ealdgyth and a scop came to sing to them. Edmund called for a pot of wine. It was sweet and dark in the candlelight. Edmund filled a horn with unwatered wine and took a long drink.

Baby Edward lay in a cot on the table. His nursemaid stood ready in case he should wake.

Edmund and Ealdgyth stood over their son. The boy was now a toddler who said 'Mama' and 'Dada', and 'kinga' as well.

Edmund left his son on the table, next to his horn of wine. He needed to use the privy, and he took a lantern and held it aloft as he stepped out into the night. The stars were clouded over. The moon hid her face. She could not watch.

Edmund held the lantern, a pale light against such great darkness, as he strode to the privy. It was a royal privy, with seat and bucket of lime to throw down to dampen down the stink of the midden pit.

Edmund pulled the door open. He hung the lantern on the peg and it filled the small space with a soft yellow light and the lamp-shadows swung back and forth.

Waiting in the stink below, a killer stood, spear in hand, his nose bunged up with oily rags. The midden door opened and a man came in. The killer peered up and saw the king's face as he unbuckled his belt and pushed his trousers down, lifted his kirtle as he lowered himself.

The spearman winced as he was splattered with royal shit and Edmund let out a long, slow fart.

He gripped his spear. One blow would do it. The lantern cast just enough light for him to see his target. God save our souls, he thought, and drove the spear upwards.

The scream woke Baby Edward.

A single eerie scream, like a vixen bark, but it was no fox. Ealdgyth's skin goose-pimpled. She shot to her feet.

'The king!' she said, and ran to the door.

Men were shouting. The privy door fell heavily open and Edmund staggered out, his legs bare, fell to the floor, rolled on to his back, one arm falling outwards, the other remaining folded on his chest. And then he lay, with his eyes still open, as if catching the last glimpse of the precious world, or looking for a friend, or a kind word to soothe his going.

Edmund was dead before the first man reached him. Ealdgyth put her hand to her mouth. 'Cover him!' she cried.

Someone saw the killer running through the gloom, stinking wet footsteps betraying his path.

Doom caught up with him before he reached the manor walls. Swords rang out, the blades shone in the moonlight.

Ealdgyth ran inside the hall, grabbed a naked sword and stood over her child as the hearth's flames licked red and yellow, one over another, and the dry wood crumbled.

'Search the place!' she told the king's men. 'There may be another. Let the dogs out. And bring his body in. I will clean it.'

She sat abruptly down. There was so much to think of.

'We need Godwin,' she said. She took off her brooch, a fine piece of silver and gold knotwork. 'Here! Take this token. Godwin will recognise it. Tell him what horrible fate has befallen us. Tell him to come with all speed.'

As soon as the words left her mouth Ealdgyth worried. Could she trust Godwin? She saw murder and manslaughter everywhere, but a sane voice spoke to her: 'Do not fear, Ealdgyth. You can trust Godwin.'

Godwin stopped on the borders of Hamtunscir and stared at the flooded river. The river remained in spate. Godwin looked at the swirling waters and laughed that Nature should conspire to keep him away from home. He would have to ride north. Perhaps he would head to Lundenburh first and work his way back round through Sudsexe.

The Downs rose up against the flat grey sky. There was no

sun, not even a rook's harsh call to break the stillness. But as he stood and looked into the brown and swirling waters, Godwin heard the sound of galloping hooves.

The sound stood out against the silent country. Godwin listened to it. A single horse, riding fast. His skin prickled with alarm. No one rode so hard to bring good news. Eadric has invaded, he thought. Knut has broken his oaths already.

I will not live through another battle, Godwin thought. The spark of life was too low within him. Another battle would claim his soul, and even knowing this Godwin knew that he would fight.

Godwin turned his horse. He stood in the middle of the road and waited. He did not know the horseman, but the man was waving madly.

It took the man's horse twenty paces to slow down, and it almost collided with Godwin's. It came so close, stamping and snorting.

'What haste?'

The boy waved a brooch at Godwin, but he seemed to have lost his senses, as if shocked by the news he carried.

'He is dead!' he gasped. 'Edmund is dead!'

'Do not speak so!' Godwin said.

'It is true. Edmund is dead!'

Godwin struck the boy across the cheek as if he were a fool.

'Who are you?'

'I am one of Elfhelm's folk. We arrived with Ealdgyth two days ago. This is her brooch.'

Godwin took it.

'What is your news?'

'The king is dead,' the boy said. His eyes welled up with shame and despair. 'He has been most foully murdered.'

*

Godwin rode hard back along the land he had come. The boy rode after him, but he did not turn or speak to him, and when Godwin arrived at the manor where he had left Edmund, he jumped from the horse and it staggered ten steps forward, then fell to the ground and lay breathing weakly. No one could get it back to its feet and it died before sunset.

Godwin strode across the yard mud. He threw open the doors, strode inside, looked for the one he loved, saw other faces but they were all a blur. Only Ealdgyth could talk sense to him.

'He is here,' she said. 'Inside this room.'

There were three men on guard at the door. Godwin looked at them. He did not know them. Who were these people, what had happened?

'They're my people,' Ealdgyth said.

Edmund lay on the table. He was dressed in fine robes, a sword belt about his waist, his hair neatly combed, his moustache trimmed, his mouth bound with a cloth, silver coins – ETHELRED REX – weighted down his eyelids. The stillness was palpable. Everyone in the room was breathing, except King Edmund. He lay like stone, cold and quiet and absent.

Godwin put his hand to Edmund's brow and flinched at the touch.

'He is dead,' he said.

The others looked at him as if he were mad.

Godwin put his hand out again. He touched Edmund's shoulder.

'He is dead.'

There was no answer.

'Edmund, how is it that you are dead?'

Ealdgyth had to pull Godwin away from the body. 'Godwin, he is dead,' she said. 'He is dead. But his son lives. And his child lives yet inside my womb. His son lives. I stood guard. His son lives, but they will come for him.'

'Who did this?' Godwin demanded.

They took him to see the murderer's body, but there was little to see: he had been hacked into meat and offal; his corpse was stripped naked; his genitals had been cut off and the remains were smeared in the midden filth.

Godwin turned the head over with the toe of his shoe.

The gory face that looked up at him was unrecognisable.

'I do not know him,' he said.

'It was Eadric,' Ealdgyth said.

Godwin didn't answer.

> *Open doth stand the gap where he stood*
> *Woeful the breach where grief floods in*

Godwin led the honour guard who escorted the coffin that contained Edmund's body. Edmund's favourite horse was brought forward and stood silent and quiet as the coffin was lashed to her back.

'Where shall we take him? The alderman of Hamtunscir has already sent word to Knut to welcome him as king,' one of the men said.

Godwin paused. 'We cannot take Edmund to Lundenburh,' he said. 'And he should not lie in Wincestre. Hamtunscir men were not loyal to him when he lived, so why should he honour them with his bones.' Godwin stood still for a moment, then took the reins of Edmund's horse, and the stallion stood by his side as if in solidarity.

Godwin remembered a ride he had taken long ago, his first summer with Edmund and Athelstan, when they had ridden along the Ridgeway and looked out from that ancient pathway.

'Glastonbury,' Godwin said at last. 'We shall bury him in St Dunstan's Abbey. Edmund will lie happily there.'

The coffin was loaded onto a cart, and when men knew who lay in that box they came out in silent crowds. Some wept and stretched out their hands, lamented his passing as if he was their own son.

Godwin carefully took Edmund's coffin across the Temese and up into the Berroscire downs. The Ridgeway was a set of rambling and interweaving tracks that followed the high ground straight across the belly of England. It was the road of farmers and drovers and invaders and conquerors. Alfred himself had fought his greatest battle here, and today it was the path that led Edmund to his resting place, in hallowed ground.

The grass grew tall on the humps and barrows of forgotten warriors. The wind blew stronger, the air was cleaner; where the grass had worn through, the chalk paths were white as old bone and the wind whistled softly through the dry winter grass and brittle thistles.

The sun touched the land with gold, and all the creatures of the downs came out to watch the passing of their mighty king. Deer, hares, foxes and feathered birds came close, or sat vigil. In the distance, spare and elegant, was the White Horse of Offentone, galloping over the hillside: a white horse on a field of green, like the ancient flag of the Wessex kings, staring proudly north towards the Mercian enemies.

Godwin paused there. To north and south and east and west there were fine views over the old heartland of Wessex. 'Look at your kingdom, Edmund the Undefeated, Edmund Ironside, dearest of lords!'

When they had first come here, Edmund and Godwin had been boys and they had spent the night in Wayland's Smithy, waiting for the dwarf to come to the tomb of stone. But no one came, and they strode down in the morning alive and proud of besting the night shadows and the darkest fears of their imagination.

Godwin could not face going back up there now; instead he followed the path down over the folds of the hillsides and camped in the ring pit, where men said the White Horse came to sleep at night.

His men's eyes were sad with reflected firelight. They stood and stared and looked for leadership, but Godwin was empty of words. He shook hands, pressed his cheek against other men's, clenched his jaw shut, embraced weeping warriors, and when they reached Glastonbury at the last, Godwin and three others shouldered the heavy load: eight legs swinging as they carried the king's coffin into the abbey, where it lay in state the night before the funeral.

The monks filed past, and when they sang that evening, their songs were as sweet as angel's voices.

Godwin sat all night and stared at the coffin.

St Dunstan's Abbey was one of the most ancient of the minsters of Wessex. The walls were vast and ancient; the arches hunched over them all; the high roof soared up into darkness; from the darkness the songs of the angels fell.

Outside the willows drooped their heads and wept. The Tor stood like a silent watchman as the candles lit the stained glass from inside, and the sound of the plainchant rose and fell like waves upon a distant shore.

Godwin was wearied by grief. He had been here, in this cathedral with Edmund, back in the days of the Wild Hunt. Godwin was fifteen then, Edmund seventeen. The country had turned to God for help, and the king had decreed that the whole country should fast and sing the third psalm.

They had stood in this cathedral, before the rood screen, and while Athelstan had joined in, Edmund had refused.

'Lord, how are they increased that trouble me! Many are they that rise up against me.'

'"They trouble me,"' young Edmund had laughed.

Godwin and Edmund had been bystanders then, skulking and hooded youths standing in the hall shadows, bitter and angry. But they used that anger and fashioned it well, and fought the Danes back. Godwin stopped. He was tormenting himself. He tried not to think, but at last, like a lone warrior against impossible odds, grief overcame him.

In the morning Godwin and thirty others stood and watched as Edmund Ironside, Bravest of Warriors, Dearest of Kings, was laid in a freshly dug grave by the side of the altar. The slab was lowered back over him and dropped the last inch.

Godwin crossed himself and turned away.

So that is that, he thought.

Outside, the pale winter daylight was so bright it made Godwin blink.

'Eadwig has raised the royal standard at Wincestre,' one man said. 'Which way will you fare, Godwin Wulfnothson? Will you rally to Eadwig's cause?'

Godwin sat down on the abbey steps. He was not listening.

'Wulfnothson, whither will you ride?'

Godwin squinted and then looked down at the land, which was touched with frost. His voice was uncertain. 'I promised Ealdgyth I would help her escape,' Godwin said. 'Then I shall return home.'

The image of Edmund and him sitting with feet stretched to the blaze flashed in his mind for a moment, and he screwed his will down on it, refusing to torment himself any longer.

'There is fine hunting in Contone. Come up and visit me there.'

Their breath steamed about their heads. Each made their choice, and they stood for a moment and embraced, then turned each away from the other and made their separate ways into the world.

Godwin sat down again, stretched his feet out and did not know what to do or think. The days were at their shortest. He was weary beyond measure.

Godwin saw some children gathering ivy and holly, and making their way across the frozen ruts to the village that lay a little way from the abbey gates.

It was nearing Christmastide when Offa the Fox arrived at Athelingedean. He threw a leg over his horse's neck and landed before it had come to a halt.

'So this is where Edmund plotted,' he said, and put his hands on his hips to admire the hall and then turned to look at the well-tended fields that were part of the manor. His men rode up behind him, and pulled their horses to a halt.

'And yours now, lord.'

Offa turned to look at the speaker. It was a short man with thick brown eyebrows and a slight stoop. 'Yes, it is.'

The man bowed.

'What's your name?'

'Coenwulf,' the man said. He spoke in a strong Sudsexe accent. 'I was steward to the Old Lady.'

'The Old Lady?'

'Sorry, sir. King Ethelred's mother.'

Offa Fox nodded. 'I am Offa Fox,' he said.

Coenwulf had guessed. Who else could the red-haired giant be except Eadric's trusted henchman, but he held the man's gaze and gave nothing away.

'Show me the hall. Then you can summon the freemen.' They started towards the hall, and then Offa stopped. 'You were here when the princes were young men?'

Coenwulf nodded. 'I have lived here all my life.'

'Then you will know Godwin Wulfnothson.'

Coenwulf nodded again. His voice was flat. 'Yes sire.'

'The king wants him,' Offa Fox said.

'He is not here,' Coenwulf replied.

Offa laughed. 'No. But his hall is not so far.' Both men looked westwards, to the dark heights of the Weald. Coenwulf pictured Mykelhal in better days. Pictured Godwin as the stiff and awkward eleven-year-old that Edmund brought in like the starveling that is brought from the cold into the hall and grows to strength and health. He pictured the Old Lady sitting with a honey cake in her lap, waiting for the boys to return from their hunt. From this hall he had seen everything.

'Has he been here?'

Coenwulf shook his head.

'Have you heard tidings of him?'

Coenwulf shook his head again.

Offa's ruddy eyebrows were severe, the freckles very bright, his pale blue eyes fixed Coenwulf to the spot. 'If you hear anything, then be sure to let me know.'

Coenwulf nodded, and caught the silver coin that Offa flicked towards him. 'There's more for anyone who brings me his head,' Offa said. 'Double if they lead me to his den, so I can cut it off myself.'

Coenwulf slipped the coin into the folds of his kirtle. 'I'll put word out,' he said, and then threw the hall wide open. 'Welcome Lord Offa to Sudsexe and the royal manor of Athelingedean.'

The Unlucky Man

Queen Emma heard the news of Edmund's death and a strange mix of emotions ran through her. Sorrow and grief, but delight as well, for now Edmund was dead there were opportunities for her.

She summoned Edward and Alfred to her chambers. 'Your half-brother King Edmund has been murdered,' she said. Alfred was twelve now, and he struggled to look manly as he weathered the shock. Edward, at sixteen, looked on with a sneering look as if he did not believe her. 'He has been murdered,' she repeated, and a voice in her head was singing the Kyrie eleison. 'The man is dead.'

'Mama,' Alfred said. He still used the childish diminutive. 'Who killed him?'

Emma drew in a deep breath. 'I do not know.' It was not me, she thought, though who would have imagined the Lord God would give me, his humblest servant, such a bounty?

Knut arrived at the gates of Lundenburh the next day.

Queen Emma sent word out that she would come to welcome him, and offered him the Palace of West Minster, so that he and his men should be comfortable while they waited.

She sat in her chamber. It was a stone room, with a high, plain window, the shutters of which had been thrown open, and the air and light streamed in. Emma felt a cold breath of air, as if God Himself had come down to her. She felt like the Virgin Mary waiting for the Archangel Gabriel. She closed her eyes, felt the chill breath on her neck and understood what God wanted.

It was thrilling and appalling at the same time. But it was God's will, she felt it and she decided her course, for good or ill.

'Bring my sons!' she called.

Edward and Alfred came together.

'Knut is here,' she said. She seemed almost excited, as if the danger thrilled her. 'We cannot resist him. You two must flee.'

'Where will we flee to?'

'To your uncle in Normandig. He will care for you both.'

'When can we return?' Edward asked.

'I do not know,' Emma said.

'When will we see you?' Alfred asked.

'Hurry along with you both.'

Emma put her sons on to the boat with a kiss and a hug, but she did not wait to see their captain push off but hurried back to organise the meeting with Knut.

The Danes stood in a great and excited crowd and awaited her arrival.

'Let us ride out to meet her,' Knut said, and in a moment they were all riding towards her, and some of her party seemed to take fear, as if the Danes were meaning to run them down, but she stayed resolute and commanded them to stay.

Knut liked that. He pulled his horse to a stop with a fine flourish, bringing it from a gallop to a halt almost on the spot. He bowed gracefully.

'Greetings, Emma, daughter of Richard, Duke of Normandig.'

Emma bowed her head. She was decked out in a robe of red velvet, with her hair bound in her wimple, but with a few coy strands of gleaming blond hair flapped in the breeze. 'Greetings, Knut Sweinson, King of All England.'

There was a brief moment of bows as each man was introduced, and then Emma said, 'It was my part to defend the city of Lundenburh while King Edmund lived, but now the Lord has judged him wanting and delivered you to us as king, I hand to you the keys of the city.'

Knut was delighted. His horse stamped with enthusiasm and tossed its head and snorted.

'I have a feast prepared. Shall we ride into your city?' Emma asked.

'Excellent. Your Danish is very good.'

Emma laughed.

It was a strange thing to look at such a beauty, dressed in the finest cloth that Christendom could offer, speaking Danish like a Sealand farm girl.

'Thank you, lord. We do not forget our ancestry. We share a common lineage, do we not?'

'We do,' Knut said, but privately he scoffed at the idea. He was descended from Odin while the Norman dukes were upstart descendants from a Danish exile. His first wife had been an English Dane, and she had already given him a son. He fancied the idea of taking Emma as wife and spawning another heir on this Danish colonist. He liked the idea of his loins making a union of new and old Danish blood. He was only nineteen years old and look at what he had achieved.

So King Knut took Lundenburh and the treasury and mint, over the dead body of the loyal English moneyer, Godric, struck down by Emma's own men.

*

Knut put his first wife aside.

Emma refused to marry him until he also swore an oath to put the son by his first wife aside and to make any sons of their union king of England.

Knut started to swear, but she knew how easily men made wrongful oaths and later relinquished their hold. She brought her favourite relics and threw open the caskets so that the skulls of St Ouen and St Augustine stared at Knut with their dark and empty sockets.

St Ouen was missing his low jaw, while the teeth of St Augustine were worn down to the roots. The saintly witnesses brought a chill to the room. Knut's skin prickled.

He put his hand out, and Emma took a tooth from a locket about her neck and added it to the pile.

'St Bridget's,' she said.

It seemed a little vulgar to put so much faith in oaths sworn over relics, but Knut put his hand out and swore.

'And that any of our sons shall be made king. None of the sons of that other woman.'

'Other woman' was how she spoke of his previous wife.

Emma insisted on having a priest come and bless the union, as if such things were needed to make a betrothal official.

She was no virgin, and Knut was quite delighted with the enthusiasm with which she took the seed from his loins.

'I want to be pregnant,' Emma said, as she lay with her backside up on a pillow. 'I will give you strong sons,' she promised, 'and they will be great rulers.'

Knut yawned. 'Well, first we must make sure all England is mine. Who shall we kill?'

Emma went through lists of names of men who could be swayed, those who could be bought or intimidated, and those who would have to be killed.

'Godwin?' Knut said. 'Is he the fair-haired man who carried the banner at Penne?'

Emma nodded. 'Yes. Fair hair, tall and strong, and a fine talker.'

There was no mistake.

'Yes, you must kill him,' she said.

Seeing which way the wind was blowing, one of the great Hamtunscir families sent armed retainers to seize Ealdgyth, but she had the sense to gather up Edward and flee. Her boat was pushing off from the Boseham quayside when the horsemen caught up with them, and they glared out as the wake widened between them, and cursed their luck.

Ealdgyth sailed far, and fortune buffeted her ever eastwards, till she found a haven in the Kingdom of the Huns, where she hoped that her son would be beyond even the reach of Knut's killers and where, later in the year Ealdgyth gave birth to another son, whom she named Edmund, in honour of his father.

Eadwig was not so lucky. He raised his banner and no one came and he was seized and slain as he tried to board a ship to Flandran.

One by one killers went through Queen Emma's list. Men were drowned or beaten to death, or hung from their necks from gibbet trees.

Godwin hid in wood and field. He spent another night in Wayland's Smithy, and came out again, from the great stones, still alive. But his footsteps led him slowly home and at last he turned his horse along the road to Contone. He stopped and looked up and saw the shoulders of the Downs appearing through the low grey clouds. He was alone and feared the faces of the wives and children of the men he had led to their deaths.

*

A lone horseman, dark in the midwinter landscape, a week after a bleak and cheerless Yuletide. He had tears in his eyes as the people came out, women in shawls, old man with their cloaks pulled tight about them, their feet in mud as they stared at him with blank dark eyes.

Godwin came closer. He wiped his eyes to clear his sight.

They stared at him.

Arnbjorn, Wulfnoth's old steward, limped out. 'Lord Godwin!' he said. 'We heard that you were dead, that all were dead. Lord Godwin, it is you! Oh, thanks be to the Lord God, Maker of Heaven and Middle Earth.'

They pulled Godwin off his horse and hurried him inside and threw wood on the fire and sat around. It was an odd feeling. There were no young men there – just women and old men and boys – except Godwin.

He looked about and their faces were still trusting and loyal. Even Kendra. It struck him that she was the last of the ship-full who had been with Wulfnoth. He looked at her for support, then began to speak.

They drank him up, drank all his words, and sniffed and one by one the women began to cry as they learnt how their men had stood in battle and bravely given themselves for kin and king and lord and country.

'What will you do?' Kendra asked in the morning.

Godwin could not bring himself to go to Knut and plead for mercy. 'I will stay here,' he said, 'till Knut comes to kill me.'

Of course it would not be Knut who would come. Just a spear in the fields, or a band of men, brave with numbers. A shoddy death.

Kendra waited for the right moment. There was none, so she spoke anyway.

'Men have been here.'

'Who?'

'Offa Fox.'

Godwin said nothing. He sat alone, staring into the fire. He did not ask any questions about what happened, could not hear.

'Sing for me,' he said after a long pause.

Kendra tried, but her voice broke and she had to bite back the tears.

Godwin looked up, and she saw pain in his eyes. Unbearable pain. Sing for me, his look implored, and she drew in a deep breath.

Coenwulf was up early the next morning, the silver coin sweaty in his hand. He hurried through the hall and knocked on Offa Fox's closet door.

'Lord!' he called, but there was no answer. He set the candle down and lifted a first to rap against the door. He rapped again, and this time there was a grunt.

'It's Coenwulf,' he called. 'Open the door, I have news of Godwin Wulfnothson.'

From inside the sleeping closet there was another grunt and the sound of furs being thrown back, and a heavy tread before the latch was lifted and the door swung open. The candle cast enough light to illuminate Offa's hairy shins, his naked legs and the kirtle he had thrown over his shoulders, which hung half way down his thighs.

It illuminated Coenwulf's face. 'What time is it?' Offa blinked.

'The third watch,' Coenwulf said.

Offa's face was screwed up with sleep. 'What news?' he yawned.

'You wanted Godwin?' Coenwulf said.

'He is here,' came a voice. This time it was not Coenwulf

who spoke. A figure stepped forward, and the candle threw enough light across his face for Offa to see who the third man was.

Godwin smiled. 'You've paid my hall two visits, and yet I have never been there to welcome you.' Godwin drew his sword. It gleamed red. Offa shouted, but the sound was quickly stifled, and Coenwulf lifted the light.

Offa lay on his bed, his freckled skin stained with gouts of dark blood. Godwin wiped his blade clean on the furs, and took Coenwulf's arm.

'You cannot stay here,' he said, and blew the candle out.

The manor of Burne lay on the coast, six miles due south of Contone. The settlement there was not as large or prosperous as its royal neighbour, Bosenham, but there was a modest Benedictine minster and a small village of workshops and long-houses spread out along the fowl-filled fens that gave a great harvest of reeds for thatching. It was the place Wulfnoth used to go to when he needed to pray, and it was where he had kept all the charters for his lands.

Godwin had not been there for a long time.

The slow creak of the mill drifted over the flat fields as he paused his horse at the end of the avenue of old and twisted yews that lined the approach to the abbey gates, like silent watchmen. The yews were malevolent in the gloomy evening light, like old hags with twisted arms and backs and fingers. The trees were deep in winter dreams, and Godwin kicked his horse onwards and ignored the strange shadows that flickered at the corner of his vision.

The abbey was secluded from the world by a deep ditch and palisade, but the roofs of the buildings were visible from outside, and a blacksmith was banging away on his stone as Godwin called to get a door ward's attention. It was a long moment before anyone appeared.

'I am Godwin, son of Wulfnoth.'

His words seemed less weighty after Edmund's death, but if they had charm, they still had a power on those closed doors, and after a long pause each leaf heaved wide open and Godwin heel kicked the reluctant horse inside. A pale-skinned novice led Godwin into a low wattle room where a small fire burnt.

Through the doorway he caught glimpses of robed monks, hurrying in unspeaking groups. It was time for vespers, which came early in winter.

Singing rose into the evening darkness, more piercing for the sudden release from silence, plainchant, thin and high and beautiful: '*Deus, in adiutorium meum intende*' – Oh Lord, come to my aid.

Godwin felt himself transported from the world of blood and mud and violence to a purer land of authority and order and peace, and then a voice spoke to him that startled him.

'Wulfnothson,' a hooded monk whispered and Godwin found his gaze had been drawn deep into the flames. 'Come, the abbot will see you now.'

A candle threw back the darkness and the monk did not turn or speak as he led Godwin to a low hall, much like any lord's hall, except that rather than carvings of dragons and warriors, the doorposts were entwined with crosses and foliage and the lives of saints. It took a moment for Godwin's eyes to get accustomed to the warmth and the dark, for the abbot's chamber was lit only by a great fire that glowed more than it burnt. By the fire, a heavy carved chair had been set, and on it, almost dwarfed by its grandeur, a bent and white-haired figure slumped in sleep.

Godwin waited and the old man suddenly opened his eyes and looked up and smiled.

'Ah! Godwin, son of Wulfnoth.' Abbot Oswi had seemed old even when Godwin was a boy, but now he appeared ancient. He spoke in a small but firm voice and beckoned Godwin forward into the fire's glow. The old man's liver-spotted hand gestured to a stool at his side. 'Your father was a frequent visitor in his time. As you were, if I remember aright.'

'Indeed,' Godwin said, a little lost for words.

'So the king is dead.'

'And buried.'

'Died of his wounds,' Abbot Oswi said.

'Indeed.'

Abbot Oswi gave the young man a penetrating look. 'But this is past news. Why are you here? I am sure that Wulfnoth's son has not come to my simple dwelling to pray with me.'

'No,' Godwin said. 'I am lost, Father. My lord is dead and the Dane hunts me.'

Oswi drew in a deep breath and let it out slowly, without an answer. The old man pushed himself up and used the back of the chair for support as he took one of the three books he had on a shelf above the fire. He retraced his steps and eased himself back into the chair, then set the leather volume on his lap and patted it as if it were a cat.

'Do you know what this is?'

Godwin shook his head.

'This is the first book of the *Historia ecclesiastica gentis Anglorum*,' the abbot said. 'I brought it with me when I left Peterborough and I have kept it since.' He patted the book again and his fingers stroked the silver catch. 'The novices read it to me to practise their Latin.'

Oswi forgot why he had brought the book and started to speak before he had quite grasped the thread again. 'This was written by the Venerable Bede. Well, not this one. This is a copy.' Oswi

473

paused. 'Ah, yes! That's it. Bede has been much on my mind. He wrote this nearly five hundred years ago. Listen.' Oswi read in Latin and then English. '"The island began to abound with plenty, and with plenty, luxury increased and this was attended with all sorts of crimes: in particular, cruelty, hatred of truth, love of falsehood, drunkenness, litigiousness, envy and other crimes. And a sudden vengeance for the people's horrid wickedness."

'Do you know what that vengeance was, or who these people were?'

Godwin told him.

'Yes. *We* were sent to punish the Britons for their crimes – Angles, Saxons and Jutes. We punished them for their sins.'

Godwin's gaze was again drawn to the burning flames. The old man was rambling. Godwin hesitated before interrupting. 'So the Danes are sent to punish us?'

Oswi nodded.

'But I did not sin. I kept my oaths. My lord was anointed.'

'And he died for us all so that peace could reign.'

Godwin looked unsatisfied.

Oswi looked at him. 'God wants peace. Go to the king.'

'No, I cannot,' Godwin said. 'I swore myself to Edmund.'

'Edmund is dead.' Oswi leant forward. 'Godwin Wulfnothson, Edmund is dead. All know of your loyalty. You kept your oaths, followed your lord through fire and hunger, cold and battle. But God wants peace. Think of what you might do as a powerful man. Use your talents to bring peace and prosperity and lawfulness back to England.'

Godwin trembled at the thought.

'He'll kill me,' Godwin said.

'It is no small thing to be martyred.'

Godwin laughed.

'Godwin, the men you feasted and fought with are gone. You

474

have survived where others have failed. You are brave and capable, England needs you. Give the people peace and order. Go, young Wulfnothson,' Oswi said at last, and put his hand out to bless Godwin's head. 'Go in peace, Wulfnothson, and do God's bidding.'

Godwin left Coenwulf at the abbey, in the care of the monks, but he did not go back to Contone. He found a high shieling and set a watch on the land about, and sent word for Kendra to come to him.

She found the spot the next afternoon, behind a simple windbreak of thorn trees. A tiny fire of a few sticks smouldered. He looked wild with a week's stubble on his chin.

'Oh thank God you are well!' she said. 'We heard of Offa's death. They have come, looking for you.' She stopped herself.

'Go on,' Godwin said.

'They beat Arnbjorn. We did not tell them anything.'

'I am sorry that you have all suffered.'

'We have not suffered,' she said. 'And if we have we would gladly suffer three times over.'

'I asked you here to say goodbye,' Godwin said.

'Don't,' she replied.

'Why not?'

She laughed bitterly because she had had this conversation once before. 'they will kill you, that is why!'

Godwin did not answer. He looked out of the open doorway, and his sight was draw to the high place where Agnes left offerings. 'I have asked my lands to be given to the abbey at Burne. Let the monks pray for my father, and the soul of King Edmund. And there is a man there named Coenwulf. If he needs anything . . .'

Kendra nodded. 'And what of my lord Godwin?'

'Think of me,' he said. 'Let men say that Godwin Wulfnothson kept his oaths and that he was a good friend of the king.'

Later that afternoon Kendra stood by the patch of thorn trees and watched as Godwin went, a dark figure diminishing into the short midwinter day. He did not turn and she did not wait. They had said their goodbyes, so she turned away and without looking back she made her way slowly homewards, heard only her own footfalls and the sigh of the wind in the winter grass.

In Mykelhal a fire was lit, and Agnes sat grinding corn. She looked up as Kendra entered.

Kendra drew in a deep breath as she sat down at the hearthside. 'So,' she said. 'He's gone.'

It was January, Solmonath – the month of the Reborn Sun – a month of beginnings and new hopes, but Godwin saw little hope ahead.

The world was darkening, clouds gathered and the winds were bleak and northerly. They skinned his hands, and chapped his lips. All winter journeys were wearisome, but this one was the hardest Godwin ever took. It was tasteless, colourless, joyless.

In truth he felt as though life had ended when he sat vigil in St Dunstan's Abbey; or the last day he had seen Edmund standing in his hall door, and this surprised him; or on the day he lay sick in Contone and heard that Edmund had taken Eadric back.

Candlemas 1017. Knut sat at West Minster and looked at the great and good men of the land who had gathered. This was his victory feast and all of England was there, great and small, thegn and alderman and bishop. It was a fine feast, dialogue by day, dancing, saga-telling and skaldic poetry by night. Joy shone like grease on their ruddy faces; laughter flowed like wine along the benches; peace had come and England was united at last.

Up to the hall one man rode. The sound of the slow-tripping hooves drifted into the hall. A man dismounted, left his sword at the door. Serving men were hurrying with the dishes for the top table. There were all manner of delicacies: heron and goose, partridge, pigeon, a dozen cranes and ten dozen curlews. The lower tables were already being served with simpler dishes of mutton and beef.

The doors were thrown open. The feast fell silent. Knut wiped his fingers on the linen tablecloth and smiled.

'Godwin Wulfnothson,' the door ward announced.

Knut sat back and waited.

Godwin's stomach felt hollow as he stood in the hall at West Minster. The high table where he had once sat with Edmund now held a row of turncoats and foreign warlords. It was all he could do to briefly bow.

'I am Godwin Wulfnothson, servant of the late King Edmund. Greetings Knut, King. We swore oaths of peace at Derheste. I have kept to mine, and expect you to keep to yours.'

A smile played about Knut's lips. 'I remember my oaths, but you have been long in coming to my hall.'

'I am a slow traveller,' Godwin said. 'Less fast than others who are buffeted east and west by the slightest breeze.'

Approach, Knut beckoned. Godwin walked up to the table. He kissed Knut's signet ring and paused before Emma and kissed her hand as well.

'Congratulations, lady,' he said. 'Are Edward and Alfred here? I should go to them and give them my respects.'

'They had to go to Normandig,' Knut said.

Godwin nodded. He stopped before Eadric and did not bow.

'Greetings, Alderman Eadric,' he said, but there was no greeting in his tone.

Eadric smiled. He did not hear what Godwin said; he did not care; who was Godwin, but the defeated friend of a dead king?

'I said, where is Offa Fox?' Godwin said.

Eadric looked at him. He paused before he spoke and read the look in Godwin's eye. 'Perhaps you know?'

'That I do,' Godwin said. 'He met my sword, and fell down dead.'

Eadric said nothing.

Knut was not interested in petty squabbles. 'Well,' he said, in a tone that appeared friendly, 'sit and eat. You have come in peace, and in peace you shall leave.'

Godwin sat. He did not eat or drink. No one talked to him. He could not bring himself to make conversation. At one point Emma caught Godwin's stare, and her cheeks coloured and she quickly looked away.

Yes, Godwin thought, you are guilty too.

At the end of the feast Knut gave out arm-bands and fabulous gifts. Godwin knew many of them by sight, for they were spoils taken from the dead at Assandune. Thorkel was given the jewelled hilt that hung at Ulfcytel's side. Eric the gold cross that was mounted on the White Dragon banner of the Wessex kings.

Knut went through the whole company presenting chief supporters with gold arm-bands that he passed across the table on the end of his sword. He was magnanimous to all. Eadric eager as a whore. Godwin guessed how he had bought Knut's favour and it sickened him.

At the end of the feast Knut stood up on the high table so that all could hear him. His booming voice carried throughout the whole hall, and men shushed for silence.

'Alderman Eadric,' Knut said, and Eadric stood and bowed, 'I promised you that when I was king I would raise you up above all other men, so that you would be the highest in the kingdom.'

Eadric smiled and made little bows to each table. Godwin could not watch.

Eadric continued to bow and scrape.

'And so I shall,' Knut declared.

Godwin tried not to hear Eadric speak. He hated the man's accent, hated his words. Hated everything about him.

'I am humbled, my king, and am glad to have served you well,' Eadric began.

'Humbled is good,' Knut said.

At that moment ten men entered the room through the king's dressing-room door. Eadric looked expectant, like a favourite hound that sees the best bone being brought into the hall and starts to drool.

'Alderman Eadric,' Knut said, 'in return for the service you did for your lord – by breaking your oaths to him and me, and fleeing from battle – I shall keep my promise to raise you above all other men. Seize him!'

Eadric paused as if this were some kind of jest, but from the strength of the hand-locks he quickly found it was no joke. He started to speak, but one of the Danes who had grabbed him struck his mouth. Blood flew out and Eadric spat out teeth not words. They pulled him away from the high table and dragged him down the middle of the hall.

There was silence except for the sound of Eadric's muffled pleas.

'I shall raise you above all men, Eadric Oath-Breaker.'

Eadric was hustled from the hall, and Knut put out his arm. Queen Emma took it and Knut led her outside, the whole company pressed behind.

Godwin seemed as one woken from a long slumber. All

about him men were laughing and chattering in delight and excitement, but Godwin sat stone-still and his eyes smarted. He stood and followed in the flow of the crowd.

The whole company stood on the hall steps and watched. On the top step, Knut stood, the flicker of a smile on his face as a rope was tossed over a tree branch. Eadric's wrists were bound behind his back. He was trussed like a swine for slaughter, and as he was led before the king there was a great cheer from those assembled. They pushed forward like the crowd at a fistfight, but Knut put out his hands for silence.

'Eadric of Mercia, you were ever a traitor. Hang him from the highest tree, so that all men may see how we deal with traitors and turncoats. Let all witness the price of disloyalty!'

Knut and the Danes treated the event like a party. Musicians were brought to play a dancing tune, and beer was passed from hand to hand, and the gold-giver gave Eadric a rough neck-ring that day, as the small figure rose slowly into the air with each haul on the rope.

'Gently!' the Danes shouted to the men who were pulling on the other end of the rope. 'Don't snap his neck – let's see him dance!'

Someone – a red-haired Dane with three fingers missing on his sword hand – thrust a beer at Godwin and Godwin took it and found himself rather enjoying this Danish way of doing things. Only Archbishop Wulfstan looked a little disapproving as he stood beneath the struggling man and said the last rites.

Godwin later learnt that that they were hearing a popular Danish dance tune and in the years that followed it was often performed throughout the country, and always brought a tear and a smile.

The Danes sang and cheered and they quickly forgot the man who was struggling on the end of his gibbet, but the

English did not forget. Godwin watched him very closely. He did not take his eyes off Eadric's face and hoped that Eadric saw him there.

Eadric took almost half an hour to die. His heels kicked and the music had long since stopped before his feet did. At the last there were a few convulsive struggles, before stillness, and his soul had gone to judgement.

Eric of Hlathir cut him down and took a wood axe and struck off his head. He laughed as he lifted Eadric's head by the hair and threw it towards the water-filled ditch, as a man might throw a turnip by its leaves. After they kicked it about the West Minster lawns, Eadric's severed head was eventually stuck on a spear above Crepelgate – a gory reminder, so that all might see the price of treachery.

That night Godwin dreamt that Edmund came to him. Godwin thrilled to see him, even if it was only in a dream, and Edmund held his hands out to him. 'When Knut kills you I will be here. I will look after you.'

Godwin woke with a start, but the night was dark and calm, and even though Emma reminded Knut that he had to kill Godwin, Knut wavered and went out of his way the next day to invite Godwin on a hunt.

Godwin bowed. He felt he owed Knut that at least, in return for killing Eadric, but he let the other men push their horses towards the quarry, left his spear un-blooded, had less to prove than the others. Knut hung back as well. Godwin found himself alone with the king, and wished someone else were here to make conversation.

'Godwin of Sudsexe?' King Knut said as the riders rode back from the hunt.

Godwin looked up in surprise. 'Yes, lord.'

'You were Edmund's man, were you not?'

'Yes, lord.'

'When Ethelred died, all men came to me and declared me king, but you did not come to Hamtun to swear an oath to me.'

'No, lord.'

'And you did not swear to my father.'

'No, lord,' Godwin said, and he laughed briefly, despite himself. 'I had sworn an oath to Edmund, and I was with him when he was made king.'

Knut turned to him. 'Why?'

'He was a good man, and a good king, and I loved him like a brother.'

Godwin opened his mouth, but stopped himself saying how he hated the Danes and how they had blighted his childhood.

'You were a hostage in Ethelred's court, were you not?'

'I was,' Godwin said, surprised that the king should know so much about him. There was a look in Knut's eyes, as if he knew the answers to all the questions he was asking, and at last Knut seemed satisfied. 'They tell me there are three deer ahead,' he said. 'We should hurry to catch them.'

Next day a messenger came to summon Godwin to Knut's private chambers.

This is it, Godwin thought. I will be seized and killed. As he prepared himself he was in a strangely glad mood.

He felt the blood tingle in his palms as he dressed, slowly and solemnly, like a hero in poems who dresses for a battle he knows he cannot win. He tipped the man who had cared for his horse, and asked him to care for his servants, if he should not return.

'You sound like someone on his death bed,' the man said.

'Well, who knows,' Godwin said.

Godwin patted the man's shoulder and then leapt up on to his saddle, Næling at his belt, and the night wind chasing like hounds across the sky.

Knut was just doing what he had to do to keep the kingdom together, he told himself.

When Godwin arrived, he was brought into a small chamber where the king was holding a private feast.

It was a small gathering of no more than twenty and Godwin did not know why he had been included in this group. He took the seat farthest from the king and said little, yet listened well.

'What say you, Godwin?' Knut called across the chamber at one point, and Godwin stammered because he had not heard what they were talking about.

'We were talking of Norman, Leofric's son. He was plotting against me.'

Godwin knew the lad. A pleasant fellow, but no conspirator.

'Did you know of Norman's plot?' Knut asked.

Godwin saw the look in Knut's eye, as if he knew the answer again.

'I did not, lord, and if I had I would have knocked some sense into the lad.'

'You would not have told me?'

Godwin paused for a moment. 'You know, lord, if I heard of another plot that meant harm to you, I would come and tell you.'

There were some murmurings from around the room, but Knut seemed pleased.

That night Godwin got quite drunk, and he found himself being given a bolster to sleep on when the feast was over. They'll kill you in your sleep, Godwin thought, and he wished that it had been done before, more cleanly, when he could face it like the Dane warrior who took the executioner's blade-strike full in the face.

But Knut kept Godwin around. Friends close, and enemies closer. A year after the battle at Assandune Knut was looking around for men to help him rule.

'I like you, Godwin,' Knut said. It was a simple and straightforward sentence. 'I want to make you alderman.'

Godwin choked on his ale.

'I need men like you.'

'Thank you, lord.' But inside Godwin groaned. He was sick of cajoling men into battle, and now he had to cajole them to pay up their taxes instead.

'Good,' he said. 'You are not married, are you?'

'No,' Godwin said.

'I have a cousin who is not married. Her name is Gytha. She is the daughter of a warrior named Thorgil Sprakling, whose mother was daughter of Harald Bluetooth.'

Knut went on for some time and Godwin did not quite understand what was being offered.

'You would like me to marry her?' Godwin said at last.

Knut looked at him as if he were stupid. 'Yes.'

'Is she very ugly?'

Knut's cheeks coloured. 'No,' he said. 'She is a very pretty woman, tall and broad and strong, who will give you good children.'

Godwin's mouth opened. 'Well,' he said, 'thank you!'

Godwin was away from Contone for a long time, and when he came home he avoided Kendra. She waited for him in her room, but he did not come.

When Godwin did appear, he had been at the beer. He wandered down to the brew house and found Agnes and Kendra, and did not feel as if he was the lord of the manor any more, felt he was somehow a visitor.

'All well?' he said and the women's expressions did not change.

'All's well,' Agnes told him, and Godwin came in and warmed his hands on the fire, but he wasn't exactly sure why he had come or what he had meant to achieve, and when Kendra turned round she saw that Godwin had gone.

In time Knut's brother Harald died and Knut became king of England and Danemark and Norway. He favoured England over his other kingdoms, became more English than the English, and Archbishop Wulfstan found him a willing pupil. He lectured Knut on England and the English – their laws, their Church and their many and confusing saints – and Godwin, amongst others, introduced him to the legends and the feuds, the wells with the sweetest water and the best places for hunting hare or hind or hart.

One of Knut's first actions was to reorganise the government under jarls. The old kingdoms of Mercia and Wessex, Northymbria, Cantware and East Anglia were all made jarldoms. His father's warlords were the first jarls, a word which the English found difficult to pronounce and changed to 'earl'.

But Thorkel and Eric knew Knut when he was a pimply boy, and Knut never really forgave them for that. Eric remained earl of Northymbria till his ship sank somewhere between Norway and Orkney, and as the Northymbrians, when they were a kingdom, had a tradition of taking their kings from the Norwegian royal line, Knut made another Norwegian, named Siward, earl.

Thorkel managed to keep his tongue for a few years, before smarting too much under a young man's rule, and he rebelled in the end, and died in exile.

In 1018 Knut spoke to Godwin. 'I want you to be earl of Wessex.'

'No,' Godwin told him.

Knut seemed surprised.

'I am no earl,' Godwin said.

'Why not?'

'I am only a thegn's son.'

Knut didn't give a toss if he was a thegn's son or not. 'You will be earl. I have decided.'

Godwin protested, but Knut was firm.

'You keep your oaths,' Knut said simply, as if that was the only reason he needed.

All summer of 1026 Knut was abroad putting down a rebellion in Norway. When he left he asked Godwin to be regent. Godwin accepted, but it was all the work without the crown. He trudged through the duties and wondered why God had let the whole country fight so hard to such little end.

Was it for this? he wondered as he stared at the hall of Danes and English singing Danish songs. For wealth and prestige and power?

No, he thought. It was not. Edmund and Godwin fought for England and Bede's Angelkyn – the English people – Dane, Saxon, Jute and Angle. Sadness came back to him that evening at hall, as an Icelandic poet hammered out his skaldic verses, and Godwin looked about at the men who were his age when he took Contone back from Ulf, and they seemed spoilt and callow and strangely foreign.

Many of them *were* foreign, he thought, for they were Dane's sons, or lads of pure Danish blood who spoke English with their fathers' accents. But even the English boys were different. England was different. The England Godwin had grown up in was lost and gone, and lingered only in memory.

For three days there was feasting and then a week of law courts, and Godwin sat in judgement on them and gave out doom like a king of old. He listened to their cases and their oaths in the law courts, watched men grip hot irons or submit themselves to ordeals of water and flame and combat, and he was Justice, lifting his steady scales, and judged them fairly.

On the twelfth day Godwin tired of listening to the cases and the babble of evening poets and decided they would go hunting. His men had found boars rooting in the next valley, and Godwin had some young hounds that needed blooding.

Godwin sat in his private chamber in Contone and watched the flames curl on each other. In Mykelhal the men were already gathering. He could hear their excited and hungry voices, could feel the slow drag of the feast tug at him, as the tide tugs at the safely moored boat.

Kendra had been watching Godwin from the doorway, and when it was ready she brought him a horn of spiced ale.

'Are you well, my lord?' she said.

Godwin looked up and forced a smile.

'Ah, Kendra,' he said, and took the proffered horn. 'Thank you.'

Kendra lingered for a moment.

Godwin was in a strange mood, and as she walked away, he called her back.

'Kendra.' He pulled a stool across for her. 'Please,' he said, 'sit.' Godwin took in a long deep breath and let it out again. 'You know,' he said at last, 'do you think my sons will understand why it was that we had to fight? Will they care about our stories? The battles we fought, the friends we lost?'

'Of course,' Kendra said.

'I don't think they will,' Godwin said. 'They will look at us as old fools who messed up at every step.'

'You were no fools. You, Edmund, Beorn, Caerl, you were the

tallest of the tall, the bravest and most courageous men in England.'

'And they're dead.'

'But the cause you fought for is not dead. The hills and rivers and people remain. There are many athelings in exile. One day one of them might return. It might be that the real battle has not yet been fought.'

Godwin looked up. Her speech had snagged his attention but he did not feel her confidence. 'This morning my son said, "Father, why did you fight against the king?" I replied that there were two kings then and that I fought for the one who was murdered.'

'Who murdered him?' the conversation had run.

'An alderman named Eadric.'

'Why did he murder him?'

'Because he wanted favour with Knut.'

'And did he win favour?'

'Yes,' Godwin said. 'Knut raised him higher than all the other men. By his neck!'

'And did you know this Eadric?'

'I did,' Godwin said. 'He drove my father into exile. Murdered good men.'

And he killed my beloved lord.

'I think your father must have been a coward,' his son had said.

'Your father was no coward,' Kendra said.

The look in her eyes was clear and sharp.

Godwin looked away. 'No, he was not,' he said. There was a long pause. 'I cannot even remember his face. Cannot picture him or hear him speak.'

Kendra kept her own counsel and Godwin fell quiet for a while.

'I will raise my sons differently,' Godwin said. 'I will never swear wrongful oaths, never abandon them as my father abandoned me.' Kendra took the ale-jug from the hearth stone and poured more steaming beer into his horn. 'Listen to them. They want their bellyfull tonight. Damned Danes.' Godwin let out a sigh. 'I am in foul spirits tonight, Kendra. And I know not why. Sing to me,' he said at last, but there was a moment's pause.

'What should I sing?'

Godwin asked for the song he had first heard her sing: a sad tune that matched his mood.

'Yes, that one,' he said and she sat straight and tall and as the Danes in the hall burst into their first drinking songs, Kendra began. Her voice was quiet at first, and very beautiful, like a balm to Godwin, and even the mice in the roof-thatch stopped scrabbling to listen.

Those years with Edmund were like a strange and melancholy dream.

Godwin sat in the feast hall that night and stared at the close-pressed warriors on the benches. I was there and this is how it happened and we should have beaten the Danes without Eadric. We would have beaten them, Godwin thought, and only God's will had made it otherwise, and he felt old and weary and nostalgic for the lost days of England, when he was Edmund Ironside's man.

But Kendra's words had found a crack, as the thorn bush that falls on rocks and finds a crevice where roots can grow. Emma's sons were in Normandig, but Godwin did not hold high opinions of either. Edmund had two sons, and Godwin wondered where they were now, and whether they took after their father.

Kendra watched Godwin as he sat and stared into the hall fire. His gaze was drawn deep into the flames, and his face softened for a moment.

Silent and empty, Kendra hummed to herself, former hall of laughter,

> The once-lord wanders
> Sorrow and longing as companions
> The solitary man awaiting God's mercy.

AUTHOR'S NOTE

When starting to tell the events of 1066, I found it almost impossible to understand the whole tale without recounting that other (and much less famous) conquest of England which took place fifty years earlier: for what fell on the 14 October 1066, at the Battle of Hastings, was an Anglo-Danish state, established by Knut, and with it fell King Harold who was himself half-Danish, and a member of the Danish not English royal family.

King Ethelred is sadly famous, mainly because of the nickname he has since acquired: Ethelred the Unready. Although his unreadiness is legendary, the name actually comes from an Old English pun on the name Ethelred, which means 'Noble-Council': so Ethelred Unread means 'Noble-Council No-Council'.

For the men and women that lived through Ethelred's reign it was an unmitigated disaster. The struggles of Edmund Ironside, fierce and bright and spectacular, are sadly much more neglected. But the battle summer of 1016, and the defeats inflicted upon the Danes, gives the lie to the contemporary trend amongst some to say that Ethelred was not such a bad king after all.

When trying to make sense of these years the gaps in information are more prominent than the stepping-stones of facts. But, with knowledge of the society and the culture, it is possible to make educated guesses at what and why and how.

Godwin Wulfnothson was the topic of much posthumous slander from Norman chroniclers, who were keen on embroidering history, and there is little sure information about his early years. Later Norman chroniclers have him variously as an oath breaker, thief of church land and as farm-boy, who curries favour with Knut by happening to help one of the Danes out after battle. This last tale is as fanciful as many of those that sprang up about the Saints of the times, who were cared for by otters, gulls and considerate housekeeping foxes. What we do know was that Godwin rose rapidly to be the most powerful man apart from the king. He was first made Earl of Wessex and then regent of England, and no doubt contributed in a large part to the period of peace and prosperity in England, that were in complete contrast to the long decline of Ethelred's reign, and which lasted until 1065.

So what do we know about young Godwin? It is assumed by most historians that the Wulfnoth Cild who the *Anglo Saxon Chronicle* lists as being exiled was the father of the Godwin who emerges from the fighting. Godwin's name appears again when the manor of Contone is returned to him in the will of Athelstan Atheling. Then he slips from the records, to return a few years later married to Knut's cousin, and then on to become King Knut's most trusted servant. Bringing what we know about the society and times and people he was living amongst, it is possible to make sensible guesses at what might have filled these gaps.

It is often asked which are real characters and which are invented. Beyond Godwin and the royal family and noblemen, most other characters are inventions. Some exist because I wanted to depict Anglo Saxon society, in a manner that shows how the common people were affected by the actions of the great. Others lend their existence because of known facts. For example, Godwin's daughter Edith was known to be fluent in

Irish, and there seems to have been a connection between the family and Dublin, as the next book will show. So the novel started in Dublin, and then Kendra appeared, and once she appeared I liked her too much to leave her behind in Viking Dublin.

As for fact and fiction: I have been guided by the facts wherever possible, even when some events, such as Queen Emma's marriage to Knut, seem too strange to be credible. But fact is sometimes stranger than fiction, and in the few accounts many of the participants had an eye to their reputations in future years: and Queen Emma's Encomium is a brave attempt to paper over the decisions she made through this and later years.

Of the places mentioned within this book, a surprising number are still standing and you can put your feet, quite literally, in the place of the men who lived at this time. Some of the more interesting ones include the tiny Saxon stone church, now isolated in a field outside Contone, which was probably built by Godwin. The chapel at Deerhurst, where Knut and Edmund exchanged oaths still stands, although the abbey is gone, and the chapel is now the village church. And another is the church at Assandune, which Knut had built to mark his victory, and which was ready to be consecrated just four years later, in 1020. Others, such as Wayland's Smithy, retain the ancient aura they must have had in Anglo-Saxon times.

The shires, the Anglo-Saxon system of government, remained functioning units of government into the twentieth century, and in some parts of the country hundreds, ridings and parts were still the basic form of government until the local government reforms of 1974.

Positions such as Shire Reeve are still found in the USA, in its modern derivation of Sherriff. The many meeting places, where each month the men of the hundred met to hear and witness the court proceedings lie all around us: mounds, prominent oaks, crossroads and places where the parishes meet – although most of us drive past them each day blithely unaware. But look at any village map, or medieval street pattern of our towns and cities, and the geography of rods, strip fields and smallholdings still define many of the boundaries we live within.

A note on battle. Some people may be surprised at the amount and severity of physical injury men suffered, succumbed to, and survived in battle but from mass graves discovered at Towton and at Fishergate, we have graphic evidence of medieval warfare, and by using modern forensic methods, can piece together even the order in which they were received, and which blow it was did for each numbered skeleton. Many Norse sagas speak of the slash under the shield edge, and evidence from the Fishergate burials show a large number of femur injuries.

On language: the difference between words of a French and Old English/Norse etymology is still clearly apparent in the modern language. For example, Germanic words, say 'kingly', have their feet firmly fixed on the ground, while French derived words – the parallel in this case being 'majesty' – tend to have their noses in the air.

I've been lenient on words that entered the language through Latin, but otherwise I have tried wherever possible to stick to words with an Old English or Old Norse etymology. These add a certain air to the novel, one that I happen to like.

A final note should be made on places where I have modernised spellings: chiefly in the case of personal names.

Old English parents liked to alliterate the names of their children with the names of their parents. This leads to families full of names that (with no thought at all towards twenty first century writers or readers) start with the same prefix. A good example of this is the ninth-century King Æthelwulf of Wessex who named his successive offspring Æthelstan, Æthelswith, Æthelbald, Æthelburt, Æthelred and Ælfred (in this case, Alfred the Great). While I personally savour the look and 'feel' of these names and letters, 'Æthel' to take just one example, is so common that reading the histories of the periods many readers can quickly become overwhelmed with the number of various Æthel-men running various bishoprics, abbeys, shires and countries.

In deference to readers who find this overwhelming, I have chosen to simplify most names to their modern counterparts. This leads inevitably to anachronisms, as the letter 'æ' is written either as an 'a' or an 'e' in modern English (Æthelred is written as Ethelred, while Æthelstan is written Athelstan though in fact the beginning prefix, meaning 'Noble' is identical).

I'd like to thank everyone who has played a part in this novel, great and small, and for any remaining inconsistencies, anachronisms and errors, I accept full blame.

Now you can order superb titles directly from Abacus

☐ Ciao Asmara   Justin Hill   £13.00
☐ Passing Under Heaven   Justin Hill   £11.99

The prices shown above are correct at time of going to press. However, the publishers reserve the right to increase prices on covers from those previously advertised, without further notice.

─────────────── ⟨ABACUS⟩ ───────────────

Please allow for postage and packing: **Free UK delivery.**
Europe: add 25% of retail price; Rest of World: 45% of retail price.

To order any of the above or any other Abacus titles, please call our credit card orderline or fill in this coupon and send/fax it to:

Abacus, PO Box 121, Kettering, Northants NN14 4ZQ
Fax: 01832 733076   Tel: 01832 737526
Email: aspenhouse@FSBDial.co.uk

☐ I enclose a UK bank cheque made payable to Abacus for £ . . . .
☐ Please charge £ . . . . . . to my Visa/Delta/Maestro

| | | | | | | | | | | | | | | | | | | |
|—|—|—|—|—|—|—|—|—|—|—|—|—|—|—|—|—|—|—|—|

Expiry Date ☐☐☐☐   Maestro Issue No. ☐☐

NAME (BLOCK LETTERS please) . . . .

ADDRESS . . . .

. . . .

. . . .

Postcode . . . . Telephone . . . .

Signature . . . .

Please allow 28 days for delivery within the UK. Offer subject to price and availability.